THE MYTHICS

1. HEROES REBORN

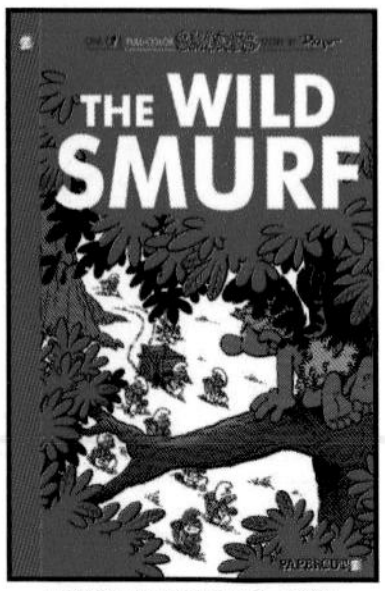
THE WILD SMURF
PAPERCUTZ

THE SMURFS #21

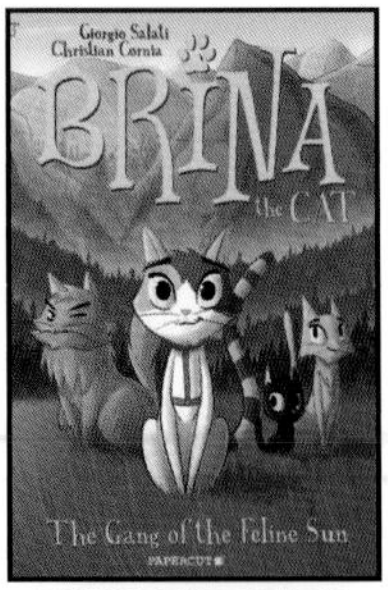
Giorgio Salati
Christian Cornia
BRINA the CAT
The Gang of the Feline Sun
PAPERCUTZ

BRINA THE CAT #1

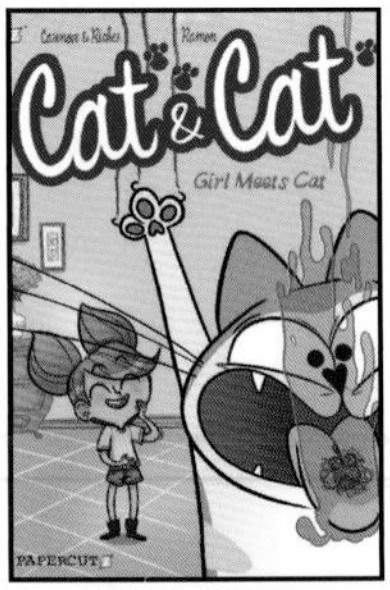
Cat & Cat
Girl Meets Cat
PAPERCUTZ

CAT & CAT #1

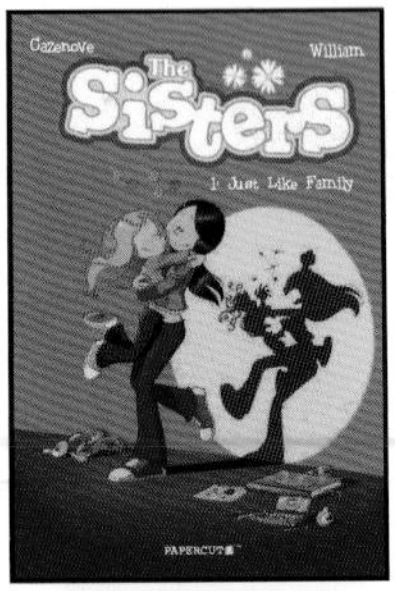
Cazenove
William
The Sisters
It Just Like Family
PAPERCUTZ

THE SISTERS #1

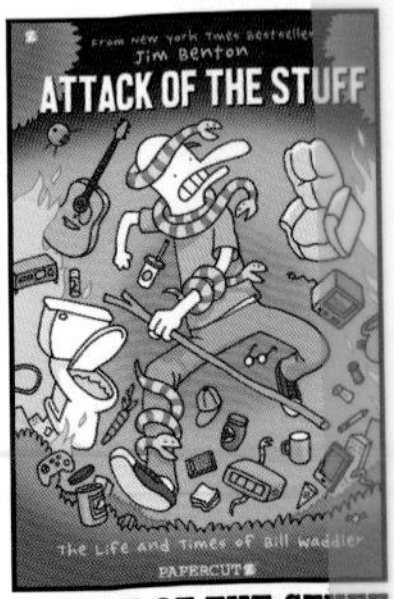
Jim Benton
ATTACK OF THE STUFF
The Life and Times of Bill Waddler
PAPERCUTZ

ATTACK OF THE STUFF

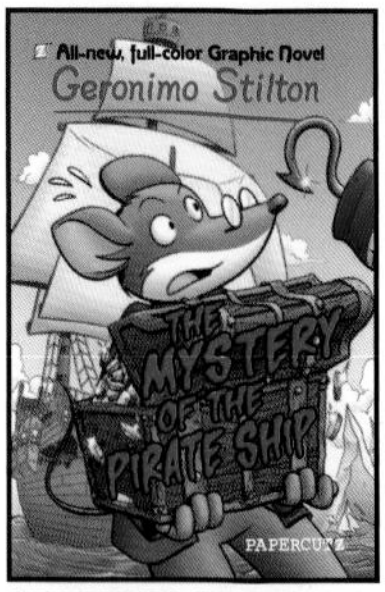
All-new, full-color Graphic Novel
Geronimo Stilton
THE MYSTERY OF THE PIRATE SHIP
PAPERCUTZ

GERONIMO STILTON #17

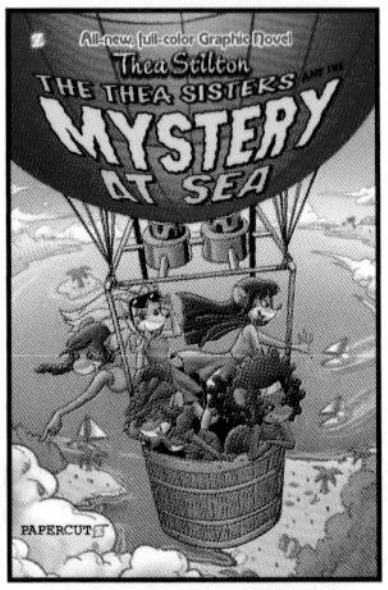
All-new full-color Graphic Novel
Thea Stilton
THE THEA SISTERS
MYSTERY AT SEA
PAPERCUTZ

THEA STILTON #6

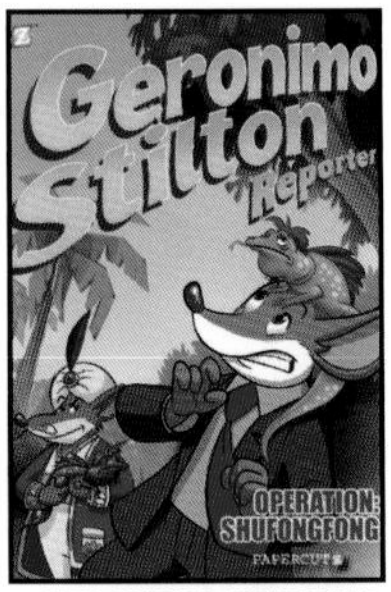
Geronimo Stilton
Reporter
OPERATION: SHUFONGFONG
PAPERCUTZ

GERONIMO STILTON RREPORTER #1

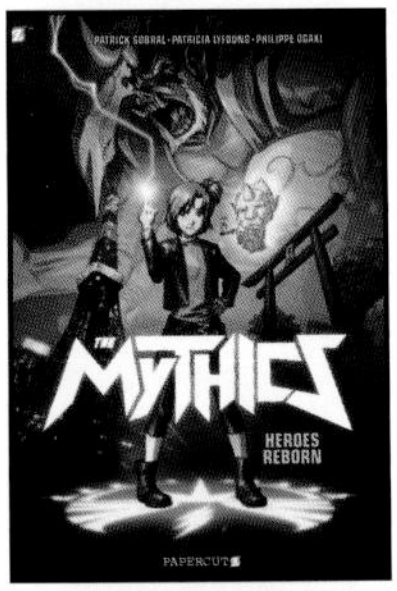
MYTHICS
HEROES REBORN
PAPERCUTZ

THE MYTHICS #1

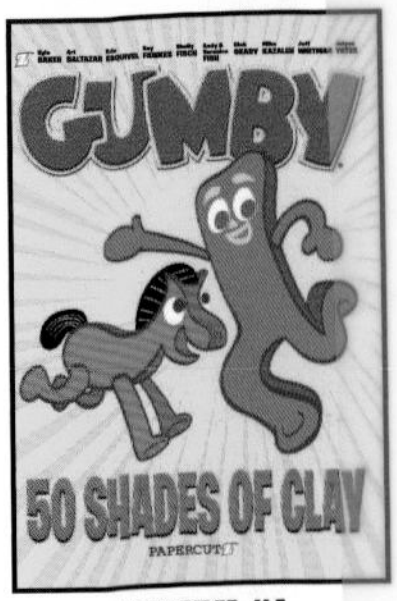
GUMBY
50 SHADES OF CLAY
PAPERCUTZ

GUMBY #1

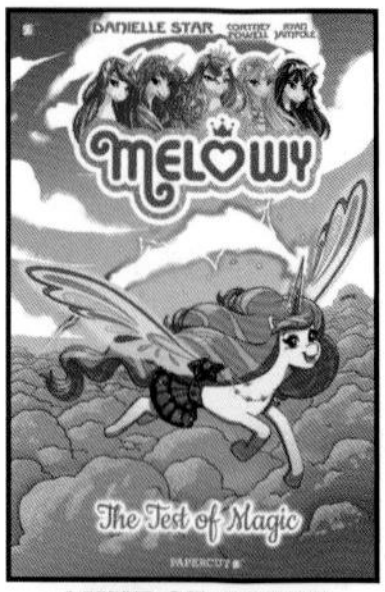
DANIELLE STAR
MELOWY
The Test of Magic

ANNE OF GREEN BAGELS #1

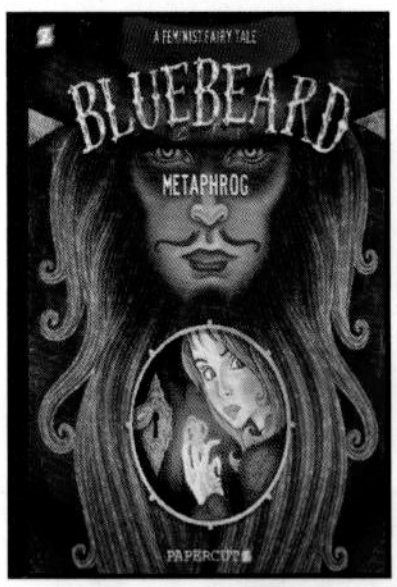
A FEMINIST FAIRY TALE
BLUEBEARD
METAPHROG
PAPERCUTZ

BLUEBEARD

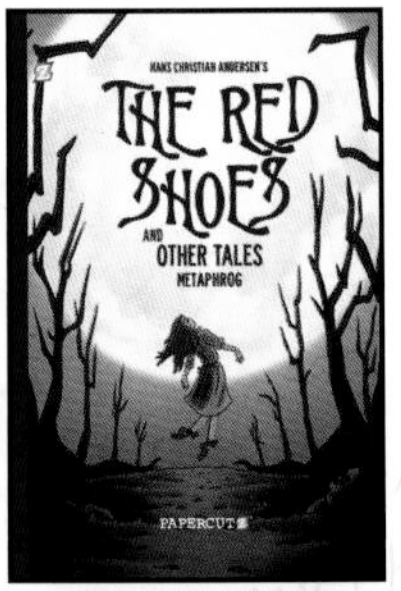
HANS CHRISTIAN ANDERSEN'S
THE RED SHOES
AND OTHER TALES
METAPHROG
PAPERCUTZ

THE RED SHOES

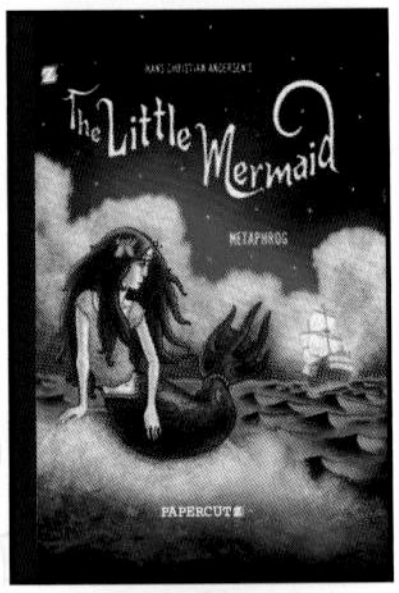
The Little Mermaid
METAPHROG
PAPERCUTZ

THE LITTLE MERMAID

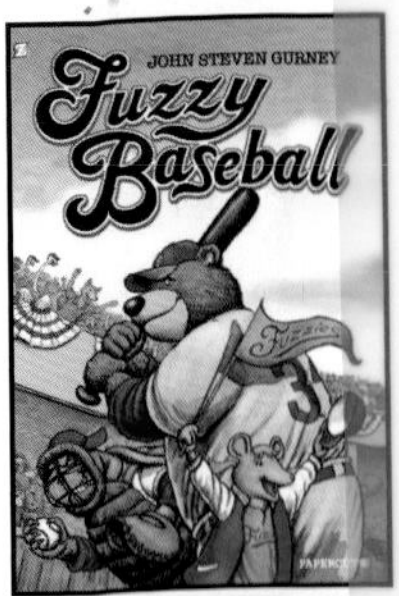
JOHN STEVEN GURNEY
Fuzzy Baseball
PAPERCUTZ

FUZZY BASEBALL

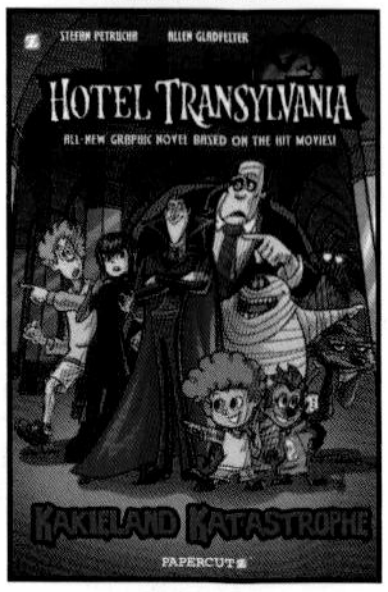
STEFAN PETRUCHA
ALLEN GLADFELTER
HOTEL TRANSYLVANIA
ALL-NEW GRAPHIC NOVEL BASED ON THE HIT MOVIES!
KAKIELAND KATASTROPHE
PAPERCUTZ

HOTEL TRANSYLVANIA #1

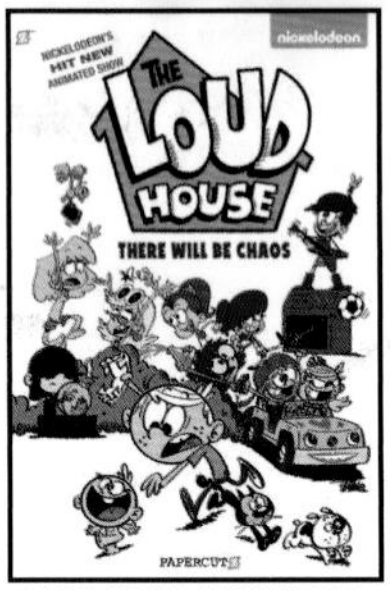
NICKELODEON'S HIT NEW ANIMATED SHOW
nickelodeon
THE LOUD HOUSE
THERE WILL BE CHAOS
PAPERCUTZ

THE LOUD HOUSE #1

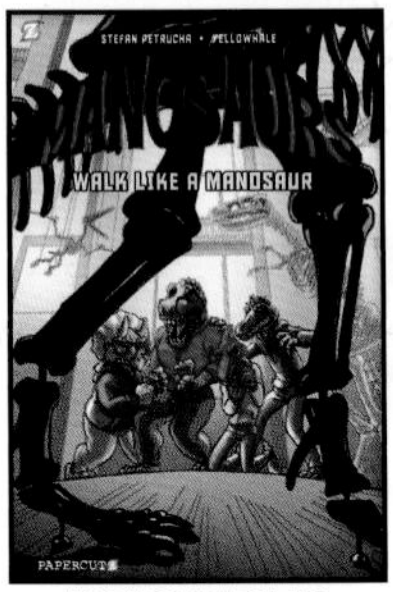
STEFAN PETRUCHA
YELLOWHALE
MANOSAURS
WALK LIKE A MANOSAUR
PAPERCUTZ

MANOSAURS #1

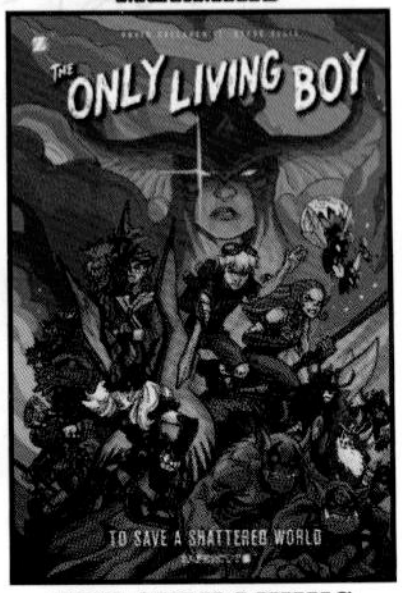
THE ONLY LIVING BOY
TO SAVE A SHATTERED WORLD
PAPERCUTZ

THE ONLY LIVING BOY #5

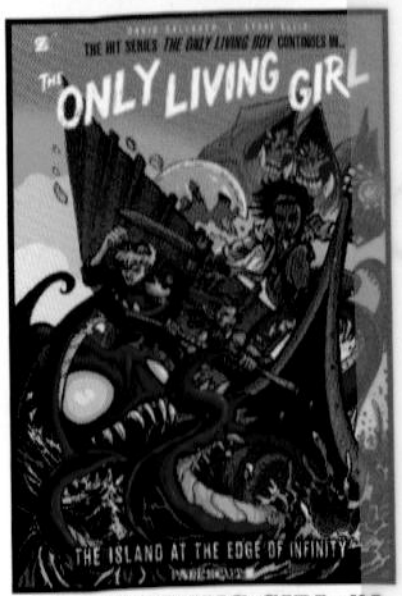
THE ONLY LIVING GIRL
THE ISLAND AT THE EDGE OF INFINITY
PAPERCUTZ

ONLY LIVING GIRL #1

MORE GREAT GRAPHIC NOVEL SERIES AVAILABLE FROM

PAPERCUTZ™

papercutz.com

All available where ebooks are sold.

THE MYTHICS

PART 1 : YUKO

Script by
PHILIPPE OGAKI

Art by
JENNY

Color by
MAGALI PAILLAT & **VALÉRIANE DUVIVIER**

Les Mythics [The Mythics], volumes 1,3, and 4 © Éditions Delcourt-2018
Originally published in French as "Yuko," "Amir," and "Abigail"
English translation and all other editorial material © 2020 Papercutz. All rights reserved

Created by PATRICK SOBRAL, PATRICIA LYFOUNG, and PHILIPPE OGAKI

Part 1- Yuko
Script — PHILIPPE OGAKI
Art — JENNY
Color—MAGALI PAILLAT and VALÉRIANE DUVIVIER

Part 2- Amir
Script and Art — PHILIPPE OGAKI
Color — MAGALI PAILLAT

Part 3- Abigail
Script — PATRICK SOBRAL with help from FABIEN DALMASSO
Art — DARA
Color — MAGALI PAILLAT

Original editor — THIERRY JOOR

Special thanks to SÉVERINE AUPERT, LUCIE MASSENA, and LINA DI FLAMMINIO

Papercutz books may be purchased for business or promotional use. For information on bulk
purchases please contact Macmillan Corporate and Premium Sales Department at
(800) 221-7945 x5442

Translation — ELIZABETH TIERI
Lettering — WILSON RAMOS JR.
Production — BIG BIRD ZATRYB
Managing Editor — JEFF WHITMAN
Editorial Intern — IZZY BOYCE-BLANCHARD
Jim Salicrup
Editor-in-Chief

J-GN
MYTHICS
474-9209

PB ISBN: 978-1-5458-0434-6
HC ISBN: 978-1-5458-0433-9

Printed in China
Distributed by Macmillan

First Papercutz Printing

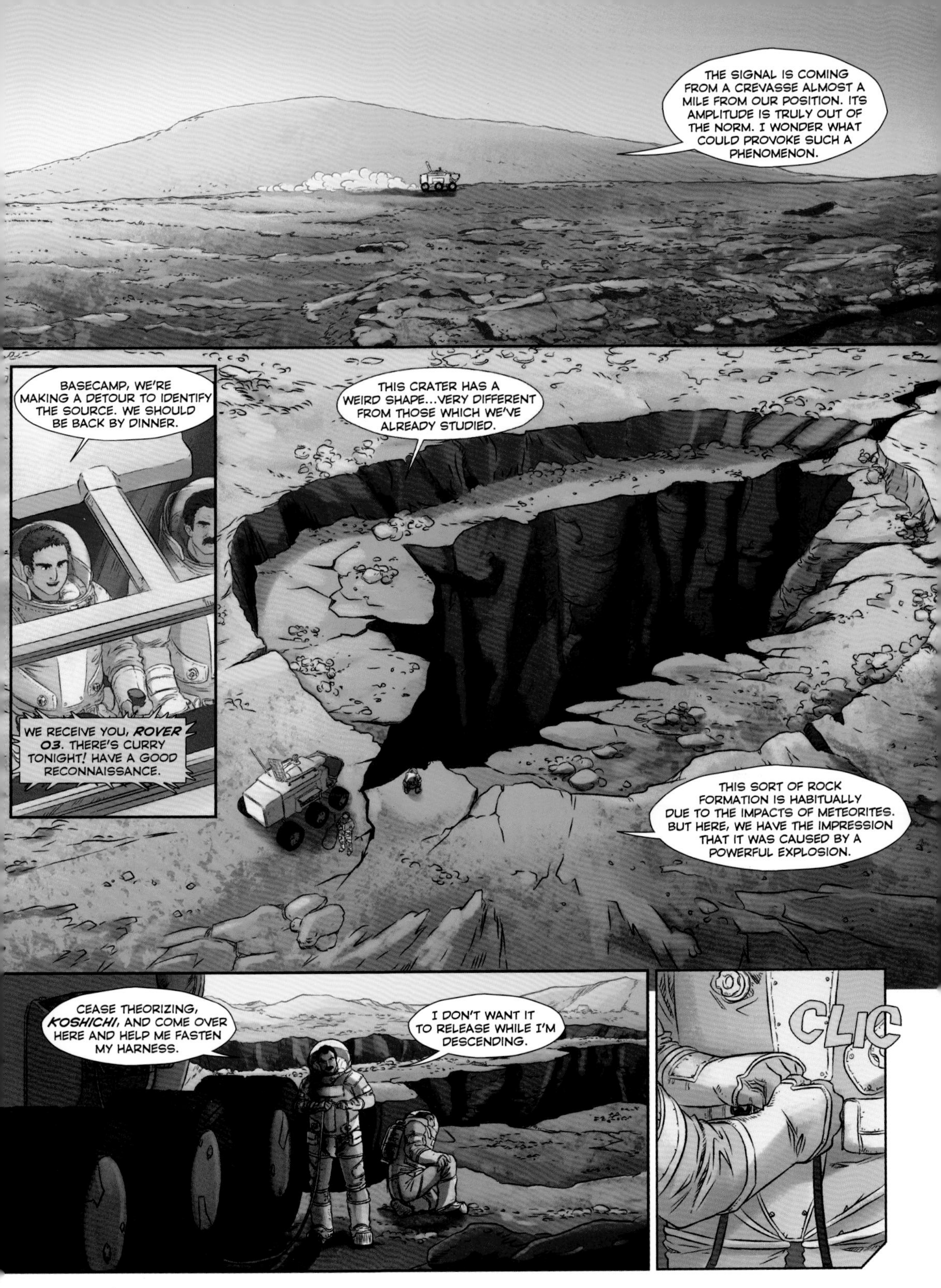
THE SIGNAL IS COMING FROM A CREVASSE ALMOST A MILE FROM OUR POSITION. ITS AMPLITUDE IS TRULY OUT OF THE NORM. I WONDER WHAT COULD PROVOKE SUCH A PHENOMENON.
BASECAMP, WE'RE MAKING A DETOUR TO IDENTIFY THE SOURCE. WE SHOULD BE BACK BY DINNER.
WE RECEIVE YOU, *ROVER 03*. THERE'S CURRY TONIGHT! HAVE A GOOD RECONNAISSANCE.
THIS CRATER HAS A WEIRD SHAPE...VERY DIFFERENT FROM THOSE WHICH WE'VE ALREADY STUDIED.
THIS SORT OF ROCK FORMATION IS HABITUALLY DUE TO THE IMPACTS OF METEORITES. BUT HERE, WE HAVE THE IMPRESSION THAT IT WAS CAUSED BY A POWERFUL EXPLOSION.
CEASE THEORIZING, *KOSHICHI*, AND COME OVER HERE AND HELP ME FASTEN MY HARNESS.
I DON'T WANT IT TO RELEASE WHILE I'M DESCENDING.
CLIC

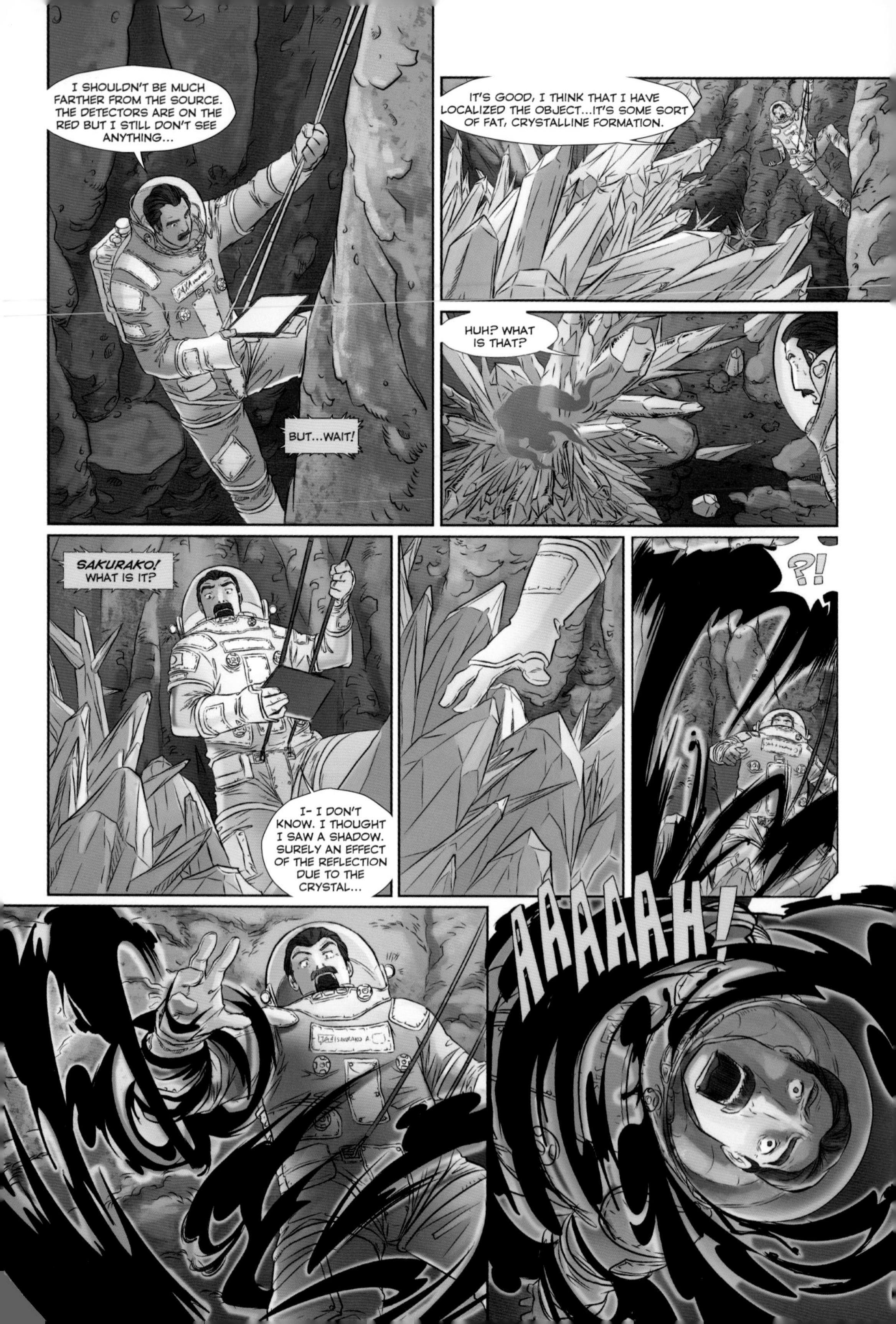
I SHOULDN'T BE MUCH FARTHER FROM THE SOURCE. THE DETECTORS ARE ON THE RED BUT I STILL DON'T SEE ANYTHING...
BUT...WAIT!
IT'S GOOD, I THINK THAT I HAVE LOCALIZED THE OBJECT...IT'S SOME SORT OF FAT, CRYSTALLINE FORMATION.
HUH? WHAT IS THAT?
SAKURAKO! WHAT IS IT?
I- I DON'T KNOW. I THOUGHT I SAW A SHADOW. SURELY AN EFFECT OF THE REFLECTION DUE TO THE CRYSTAL...
?!
AAAAAH!

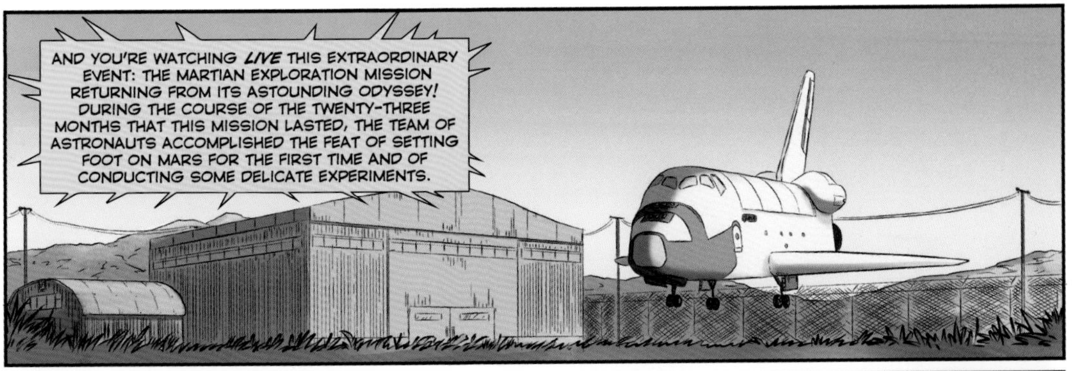
AND YOU'RE WATCHING *LIVE* THIS EXTRAORDINARY EVENT: THE MARTIAN EXPLORATION MISSION RETURNING FROM ITS ASTOUNDING ODYSSEY! DURING THE COURSE OF THE TWENTY-THREE MONTHS THAT THIS MISSION LASTED, THE TEAM OF ASTRONAUTS ACCOMPLISHED THE FEAT OF SETTING FOOT ON MARS FOR THE FIRST TIME AND OF CONDUCTING SOME DELICATE EXPERIMENTS.

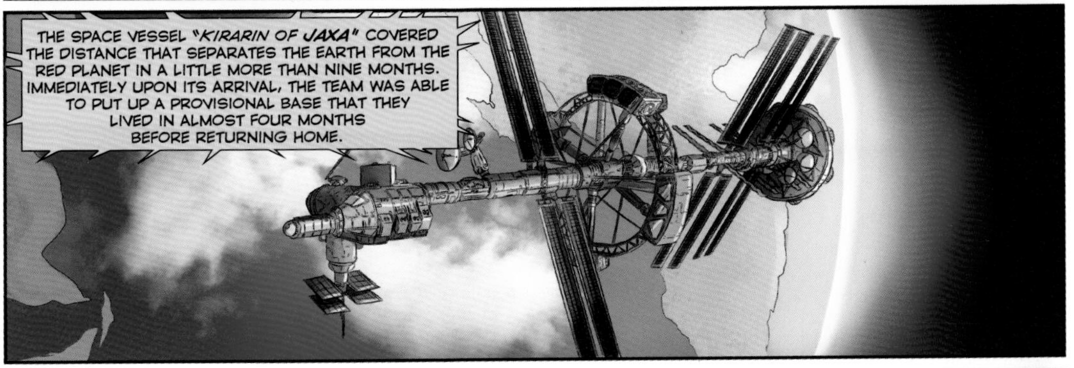
THE SPACE VESSEL *"KIRARIN OF JAXA"* COVERED THE DISTANCE THAT SEPARATES THE EARTH FROM THE RED PLANET IN A LITTLE MORE THAN NINE MONTHS. IMMEDIATELY UPON ITS ARRIVAL, THE TEAM WAS ABLE TO PUT UP A PROVISIONAL BASE THAT THEY LIVED IN ALMOST FOUR MONTHS BEFORE RETURNING HOME.

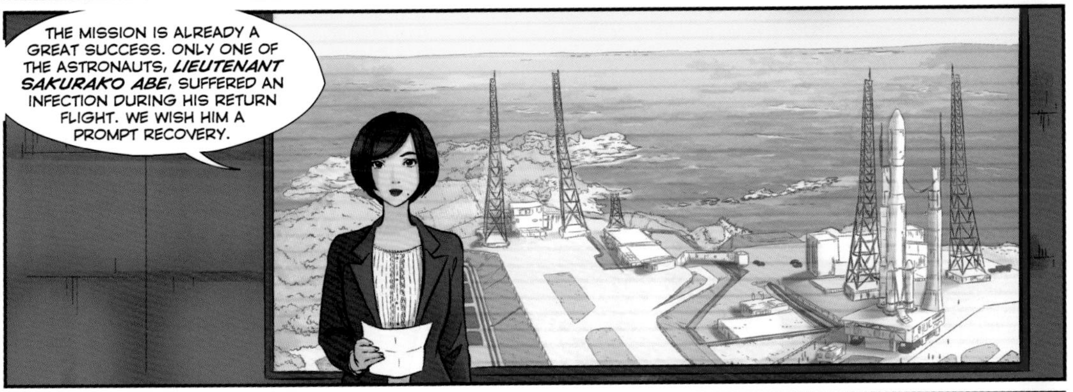
THE MISSION IS ALREADY A GREAT SUCCESS. ONLY ONE OF THE ASTRONAUTS, ***LIEUTENANT SAKURAKO ABE***, SUFFERED AN INFECTION DURING HIS RETURN FLIGHT. WE WISH HIM A PROMPT RECOVERY.

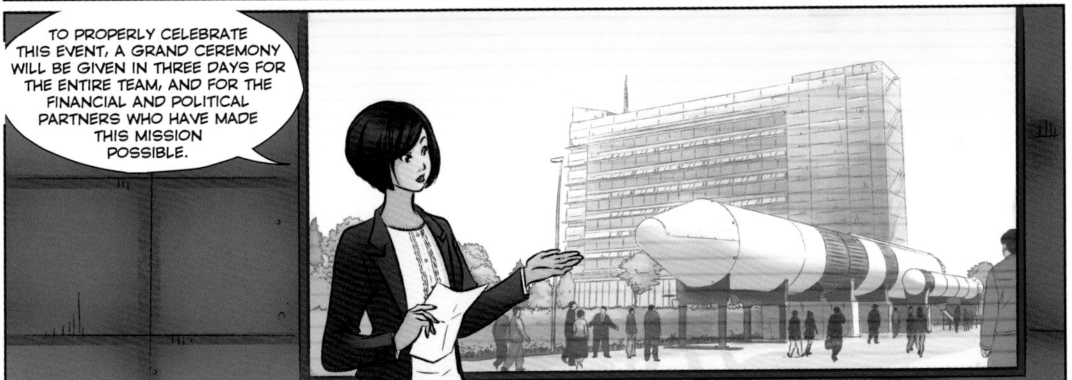
TO PROPERLY CELEBRATE THIS EVENT, A GRAND CEREMONY WILL BE GIVEN IN THREE DAYS FOR THE ENTIRE TEAM, AND FOR THE FINANCIAL AND POLITICAL PARTNERS WHO HAVE MADE THIS MISSION POSSIBLE.

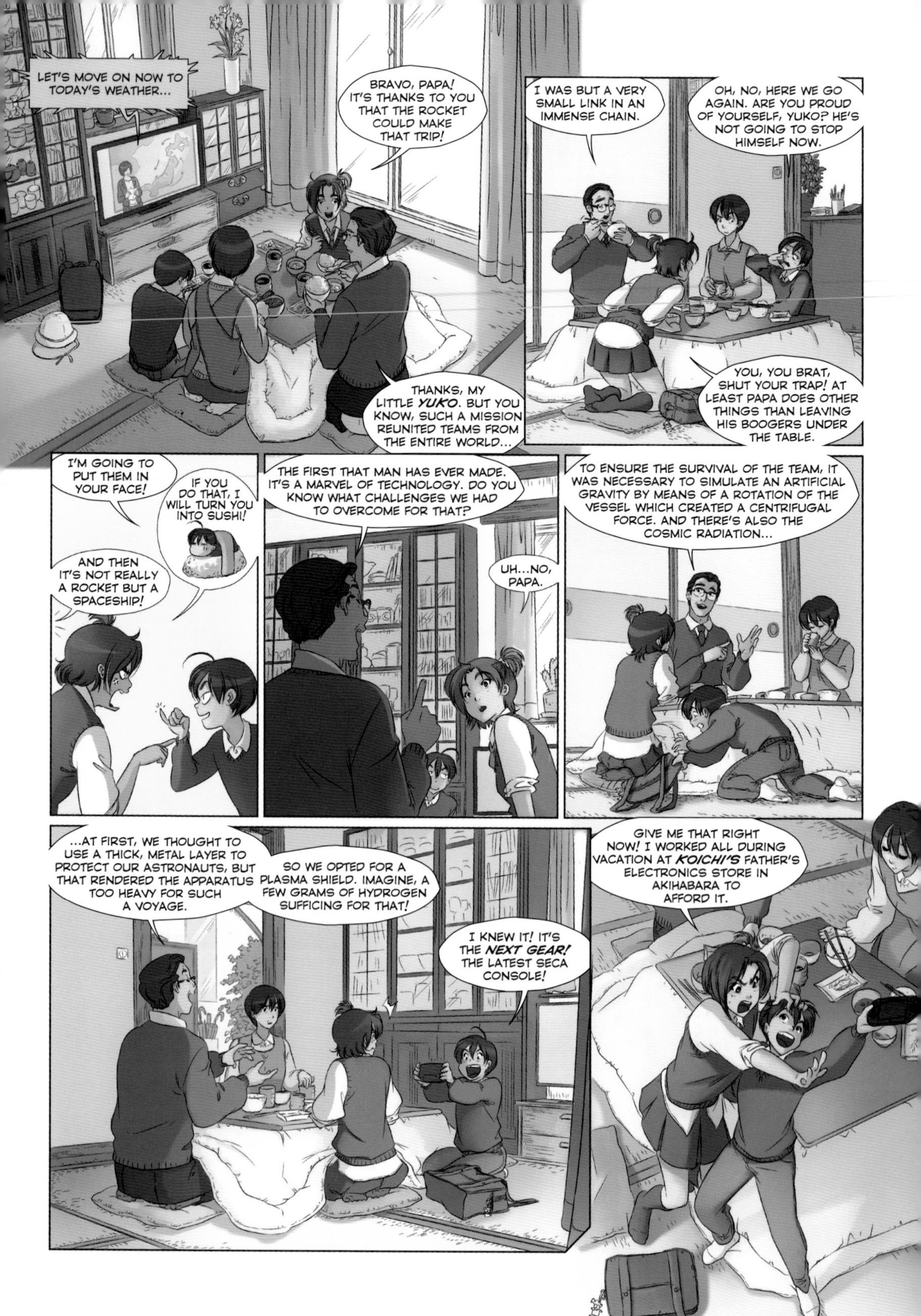

LET'S MOVE ON NOW TO TODAY'S WEATHER...
BRAVO, PAPA! IT'S THANKS TO YOU THAT THE ROCKET COULD MAKE THAT TRIP!
THANKS, MY LITTLE YUKO. BUT YOU KNOW, SUCH A MISSION REUNITED TEAMS FROM THE ENTIRE WORLD...
I WAS BUT A VERY SMALL LINK IN AN IMMENSE CHAIN.
OH, NO, HERE WE GO AGAIN. ARE YOU PROUD OF YOURSELF, YUKO? HE'S NOT GOING TO STOP HIMSELF NOW.
YOU, YOU BRAT, SHUT YOUR TRAP! AT LEAST PAPA DOES OTHER THINGS THAN LEAVING HIS BOOGERS UNDER THE TABLE.
I'M GOING TO PUT THEM IN YOUR FACE!
IF YOU DO THAT, I WILL TURN YOU INTO SUSHI!
AND THEN IT'S NOT REALLY A ROCKET BUT A SPACESHIP!
THE FIRST THAT MAN HAS EVER MADE. IT'S A MARVEL OF TECHNOLOGY. DO YOU KNOW WHAT CHALLENGES WE HAD TO OVERCOME FOR THAT?
UH...NO, PAPA.
TO ENSURE THE SURVIVAL OF THE TEAM, IT WAS NECESSARY TO SIMULATE AN ARTIFICIAL GRAVITY BY MEANS OF A ROTATION OF THE VESSEL WHICH CREATED A CENTRIFUGAL FORCE. AND THERE'S ALSO THE COSMIC RADIATION...
...AT FIRST, WE THOUGHT TO USE A THICK, METAL LAYER TO PROTECT OUR ASTRONAUTS, BUT THAT RENDERED THE APPARATUS TOO HEAVY FOR SUCH A VOYAGE.
SO WE OPTED FOR A PLASMA SHIELD. IMAGINE, A FEW GRAMS OF HYDROGEN SUFFICING FOR THAT!
I KNEW IT! IT'S THE NEXT GEAR! THE LATEST SECA CONSOLE!
GIVE ME THAT RIGHT NOW! I WORKED ALL DURING VACATION AT KOICHI'S FATHER'S ELECTRONICS STORE IN AKIHABARA TO AFFORD IT.

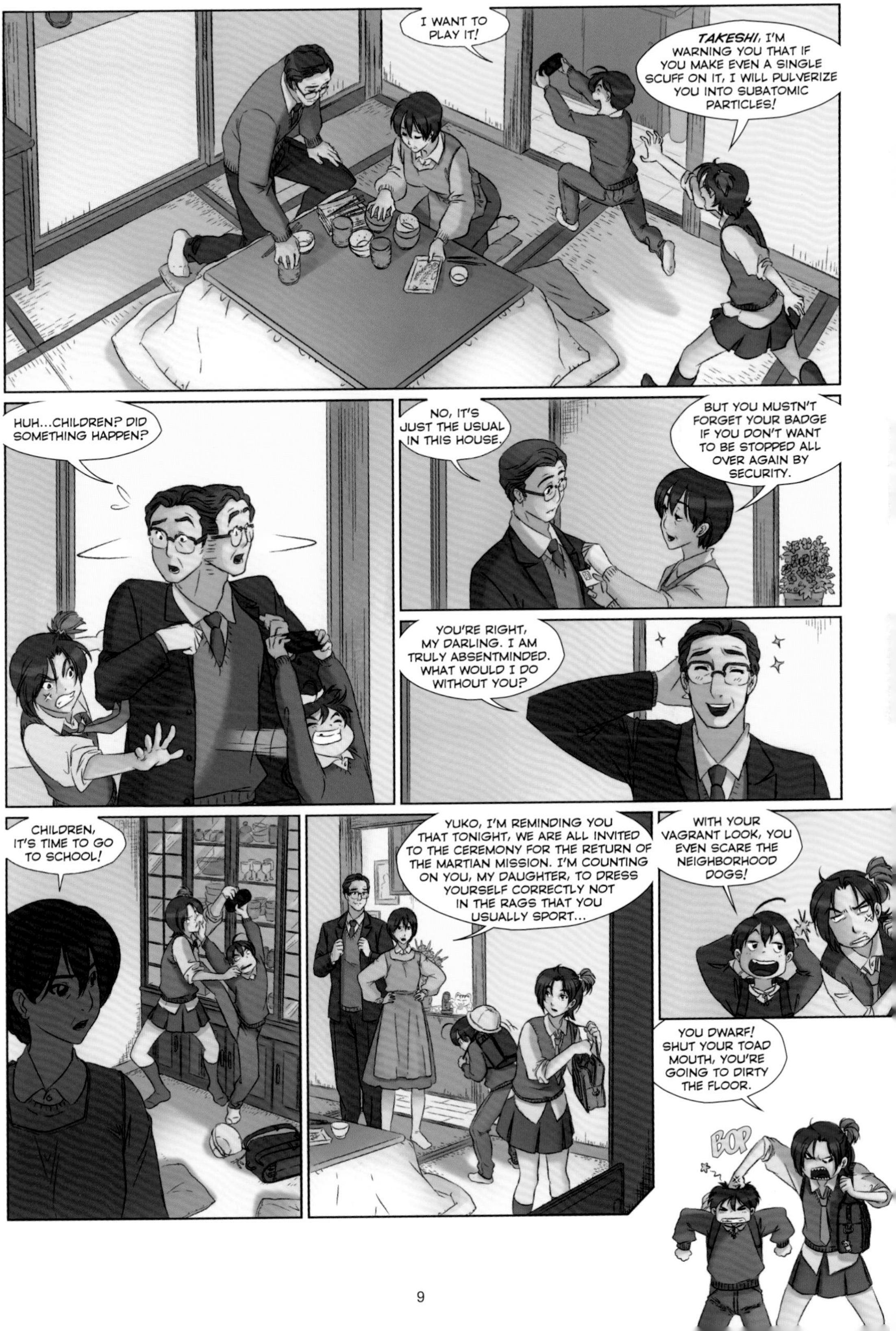
I WANT TO PLAY IT!
TAKESHI, I'M WARNING YOU THAT IF YOU MAKE EVEN A SINGLE SCUFF ON IT, I WILL PULVERIZE YOU INTO SUBATOMIC PARTICLES!
HUH...CHILDREN? DID SOMETHING HAPPEN?
NO, IT'S JUST THE USUAL IN THIS HOUSE.
BUT YOU MUSTN'T FORGET YOUR BADGE IF YOU DON'T WANT TO BE STOPPED ALL OVER AGAIN BY SECURITY.
YOU'RE RIGHT, MY DARLING. I AM TRULY ABSENTMINDED. WHAT WOULD I DO WITHOUT YOU?
CHILDREN, IT'S TIME TO GO TO SCHOOL!
YUKO, I'M REMINDING YOU THAT TONIGHT, WE ARE ALL INVITED TO THE CEREMONY FOR THE RETURN OF THE MARTIAN MISSION. I'M COUNTING ON YOU, MY DAUGHTER, TO DRESS YOURSELF CORRECTLY NOT IN THE RAGS THAT YOU USUALLY SPORT...
WITH YOUR VAGRANT LOOK, YOU EVEN SCARE THE NEIGHBORHOOD DOGS!
YOU DWARF! SHUT YOUR TOAD MOUTH, YOU'RE GOING TO DIRTY THE FLOOR.
BOP

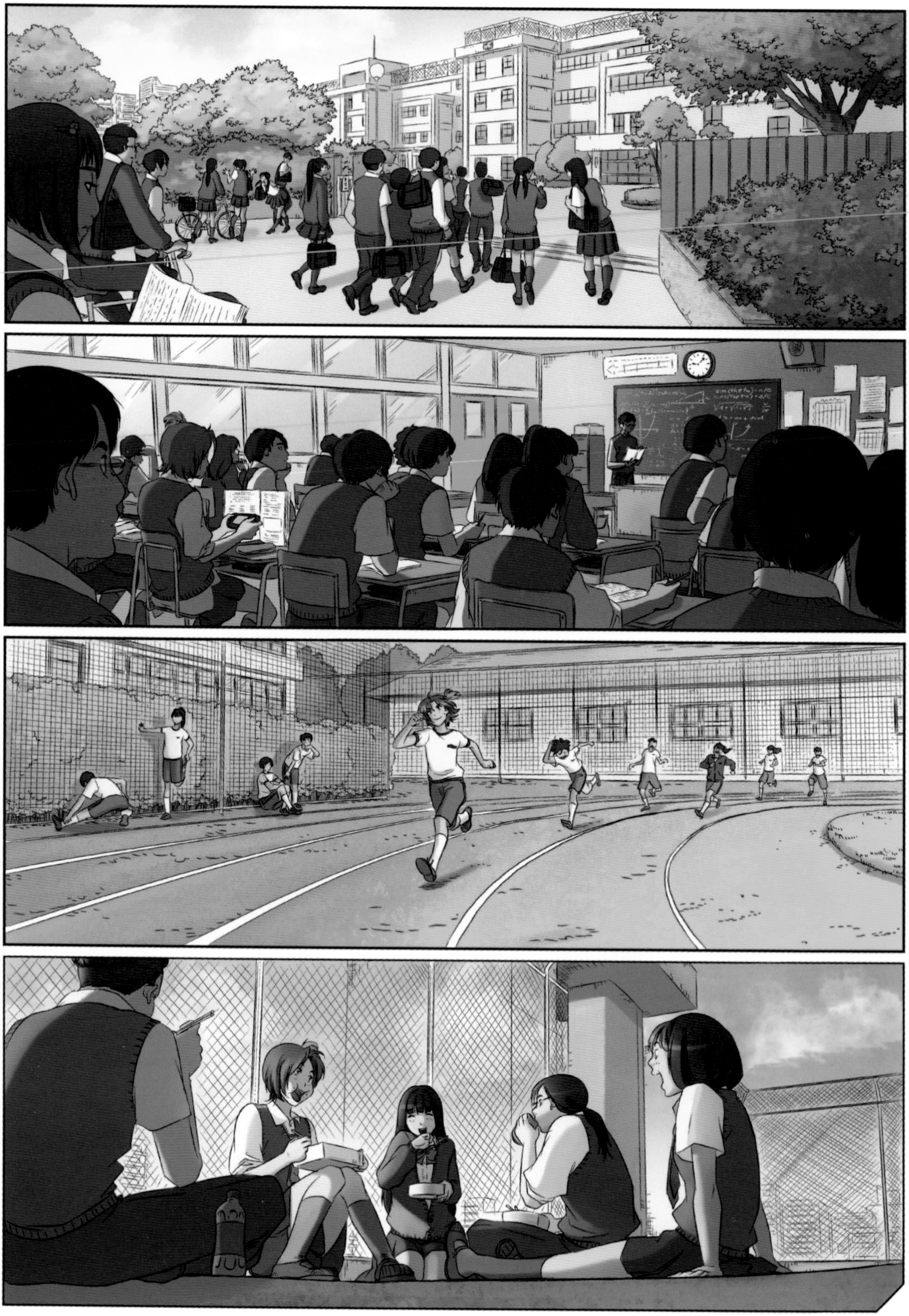

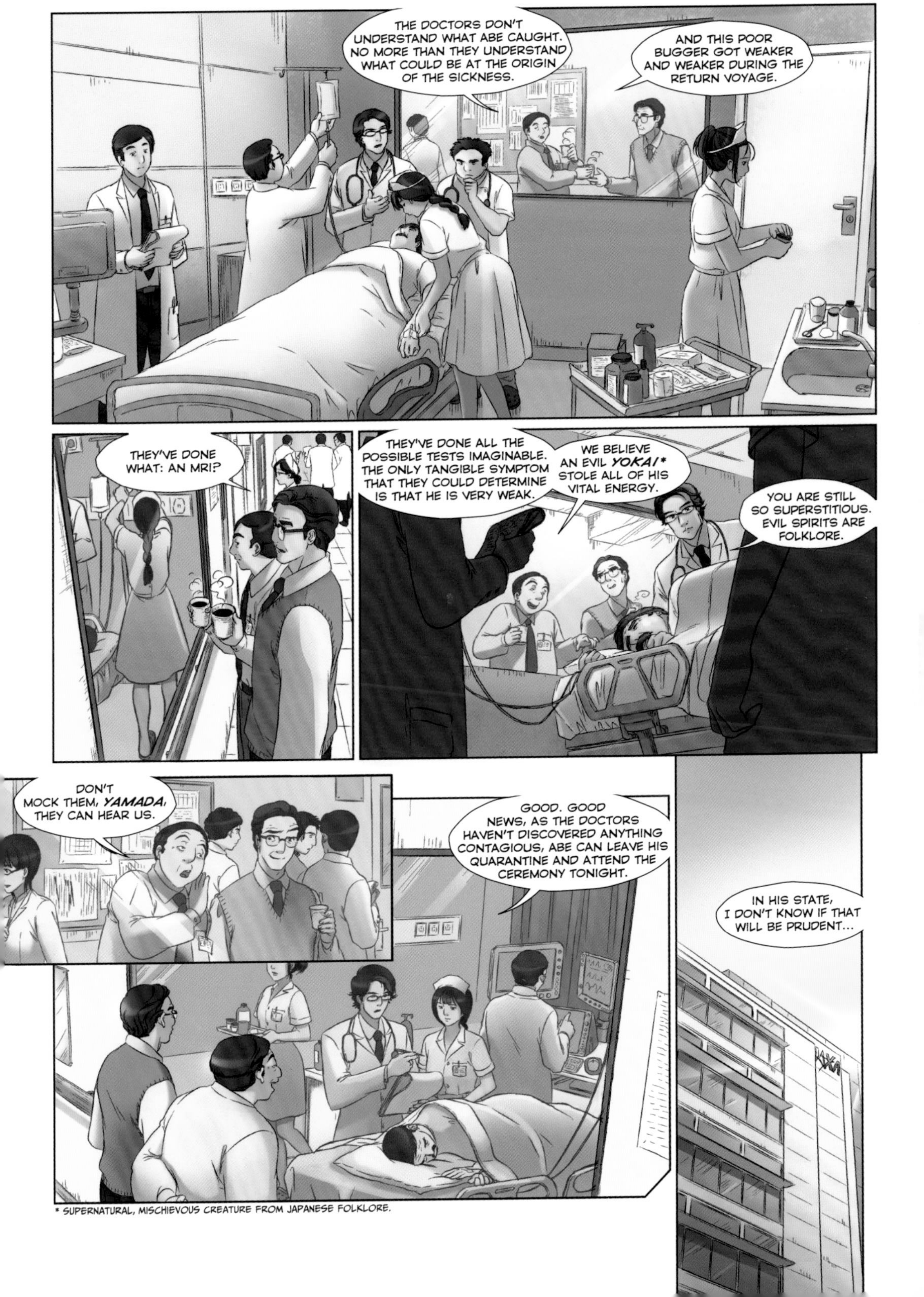
THE DOCTORS DON'T UNDERSTAND WHAT ABE CAUGHT. NO MORE THAN THEY UNDERSTAND WHAT COULD BE AT THE ORIGIN OF THE SICKNESS.
AND THIS POOR BUGGER GOT WEAKER AND WEAKER DURING THE RETURN VOYAGE.
THEY'VE DONE WHAT: AN MRI?
THEY'VE DONE ALL THE POSSIBLE TESTS IMAGINABLE. THE ONLY TANGIBLE SYMPTOM THAT THEY COULD DETERMINE IS THAT HE IS VERY WEAK.
WE BELIEVE AN EVIL YOKAI* STOLE ALL OF HIS VITAL ENERGY.
YOU ARE STILL SO SUPERSTITIOUS. EVIL SPIRITS ARE FOLKLORE.
DON'T MOCK THEM, YAMADA, THEY CAN HEAR US.
GOOD. GOOD NEWS, AS THE DOCTORS HAVEN'T DISCOVERED ANYTHING CONTAGIOUS, ABE CAN LEAVE HIS QUARANTINE AND ATTEND THE CEREMONY TONIGHT.
IN HIS STATE, I DON'T KNOW IF THAT WILL BE PRUDENT...

* SUPERNATURAL, MISCHIEVOUS CREATURE FROM JAPANESE FOLKLORE.

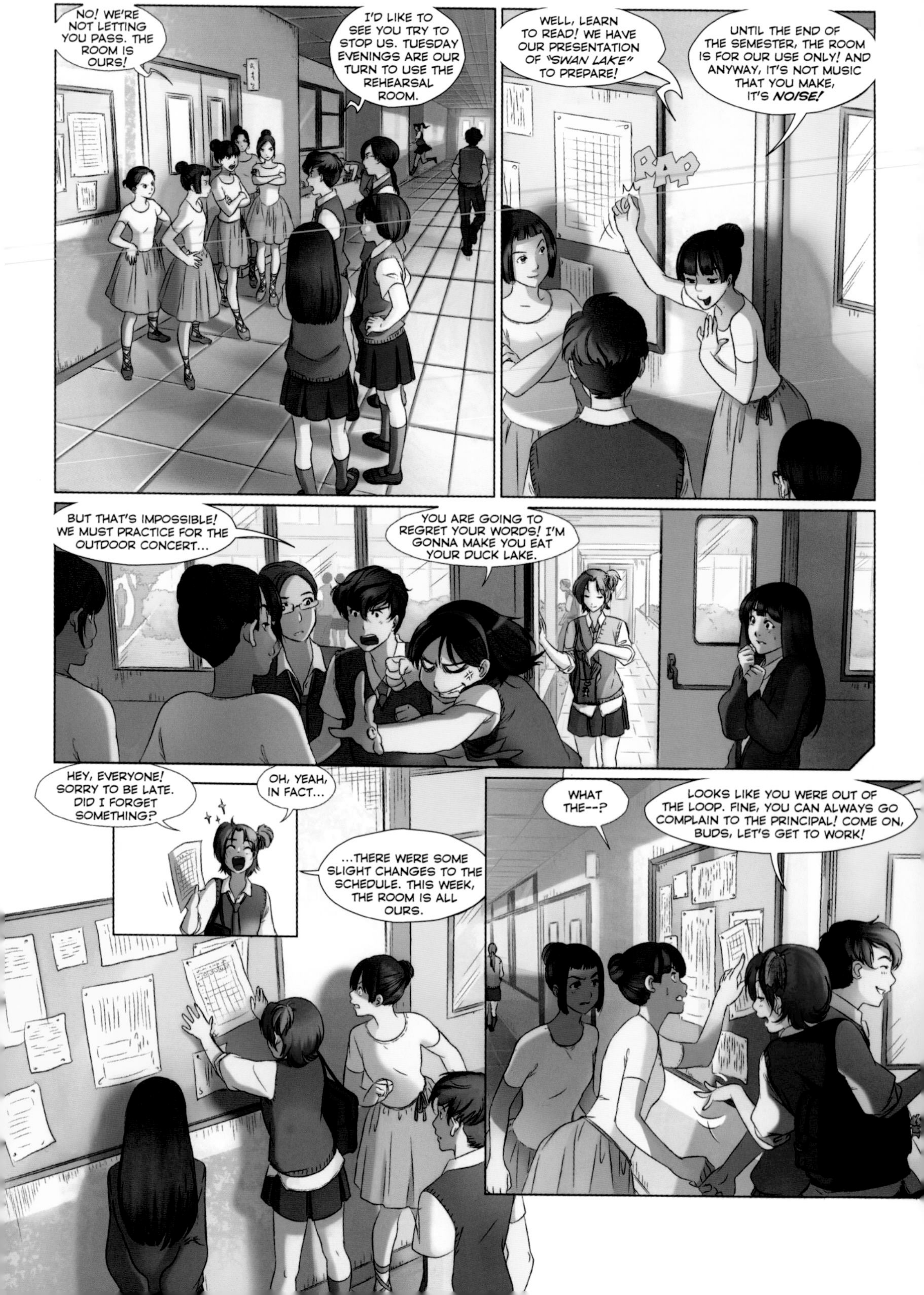
NO! WE'RE NOT LETTING YOU PASS. THE ROOM IS OURS!
I'D LIKE TO SEE YOU TRY TO STOP US. TUESDAY EVENINGS ARE OUR TURN TO USE THE REHEARSAL ROOM.
WELL, LEARN TO READ! WE HAVE OUR PRESENTATION OF "SWAN LAKE" TO PREPARE!
UNTIL THE END OF THE SEMESTER, THE ROOM IS FOR OUR USE ONLY! AND ANYWAY, IT'S NOT MUSIC THAT YOU MAKE, IT'S NOISE!
RAP
BUT THAT'S IMPOSSIBLE! WE MUST PRACTICE FOR THE OUTDOOR CONCERT...
YOU ARE GOING TO REGRET YOUR WORDS! I'M GONNA MAKE YOU EAT YOUR DUCK LAKE.
HEY, EVERYONE! SORRY TO BE LATE. DID I FORGET SOMETHING?
OH, YEAH, IN FACT...
...THERE WERE SOME SLIGHT CHANGES TO THE SCHEDULE. THIS WEEK, THE ROOM IS ALL OURS.
WHAT THE--?
LOOKS LIKE YOU WERE OUT OF THE LOOP. FINE, YOU CAN ALWAYS GO COMPLAIN TO THE PRINCIPAL! COME ON, BUDS, LET'S GET TO WORK!

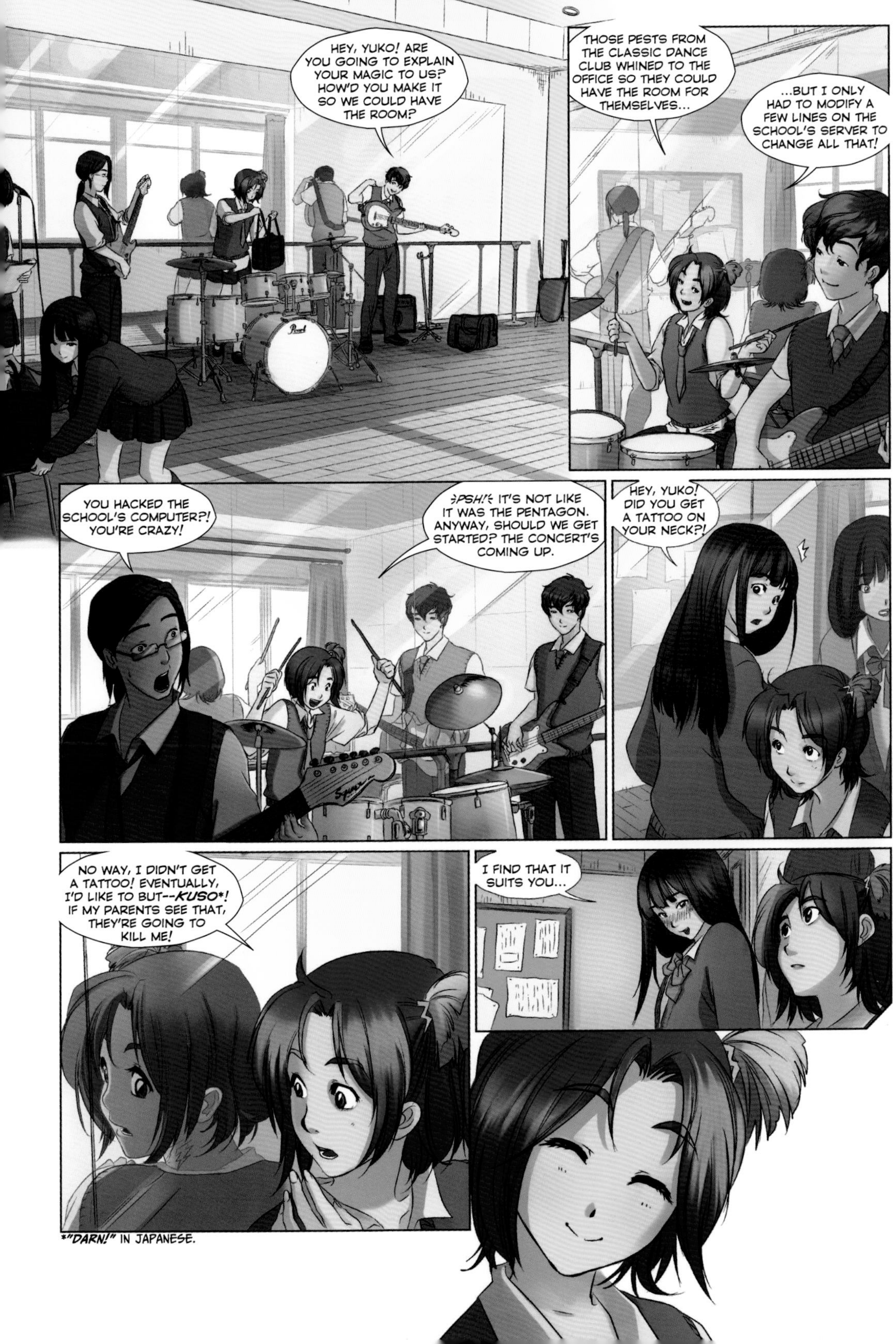
HEY, YUKO! ARE YOU GOING TO EXPLAIN YOUR MAGIC TO US? HOW'D YOU MAKE IT SO WE COULD HAVE THE ROOM?
THOSE PESTS FROM THE CLASSIC DANCE CLUB WHINED TO THE OFFICE SO THEY COULD HAVE THE ROOM FOR THEMSELVES...
...BUT I ONLY HAD TO MODIFY A FEW LINES ON THE SCHOOL'S SERVER TO CHANGE ALL THAT!
YOU HACKED THE SCHOOL'S COMPUTER?! YOU'RE CRAZY!
PSH! IT'S NOT LIKE IT WAS THE PENTAGON. ANYWAY, SHOULD WE GET STARTED? THE CONCERT'S COMING UP.
HEY, YUKO! DID YOU GET A TATTOO ON YOUR NECK?!
NO WAY, I DIDN'T GET A TATTOO! EVENTUALLY, I'D LIKE TO BUT--KUSO*! IF MY PARENTS SEE THAT, THEY'RE GOING TO KILL ME!
I FIND THAT IT SUITS YOU...

*"DARN!" IN JAPANESE.

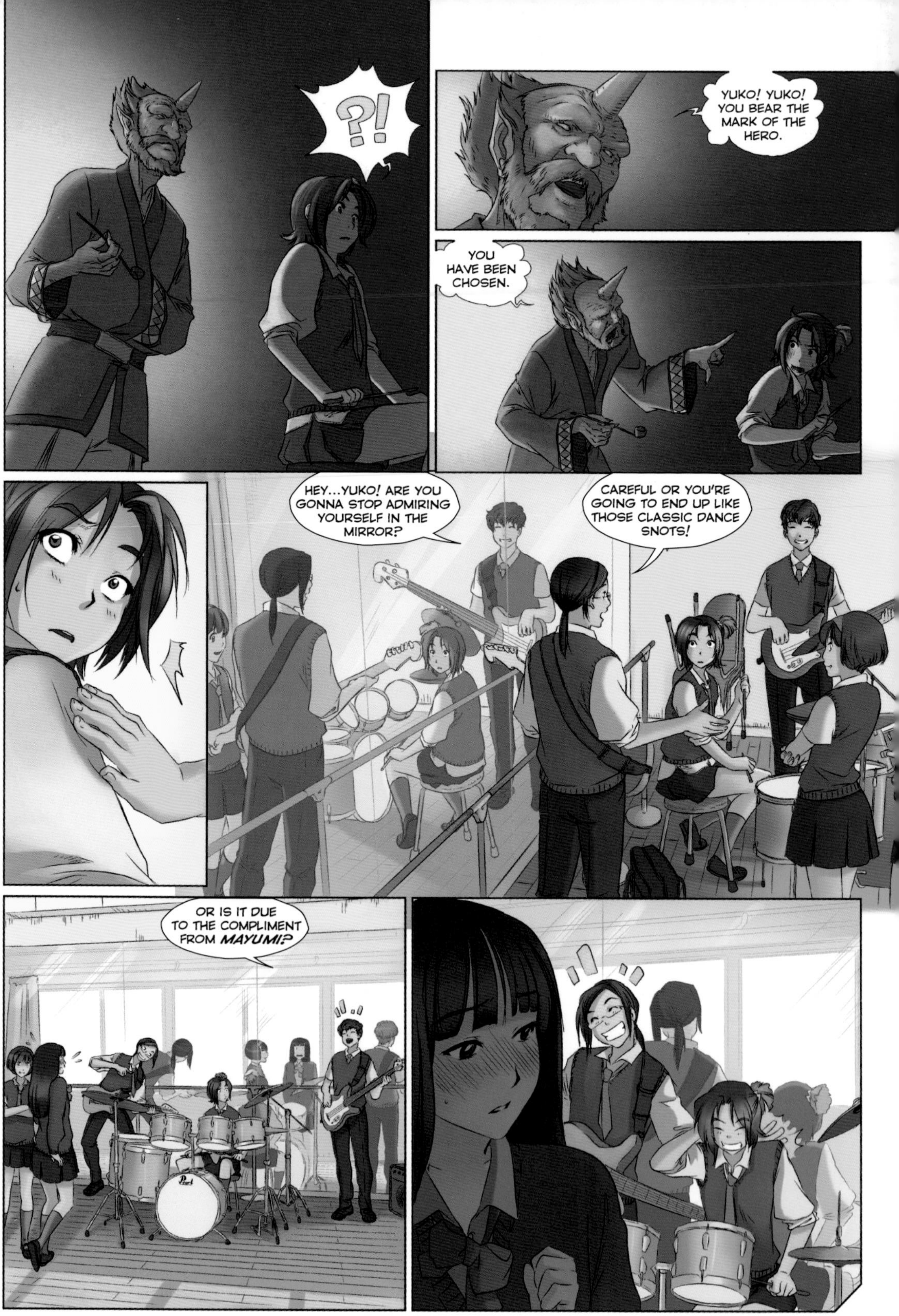
?!
YUKO! YUKO! YOU BEAR THE MARK OF THE HERO.
YOU HAVE BEEN CHOSEN.
HEY...YUKO! ARE YOU GONNA STOP ADMIRING YOURSELF IN THE MIRROR?
CAREFUL OR YOU'RE GOING TO END UP LIKE THOSE CLASSIC DANCE SNOTS!
OR IS IT DUE TO THE COMPLIMENT FROM MAYUMI?

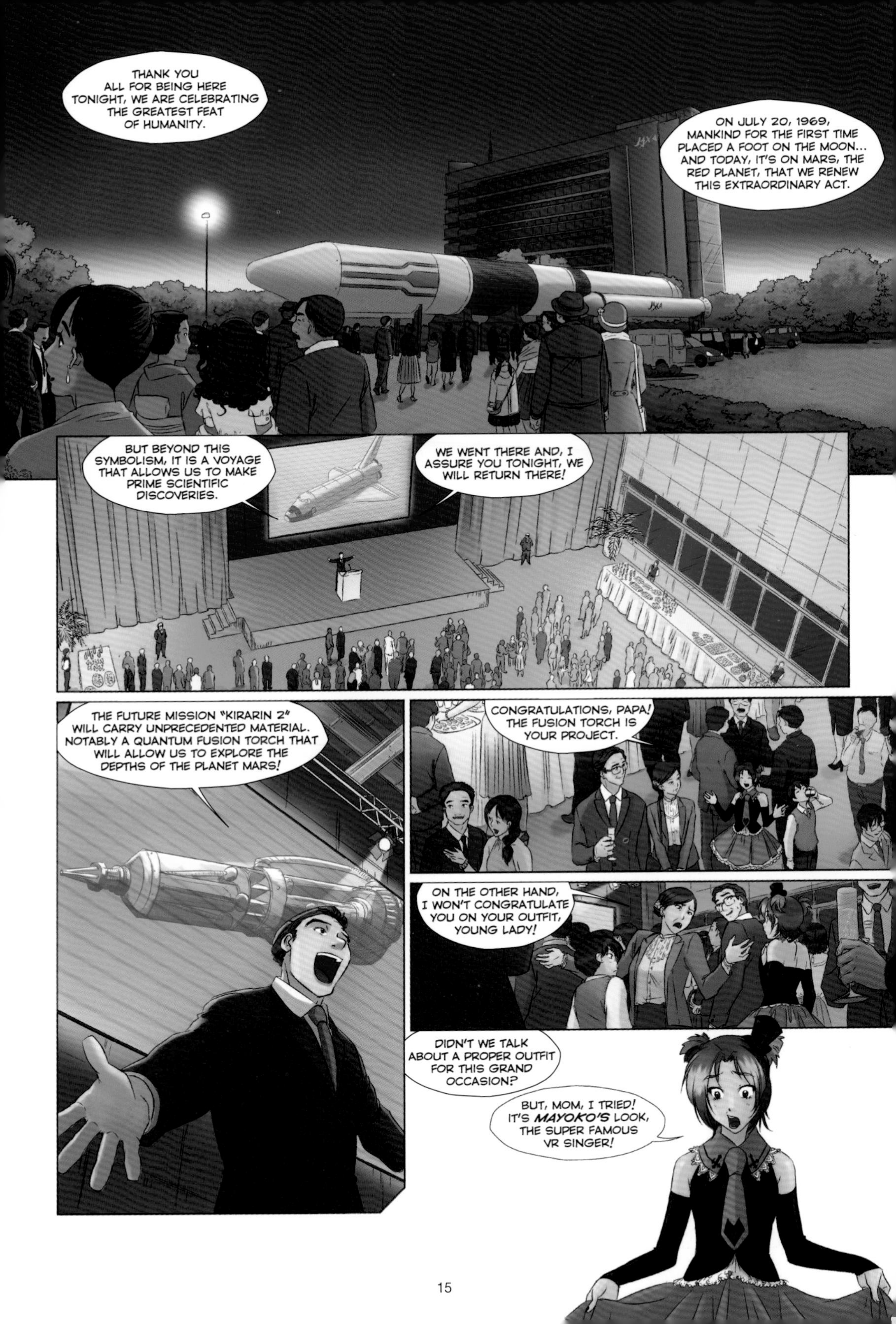
THANK YOU ALL FOR BEING HERE TONIGHT, WE ARE CELEBRATING THE GREATEST FEAT OF HUMANITY.
ON JULY 20, 1969, MANKIND FOR THE FIRST TIME PLACED A FOOT ON THE MOON... AND TODAY, IT'S ON MARS, THE RED PLANET, THAT WE RENEW THIS EXTRAORDINARY ACT.
BUT BEYOND THIS SYMBOLISM, IT IS A VOYAGE THAT ALLOWS US TO MAKE PRIME SCIENTIFIC DISCOVERIES.
WE WENT THERE AND, I ASSURE YOU TONIGHT, WE WILL RETURN THERE!
THE FUTURE MISSION "KIRARIN 2" WILL CARRY UNPRECEDENTED MATERIAL. NOTABLY A QUANTUM FUSION TORCH THAT WILL ALLOW US TO EXPLORE THE DEPTHS OF THE PLANET MARS!
CONGRATULATIONS, PAPA! THE FUSION TORCH IS YOUR PROJECT.
ON THE OTHER HAND, I WON'T CONGRATULATE YOU ON YOUR OUTFIT, YOUNG LADY!
DIDN'T WE TALK ABOUT A PROPER OUTFIT FOR THIS GRAND OCCASION?
BUT, MOM, I TRIED! IT'S *MAYOKO'S* LOOK, THE SUPER FAMOUS VR SINGER!

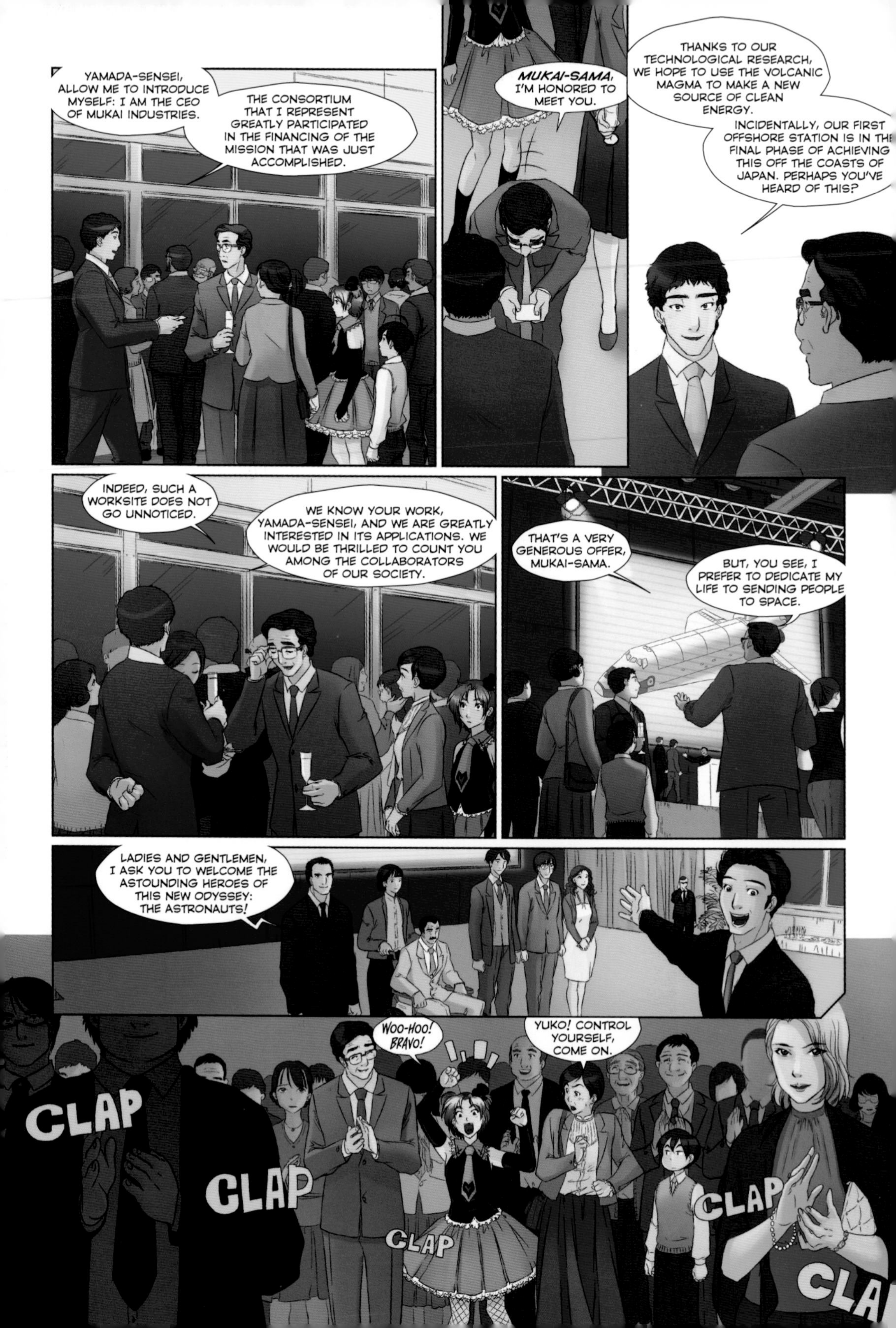
YAMADA-SENSEI, ALLOW ME TO INTRODUCE MYSELF: I AM THE CEO OF MUKAI INDUSTRIES.
THE CONSORTIUM THAT I REPRESENT GREATLY PARTICIPATED IN THE FINANCING OF THE MISSION THAT WAS JUST ACCOMPLISHED.
MUKAI-SAMA, I'M HONORED TO MEET YOU.
THANKS TO OUR TECHNOLOGICAL RESEARCH, WE HOPE TO USE THE VOLCANIC MAGMA TO MAKE A NEW SOURCE OF CLEAN ENERGY.
INCIDENTALLY, OUR FIRST OFFSHORE STATION IS IN THE FINAL PHASE OF ACHIEVING THIS OFF THE COASTS OF JAPAN. PERHAPS YOU'VE HEARD OF THIS?
INDEED, SUCH A WORKSITE DOES NOT GO UNNOTICED.
WE KNOW YOUR WORK, YAMADA-SENSEI, AND WE ARE GREATLY INTERESTED IN ITS APPLICATIONS. WE WOULD BE THRILLED TO COUNT YOU AMONG THE COLLABORATORS OF OUR SOCIETY.
THAT'S A VERY GENEROUS OFFER, MUKAI-SAMA.
BUT, YOU SEE, I PREFER TO DEDICATE MY LIFE TO SENDING PEOPLE TO SPACE.
LADIES AND GENTLEMEN, I ASK YOU TO WELCOME THE ASTOUNDING HEROES OF THIS NEW ODYSSEY: THE ASTRONAUTS!
CLAP
CLAP
WOO-HOO! BRAVO!
CLAP
YUKO! CONTROL YOURSELF, COME ON.
CLAP
CLA

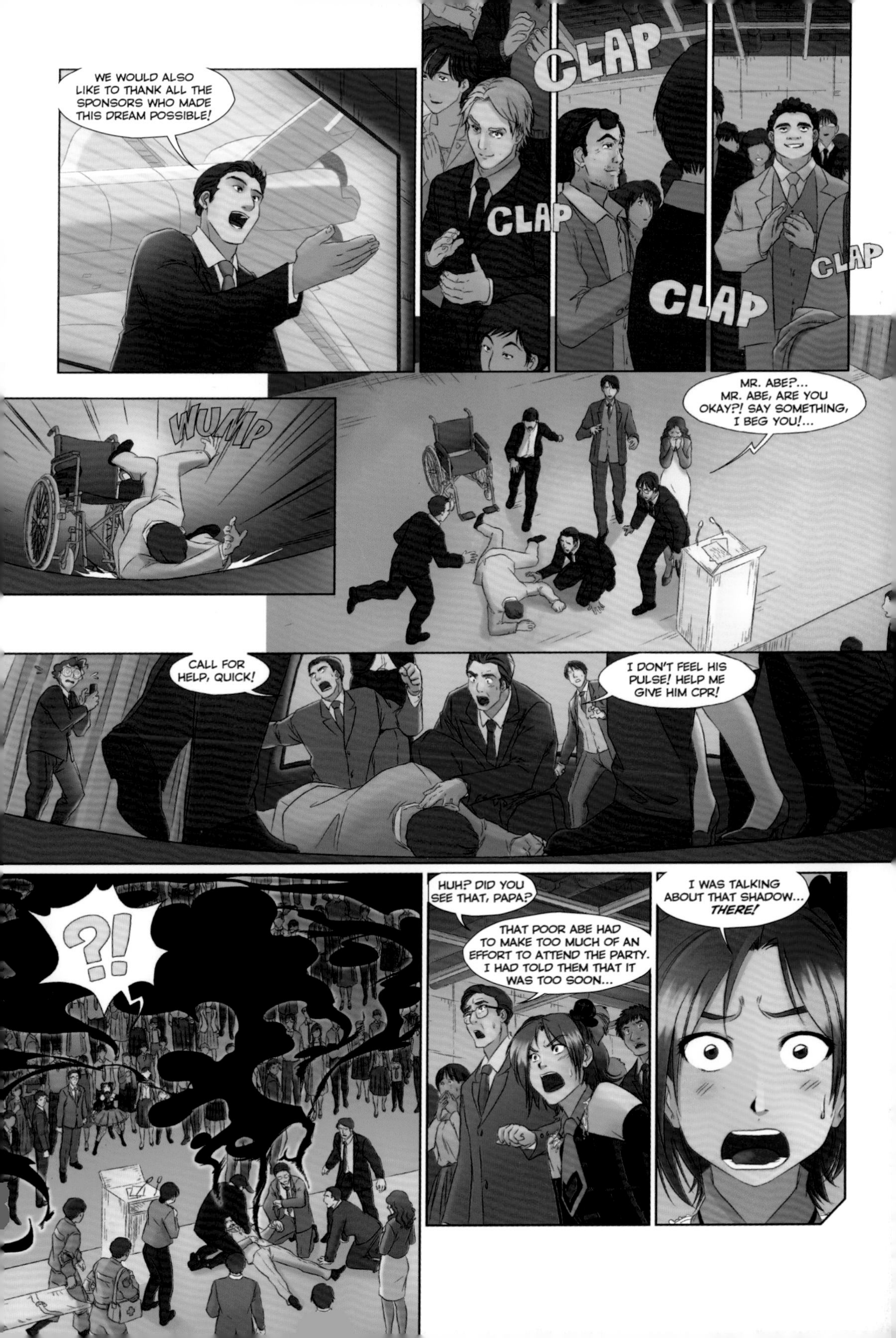
WE WOULD ALSO LIKE TO THANK ALL THE SPONSORS WHO MADE THIS DREAM POSSIBLE!
CLAP
CLAP
CLAP
CLAP
WUMP
MR. ABE?... MR. ABE, ARE YOU OKAY?! SAY SOMETHING, I BEG YOU!...
CALL FOR HELP, QUICK!
I DON'T FEEL HIS PULSE! HELP ME GIVE HIM CPR!
?!
HUH? DID YOU SEE THAT, PAPA?
THAT POOR ABE HAD TO MAKE TOO MUCH OF AN EFFORT TO ATTEND THE PARTY. I HAD TOLD THEM THAT IT WAS TOO SOON...
I WAS TALKING ABOUT THAT SHADOW... THERE!

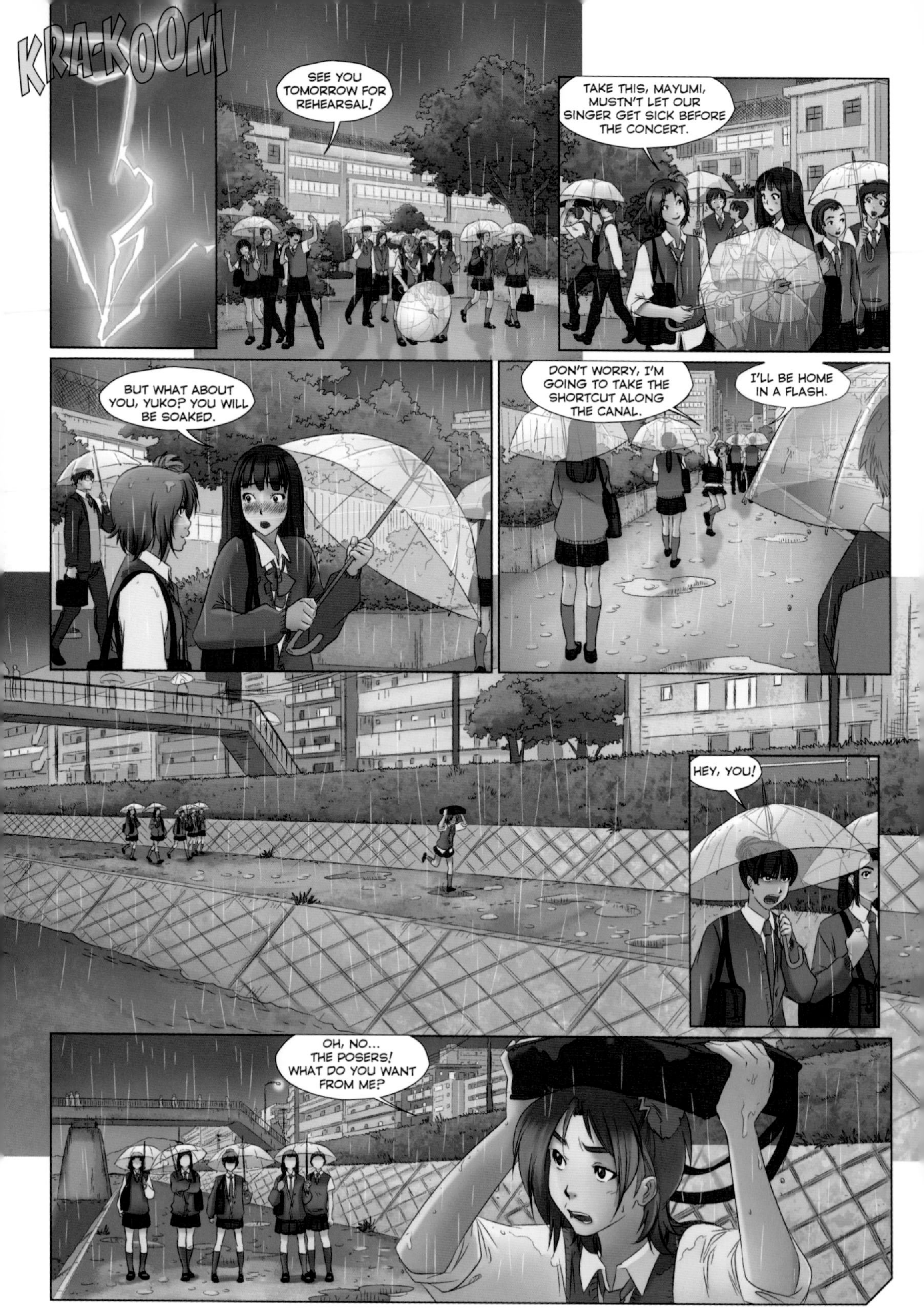
KRA-KOOM
SEE YOU TOMORROW FOR REHEARSAL!
TAKE THIS, MAYUMI, MUSTN'T LET OUR SINGER GET SICK BEFORE THE CONCERT.
BUT WHAT ABOUT YOU, YUKO? YOU WILL BE SOAKED.
DON'T WORRY, I'M GOING TO TAKE THE SHORTCUT ALONG THE CANAL.
I'LL BE HOME IN A FLASH.
HEY, YOU!
OH, NO... THE POSERS! WHAT DO YOU WANT FROM ME?

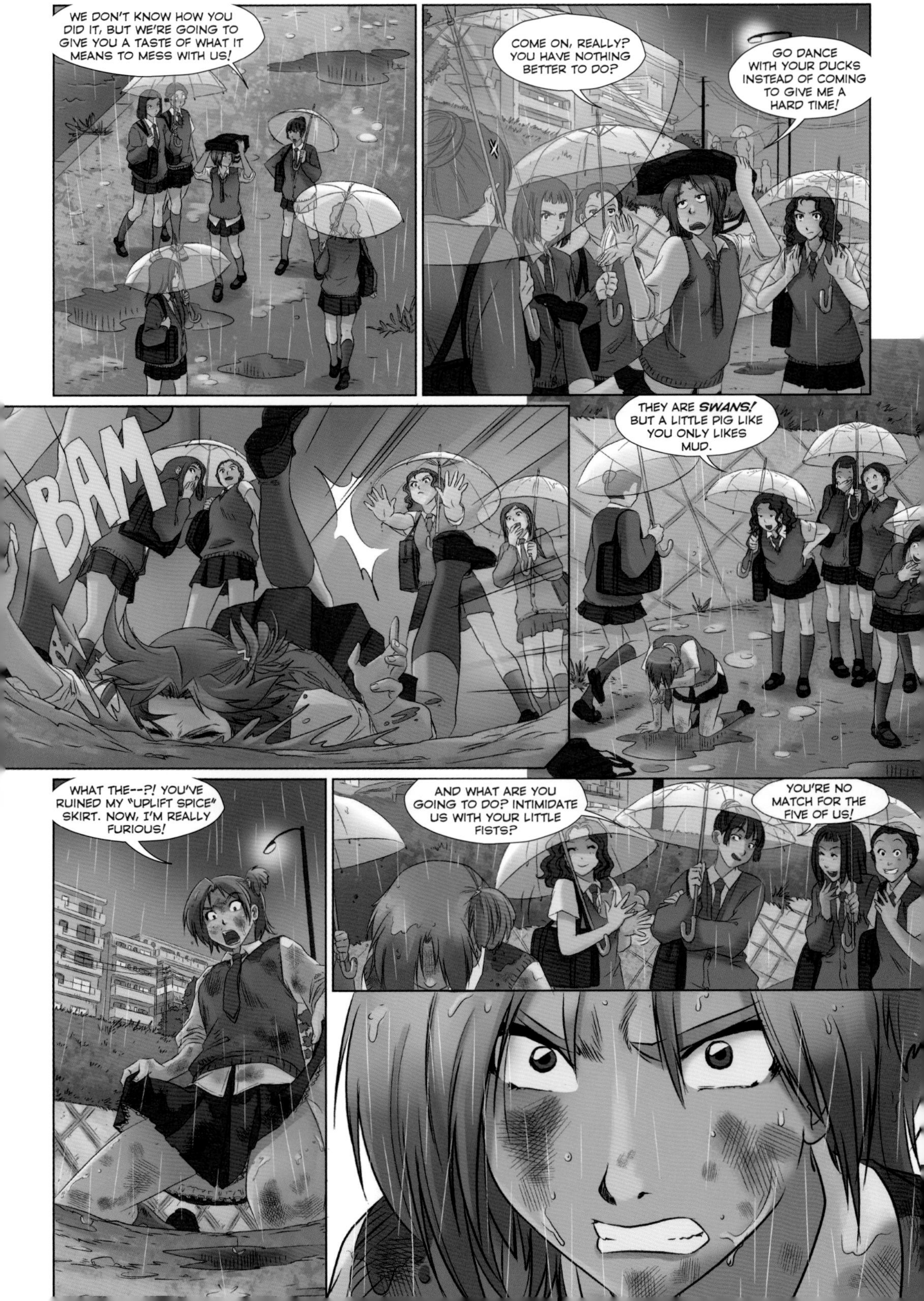
WE DON'T KNOW HOW YOU DID IT, BUT WE'RE GOING TO GIVE YOU A TASTE OF WHAT IT MEANS TO MESS WITH US!
COME ON, REALLY? YOU HAVE NOTHING BETTER TO DO?
GO DANCE WITH YOUR DUCKS INSTEAD OF COMING TO GIVE ME A HARD TIME!
BAM
THEY ARE SWANS! BUT A LITTLE PIG LIKE YOU ONLY LIKES MUD.
WHAT THE--?! YOU'VE RUINED MY "UPLIFT SPICE" SKIRT. NOW, I'M REALLY FURIOUS!
AND WHAT ARE YOU GOING TO DO? INTIMIDATE US WITH YOUR LITTLE FISTS?
YOU'RE NO MATCH FOR THE FIVE OF US!

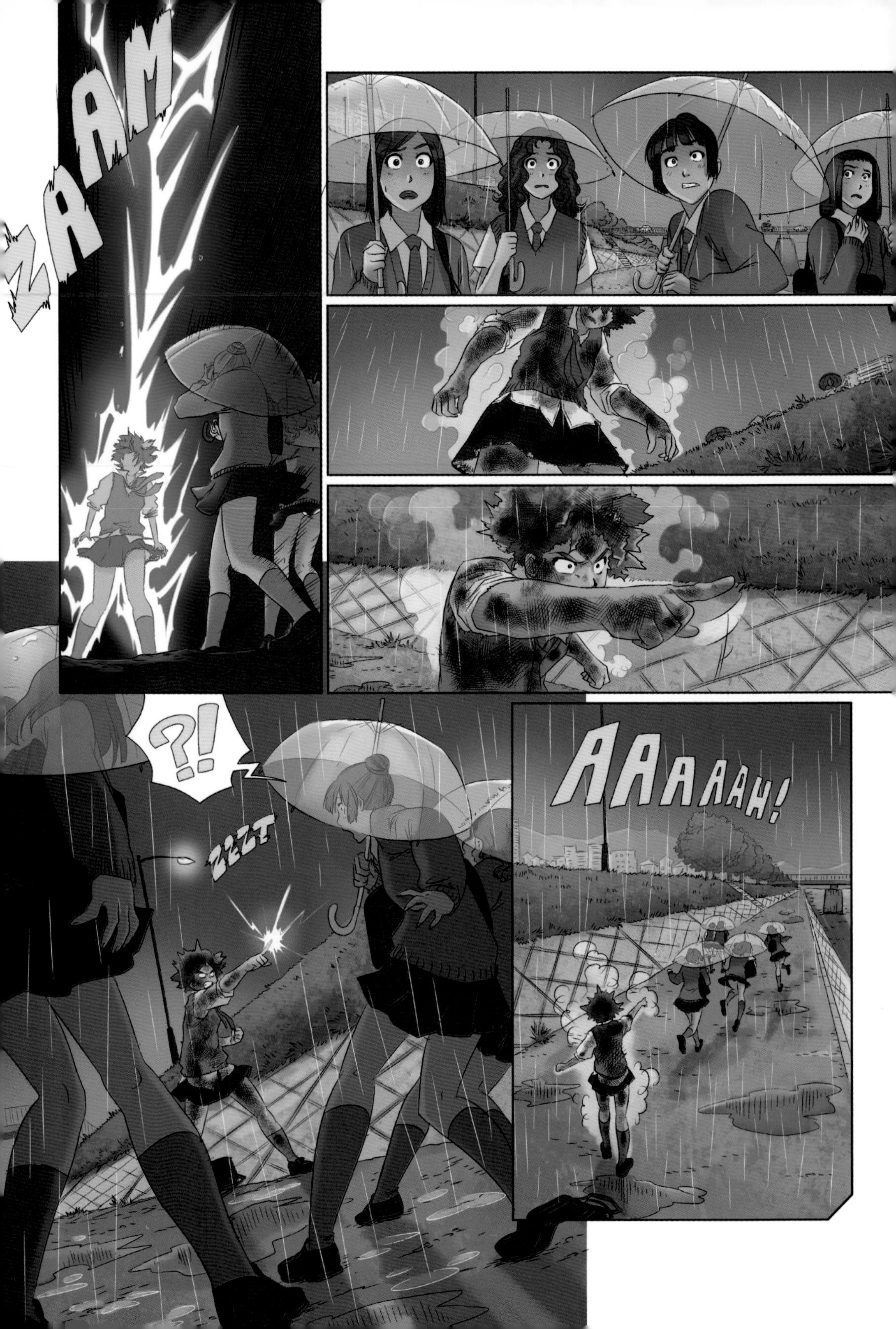
ZZAAM
?!
ZZZT
AAAAAAH!

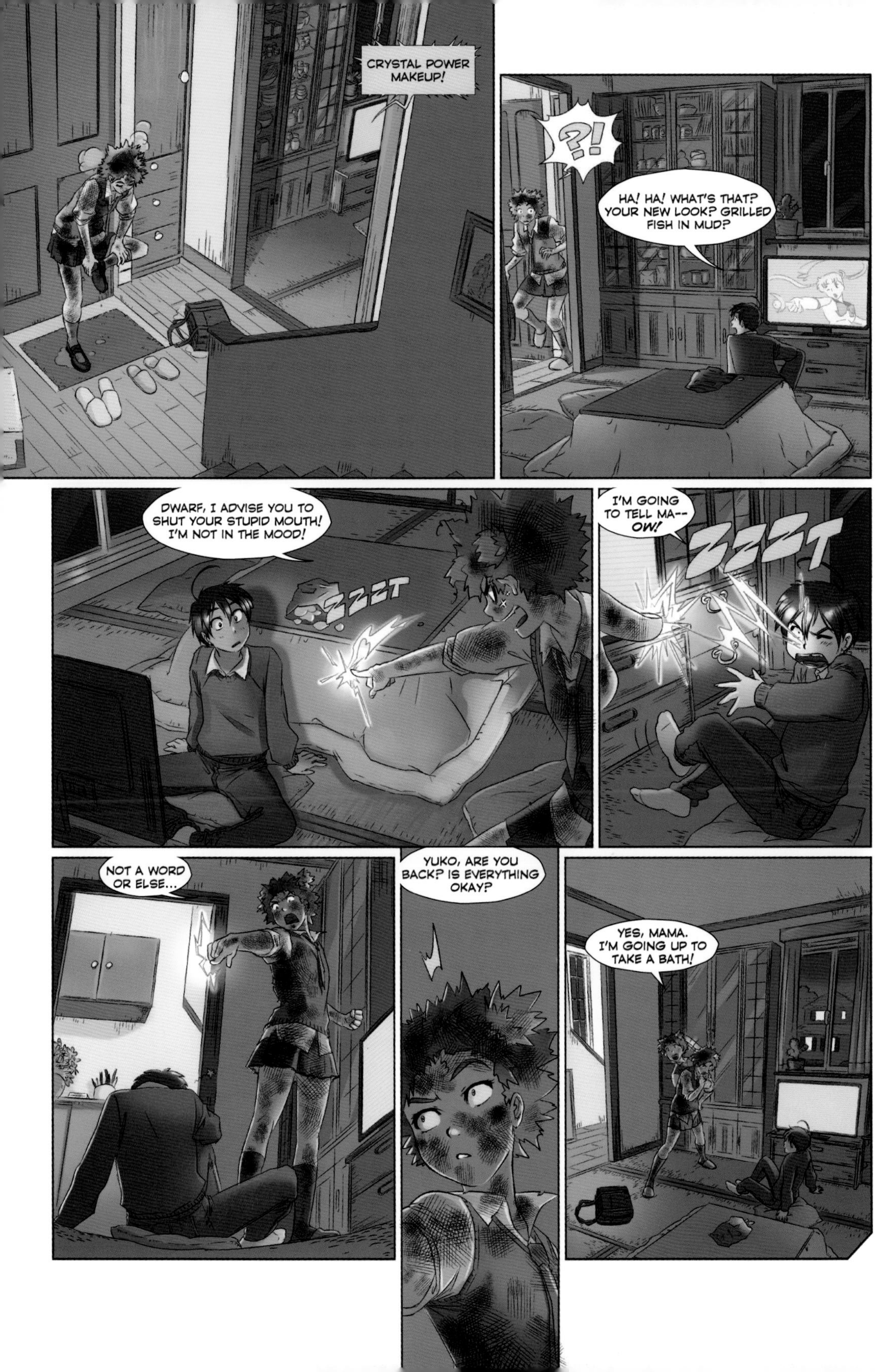
CRYSTAL POWER MAKEUP!
?!
HA! HA! WHAT'S THAT? YOUR NEW LOOK? GRILLED FISH IN MUD?
DWARF, I ADVISE YOU TO SHUT YOUR STUPID MOUTH! I'M NOT IN THE MOOD!
ZZZT
I'M GOING TO TELL MA-- OW!
ZZZT
NOT A WORD OR ELSE...
YUKO, ARE YOU BACK? IS EVERYTHING OKAY?
YES, MAMA. I'M GOING UP TO TAKE A BATH!

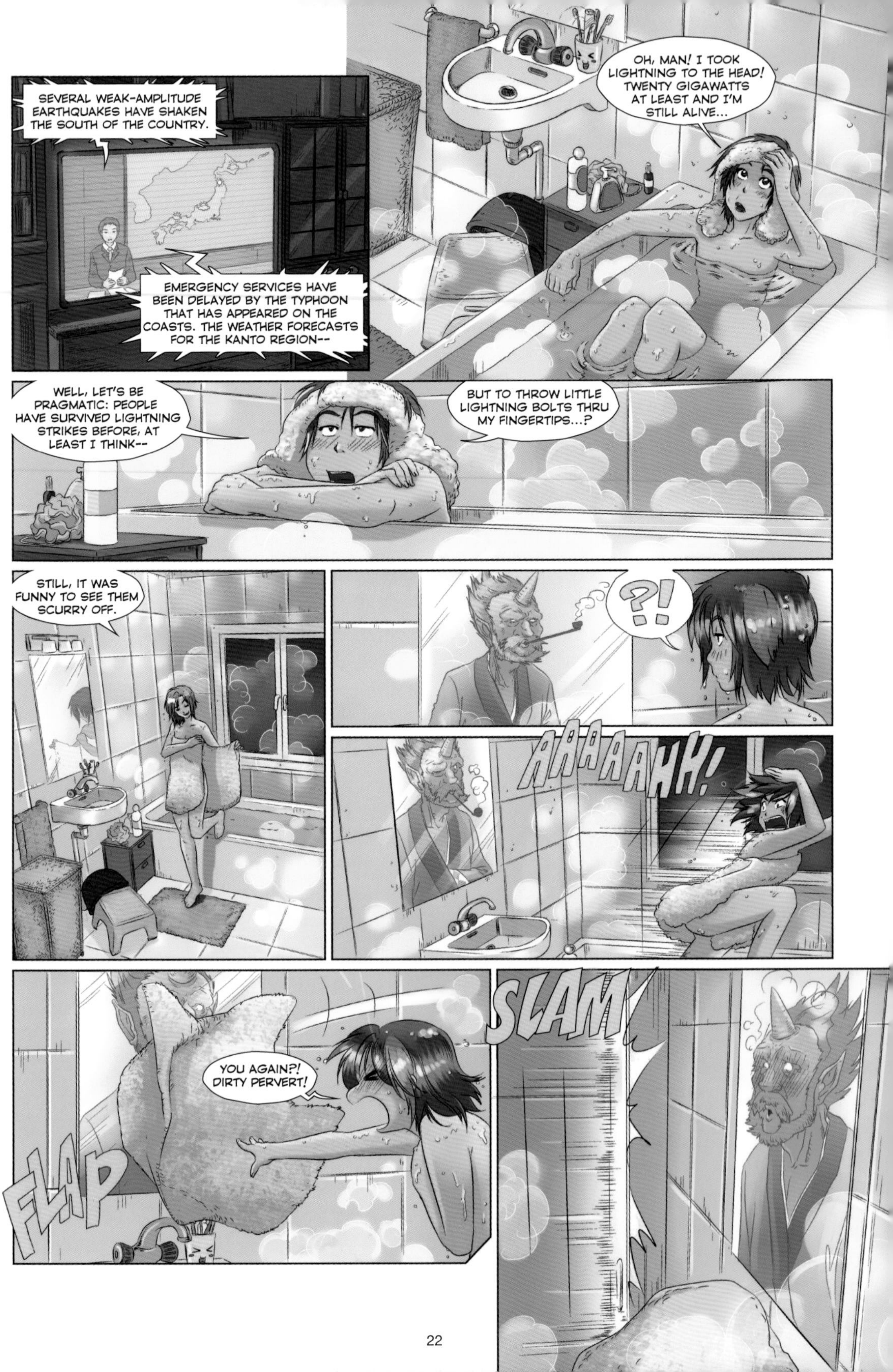
SEVERAL WEAK-AMPLITUDE EARTHQUAKES HAVE SHAKEN THE SOUTH OF THE COUNTRY.
EMERGENCY SERVICES HAVE BEEN DELAYED BY THE TYPHOON THAT HAS APPEARED ON THE COASTS. THE WEATHER FORECASTS FOR THE KANTO REGION--
OH, MAN! I TOOK LIGHTNING TO THE HEAD! TWENTY GIGAWATTS AT LEAST AND I'M STILL ALIVE...
WELL, LET'S BE PRAGMATIC: PEOPLE HAVE SURVIVED LIGHTNING STRIKES BEFORE, AT LEAST I THINK--
BUT TO THROW LITTLE LIGHTNING BOLTS THRU MY FINGERTIPS...?
STILL, IT WAS FUNNY TO SEE THEM SCURRY OFF.
?!
AAAAAAHH!
YOU AGAIN?! DIRTY PERVERT!
FLAP
SLAM

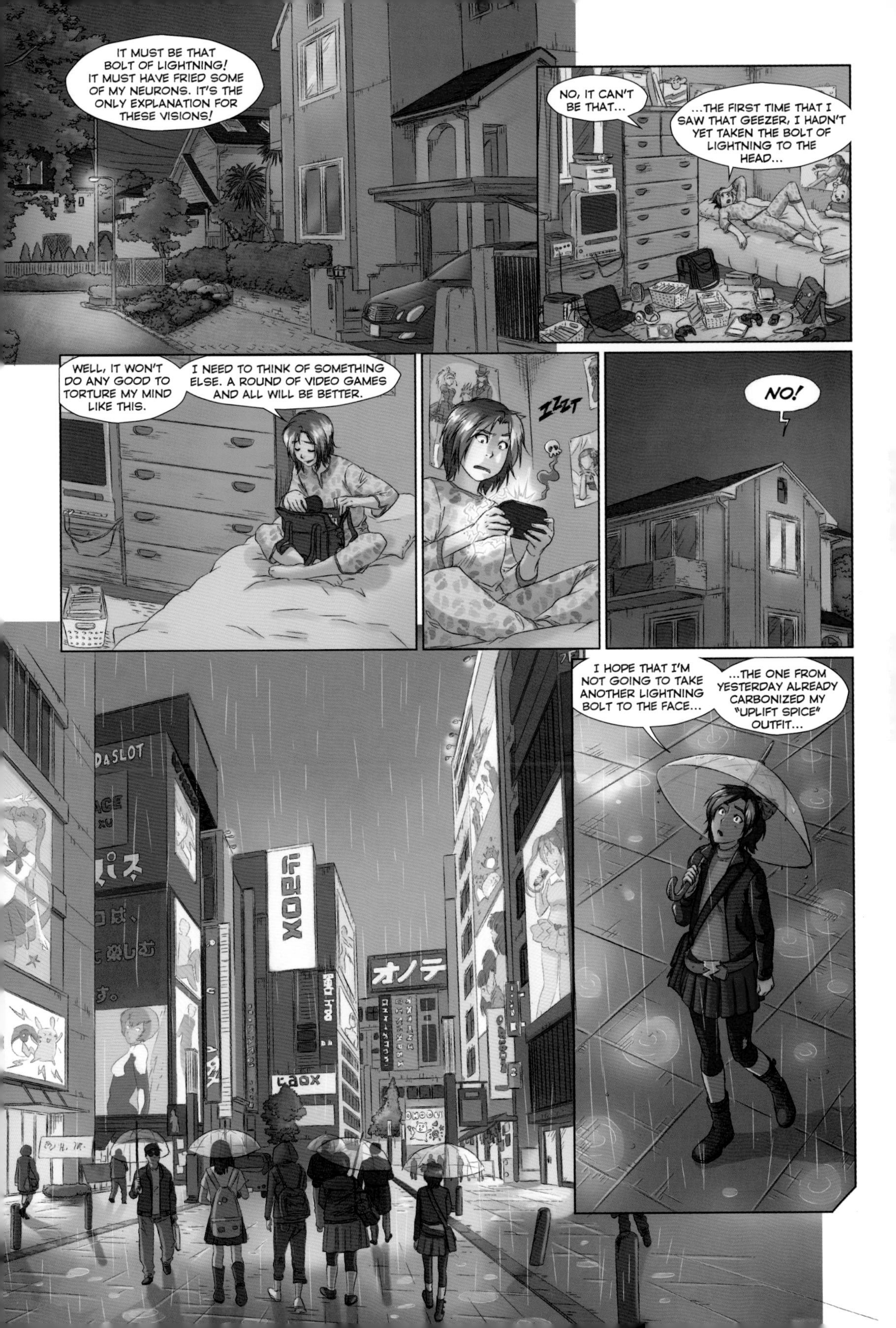

IT MUST BE THAT BOLT OF LIGHTNING! IT MUST HAVE FRIED SOME OF MY NEURONS. IT'S THE ONLY EXPLANATION FOR THESE VISIONS!
NO, IT CAN'T BE THAT...
...THE FIRST TIME THAT I SAW THAT GEEZER, I HADN'T YET TAKEN THE BOLT OF LIGHTNING TO THE HEAD...
WELL, IT WON'T DO ANY GOOD TO TORTURE MY MIND LIKE THIS.
I NEED TO THINK OF SOMETHING ELSE. A ROUND OF VIDEO GAMES AND ALL WILL BE BETTER.
ZZZT
NO!
I HOPE THAT I'M NOT GOING TO TAKE ANOTHER LIGHTNING BOLT TO THE FACE...
...THE ONE FROM YESTERDAY ALREADY CARBONIZED MY "UPLIFT SPICE" OUTFIT...

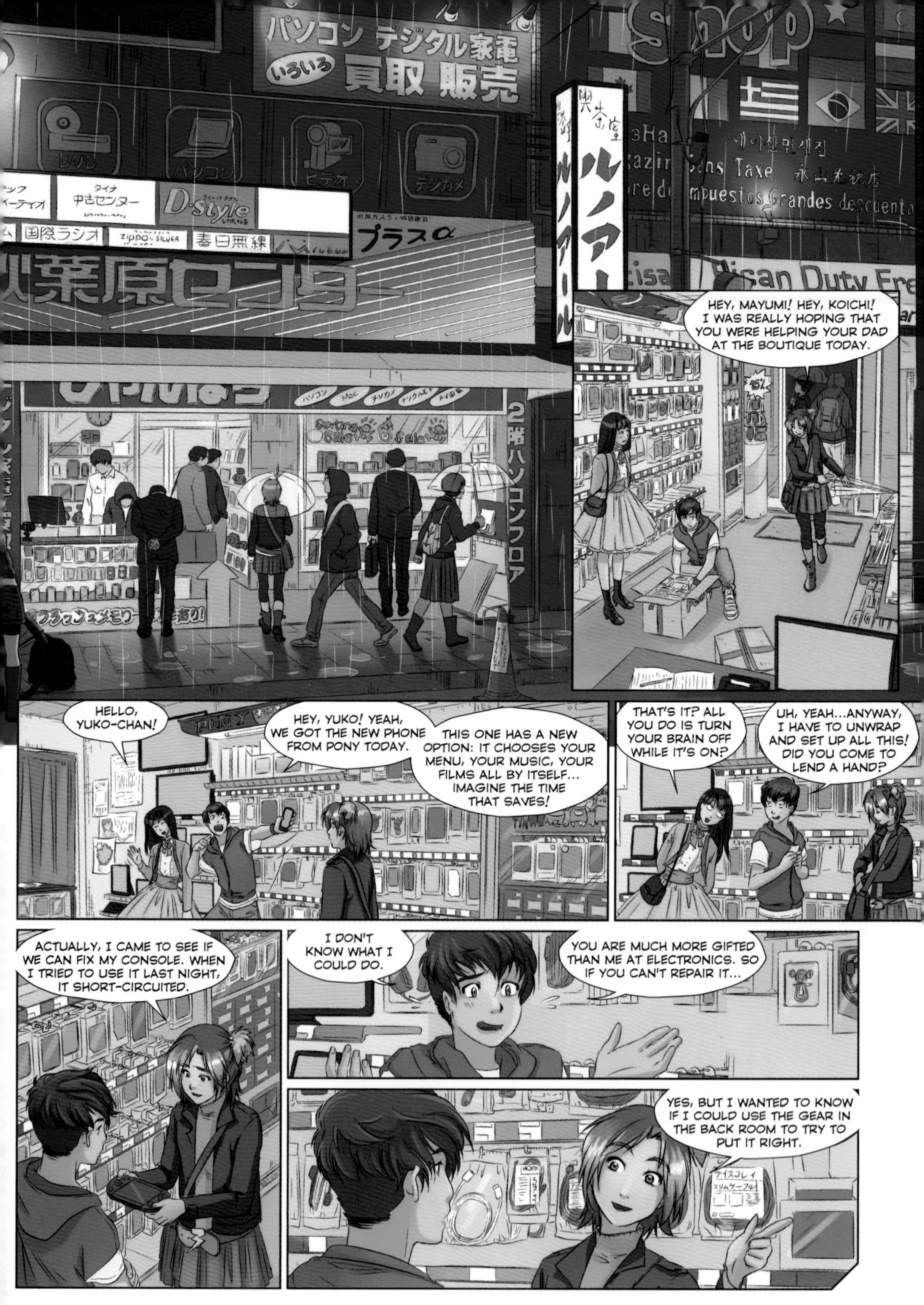

パソコン デジタル家電
いろいろ 買取 販売
DVD
パソコン
ビデオ
デジカメ
中古センター
D-style
国際ラジオ
春日無線
プラスα
shop
Sans Taxe
Grandes descuento
Duty Free
2階パソコンフロア
HEY, MAYUMI! HEY, KOICHI! I WAS REALLY HOPING THAT YOU WERE HELPING YOUR DAD AT THE BOUTIQUE TODAY.
HELLO, YUKO-CHAN!
HEY, YUKO! YEAH, WE GOT THE NEW PHONE FROM PONY TODAY.
THIS ONE HAS A NEW OPTION: IT CHOOSES YOUR MENU, YOUR MUSIC, YOUR FILMS ALL BY ITSELF... IMAGINE THE TIME THAT SAVES!
THAT'S IT? ALL YOU DO IS TURN YOUR BRAIN OFF WHILE IT'S ON?
UH, YEAH...ANYWAY, I HAVE TO UNWRAP AND SET UP ALL THIS! DID YOU COME TO LEND A HAND?
ACTUALLY, I CAME TO SEE IF WE CAN FIX MY CONSOLE. WHEN I TRIED TO USE IT LAST NIGHT, IT SHORT-CIRCUITED.
I DON'T KNOW WHAT I COULD DO.
YOU ARE MUCH MORE GIFTED THAN ME AT ELECTRONICS. SO IF YOU CAN'T REPAIR IT...
YES, BUT I WANTED TO KNOW IF I COULD USE THE GEAR IN THE BACK ROOM TO TRY TO PUT IT RIGHT.

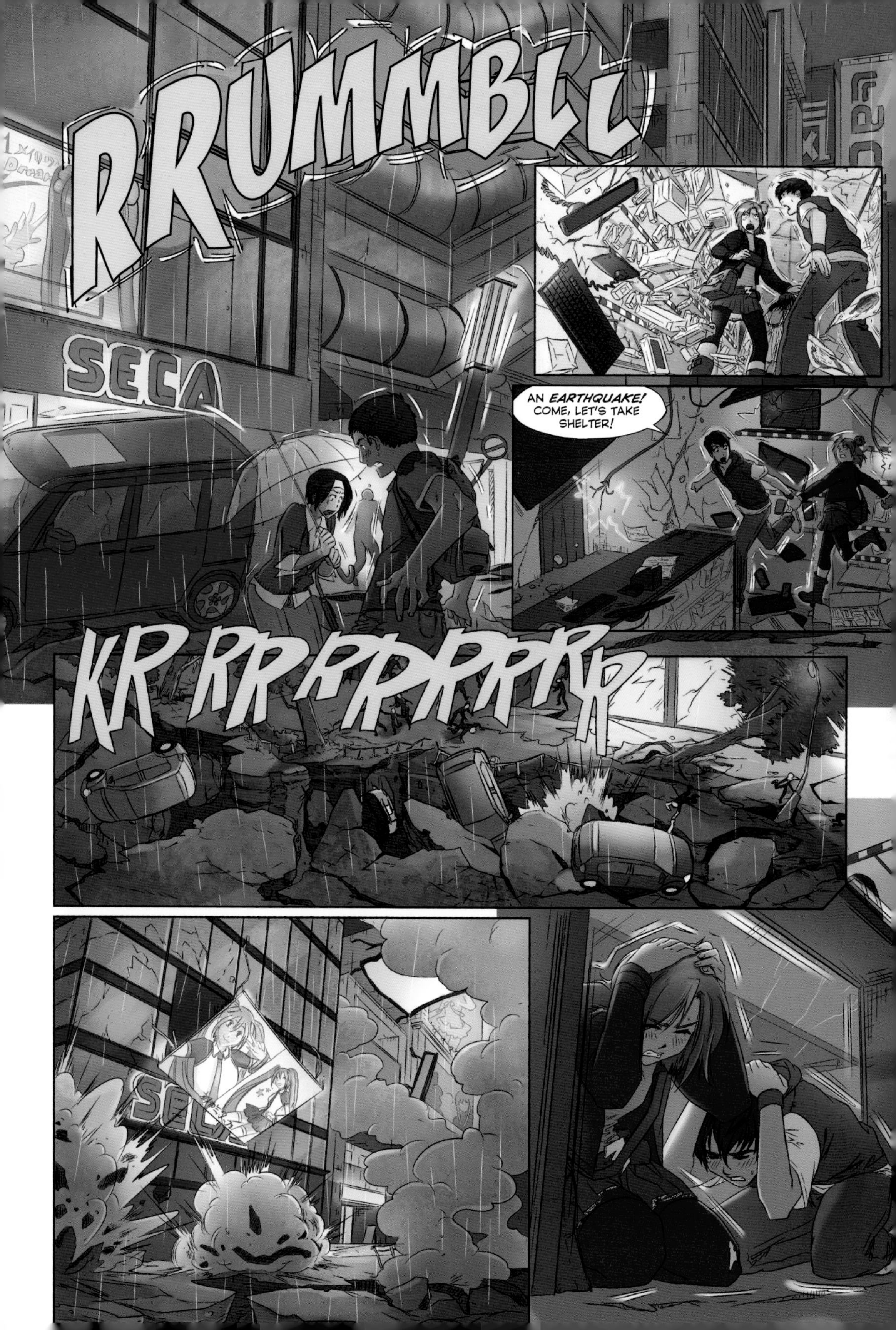
RRUMMBLL
SEGA
AN EARTHQUAKE! COME, LET'S TAKE SHELTER!
KRRRRRRRRRA

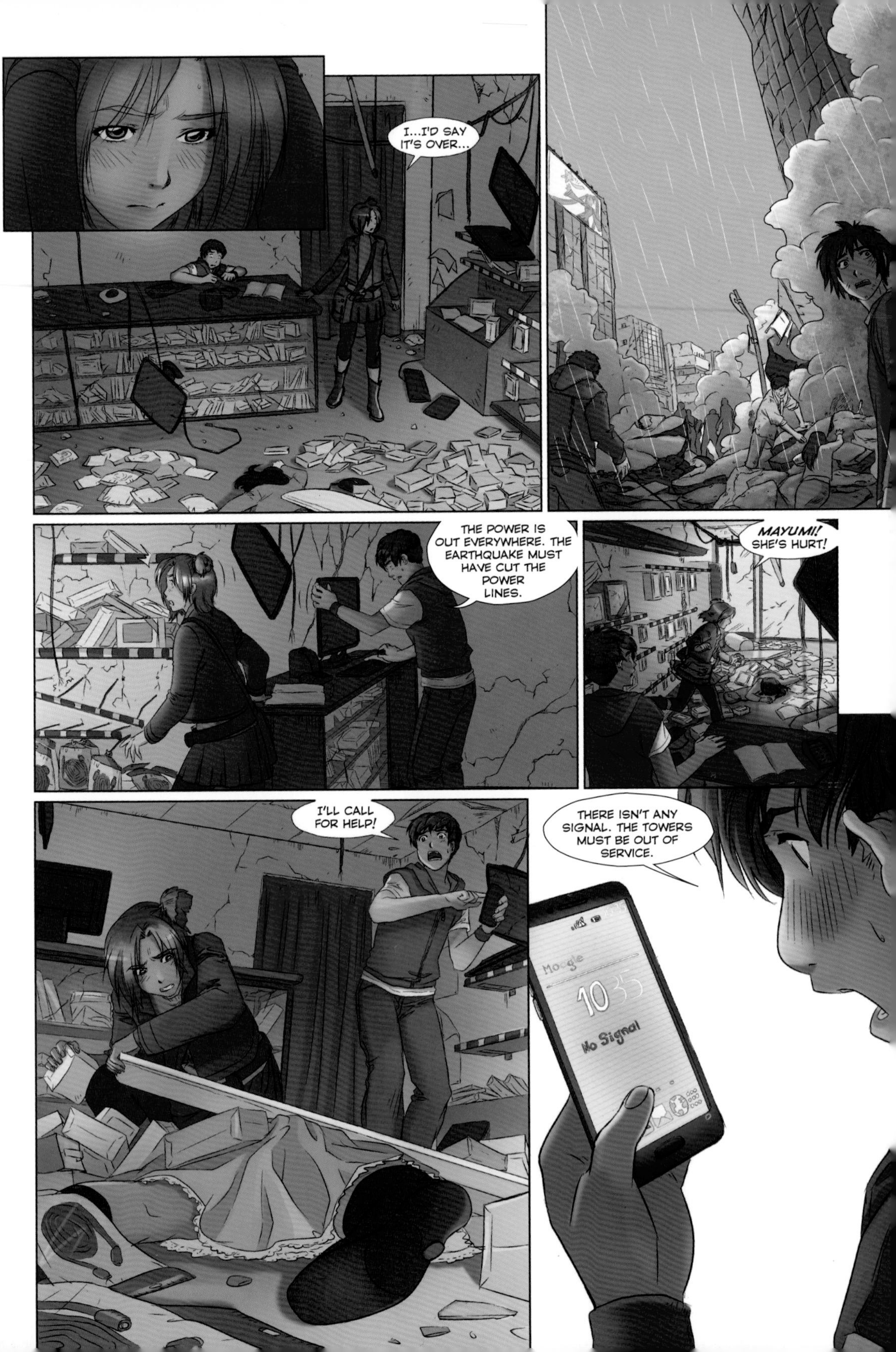

I...I'D SAY IT'S OVER...
THE POWER IS OUT EVERYWHERE. THE EARTHQUAKE MUST HAVE CUT THE POWER LINES.
MAYUMI! SHE'S HURT!
I'LL CALL FOR HELP!
THERE ISN'T ANY SIGNAL. THE TOWERS MUST BE OUT OF SERVICE.
Moogle
No Signal

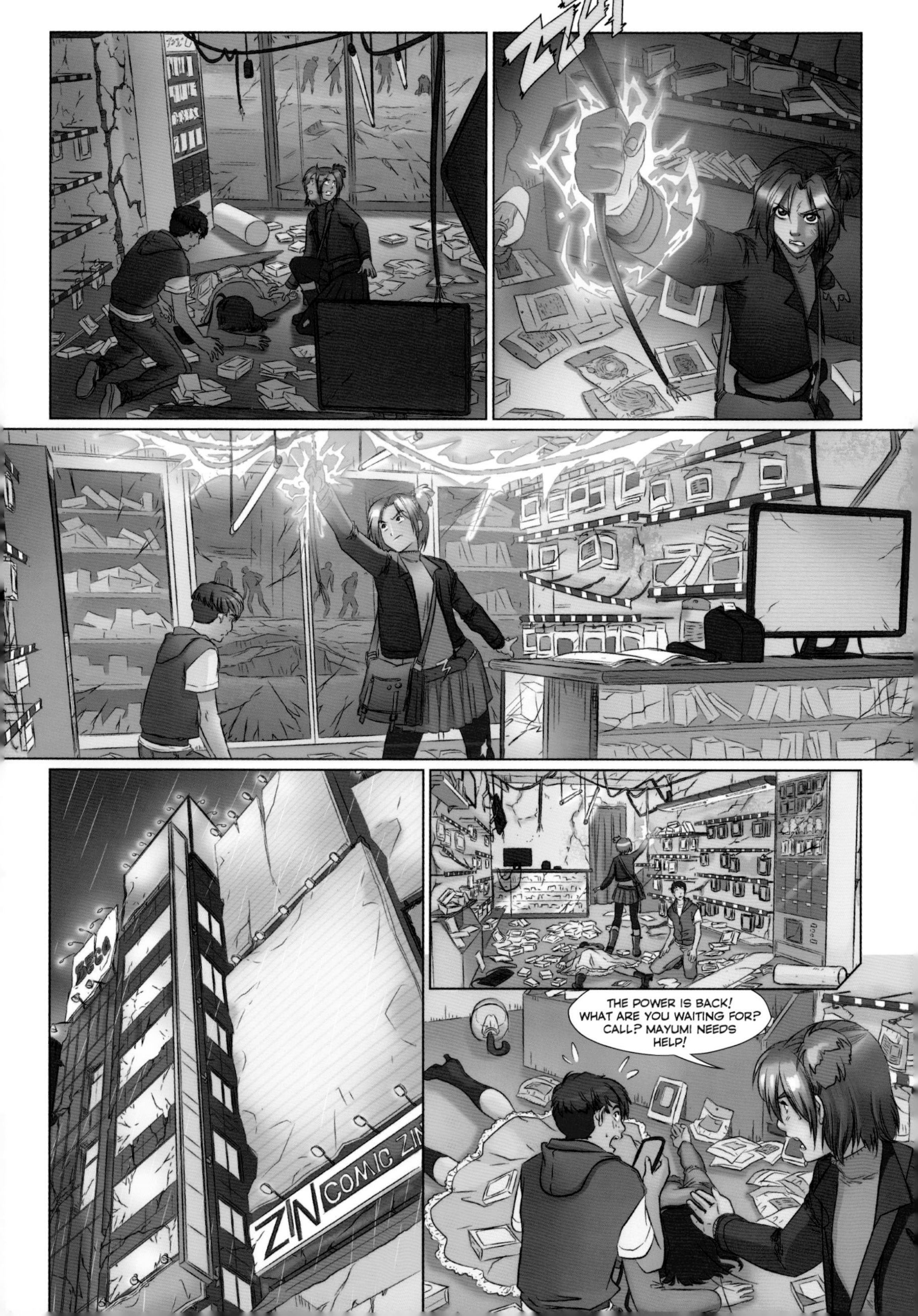
ZZZT
THE POWER IS BACK! WHAT ARE YOU WAITING FOR? CALL? MAYUMI NEEDS HELP!
ZIN COMIC ZIN

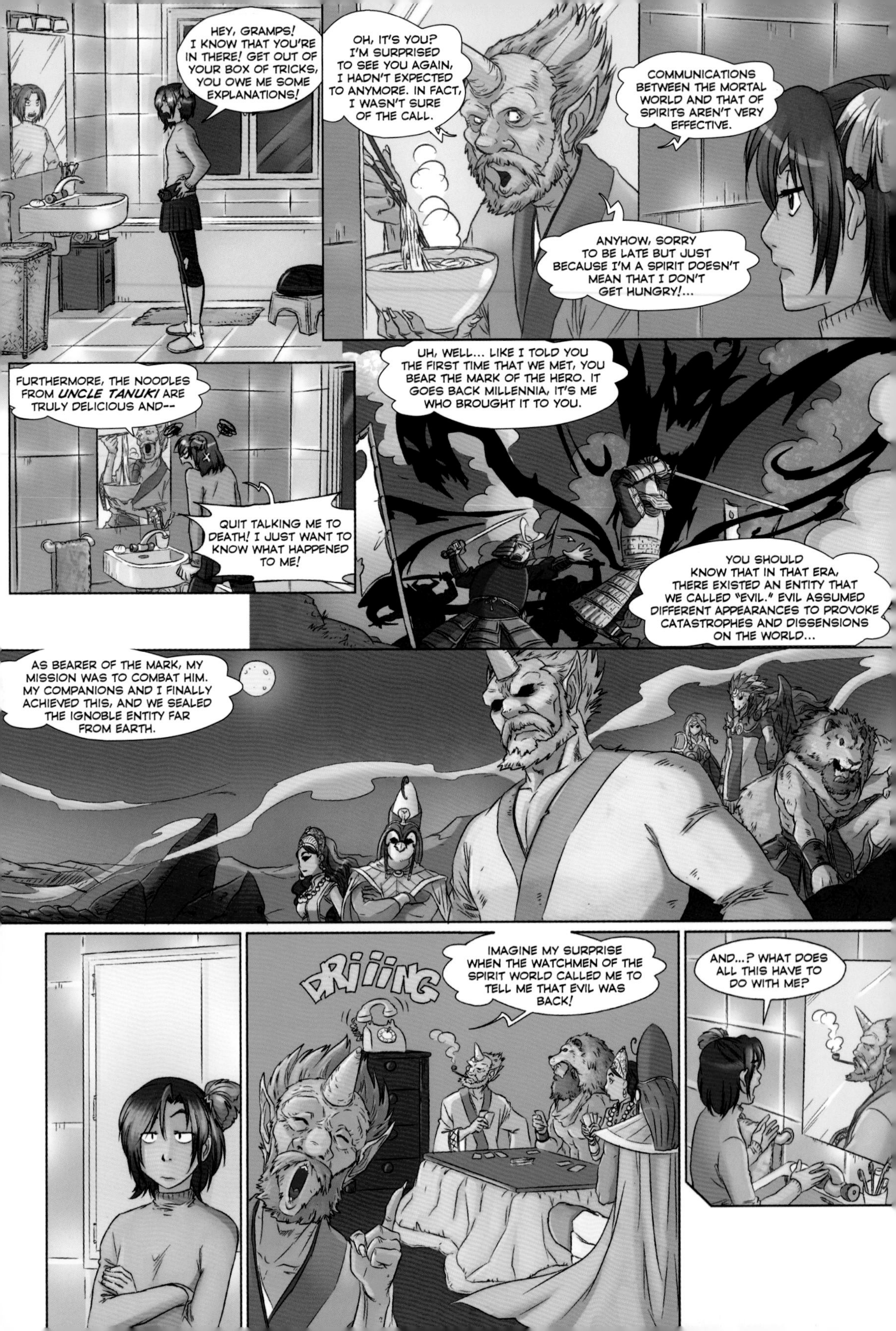

HEY, GRAMPS! I KNOW THAT YOU'RE IN THERE! GET OUT OF YOUR BOX OF TRICKS, YOU OWE ME SOME EXPLANATIONS!
OH, IT'S YOU? I'M SURPRISED TO SEE YOU AGAIN, I HADN'T EXPECTED TO ANYMORE. IN FACT, I WASN'T SURE OF THE CALL.
COMMUNICATIONS BETWEEN THE MORTAL WORLD AND THAT OF SPIRITS AREN'T VERY EFFECTIVE.
ANYHOW, SORRY TO BE LATE BUT JUST BECAUSE I'M A SPIRIT DOESN'T MEAN THAT I DON'T GET HUNGRY!...
FURTHERMORE, THE NOODLES FROM *UNCLE TANUKI* ARE TRULY DELICIOUS AND--
QUIT TALKING ME TO DEATH! I JUST WANT TO KNOW WHAT HAPPENED TO ME!
UH, WELL... LIKE I TOLD YOU THE FIRST TIME THAT WE MET, YOU BEAR THE MARK OF THE HERO. IT GOES BACK MILLENNIA, IT'S ME WHO BROUGHT IT TO YOU.
YOU SHOULD KNOW THAT IN THAT ERA, THERE EXISTED AN ENTITY THAT WE CALLED "EVIL." EVIL ASSUMED DIFFERENT APPEARANCES TO PROVOKE CATASTROPHES AND DISSENSIONS ON THE WORLD...
AS BEARER OF THE MARK, MY MISSION WAS TO COMBAT HIM. MY COMPANIONS AND I FINALLY ACHIEVED THIS, AND WE SEALED THE IGNOBLE ENTITY FAR FROM EARTH.
DRIIING
IMAGINE MY SURPRISE WHEN THE WATCHMEN OF THE SPIRIT WORLD CALLED ME TO TELL ME THAT EVIL WAS BACK!
AND...? WHAT DOES ALL THIS HAVE TO DO WITH ME?

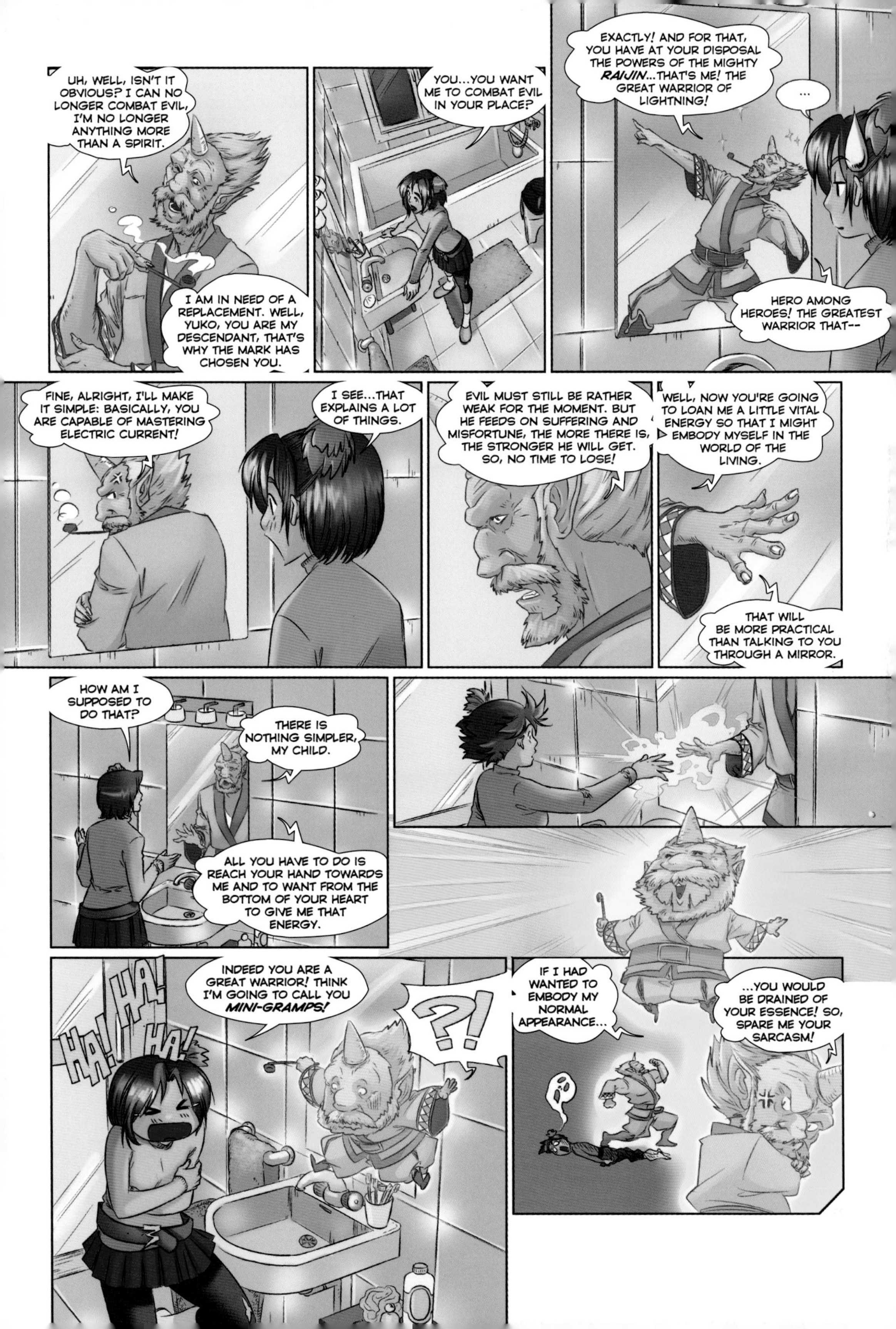
UH, WELL, ISN'T IT OBVIOUS? I CAN NO LONGER COMBAT EVIL, I'M NO LONGER ANYTHING MORE THAN A SPIRIT.
I AM IN NEED OF A REPLACEMENT. WELL, YUKO, YOU ARE MY DESCENDANT, THAT'S WHY THE MARK HAS CHOSEN YOU.
YOU...YOU WANT ME TO COMBAT EVIL IN YOUR PLACE?
EXACTLY! AND FOR THAT, YOU HAVE AT YOUR DISPOSAL THE POWERS OF THE MIGHTY RAIJIN...THAT'S ME! THE GREAT WARRIOR OF LIGHTNING!
...
HERO AMONG HEROES! THE GREATEST WARRIOR THAT--
FINE, ALRIGHT, I'LL MAKE IT SIMPLE: BASICALLY, YOU ARE CAPABLE OF MASTERING ELECTRIC CURRENT!
I SEE...THAT EXPLAINS A LOT OF THINGS.
EVIL MUST STILL BE RATHER WEAK FOR THE MOMENT. BUT HE FEEDS ON SUFFERING AND MISFORTUNE, THE MORE THERE IS, THE STRONGER HE WILL GET. SO, NO TIME TO LOSE!
WELL, NOW YOU'RE GOING TO LOAN ME A LITTLE VITAL ENERGY SO THAT I MIGHT EMBODY MYSELF IN THE WORLD OF THE LIVING.
THAT WILL BE MORE PRACTICAL THAN TALKING TO YOU THROUGH A MIRROR.
HOW AM I SUPPOSED TO DO THAT?
THERE IS NOTHING SIMPLER, MY CHILD.
ALL YOU HAVE TO DO IS REACH YOUR HAND TOWARDS ME AND TO WANT FROM THE BOTTOM OF YOUR HEART TO GIVE ME THAT ENERGY.
HA! HA! HA! HA!
INDEED YOU ARE A GREAT WARRIOR! THINK I'M GOING TO CALL YOU MINI-GRAMPS!
?!
IF I HAD WANTED TO EMBODY MY NORMAL APPEARANCE...
...YOU WOULD BE DRAINED OF YOUR ESSENCE! SO, SPARE ME YOUR SARCASM!

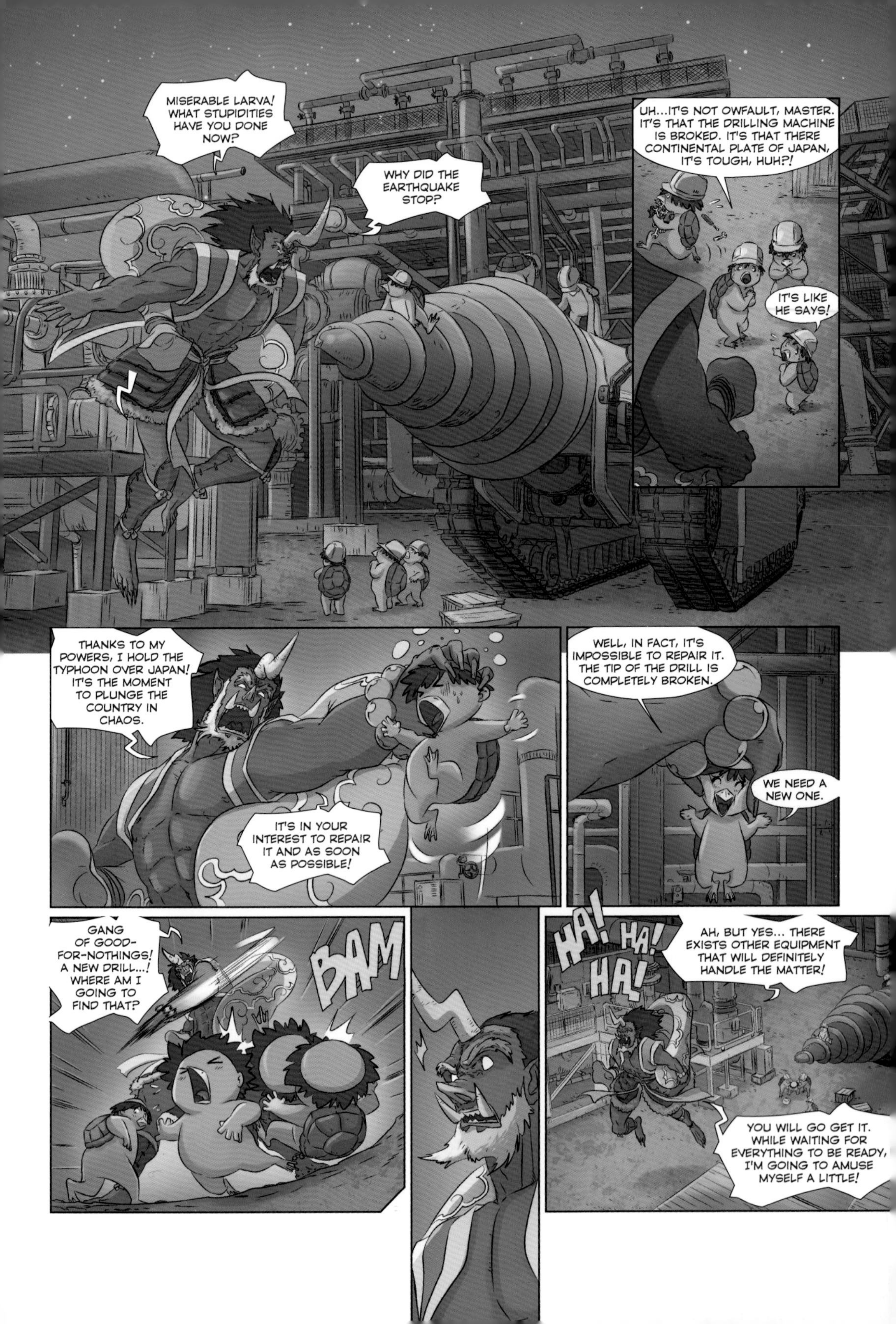
MISERABLE LARVA! WHAT STUPIDITIES HAVE YOU DONE NOW?
WHY DID THE EARTHQUAKE STOP?
UH...IT'S NOT OWFAULT, MASTER. IT'S THAT THE DRILLING MACHINE IS BROKED. IT'S THAT THERE CONTINENTAL PLATE OF JAPAN, IT'S TOUGH, HUH?!
IT'S LIKE HE SAYS!
THANKS TO MY POWERS, I HOLD THE TYPHOON OVER JAPAN! IT'S THE MOMENT TO PLUNGE THE COUNTRY IN CHAOS.
IT'S IN YOUR INTEREST TO REPAIR IT AND AS SOON AS POSSIBLE!
WELL, IN FACT, IT'S IMPOSSIBLE TO REPAIR IT. THE TIP OF THE DRILL IS COMPLETELY BROKEN.
WE NEED A NEW ONE.
GANG OF GOOD-FOR-NOTHINGS! A NEW DRILL...! WHERE AM I GOING TO FIND THAT?
BAM
HA! HA! HA!
AH, BUT YES... THERE EXISTS OTHER EQUIPMENT THAT WILL DEFINITELY HANDLE THE MATTER!
YOU WILL GO GET IT. WHILE WAITING FOR EVERYTHING TO BE READY, I'M GOING TO AMUSE MYSELF A LITTLE!

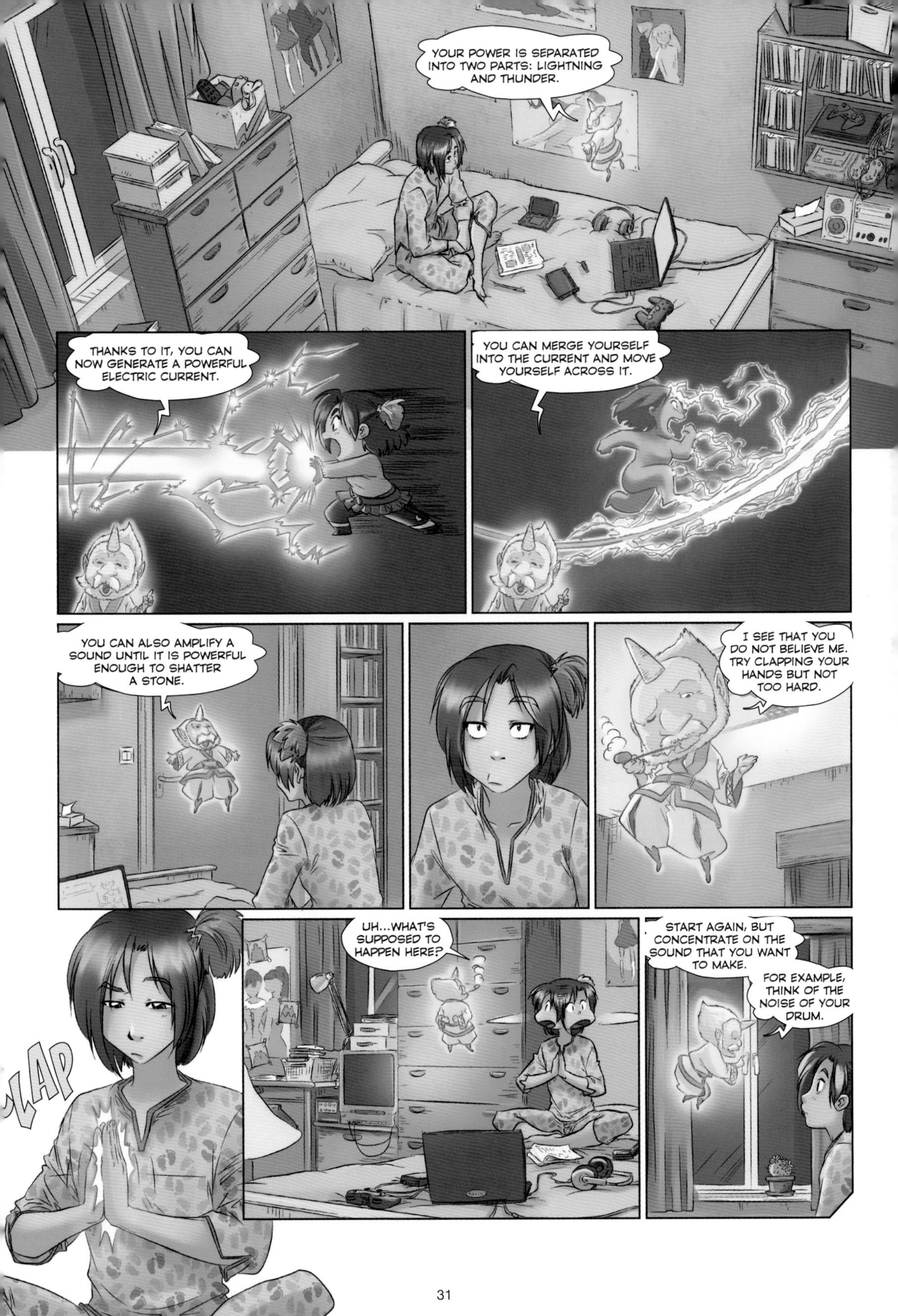
YOUR POWER IS SEPARATED INTO TWO PARTS: LIGHTNING AND THUNDER.
THANKS TO IT, YOU CAN NOW GENERATE A POWERFUL ELECTRIC CURRENT.
YOU CAN MERGE YOURSELF INTO THE CURRENT AND MOVE YOURSELF ACROSS IT.
YOU CAN ALSO AMPLIFY A SOUND UNTIL IT IS POWERFUL ENOUGH TO SHATTER A STONE.
I SEE THAT YOU DO NOT BELIEVE ME. TRY CLAPPING YOUR HANDS BUT NOT TOO HARD.
CLAP
UH...WHAT'S SUPPOSED TO HAPPEN HERE?
START AGAIN, BUT CONCENTRATE ON THE SOUND THAT YOU WANT TO MAKE.
FOR EXAMPLE, THINK OF THE NOISE OF YOUR DRUM.

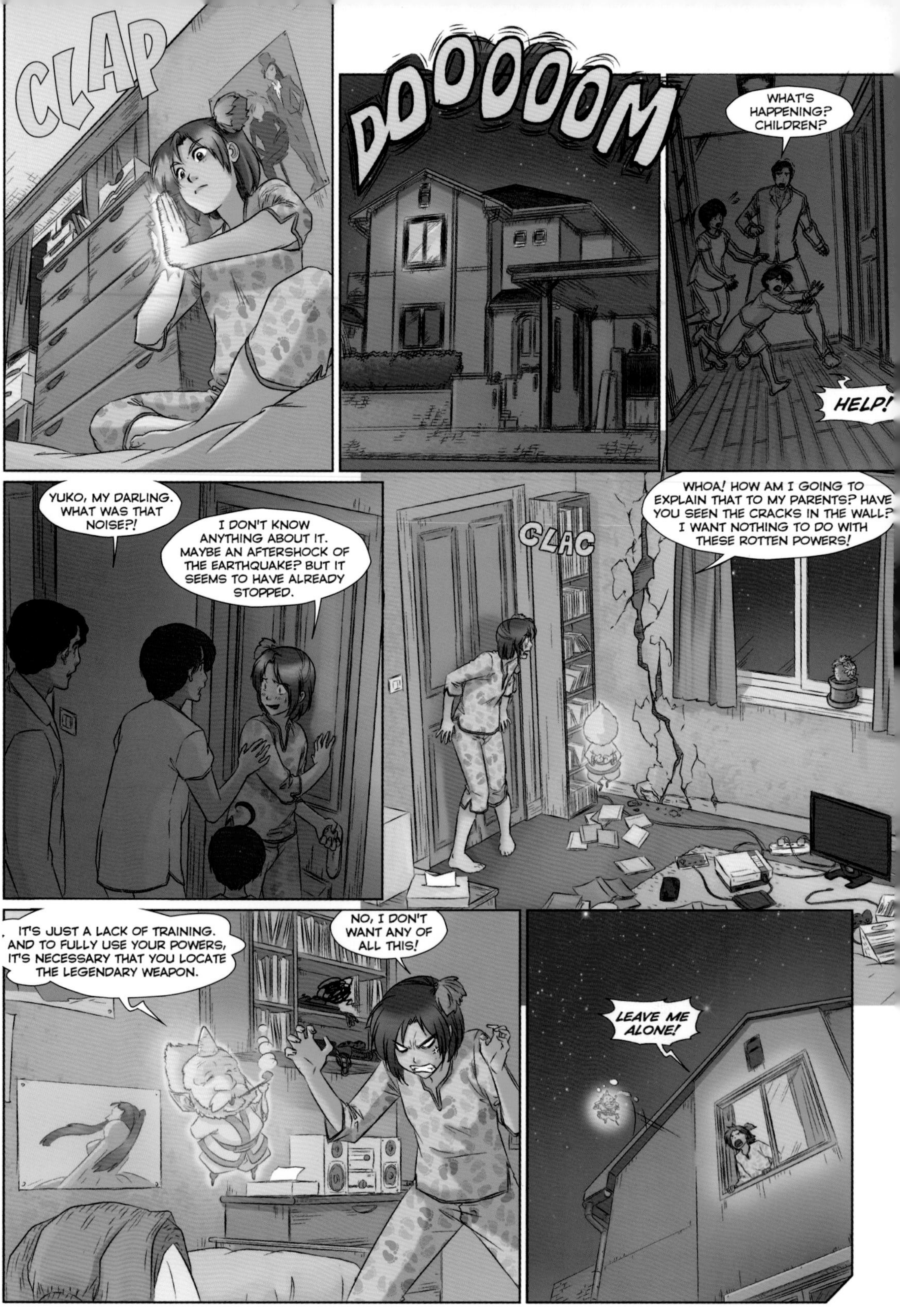
CLAP
DOOOOOM
WHAT'S HAPPENING? CHILDREN?
HELP!
YUKO, MY DARLING. WHAT WAS THAT NOISE?!
I DON'T KNOW ANYTHING ABOUT IT. MAYBE AN AFTERSHOCK OF THE EARTHQUAKE? BUT IT SEEMS TO HAVE ALREADY STOPPED.
CLAC
WHOA! HOW AM I GOING TO EXPLAIN THAT TO MY PARENTS? HAVE YOU SEEN THE CRACKS IN THE WALL? I WANT NOTHING TO DO WITH THESE ROTTEN POWERS!
IT'S JUST A LACK OF TRAINING. AND TO FULLY USE YOUR POWERS, IT'S NECESSARY THAT YOU LOCATE THE LEGENDARY WEAPON.
NO, I DON'T WANT ANY OF ALL THIS!
LEAVE ME ALONE!

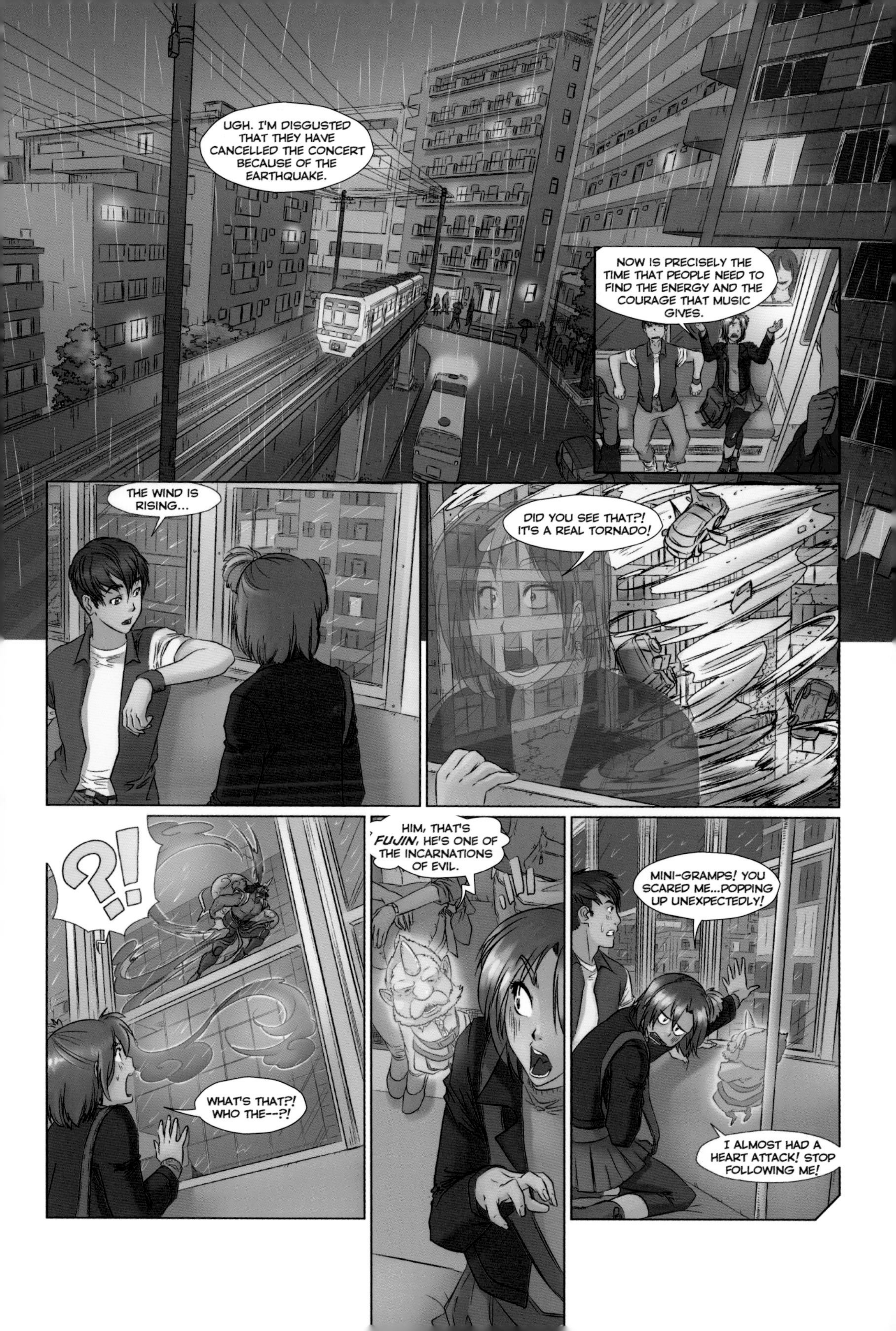
UGH. I'M DISGUSTED THAT THEY HAVE CANCELLED THE CONCERT BECAUSE OF THE EARTHQUAKE.
NOW IS PRECISELY THE TIME THAT PEOPLE NEED TO FIND THE ENERGY AND THE COURAGE THAT MUSIC GIVES.
THE WIND IS RISING...
DID YOU SEE THAT?! IT'S A REAL TORNADO!
?!
WHAT'S THAT?! WHO THE--?!
HIM, THAT'S FUJIN, HE'S ONE OF THE INCARNATIONS OF EVIL.
MINI-GRAMPS! YOU SCARED ME...POPPING UP UNEXPECTEDLY!
I ALMOST HAD A HEART ATTACK! STOP FOLLOWING ME!

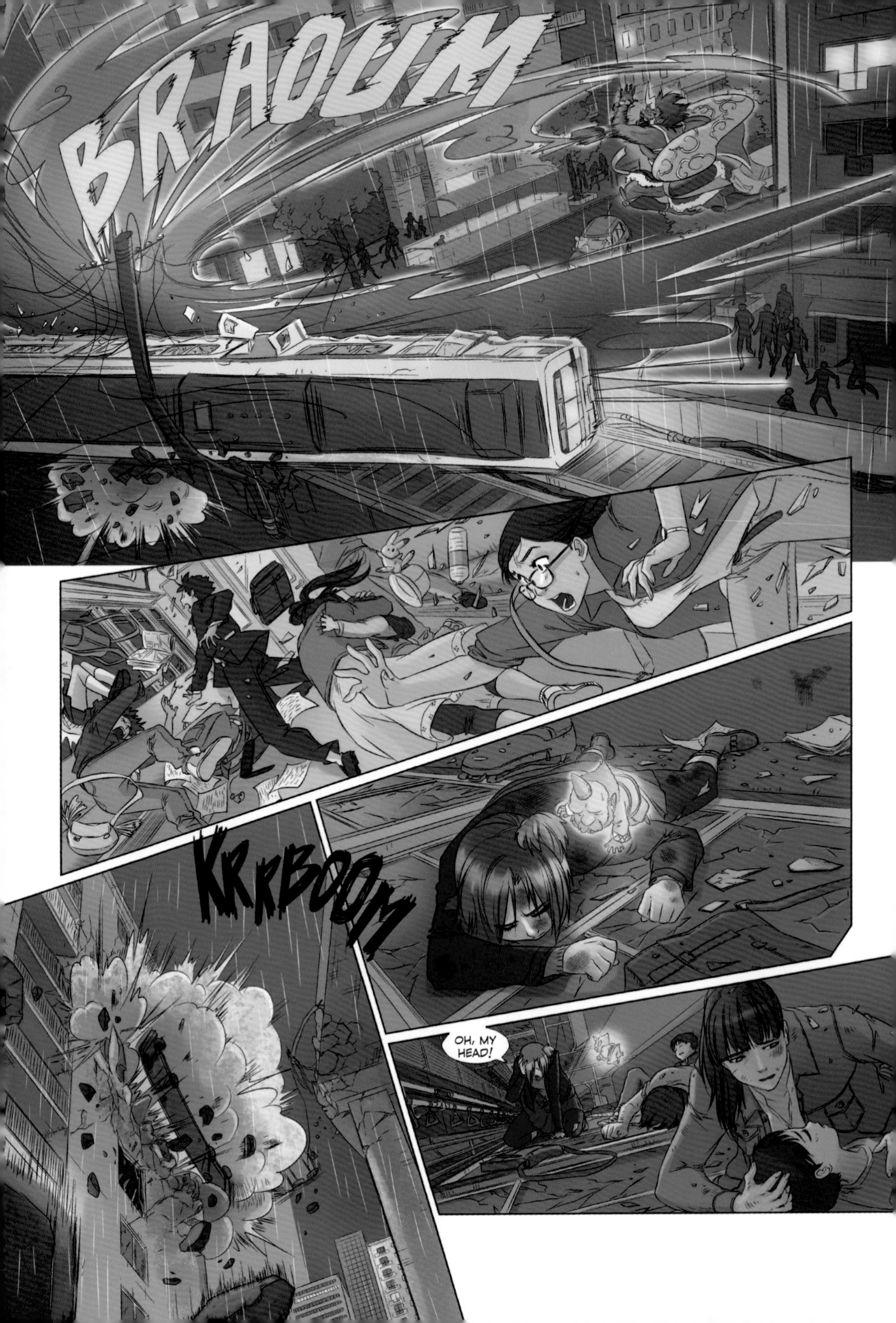
BRAOUM
KRRBOOM
OH, MY HEAD!

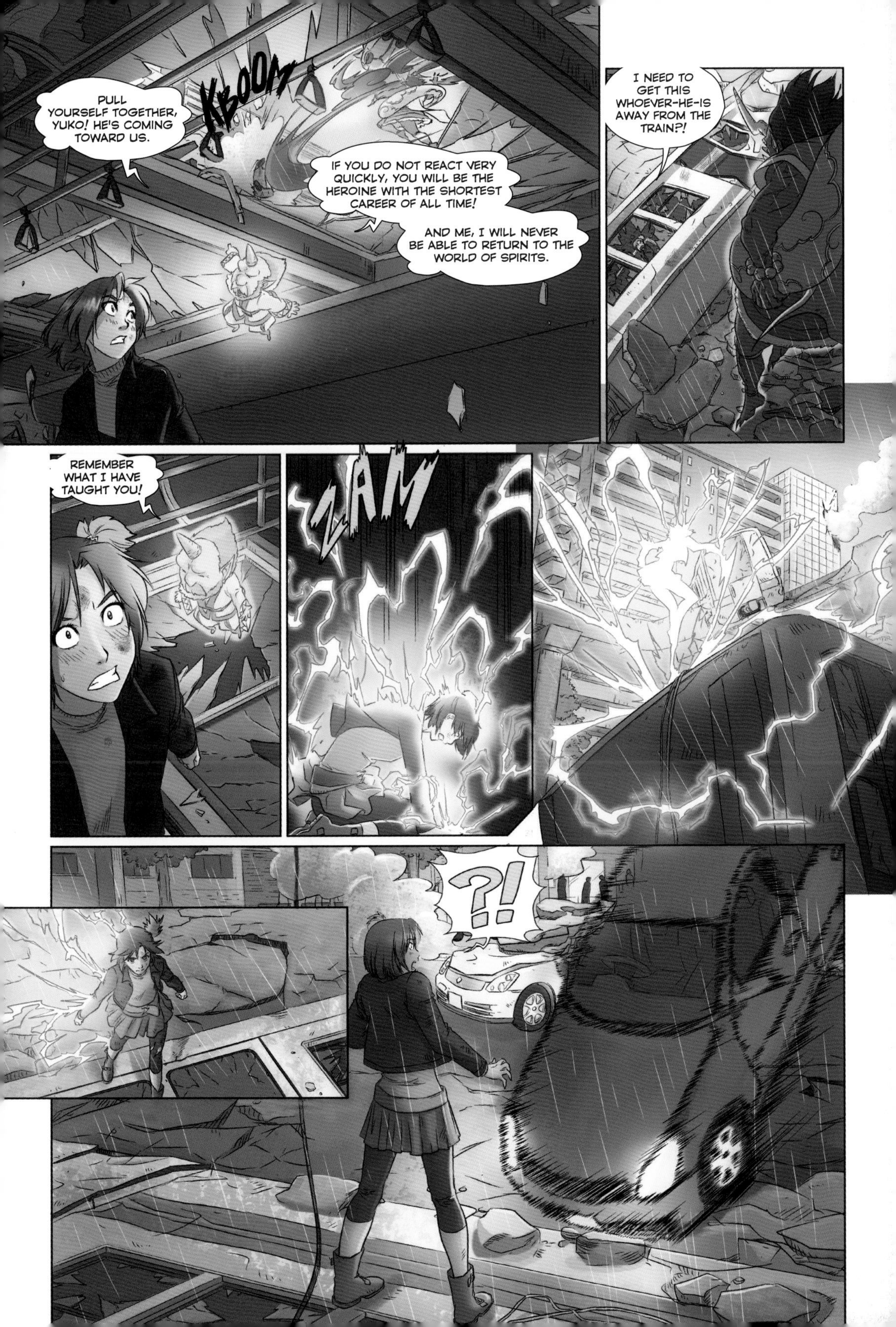
KBOOM
PULL YOURSELF TOGETHER, YUKO! HE'S COMING TOWARD US.
IF YOU DO NOT REACT VERY QUICKLY, YOU WILL BE THE HEROINE WITH THE SHORTEST CAREER OF ALL TIME!
AND ME, I WILL NEVER BE ABLE TO RETURN TO THE WORLD OF SPIRITS.
I NEED TO GET THIS WHOEVER-HE-IS AWAY FROM THE TRAIN?!
REMEMBER WHAT I HAVE TAUGHT YOU!
ZAM
?!

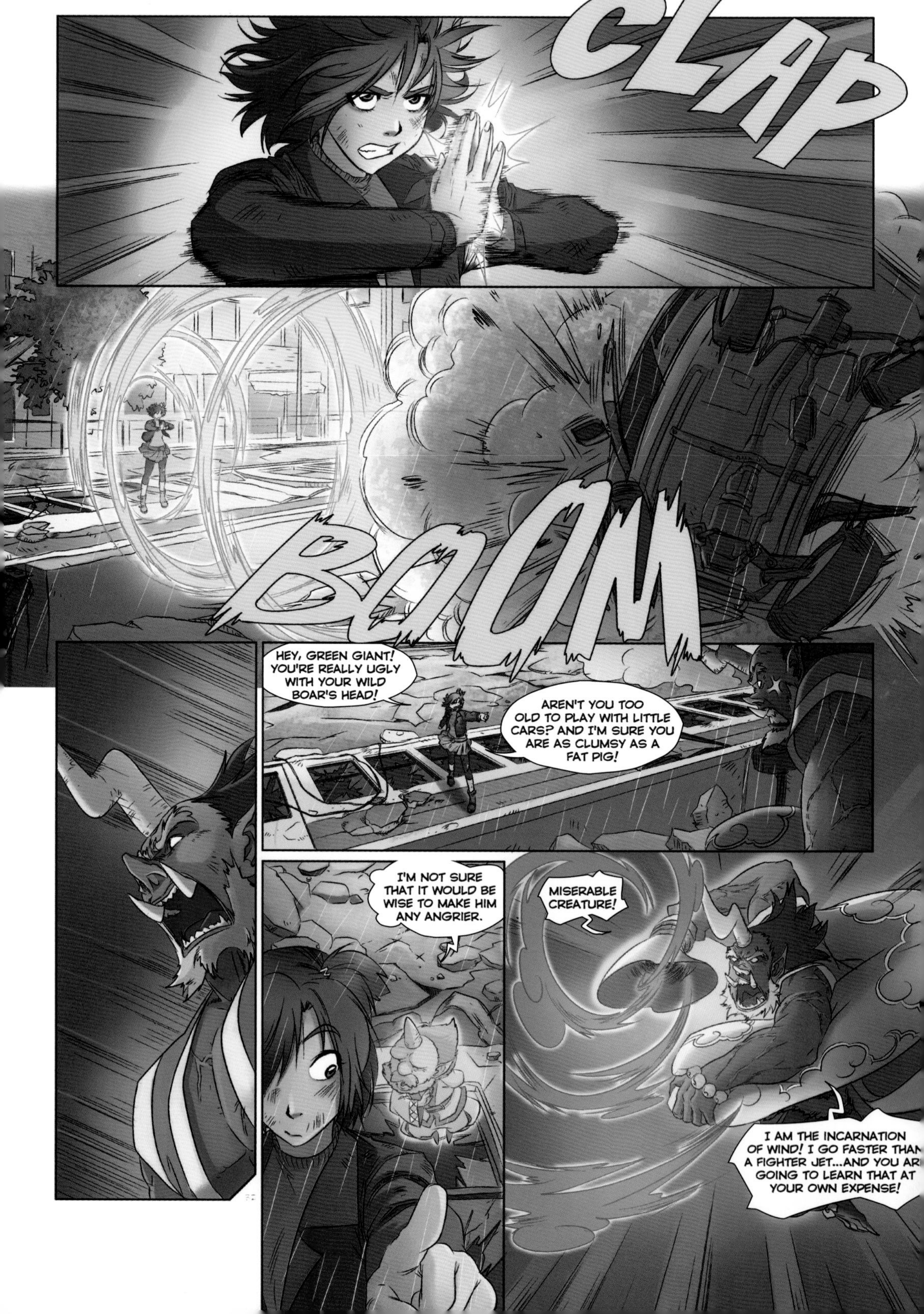
CLAP
BOOM
HEY, GREEN GIANT! YOU'RE REALLY UGLY WITH YOUR WILD BOAR'S HEAD!
AREN'T YOU TOO OLD TO PLAY WITH LITTLE CARS? AND I'M SURE YOU ARE AS CLUMSY AS A FAT PIG!
I'M NOT SURE THAT IT WOULD BE WISE TO MAKE HIM ANY ANGRIER.
MISERABLE CREATURE!
I AM THE INCARNATION OF WIND! I GO FASTER THAN A FIGHTER JET...AND YOU AR GOING TO LEARN THAT AT YOUR OWN EXPENSE!

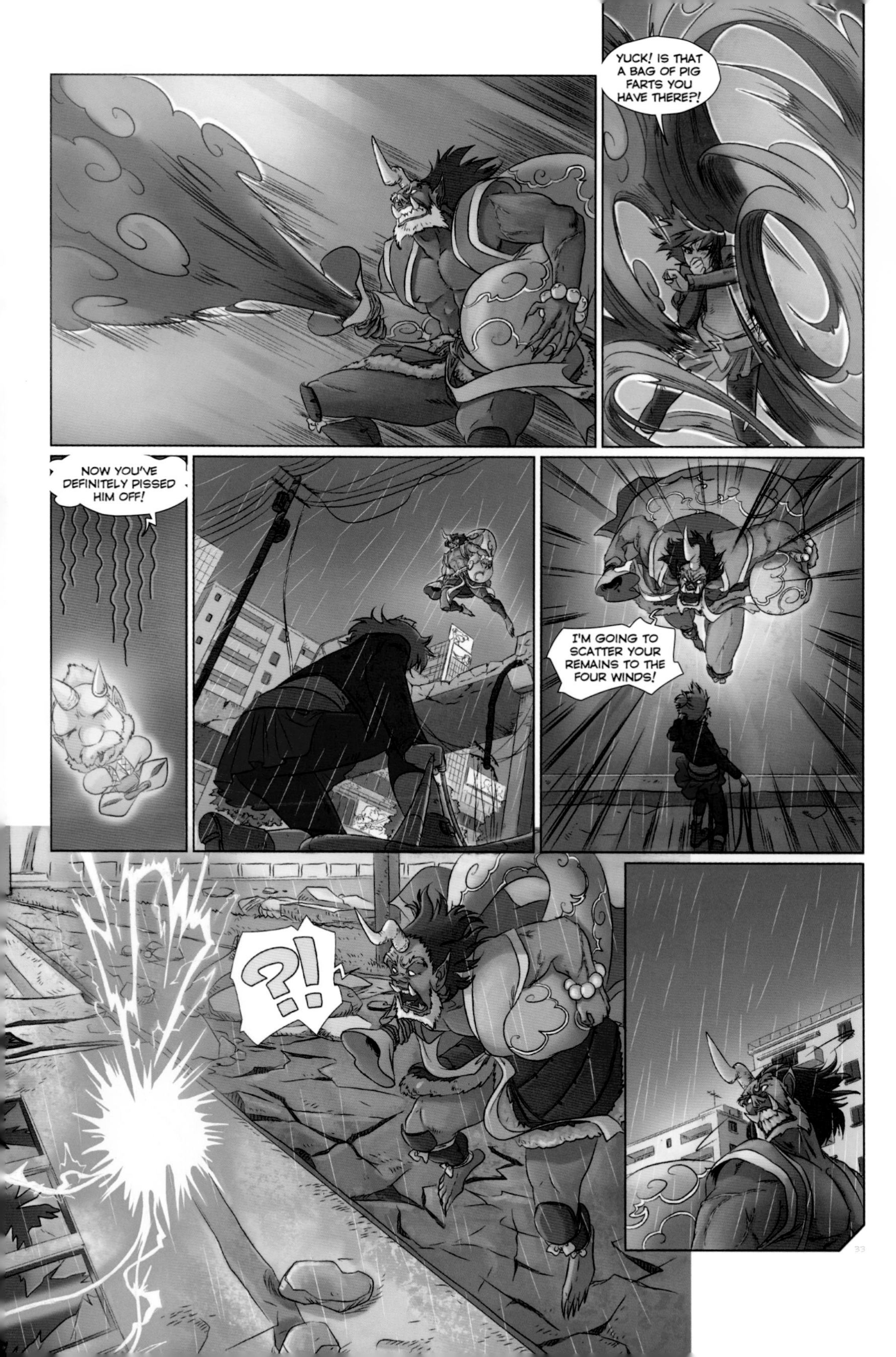
YUCK! IS THAT A BAG OF PIG FARTS YOU HAVE THERE?!
NOW YOU'VE DEFINITELY PISSED HIM OFF!
I'M GOING TO SCATTER YOUR REMAINS TO THE FOUR WINDS!
?!

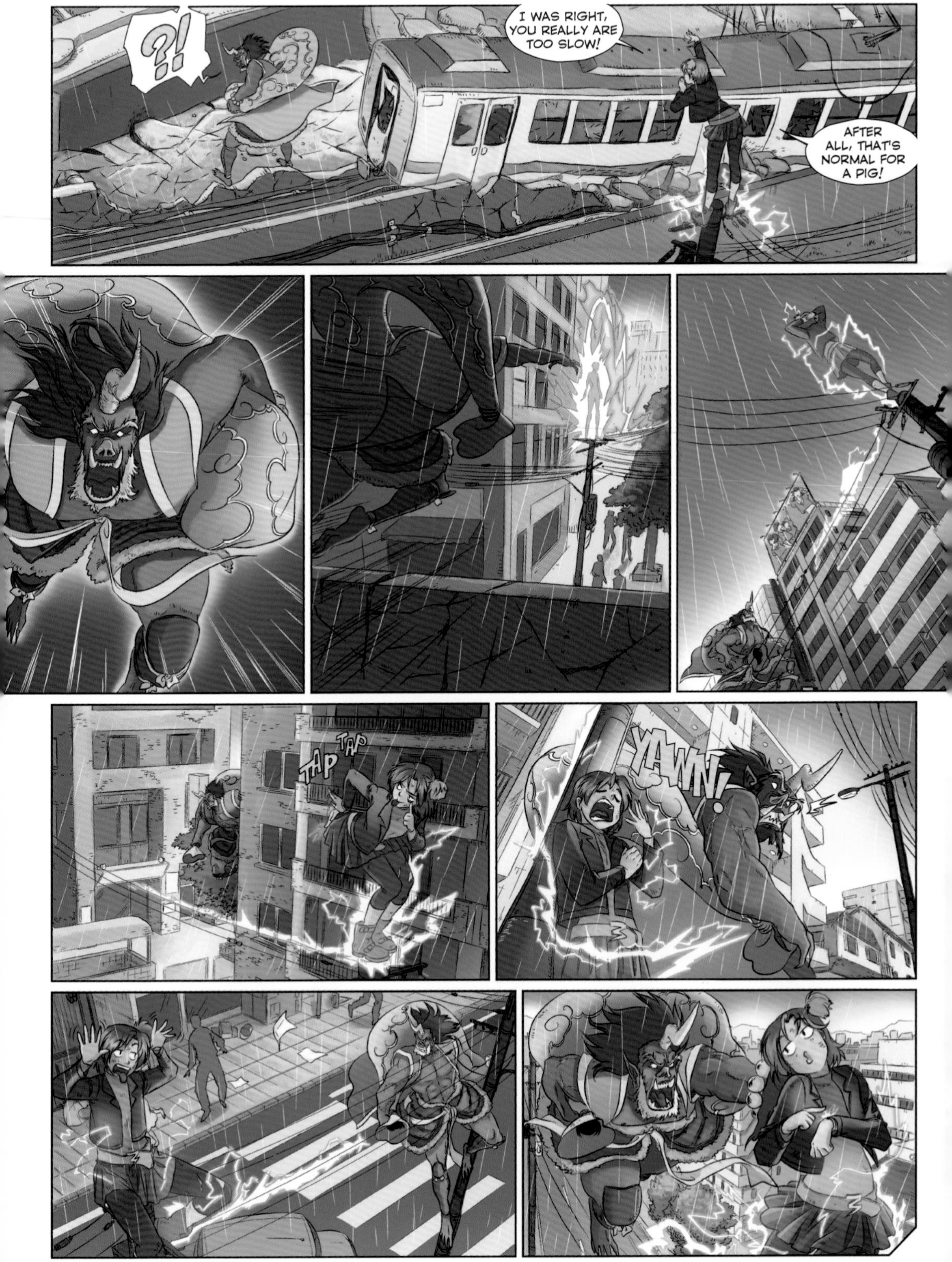
?!
I WAS RIGHT, YOU REALLY ARE TOO SLOW!
AFTER ALL, THAT'S NORMAL FOR A PIG!
TAP TAP
YAWN!

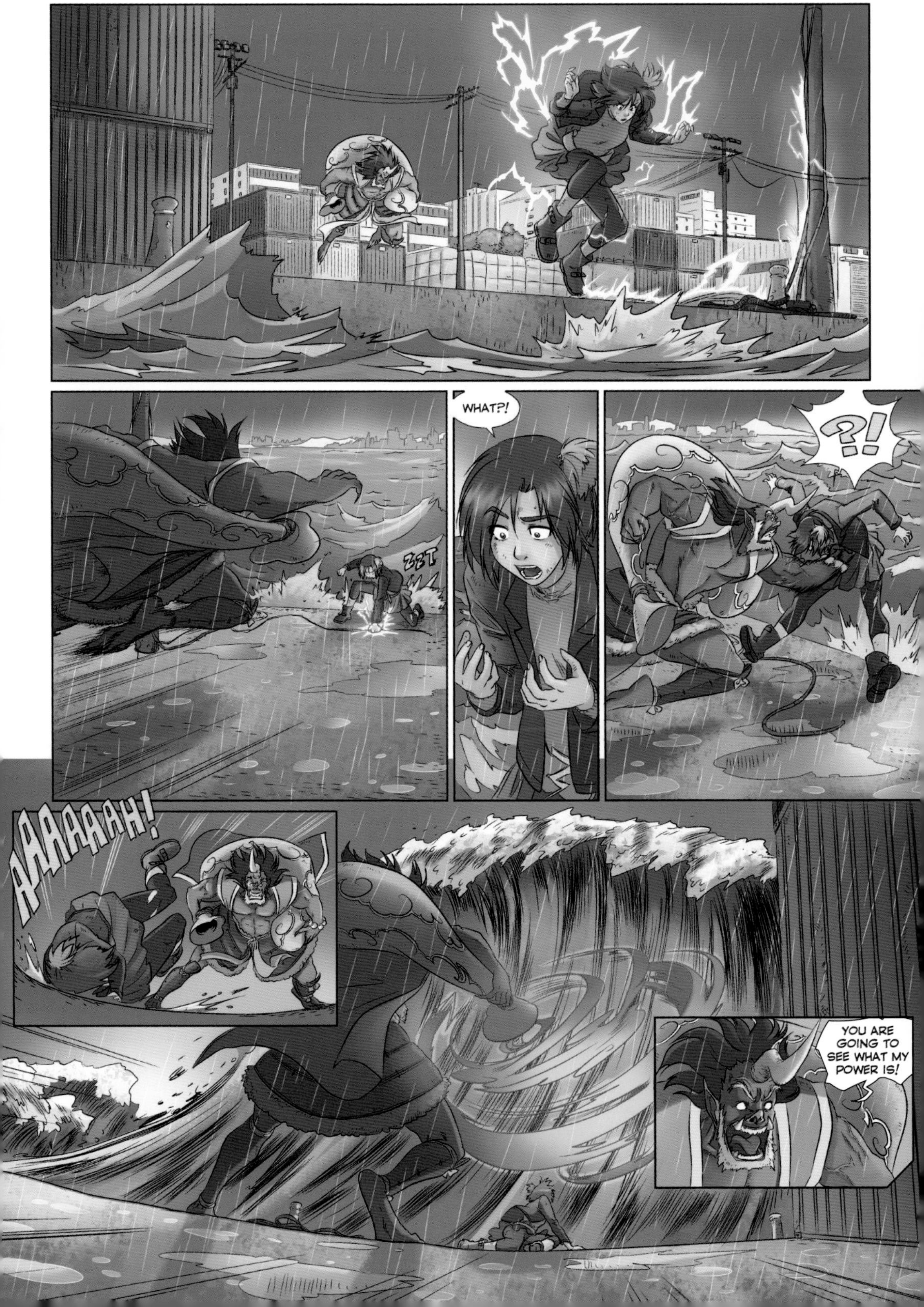

ZZT
WHAT?!
?!
AAAAAAH!
YOU ARE GOING TO SEE WHAT MY POWER IS!

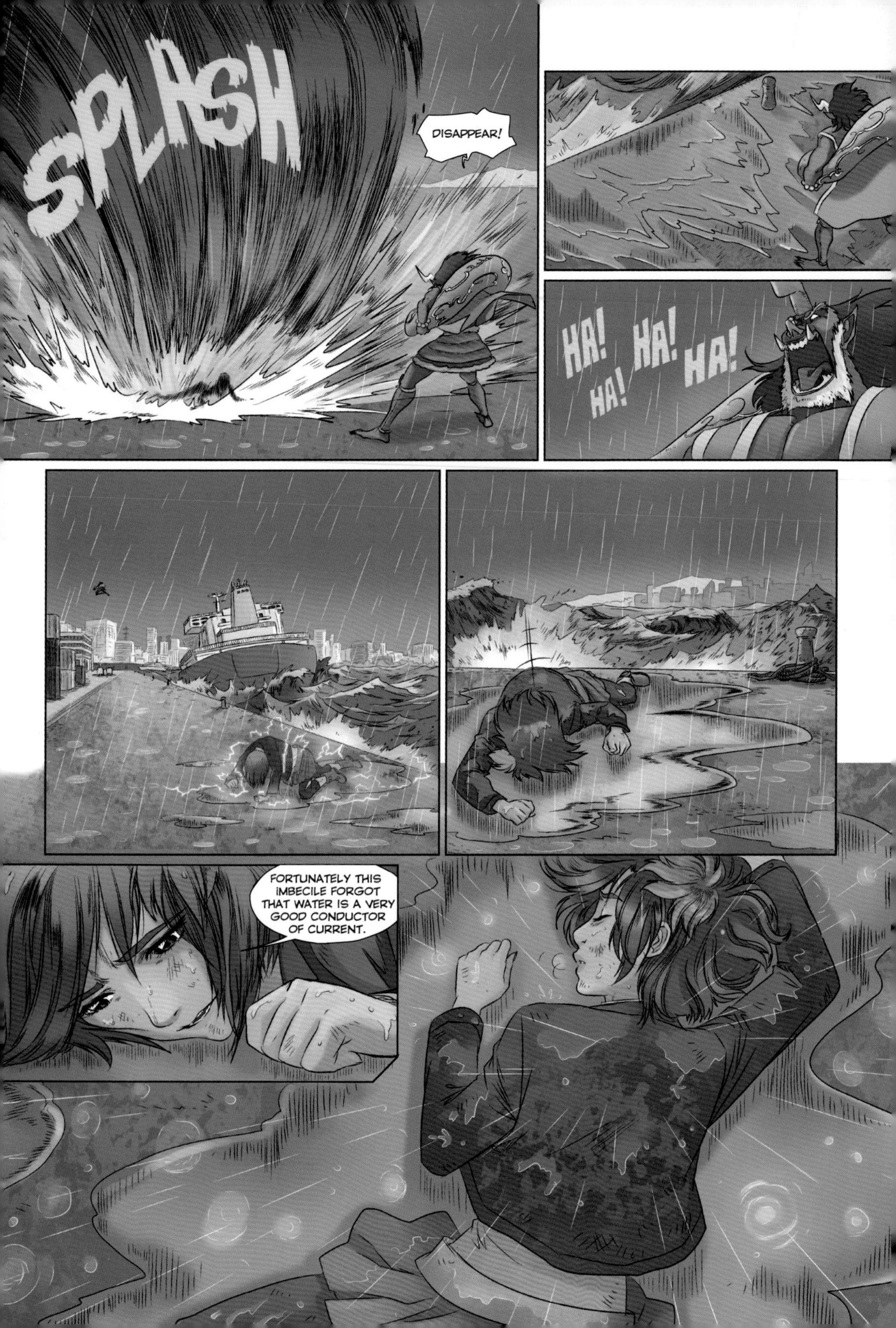
SPLASH
DISAPPEAR!
HA! HA! HA! HA!
FORTUNATELY THIS IMBECILE FORGOT THAT WATER IS A VERY GOOD CONDUCTOR OF CURRENT.

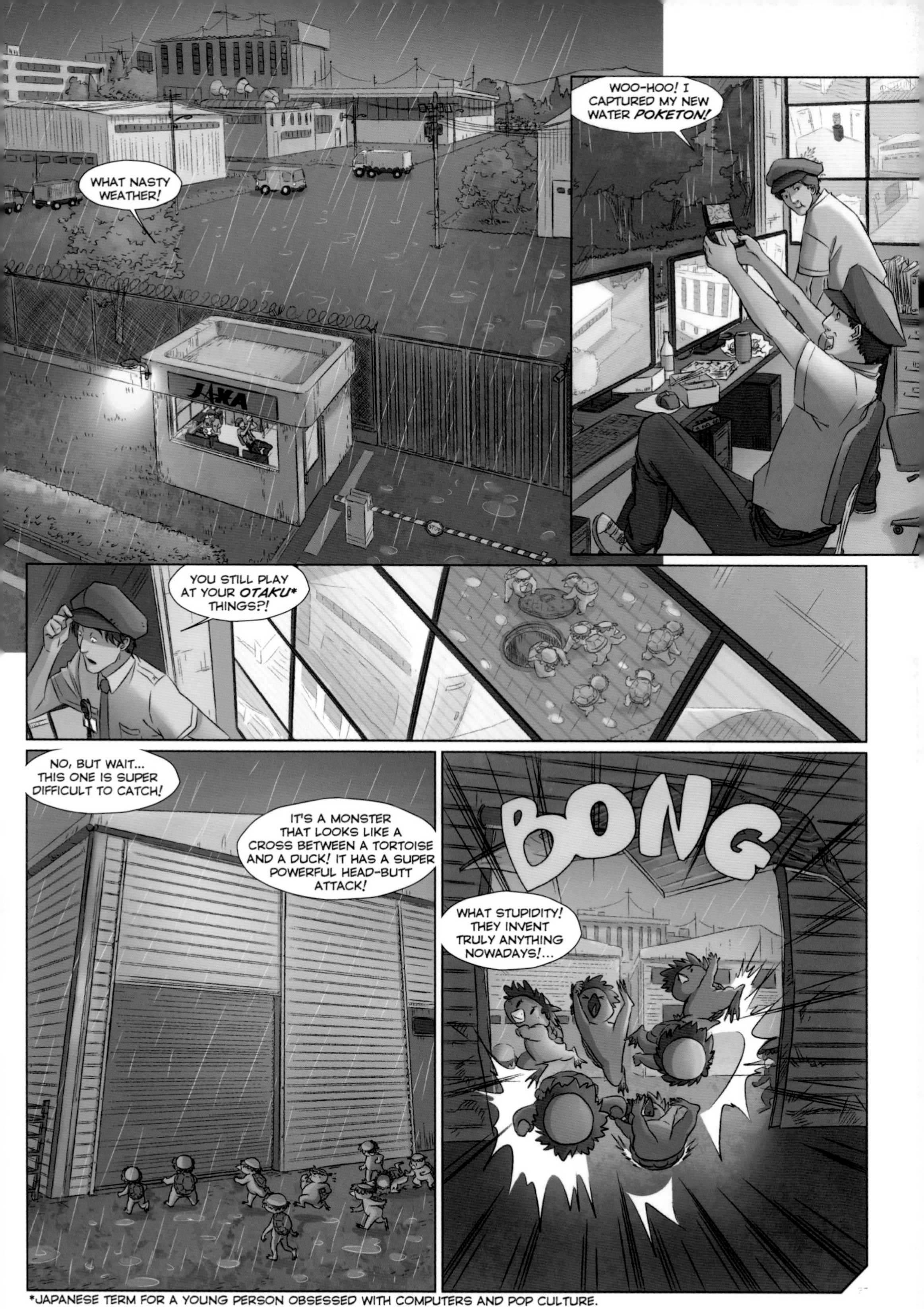
WHAT NASTY WEATHER!
WOO-HOO! I CAPTURED MY NEW WATER POKETON!
YOU STILL PLAY AT YOUR OTAKU* THINGS?!
NO, BUT WAIT... THIS ONE IS SUPER DIFFICULT TO CATCH!
IT'S A MONSTER THAT LOOKS LIKE A CROSS BETWEEN A TORTOISE AND A DUCK! IT HAS A SUPER POWERFUL HEAD-BUTT ATTACK!
BONG
WHAT STUPIDITY! THEY INVENT TRULY ANYTHING NOWADAYS!...

*JAPANESE TERM FOR A YOUNG PERSON OBSESSED WITH COMPUTERS AND POP CULTURE.

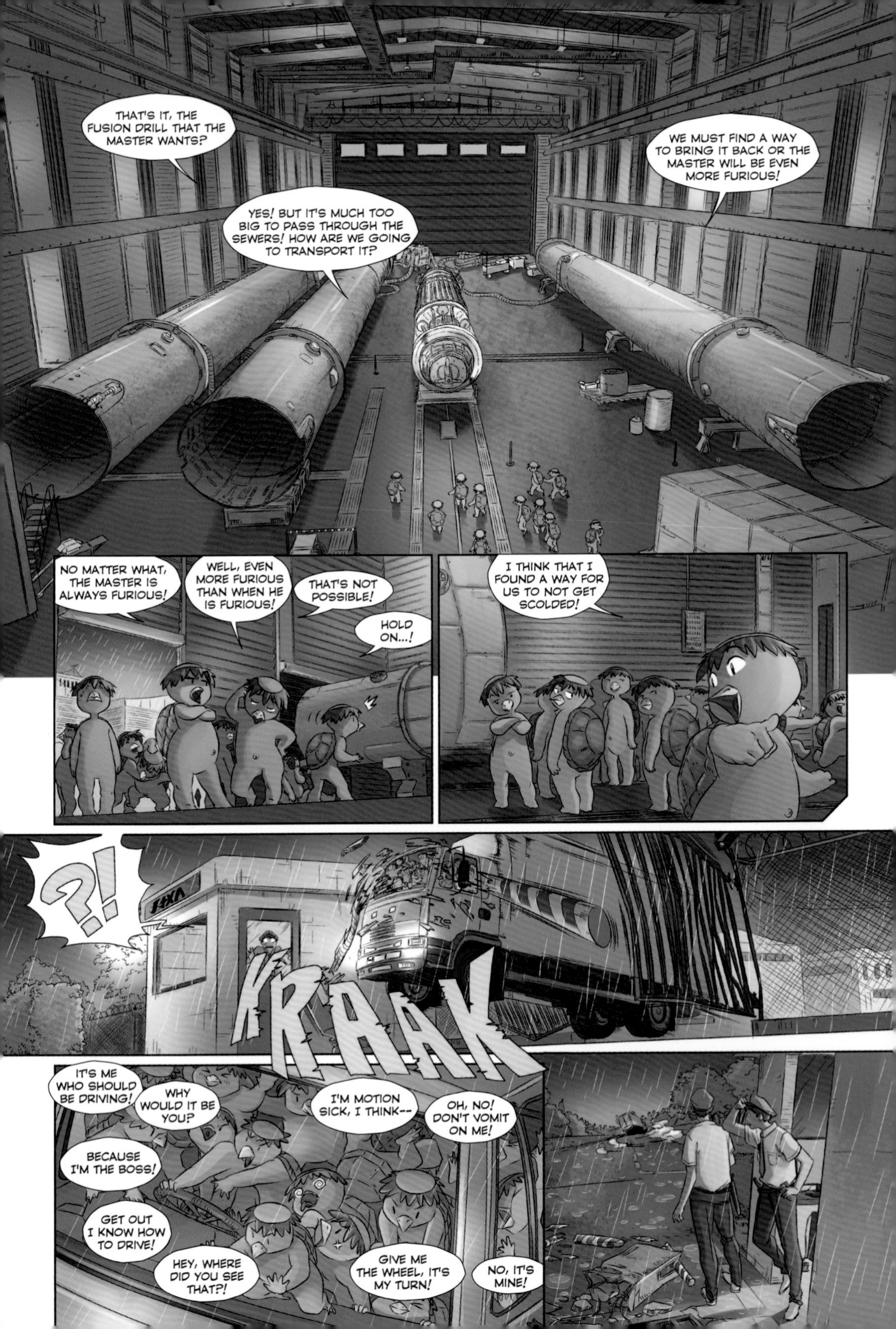
THAT'S IT, THE FUSION DRILL THAT THE MASTER WANTS?
YES! BUT IT'S MUCH TOO BIG TO PASS THROUGH THE SEWERS! HOW ARE WE GOING TO TRANSPORT IT?
WE MUST FIND A WAY TO BRING IT BACK OR THE MASTER WILL BE EVEN MORE FURIOUS!
NO MATTER WHAT, THE MASTER IS ALWAYS FURIOUS!
WELL, EVEN MORE FURIOUS THAN WHEN HE IS FURIOUS!
THAT'S NOT POSSIBLE!
HOLD ON...!
I THINK THAT I FOUND A WAY FOR US TO NOT GET SCOLDED!
?!
KRAAK
IT'S ME WHO SHOULD BE DRIVING!
WHY WOULD IT BE YOU?
BECAUSE I'M THE BOSS!
GET OUT I KNOW HOW TO DRIVE!
HEY, WHERE DID YOU SEE THAT?!
I'M MOTION SICK, I THINK--
OH, NO! DON'T VOMIT ON ME!
GIVE ME THE WHEEL, IT'S MY TURN!
NO, IT'S MINE!

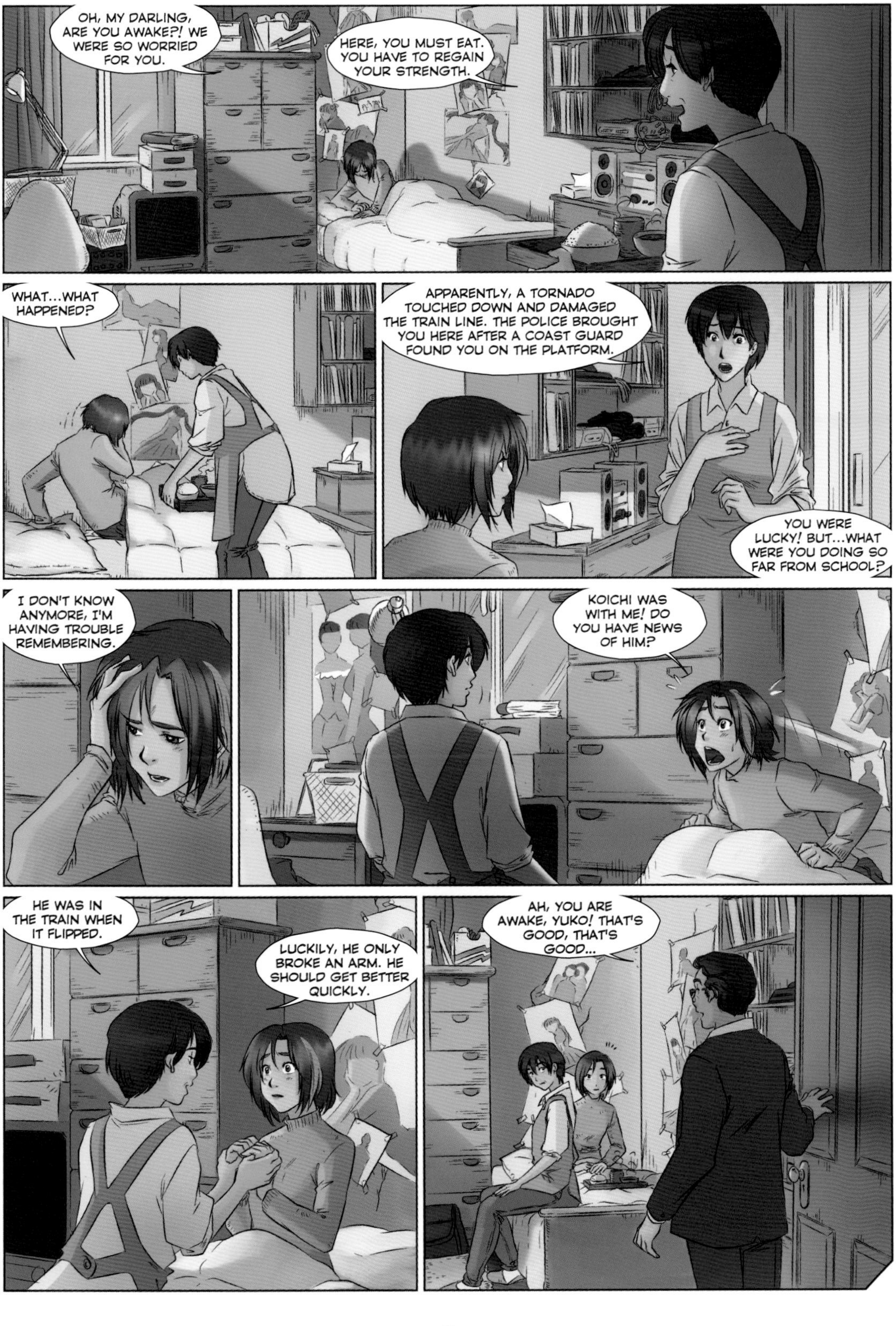
OH, MY DARLING, ARE YOU AWAKE?! WE WERE SO WORRIED FOR YOU.
HERE, YOU MUST EAT. YOU HAVE TO REGAIN YOUR STRENGTH.
WHAT...WHAT HAPPENED?
APPARENTLY, A TORNADO TOUCHED DOWN AND DAMAGED THE TRAIN LINE. THE POLICE BROUGHT YOU HERE AFTER A COAST GUARD FOUND YOU ON THE PLATFORM.
YOU WERE LUCKY! BUT...WHAT WERE YOU DOING SO FAR FROM SCHOOL?
I DON'T KNOW ANYMORE, I'M HAVING TROUBLE REMEMBERING.
KOICHI WAS WITH ME! DO YOU HAVE NEWS OF HIM?
HE WAS IN THE TRAIN WHEN IT FLIPPED.
LUCKILY, HE ONLY BROKE AN ARM. HE SHOULD GET BETTER QUICKLY.
AH, YOU ARE AWAKE, YUKO! THAT'S GOOD, THAT'S GOOD...

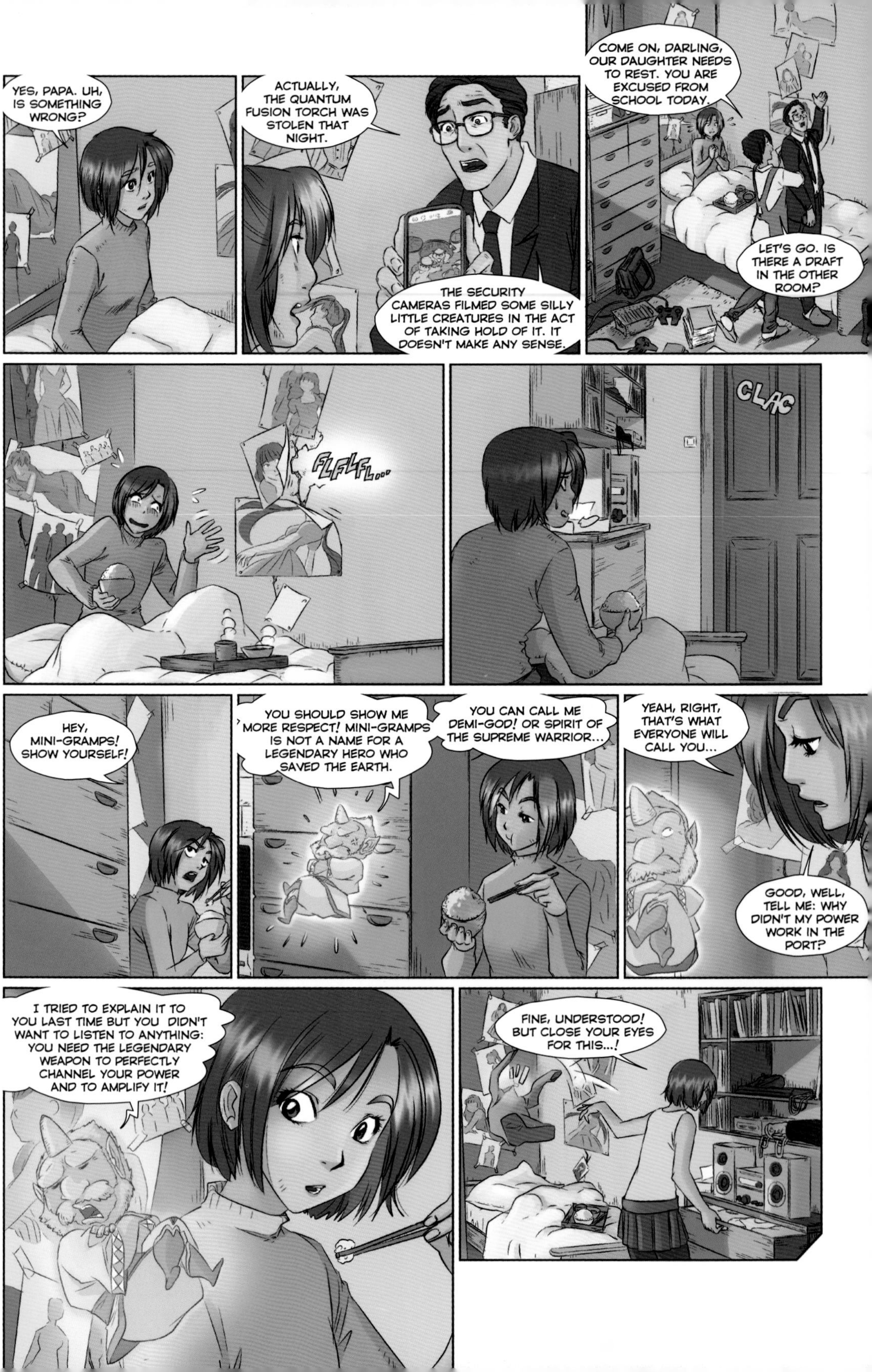
YES, PAPA. UH, IS SOMETHING WRONG?
ACTUALLY, THE QUANTUM FUSION TORCH WAS STOLEN THAT NIGHT.
THE SECURITY CAMERAS FILMED SOME SILLY LITTLE CREATURES IN THE ACT OF TAKING HOLD OF IT. IT DOESN'T MAKE ANY SENSE.
COME ON, DARLING, OUR DAUGHTER NEEDS TO REST. YOU ARE EXCUSED FROM SCHOOL TODAY.
LET'S GO. IS THERE A DRAFT IN THE OTHER ROOM?
FLFLFL...
CLAC
HEY, MINI-GRAMPS! SHOW YOURSELF!
YOU SHOULD SHOW ME MORE RESPECT! MINI-GRAMPS IS NOT A NAME FOR A LEGENDARY HERO WHO SAVED THE EARTH.
YOU CAN CALL ME DEMI-GOD! OR SPIRIT OF THE SUPREME WARRIOR...
YEAH, RIGHT, THAT'S WHAT EVERYONE WILL CALL YOU...
GOOD, WELL, TELL ME: WHY DIDN'T MY POWER WORK IN THE PORT?
I TRIED TO EXPLAIN IT TO YOU LAST TIME BUT YOU DIDN'T WANT TO LISTEN TO ANYTHING: YOU NEED THE LEGENDARY WEAPON TO PERFECTLY CHANNEL YOUR POWER AND TO AMPLIFY IT!
FINE, UNDERSTOOD! BUT CLOSE YOUR EYES FOR THIS...!

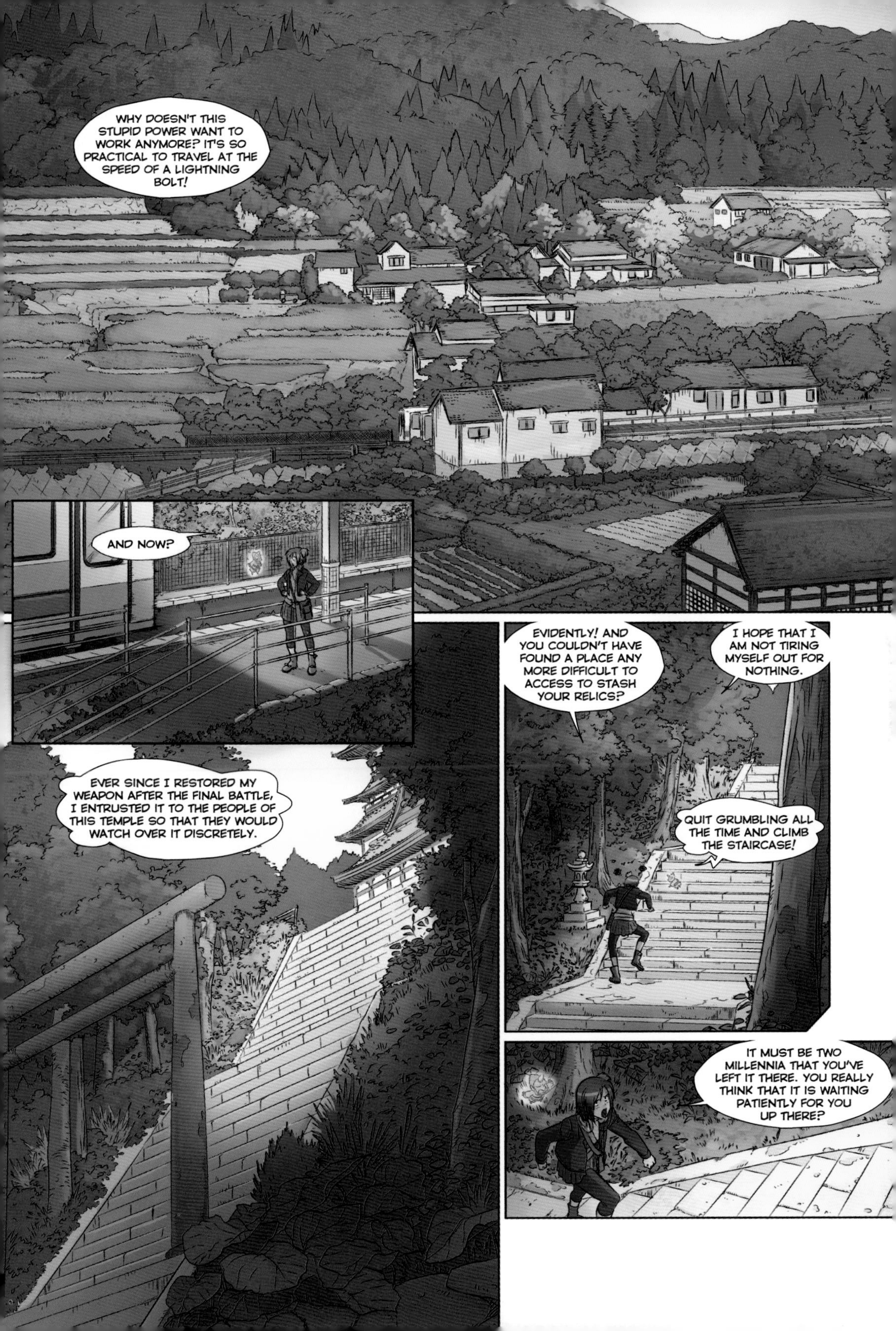
WHY DOESN'T THIS STUPID POWER WANT TO WORK ANYMORE? IT'S SO PRACTICAL TO TRAVEL AT THE SPEED OF A LIGHTNING BOLT!
AND NOW?
EVER SINCE I RESTORED MY WEAPON AFTER THE FINAL BATTLE, I ENTRUSTED IT TO THE PEOPLE OF THIS TEMPLE SO THAT THEY WOULD WATCH OVER IT DISCRETELY.
EVIDENTLY! AND YOU COULDN'T HAVE FOUND A PLACE ANY MORE DIFFICULT TO ACCESS TO STASH YOUR RELICS?
I HOPE THAT I AM NOT TIRING MYSELF OUT FOR NOTHING.
QUIT GRUMBLING ALL THE TIME AND CLIMB THE STAIRCASE!
IT MUST BE TWO MILLENNIA THAT YOU'VE LEFT IT THERE. YOU REALLY THINK THAT IT IS WAITING PATIENTLY FOR YOU UP THERE?

I FELT IT RIGHT AWAY THAT YOU WERE THE HEROINE.

MY FAMILY HAS TAKEN CARE OF THESE MAGICAL ARTIFACTS SINCE THE DAWN OF TIME.

THESE ARTIFACTS? I EXPECTED TO FIND A WEAPON...NOT A PAIR OF *TAIKO.**

AND...I CAN'T QUITE BELIEVE THAT AFTER ALL THIS TIME THEY ARE STILL HERE.

POG

*JAPANESE DRUMS

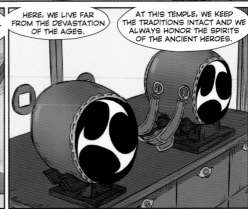

HERE, WE LIVE FAR FROM THE DEVASTATION OF THE AGES.

AT THIS TEMPLE, WE KEEP THE TRADITIONS INTACT AND WE ALWAYS HONOR THE SPIRITS OF THE ANCIENT HEROES.

IT IS TIME THAT YOU TRY THE DRUMS, YOUNG GIRL.

?!

HENCEFORTH, YOU ARE *RAIJIN,* THE SPIRIT OF THUNDER AND LIGHTNING!

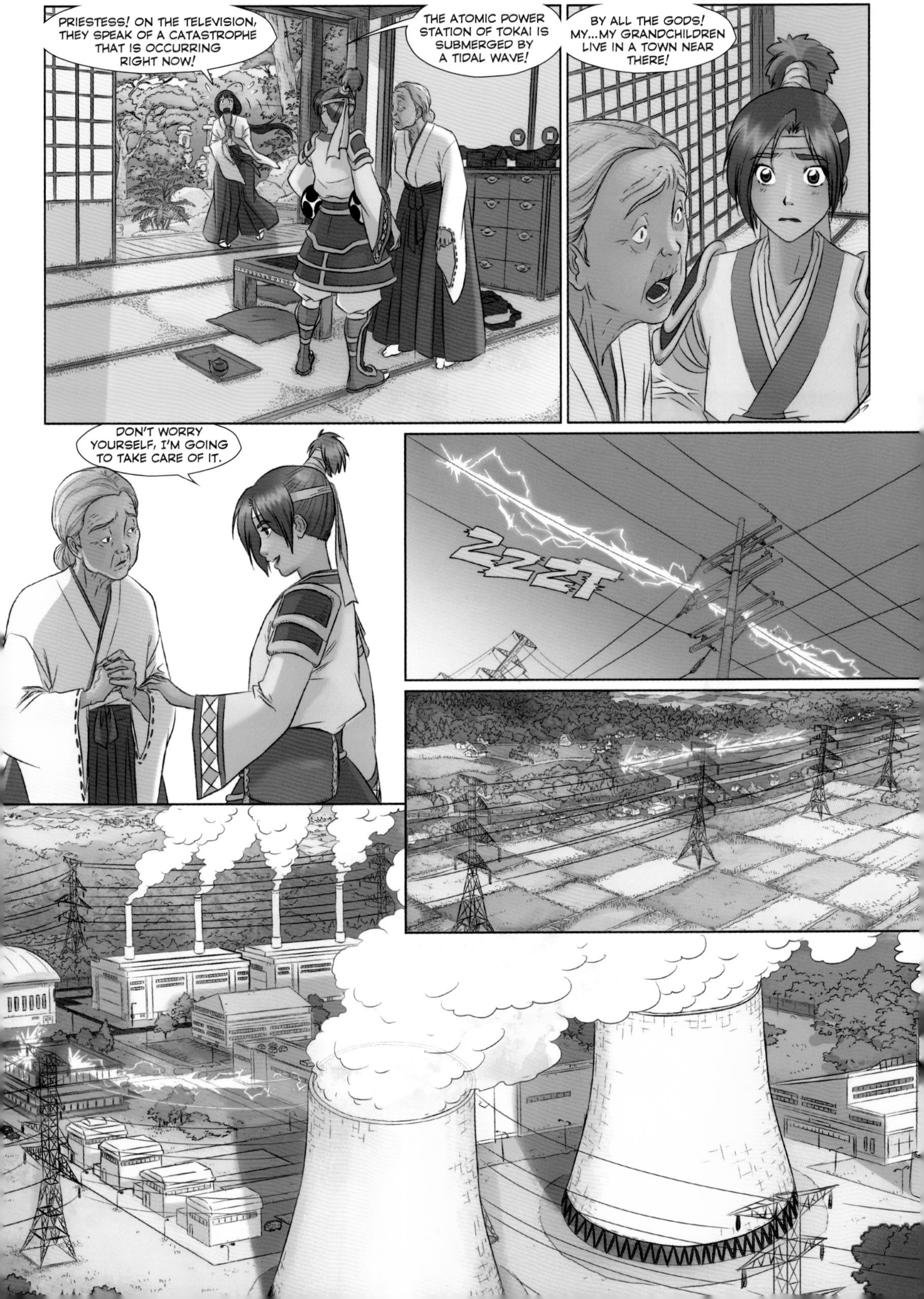
PRIESTESS! ON THE TELEVISION, THEY SPEAK OF A CATASTROPHE THAT IS OCCURRING RIGHT NOW!
THE ATOMIC POWER STATION OF TOKAI IS SUBMERGED BY A TIDAL WAVE!
BY ALL THE GODS! MY...MY GRANDCHILDREN LIVE IN A TOWN NEAR THERE!
DON'T WORRY YOURSELF, I'M GOING TO TAKE CARE OF IT.
ZZZT

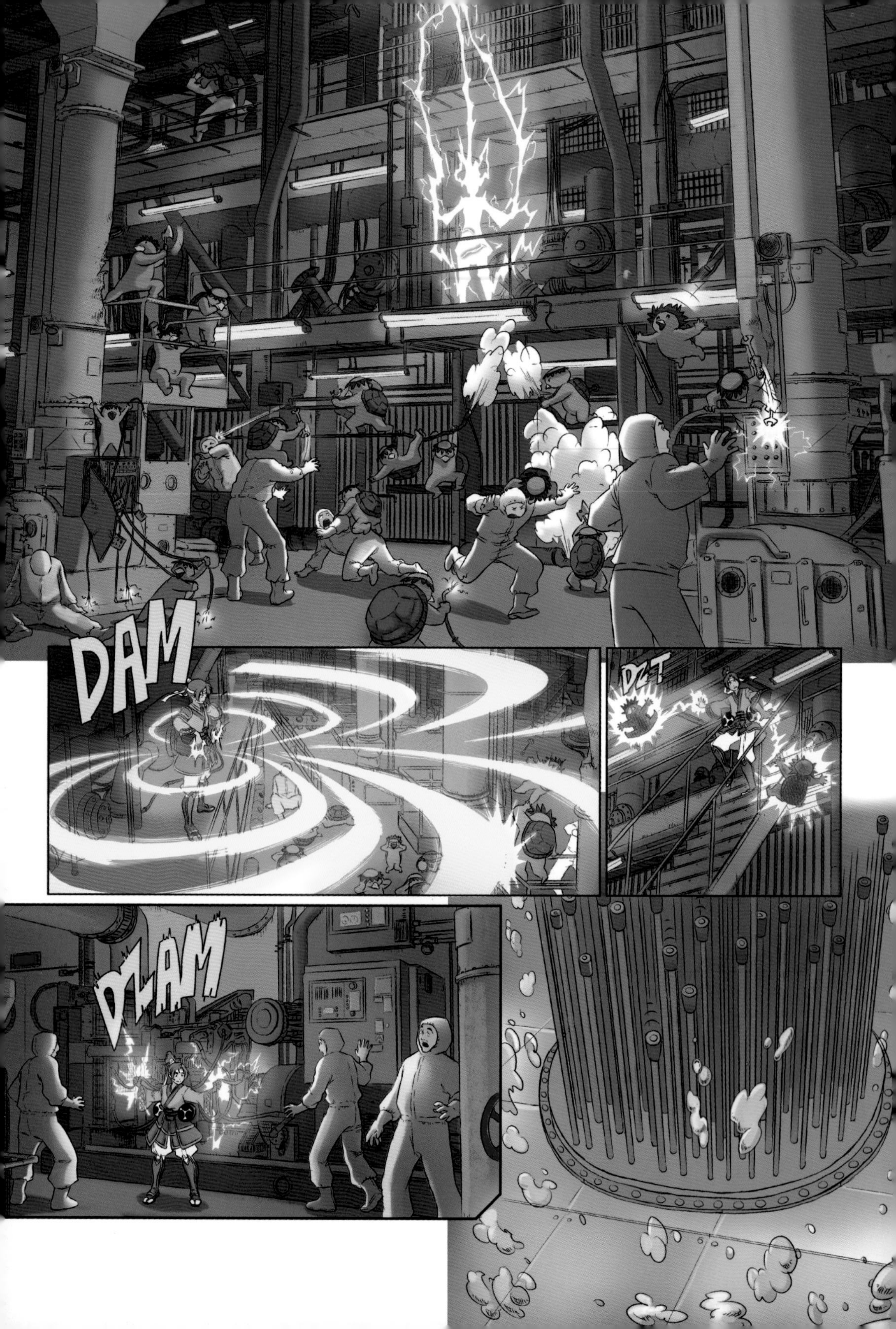
DAM
DZT
DZAM

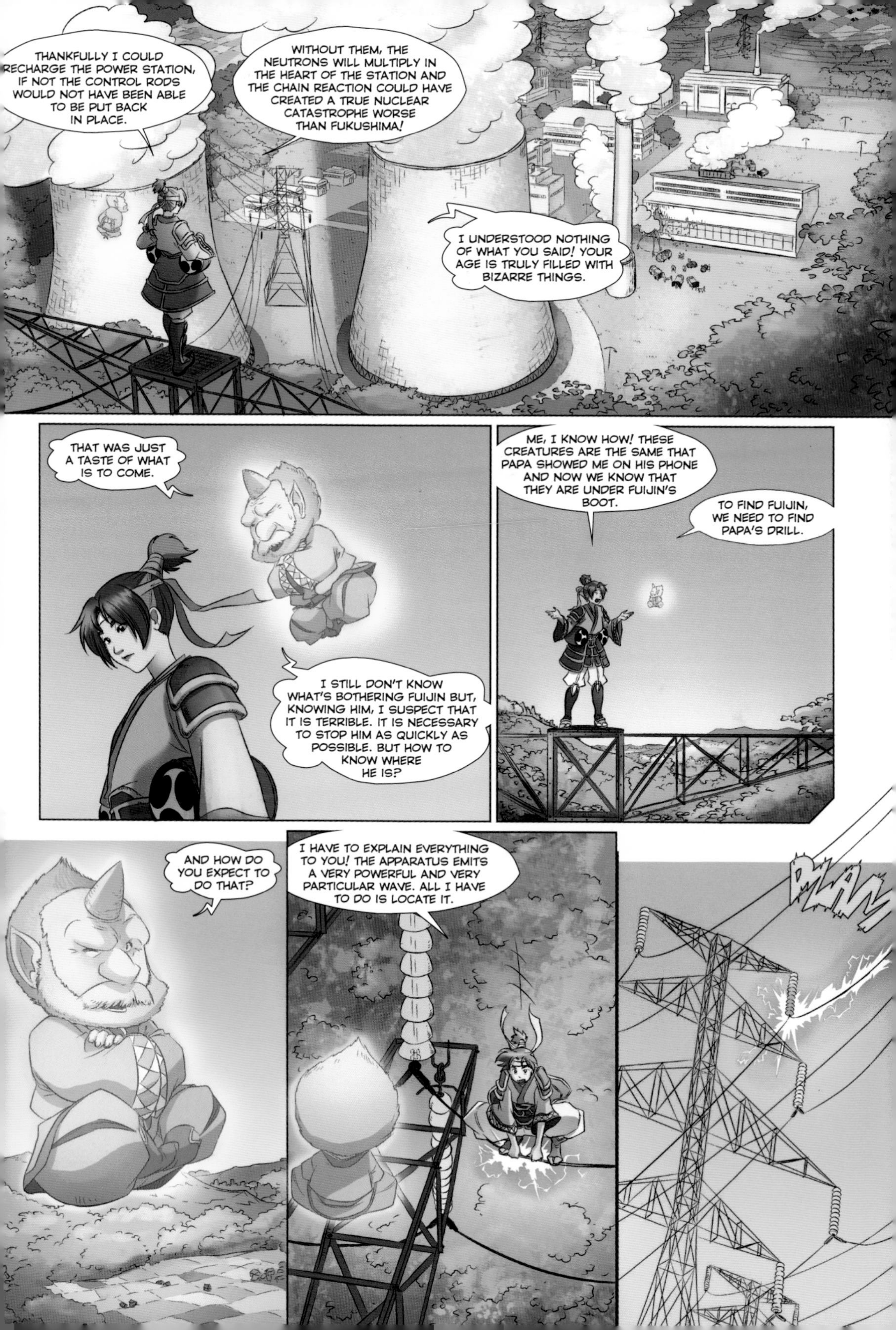
THANKFULLY I COULD RECHARGE THE POWER STATION, IF NOT THE CONTROL RODS WOULD NOT HAVE BEEN ABLE TO BE PUT BACK IN PLACE.
WITHOUT THEM, THE NEUTRONS WILL MULTIPLY IN THE HEART OF THE STATION AND THE CHAIN REACTION COULD HAVE CREATED A TRUE NUCLEAR CATASTROPHE WORSE THAN FUKUSHIMA!
I UNDERSTOOD NOTHING OF WHAT YOU SAID! YOUR AGE IS TRULY FILLED WITH BIZARRE THINGS.
THAT WAS JUST A TASTE OF WHAT IS TO COME.
I STILL DON'T KNOW WHAT'S BOTHERING FUIJIN BUT, KNOWING HIM, I SUSPECT THAT IT IS TERRIBLE. IT IS NECESSARY TO STOP HIM AS QUICKLY AS POSSIBLE. BUT HOW TO KNOW WHERE HE IS?
ME, I KNOW HOW! THESE CREATURES ARE THE SAME THAT PAPA SHOWED ME ON HIS PHONE AND NOW WE KNOW THAT THEY ARE UNDER FUIJIN'S BOOT.
TO FIND FUIJIN, WE NEED TO FIND PAPA'S DRILL.
AND HOW DO YOU EXPECT TO DO THAT?
I HAVE TO EXPLAIN EVERYTHING TO YOU! THE APPARATUS EMITS A VERY POWERFUL AND VERY PARTICULAR WAVE. ALL I HAVE TO DO IS LOCATE IT.
BLAM

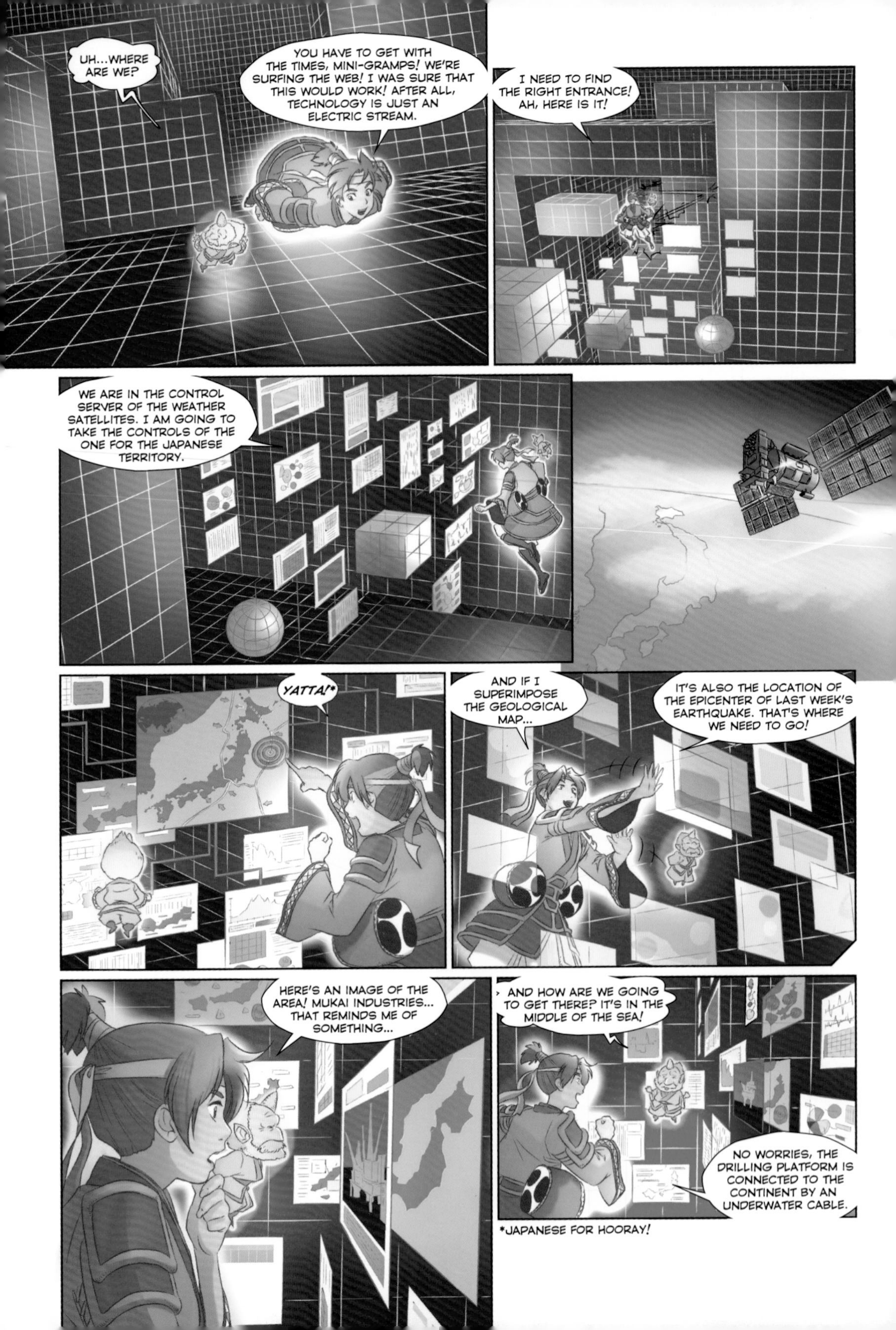
UH...WHERE ARE WE?
YOU HAVE TO GET WITH THE TIMES, MINI-GRAMPS! WE'RE SURFING THE WEB! I WAS SURE THAT THIS WOULD WORK! AFTER ALL, TECHNOLOGY IS JUST AN ELECTRIC STREAM.
I NEED TO FIND THE RIGHT ENTRANCE! AH, HERE IS IT!
WE ARE IN THE CONTROL SERVER OF THE WEATHER SATELLITES. I AM GOING TO TAKE THE CONTROLS OF THE ONE FOR THE JAPANESE TERRITORY.
YATTA!*
AND IF I SUPERIMPOSE THE GEOLOGICAL MAP...
IT'S ALSO THE LOCATION OF THE EPICENTER OF LAST WEEK'S EARTHQUAKE. THAT'S WHERE WE NEED TO GO!
HERE'S AN IMAGE OF THE AREA! MUKAI INDUSTRIES... THAT REMINDS ME OF SOMETHING...
AND HOW ARE WE GOING TO GET THERE? IT'S IN THE MIDDLE OF THE SEA!
NO WORRIES, THE DRILLING PLATFORM IS CONNECTED TO THE CONTINENT BY AN UNDERWATER CABLE.

*JAPANESE FOR HOORAY!

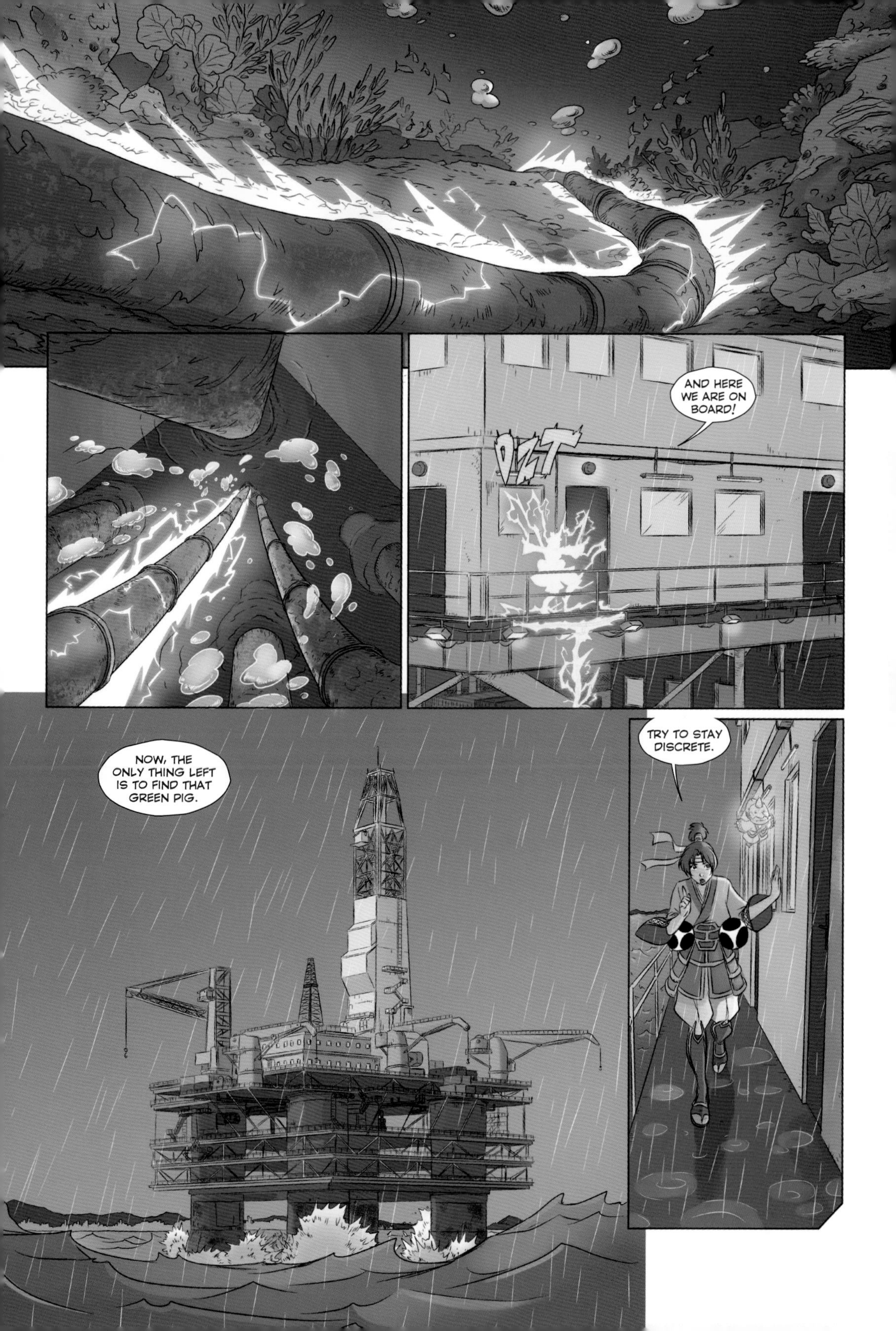
AND HERE WE ARE ON BOARD!
NOW, THE ONLY THING LEFT IS TO FIND THAT GREEN PIG.
TRY TO STAY DISCRETE.

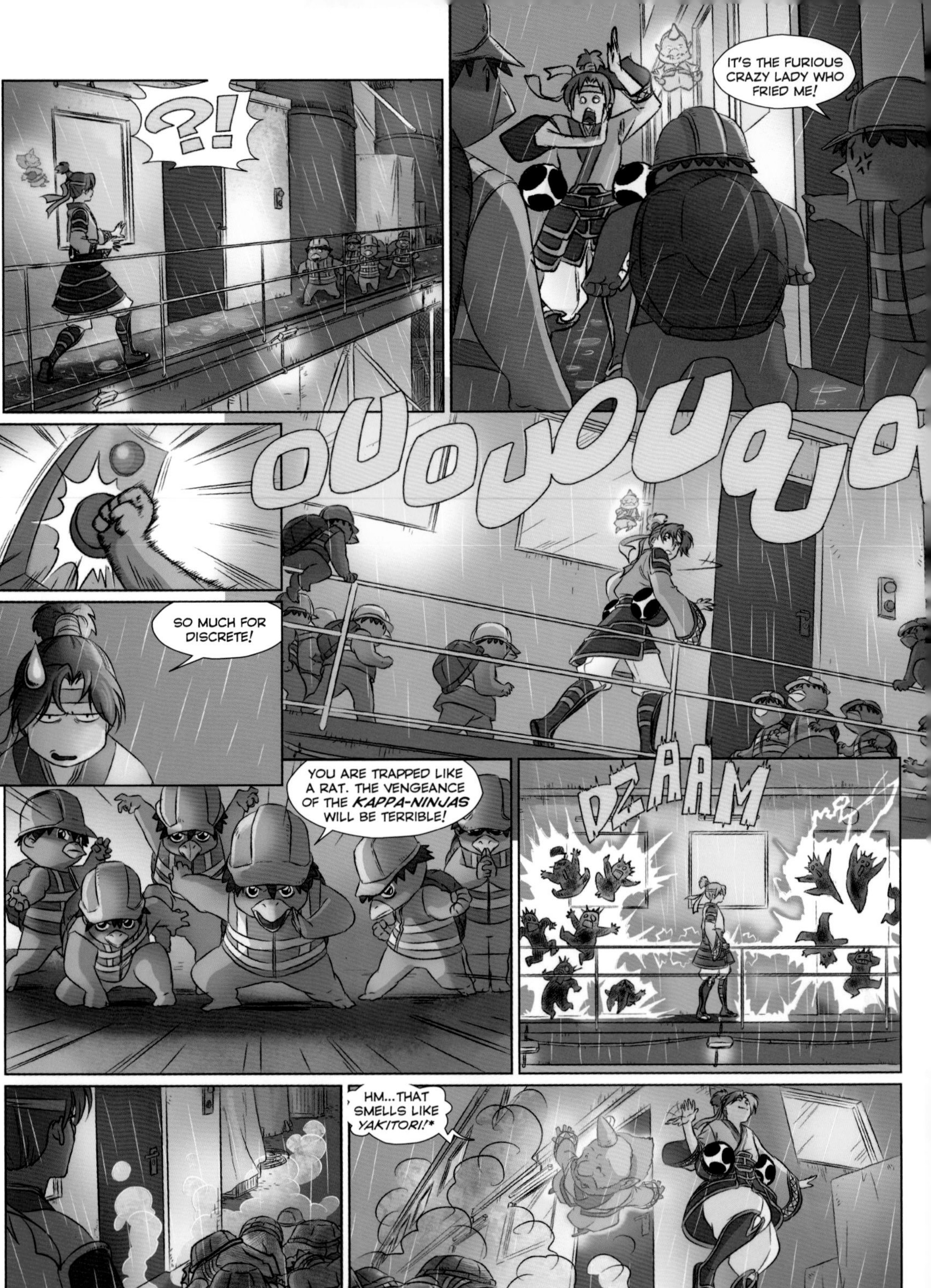
?!
IT'S THE FURIOUS CRAZY LADY WHO FRIED ME!
OUOUOUOUOUO
SO MUCH FOR DISCRETE!
YOU ARE TRAPPED LIKE A RAT. THE VENGEANCE OF THE *KAPPA-NINJAS* WILL BE TERRIBLE!
DZAAM
HM...THAT SMELLS LIKE *YAKITORI!**

*JAPANESE FOR GRILLED CHICKEN.

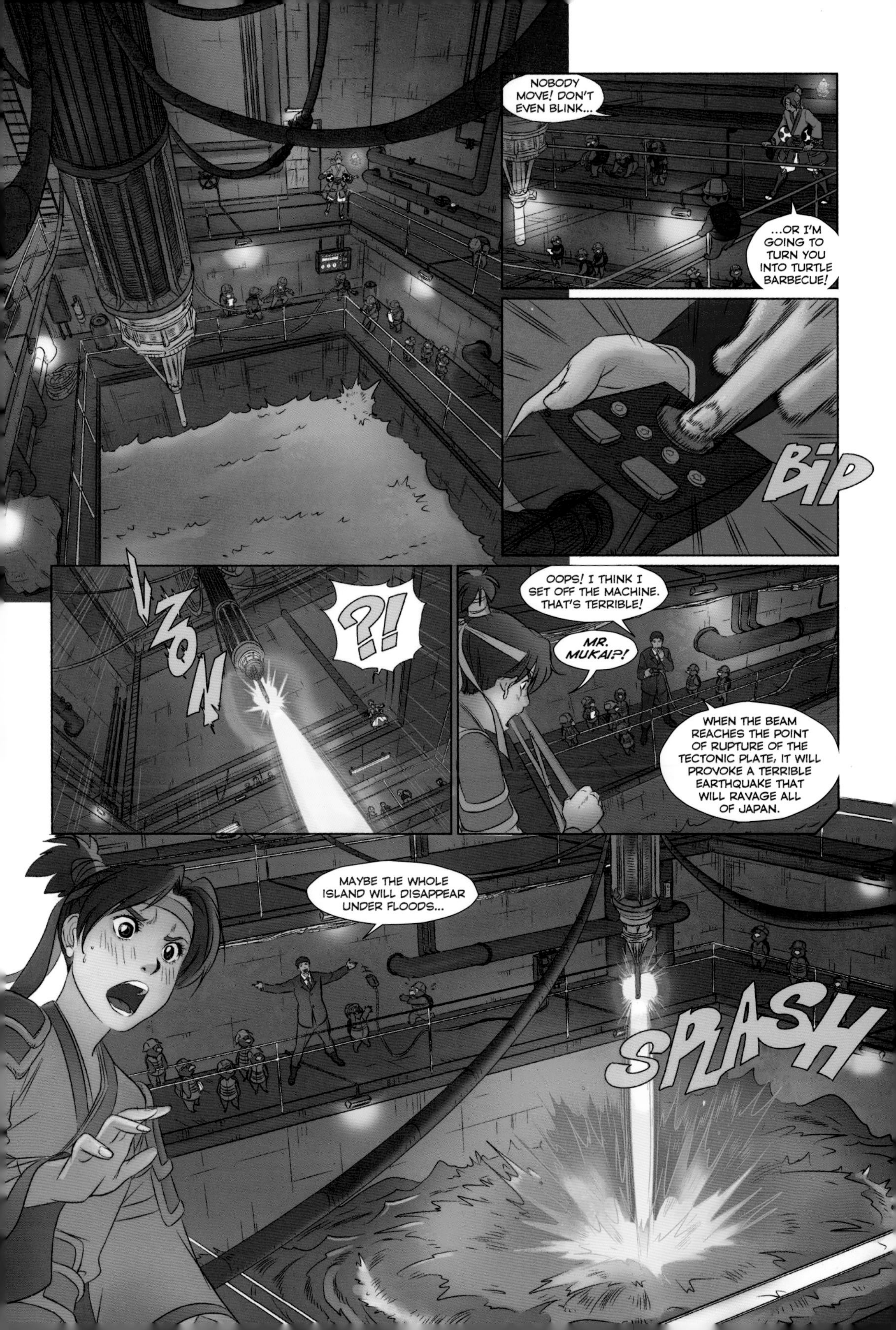
NOBODY MOVE! DON'T EVEN BLINK...
...OR I'M GOING TO TURN YOU INTO TURTLE BARBECUE!
BIP
VZOON
?!
OOPS! I THINK I SET OFF THE MACHINE. THAT'S TERRIBLE!
MR. MUKAI?!
WHEN THE BEAM REACHES THE POINT OF RUPTURE OF THE TECTONIC PLATE, IT WILL PROVOKE A TERRIBLE EARTHQUAKE THAT WILL RAVAGE ALL OF JAPAN.
MAYBE THE WHOLE ISLAND WILL DISAPPEAR UNDER FLOODS...
SPLASH

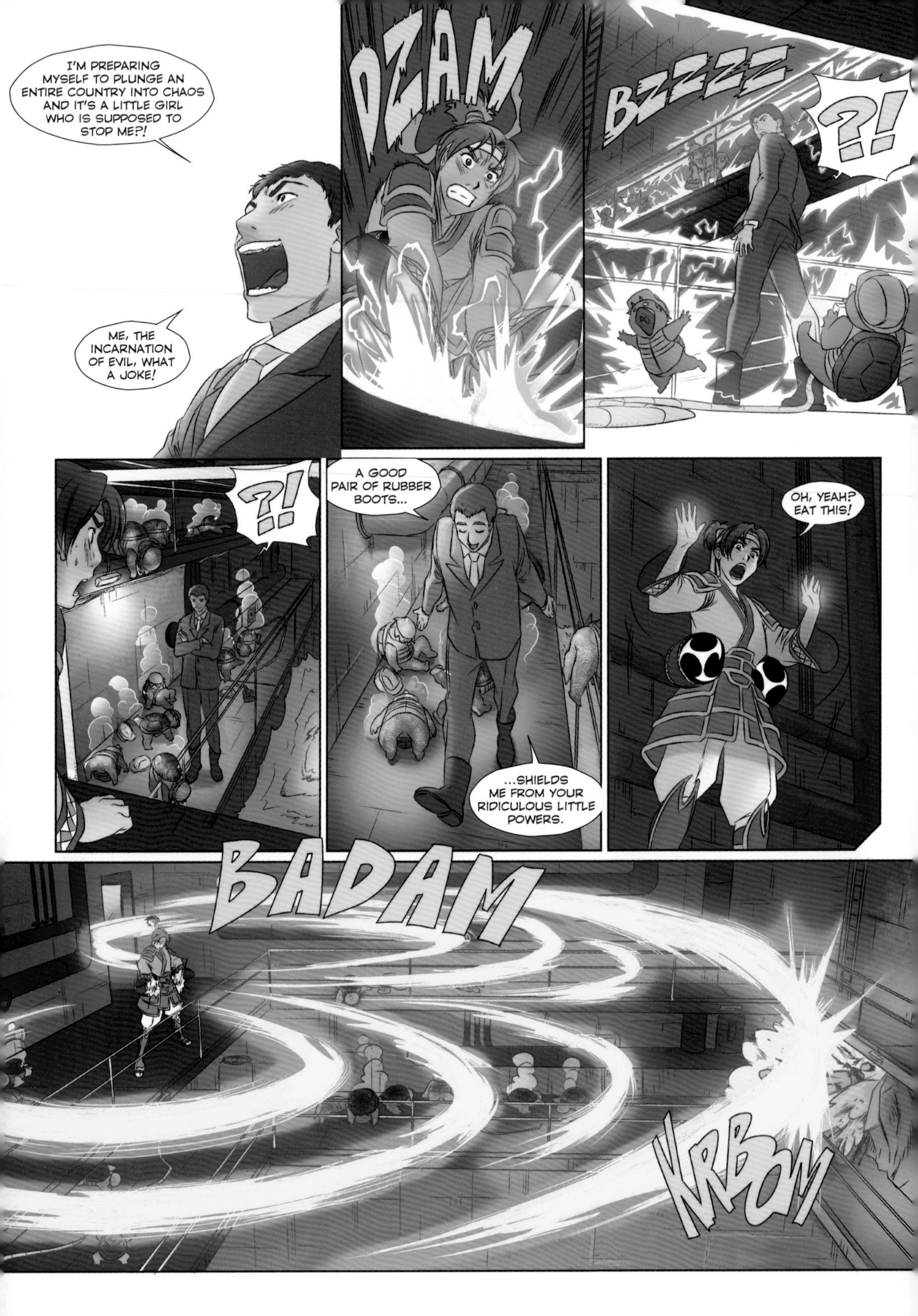

I'M PREPARING MYSELF TO PLUNGE AN ENTIRE COUNTRY INTO CHAOS AND IT'S A LITTLE GIRL WHO IS SUPPOSED TO STOP ME?!
ME, THE INCARNATION OF EVIL, WHAT A JOKE!
DZAM
BZZZZZ
?!
?!
A GOOD PAIR OF RUBBER BOOTS...
...SHIELDS ME FROM YOUR RIDICULOUS LITTLE POWERS.
OH, YEAH? EAT THIS!
BADAM
KRBOM

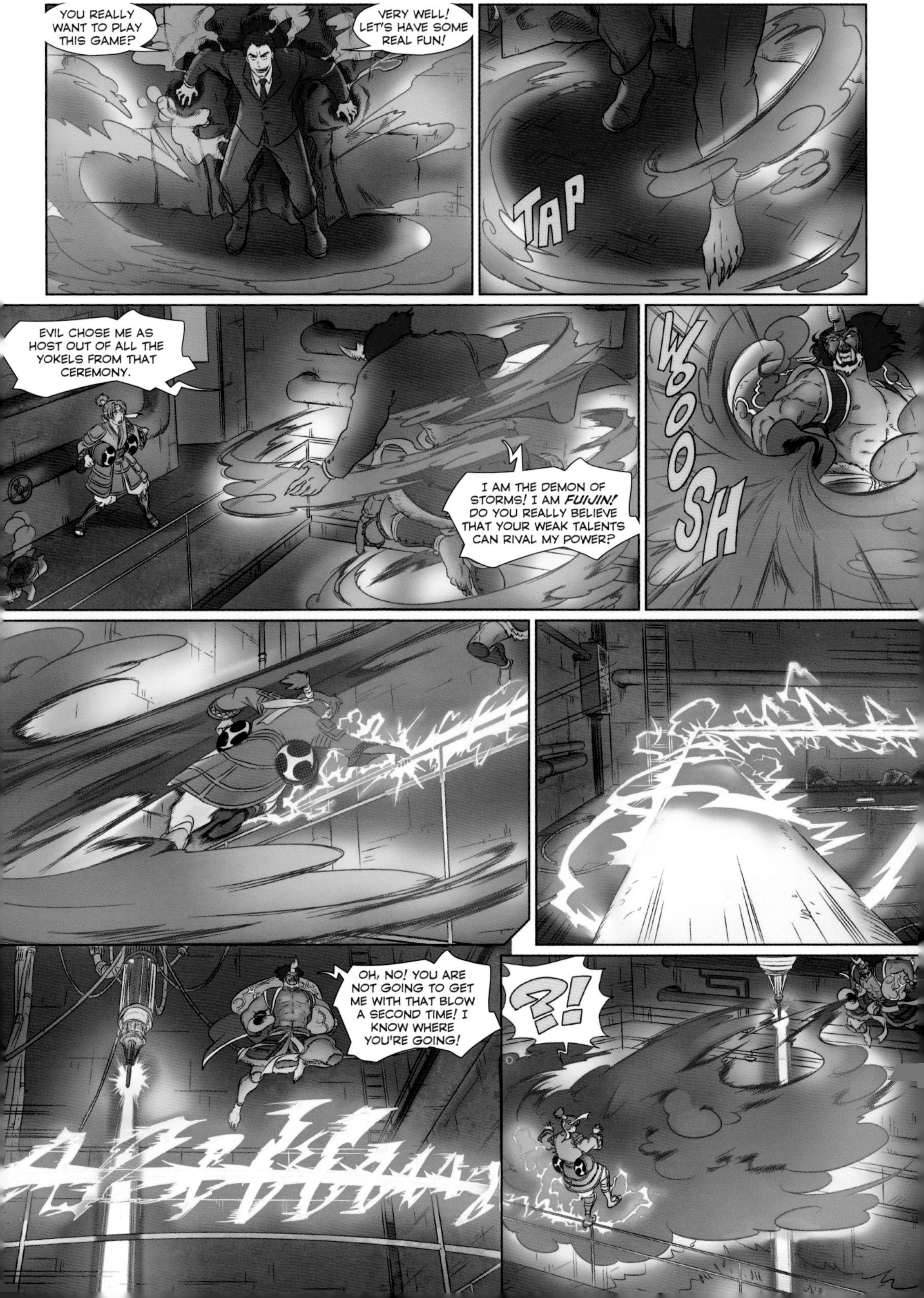
YOU REALLY WANT TO PLAY THIS GAME?
VERY WELL! LET'S HAVE SOME REAL FUN!
TAP
EVIL CHOSE ME AS HOST OUT OF ALL THE YOKELS FROM THAT CEREMONY.
I AM THE DEMON OF STORMS! I AM *FUIJIN!* DO YOU REALLY BELIEVE THAT YOUR WEAK TALENTS CAN RIVAL MY POWER?
WOOOSH
OH, NO! YOU ARE NOT GOING TO GET ME WITH THAT BLOW A SECOND TIME! I KNOW WHERE YOU'RE GOING!
?!

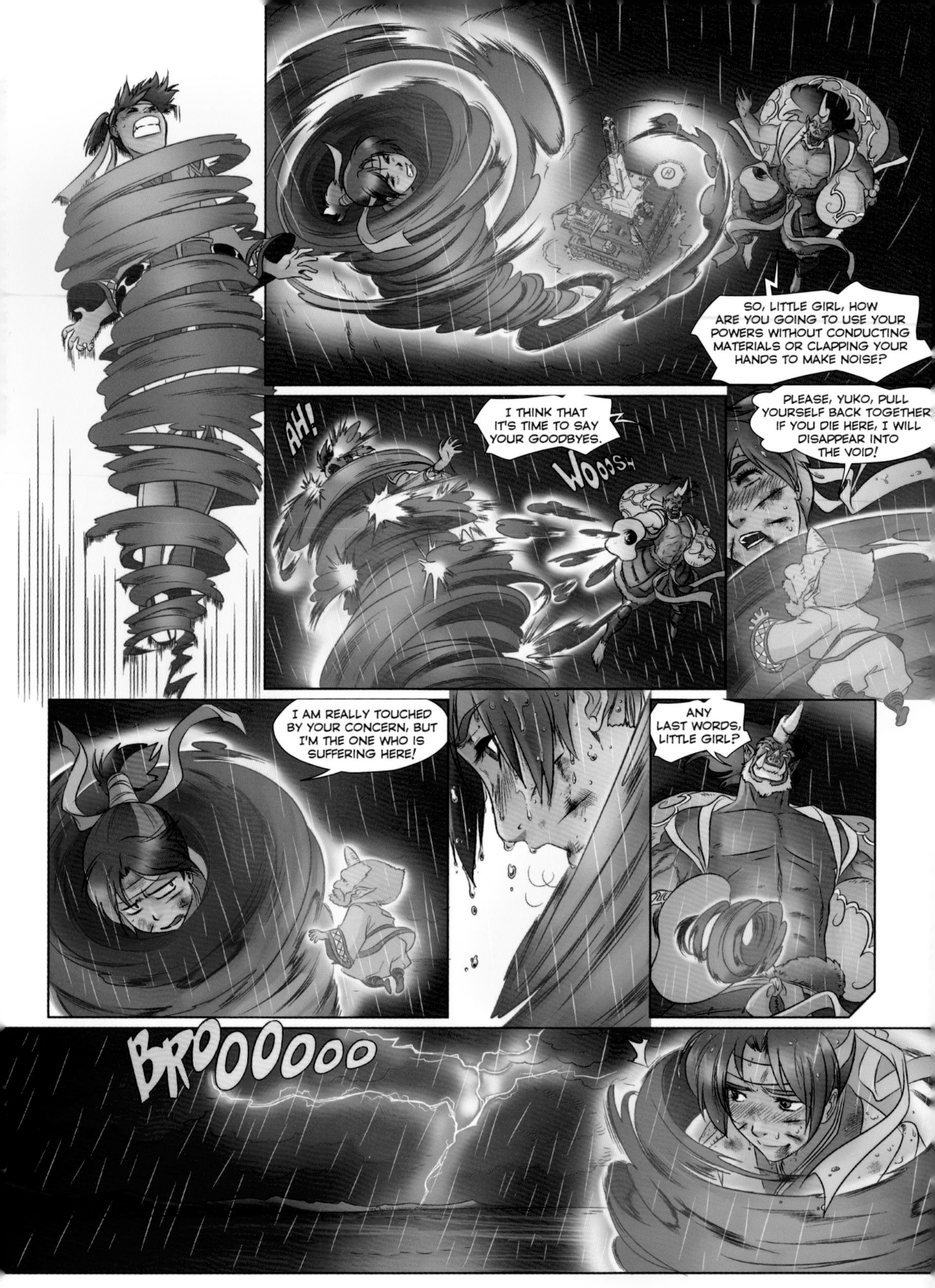
SO, LITTLE GIRL, HOW ARE YOU GOING TO USE YOUR POWERS WITHOUT CONDUCTING MATERIALS OR CLAPPING YOUR HANDS TO MAKE NOISE?
AH!
I THINK THAT IT'S TIME TO SAY YOUR GOODBYES.
WOOOSH
PLEASE, YUKO, PULL YOURSELF BACK TOGETHER IF YOU DIE HERE, I WILL DISAPPEAR INTO THE VOID!
I AM REALLY TOUCHED BY YOUR CONCERN, BUT I'M THE ONE WHO IS SUFFERING HERE!
ANY LAST WORDS, LITTLE GIRL?
BROOOOOO

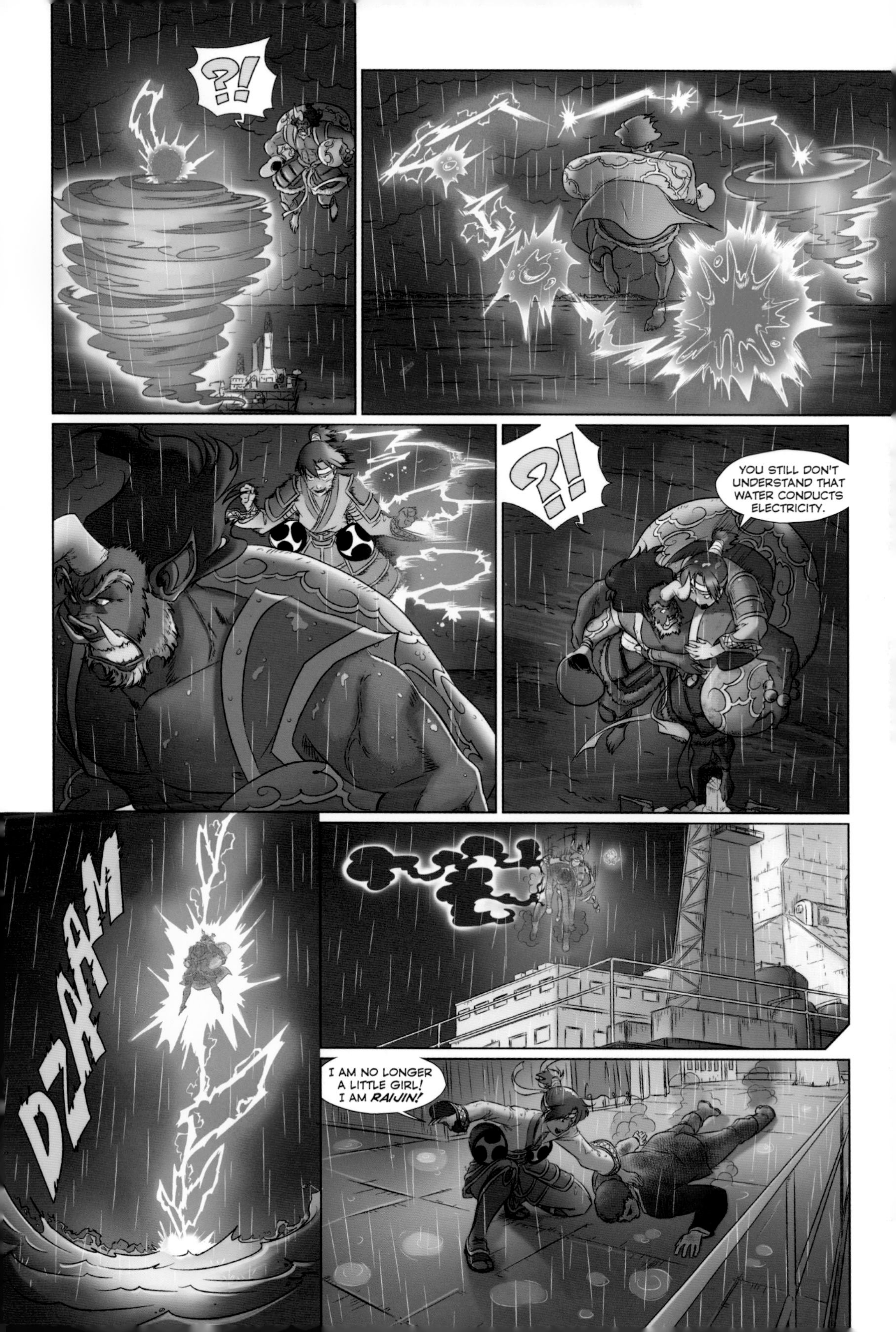
?!
?!
YOU STILL DON'T UNDERSTAND THAT WATER CONDUCTS ELECTRICITY.
DZAAM
I AM NO LONGER A LITTLE GIRL! I AM *RAIJIN!*

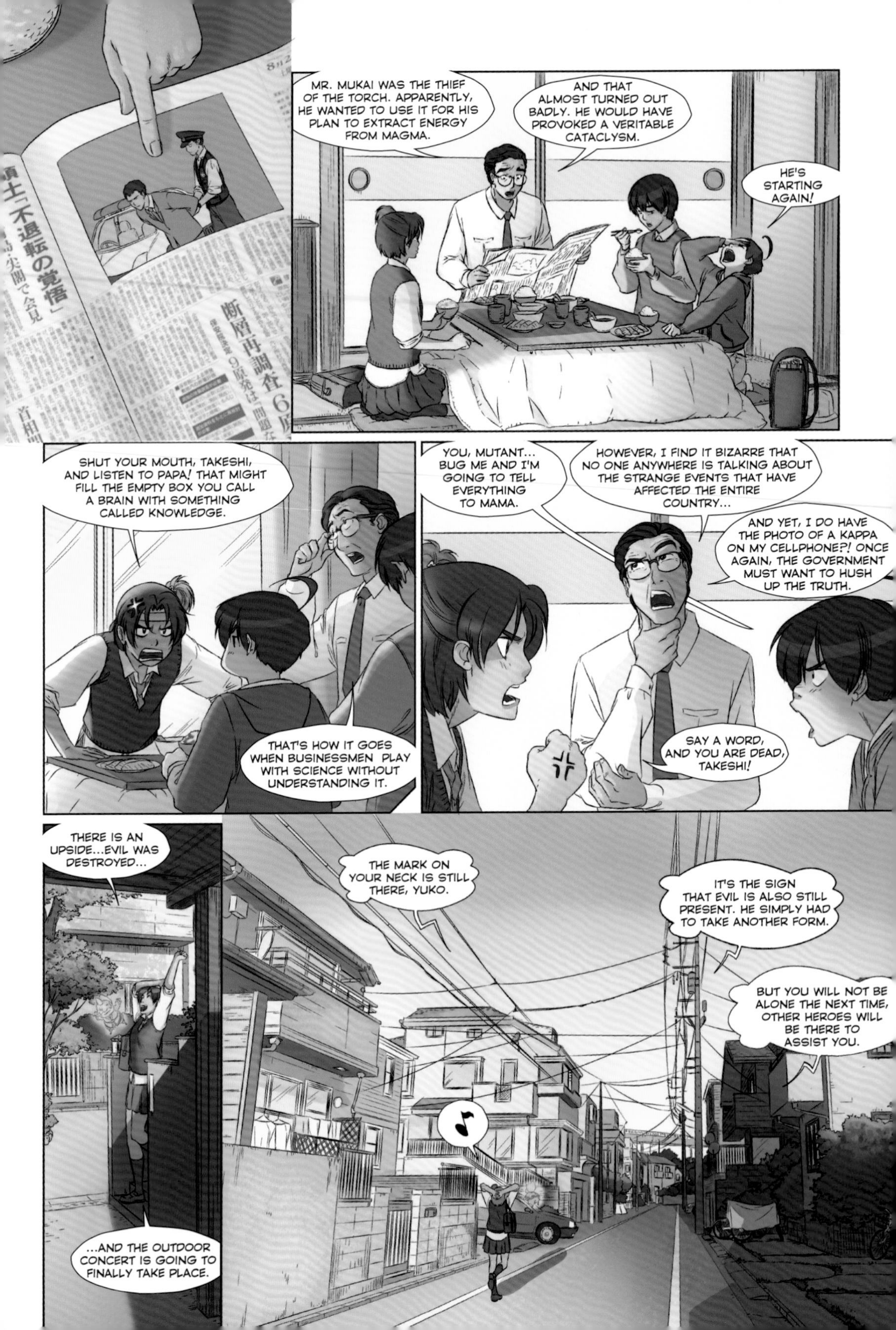
「不退転の覚悟」
断層再調査
MR. MUKAI WAS THE THIEF OF THE TORCH. APPARENTLY, HE WANTED TO USE IT FOR HIS PLAN TO EXTRACT ENERGY FROM MAGMA.
AND THAT ALMOST TURNED OUT BADLY. HE WOULD HAVE PROVOKED A VERITABLE CATACLYSM.
HE'S STARTING AGAIN!
SHUT YOUR MOUTH, TAKESHI, AND LISTEN TO PAPA! THAT MIGHT FILL THE EMPTY BOX YOU CALL A BRAIN WITH SOMETHING CALLED KNOWLEDGE.
THAT'S HOW IT GOES WHEN BUSINESSMEN PLAY WITH SCIENCE WITHOUT UNDERSTANDING IT.
YOU, MUTANT... BUG ME AND I'M GOING TO TELL EVERYTHING TO MAMA.
HOWEVER, I FIND IT BIZARRE THAT NO ONE ANYWHERE IS TALKING ABOUT THE STRANGE EVENTS THAT HAVE AFFECTED THE ENTIRE COUNTRY...
AND YET, I DO HAVE THE PHOTO OF A KAPPA ON MY CELLPHONE?! ONCE AGAIN, THE GOVERNMENT MUST WANT TO HUSH UP THE TRUTH.
SAY A WORD, AND YOU ARE DEAD, TAKESHI!
THERE IS AN UPSIDE...EVIL WAS DESTROYED...
...AND THE OUTDOOR CONCERT IS GOING TO FINALLY TAKE PLACE.
THE MARK ON YOUR NECK IS STILL THERE, YUKO.
IT'S THE SIGN THAT EVIL IS ALSO STILL PRESENT. HE SIMPLY HAD TO TAKE ANOTHER FORM.
BUT YOU WILL NOT BE ALONE THE NEXT TIME, OTHER HEROES WILL BE THERE TO ASSIST YOU.

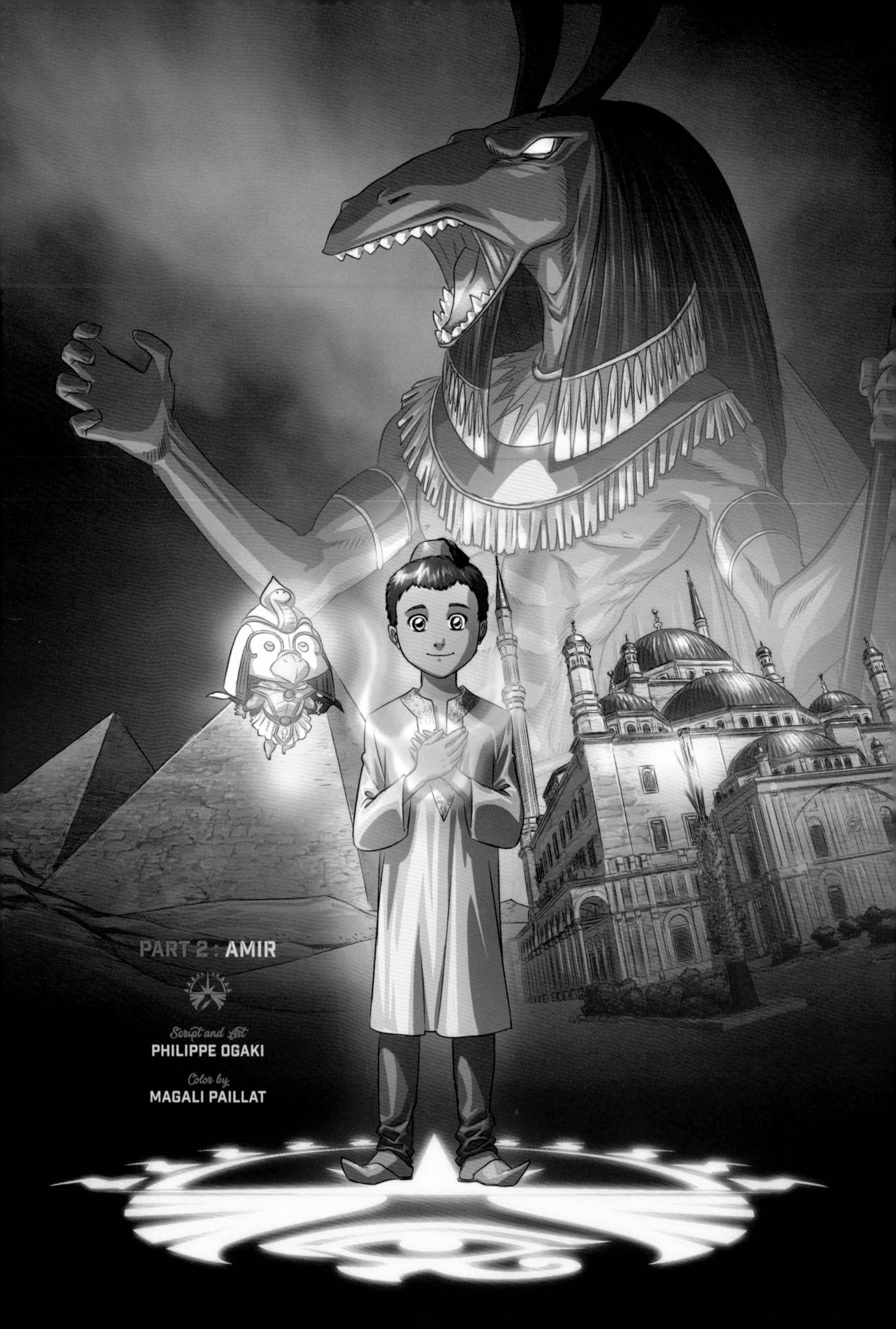
PART 2 : AMIR
Script and Art
PHILIPPE OGAKI
Color by
MAGALI PAILLAT

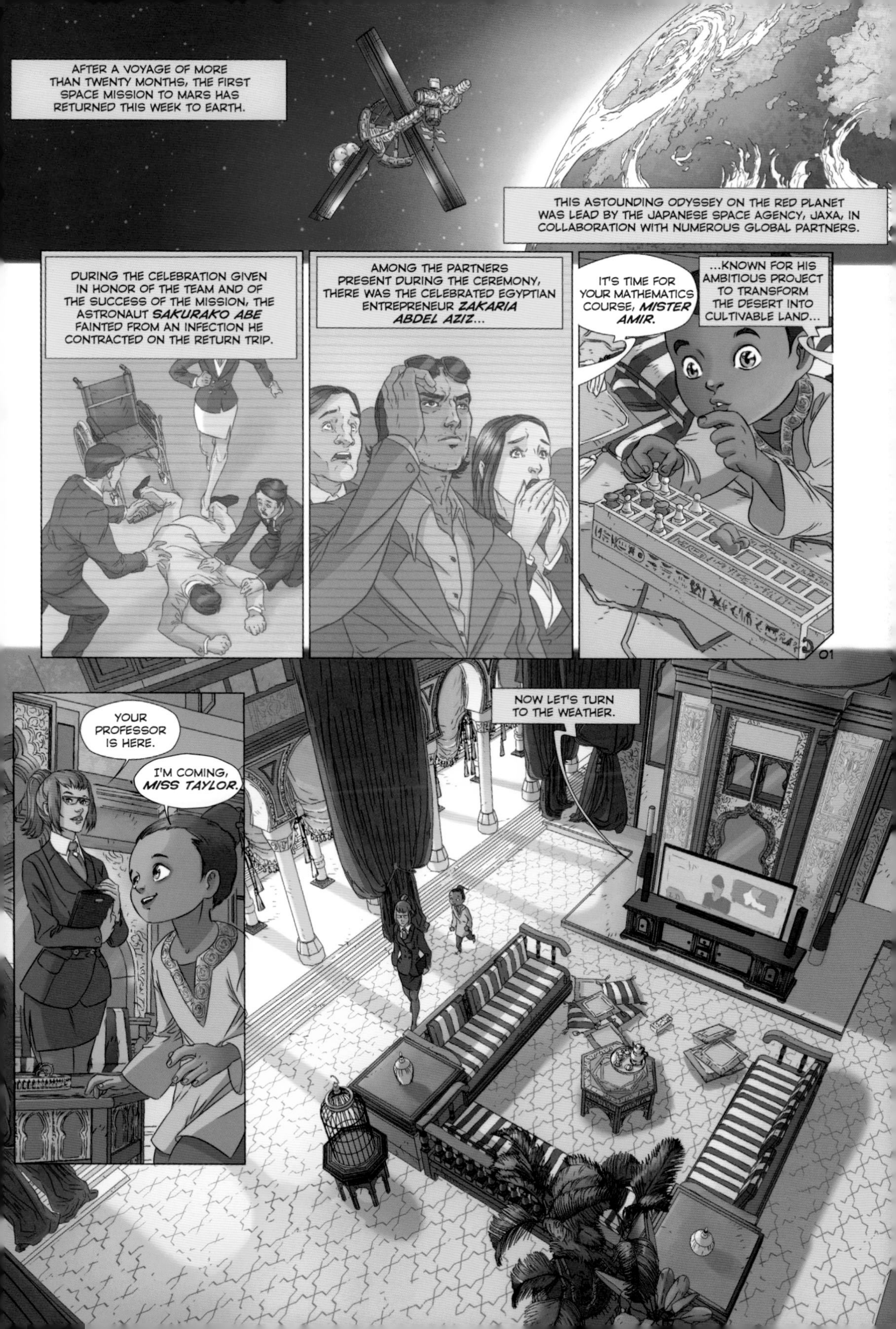
AFTER A VOYAGE OF MORE THAN TWENTY MONTHS, THE FIRST SPACE MISSION TO MARS HAS RETURNED THIS WEEK TO EARTH.
THIS ASTOUNDING ODYSSEY ON THE RED PLANET WAS LEAD BY THE JAPANESE SPACE AGENCY, JAXA, IN COLLABORATION WITH NUMEROUS GLOBAL PARTNERS.
DURING THE CELEBRATION GIVEN IN HONOR OF THE TEAM AND OF THE SUCCESS OF THE MISSION, THE ASTRONAUT SAKURAKO ABE FAINTED FROM AN INFECTION HE CONTRACTED ON THE RETURN TRIP.
AMONG THE PARTNERS PRESENT DURING THE CEREMONY, THERE WAS THE CELEBRATED EGYPTIAN ENTREPRENEUR ZAKARIA ABDEL AZIZ...
IT'S TIME FOR YOUR MATHEMATICS COURSE, MISTER AMIR.
...KNOWN FOR HIS AMBITIOUS PROJECT TO TRANSFORM THE DESERT INTO CULTIVABLE LAND...
01
YOUR PROFESSOR IS HERE.
I'M COMING, MISS TAYLOR.
NOW LET'S TURN TO THE WEATHER.

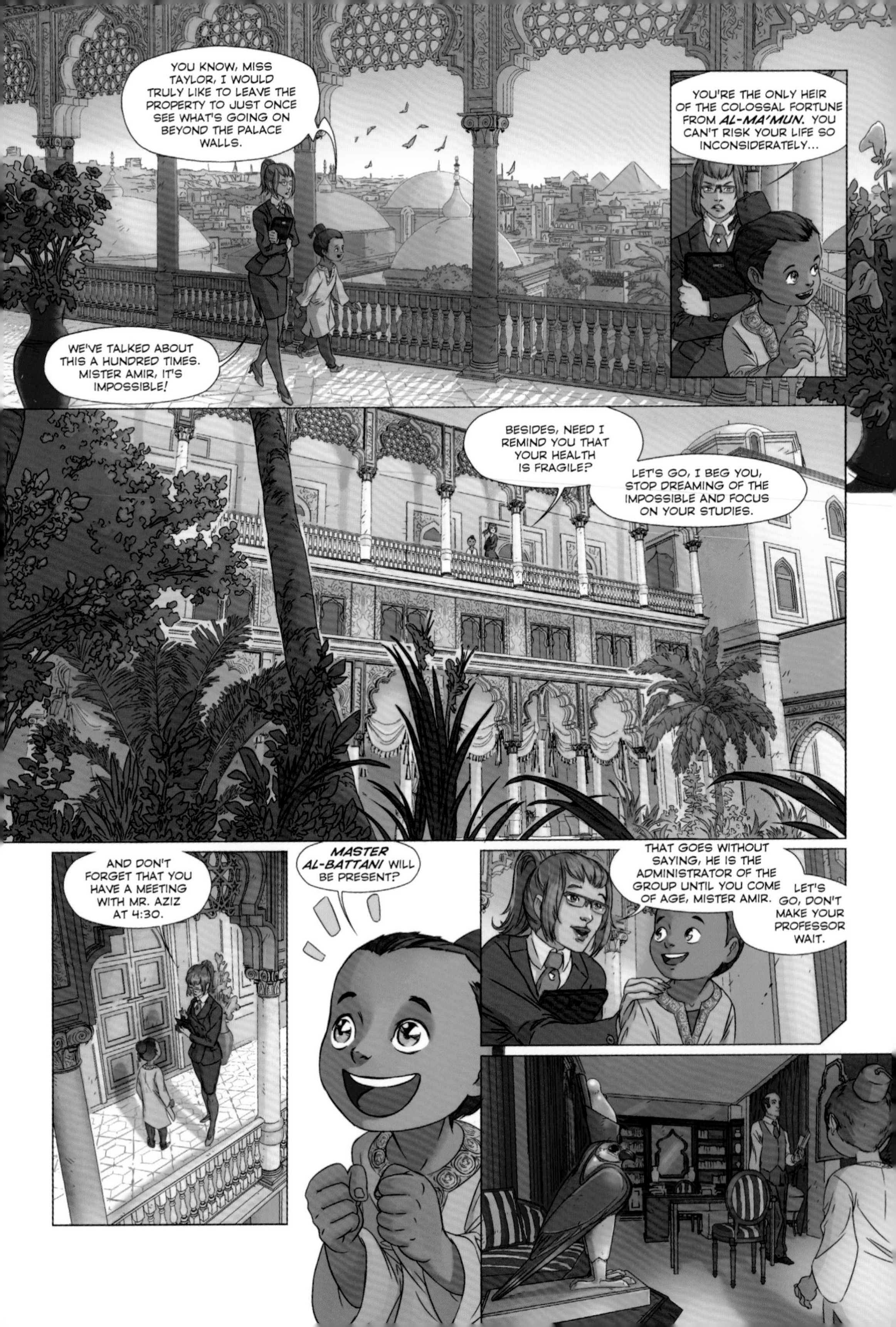

YOU KNOW, MISS TAYLOR, I WOULD TRULY LIKE TO LEAVE THE PROPERTY TO JUST ONCE SEE WHAT'S GOING ON BEYOND THE PALACE WALLS.
WE'VE TALKED ABOUT THIS A HUNDRED TIMES. MISTER AMIR, IT'S IMPOSSIBLE!
YOU'RE THE ONLY HEIR OF THE COLOSSAL FORTUNE FROM AL-MA'MUN. YOU CAN'T RISK YOUR LIFE SO INCONSIDERATELY...
BESIDES, NEED I REMIND YOU THAT YOUR HEALTH IS FRAGILE?
LET'S GO, I BEG YOU, STOP DREAMING OF THE IMPOSSIBLE AND FOCUS ON YOUR STUDIES.
AND DON'T FORGET THAT YOU HAVE A MEETING WITH MR. AZIZ AT 4:30.
MASTER AL-BATTANI WILL BE PRESENT?
THAT GOES WITHOUT SAYING, HE IS THE ADMINISTRATOR OF THE GROUP UNTIL YOU COME OF AGE, MISTER AMIR.
LET'S GO, DON'T MAKE YOUR PROFESSOR WAIT.

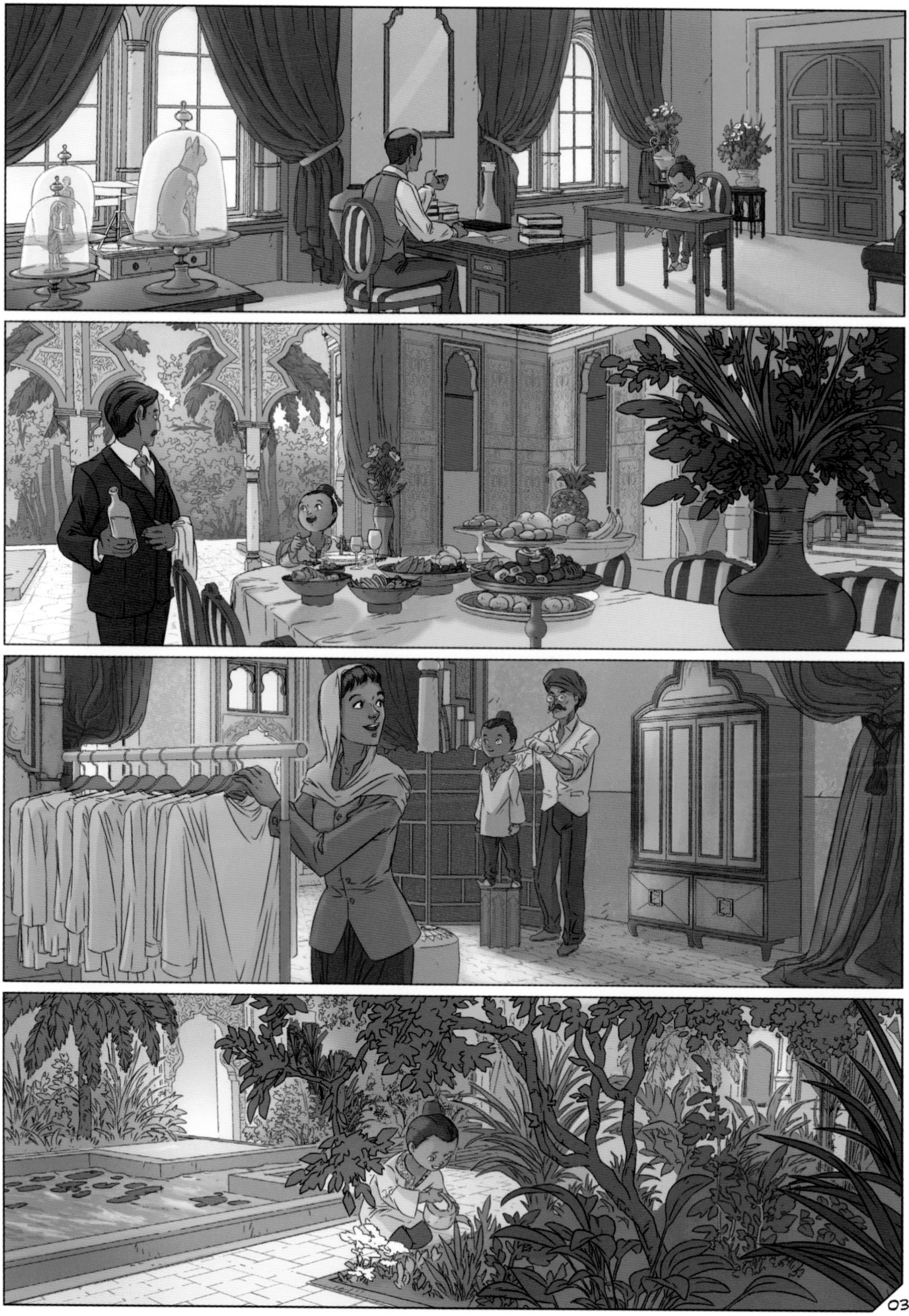
03

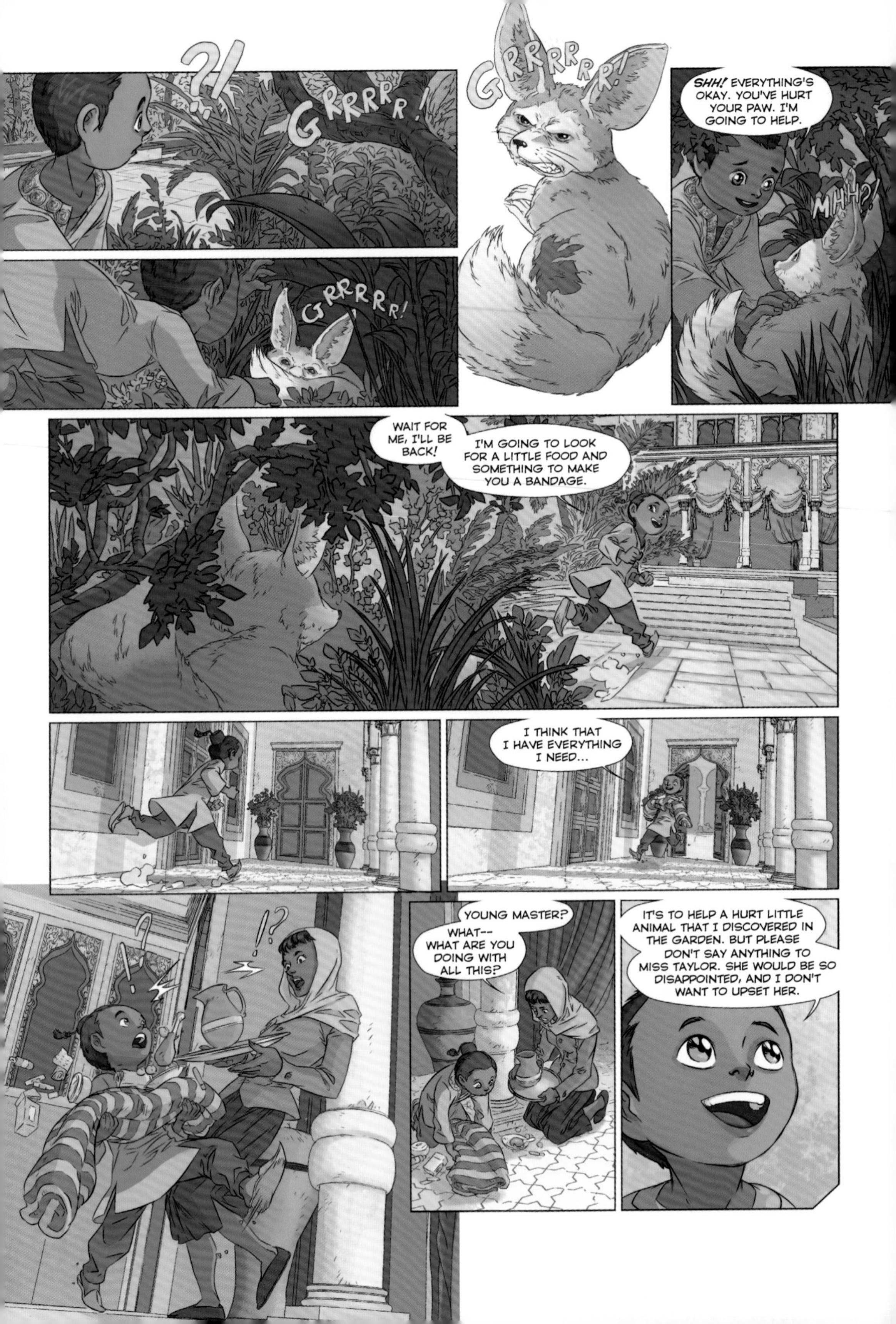
?!
GRRRRR!
GRRRRR!
GRRRRRR!
SHH! EVERYTHING'S OKAY. YOU'VE HURT YOUR PAW. I'M GOING TO HELP.
MHH?!
WAIT FOR ME, I'LL BE BACK!
I'M GOING TO LOOK FOR A LITTLE FOOD AND SOMETHING TO MAKE YOU A BANDAGE.
I THINK THAT I HAVE EVERYTHING I NEED...
!?
YOUNG MASTER?
WHAT-- WHAT ARE YOU DOING WITH ALL THIS?
IT'S TO HELP A HURT LITTLE ANIMAL THAT I DISCOVERED IN THE GARDEN. BUT PLEASE DON'T SAY ANYTHING TO MISS TAYLOR. SHE WOULD BE SO DISAPPOINTED, AND I DON'T WANT TO UPSET HER.

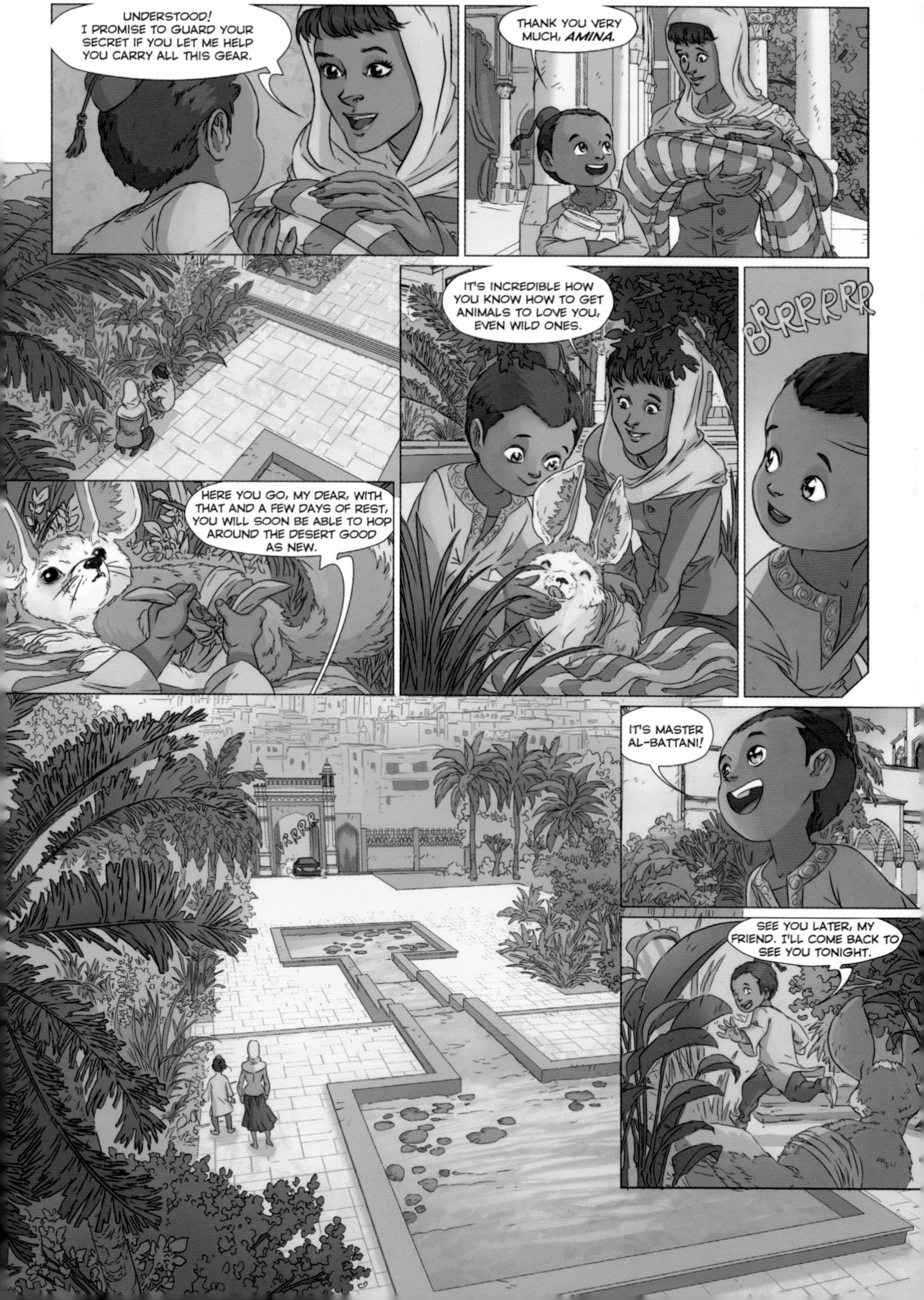
UNDERSTOOD! I PROMISE TO GUARD YOUR SECRET IF YOU LET ME HELP YOU CARRY ALL THIS GEAR.
THANK YOU VERY MUCH, AMINA.
HERE YOU GO, MY DEAR, WITH THAT AND A FEW DAYS OF REST, YOU WILL SOON BE ABLE TO HOP AROUND THE DESERT GOOD AS NEW.
IT'S INCREDIBLE HOW YOU KNOW HOW TO GET ANIMALS TO LOVE YOU, EVEN WILD ONES.
BRRRRRR
VRRRR
IT'S MASTER AL-BATTANI!
SEE YOU LATER, MY FRIEND. I'LL COME BACK TO SEE YOU TONIGHT.

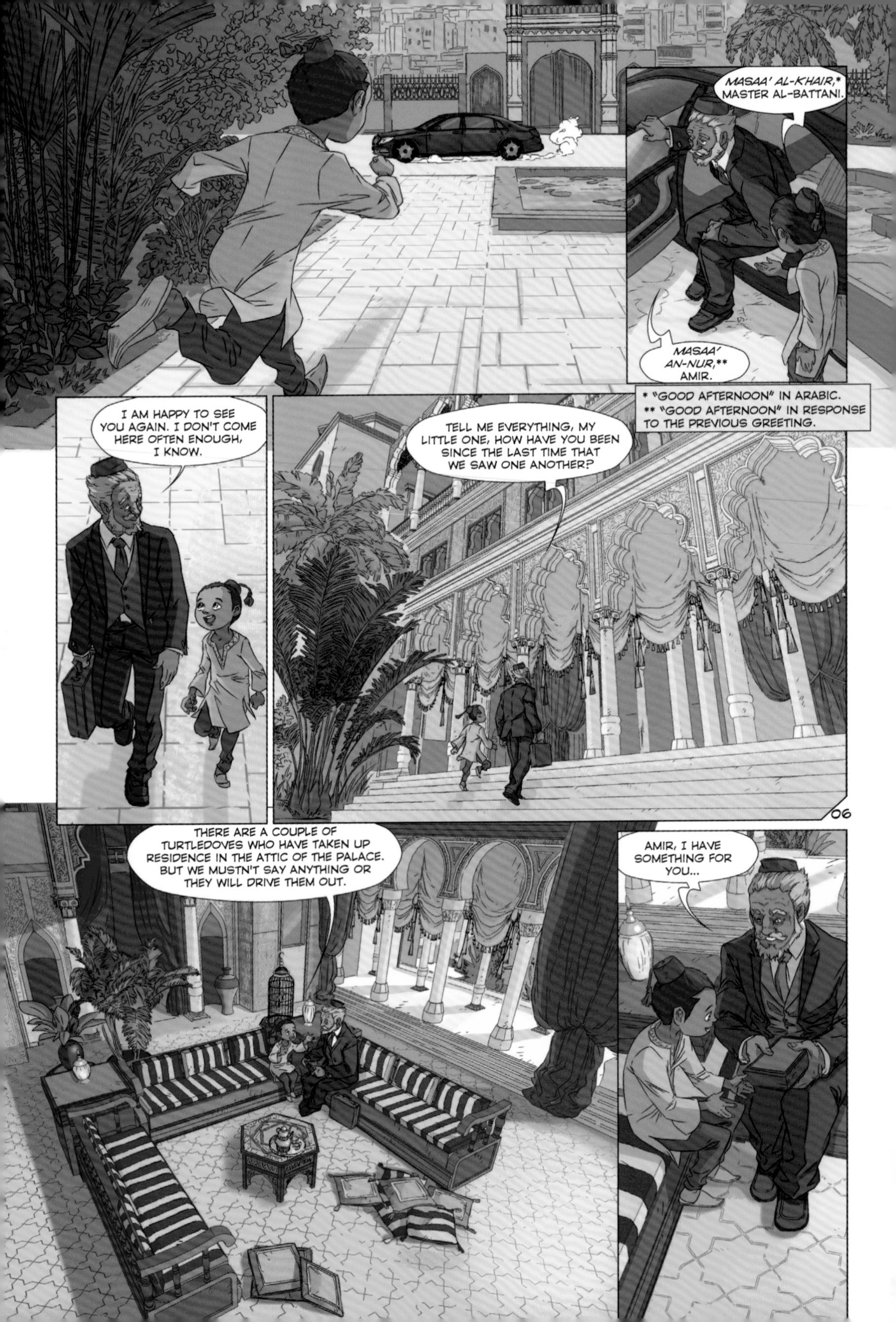

MASAA' AL-KHAIR,* MASTER AL-BATTANI.
MASAA' AN-NUR,** AMIR.
* "GOOD AFTERNOON" IN ARABIC.
** "GOOD AFTERNOON" IN RESPONSE TO THE PREVIOUS GREETING.
I AM HAPPY TO SEE YOU AGAIN. I DON'T COME HERE OFTEN ENOUGH, I KNOW.
TELL ME EVERYTHING, MY LITTLE ONE, HOW HAVE YOU BEEN SINCE THE LAST TIME THAT WE SAW ONE ANOTHER?
06
THERE ARE A COUPLE OF TURTLEDOVES WHO HAVE TAKEN UP RESIDENCE IN THE ATTIC OF THE PALACE. BUT WE MUSTN'T SAY ANYTHING OR THEY WILL DRIVE THEM OUT.
AMIR, I HAVE SOMETHING FOR YOU...

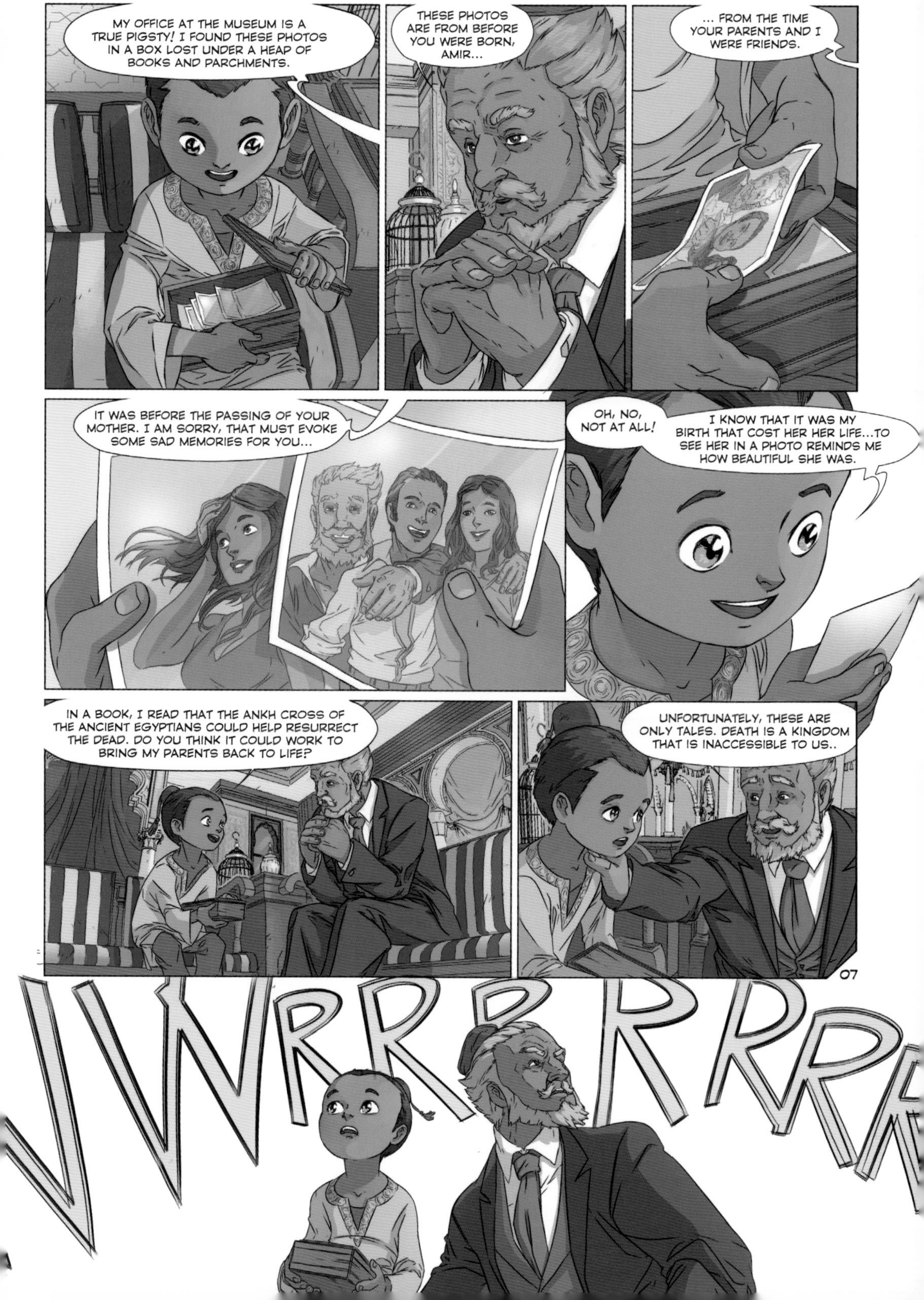
MY OFFICE AT THE MUSEUM IS A TRUE PIGSTY! I FOUND THESE PHOTOS IN A BOX LOST UNDER A HEAP OF BOOKS AND PARCHMENTS.
THESE PHOTOS ARE FROM BEFORE YOU WERE BORN, AMIR...
... FROM THE TIME YOUR PARENTS AND I WERE FRIENDS.
IT WAS BEFORE THE PASSING OF YOUR MOTHER. I AM SORRY, THAT MUST EVOKE SOME SAD MEMORIES FOR YOU...
OH, NO, NOT AT ALL!
I KNOW THAT IT WAS MY BIRTH THAT COST HER HER LIFE...TO SEE HER IN A PHOTO REMINDS ME HOW BEAUTIFUL SHE WAS.
IN A BOOK, I READ THAT THE ANKH CROSS OF THE ANCIENT EGYPTIANS COULD HELP RESURRECT THE DEAD. DO YOU THINK IT COULD WORK TO BRING MY PARENTS BACK TO LIFE?
UNFORTUNATELY, THESE ARE ONLY TALES. DEATH IS A KINGDOM THAT IS INACCESSIBLE TO US..
VVRRRRRR

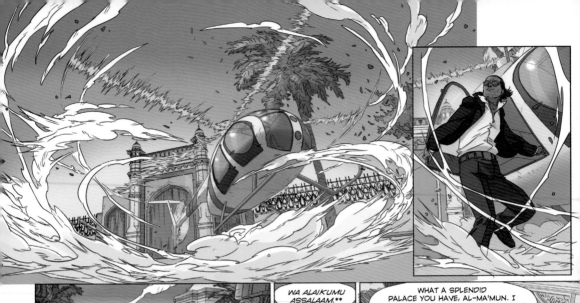

AS-SALAMU AAIYKUM.*

* A TRADITIONAL GREETING IN ARABIC, TRANSLATABLE AS "MAY PEACE BE WITH YOU."

WA ALAIKUMU ASSALAAM.**

** THE TRADITIONAL RESPONSE TO THE PREVIOUS GREETING, TRANSLATABLE AS "MAY PEACE BE WITH YOU AS WELL."

WHAT A SPLENDID PALACE YOU HAVE, AL-MA'MUN. I CAN HARDLY IMAGINE HOW PLEASANT IT MUST BE TO GROW UP IN SUCH A SETTING.

THANKS TO THESE MACHINES, WE'RE GOING TO TAKE THE WATER FROM THE NILE TO IRRIGATE CERTAIN PARTS OF THE DESERT TO MAKE THEM FERTILE.

WITH OUR PROCESS, THE DESERT WILL DIMINISH AND THEN FAMINE AND MALNUTRITION WILL BE SAD EVENTS OF THE PAST.

08

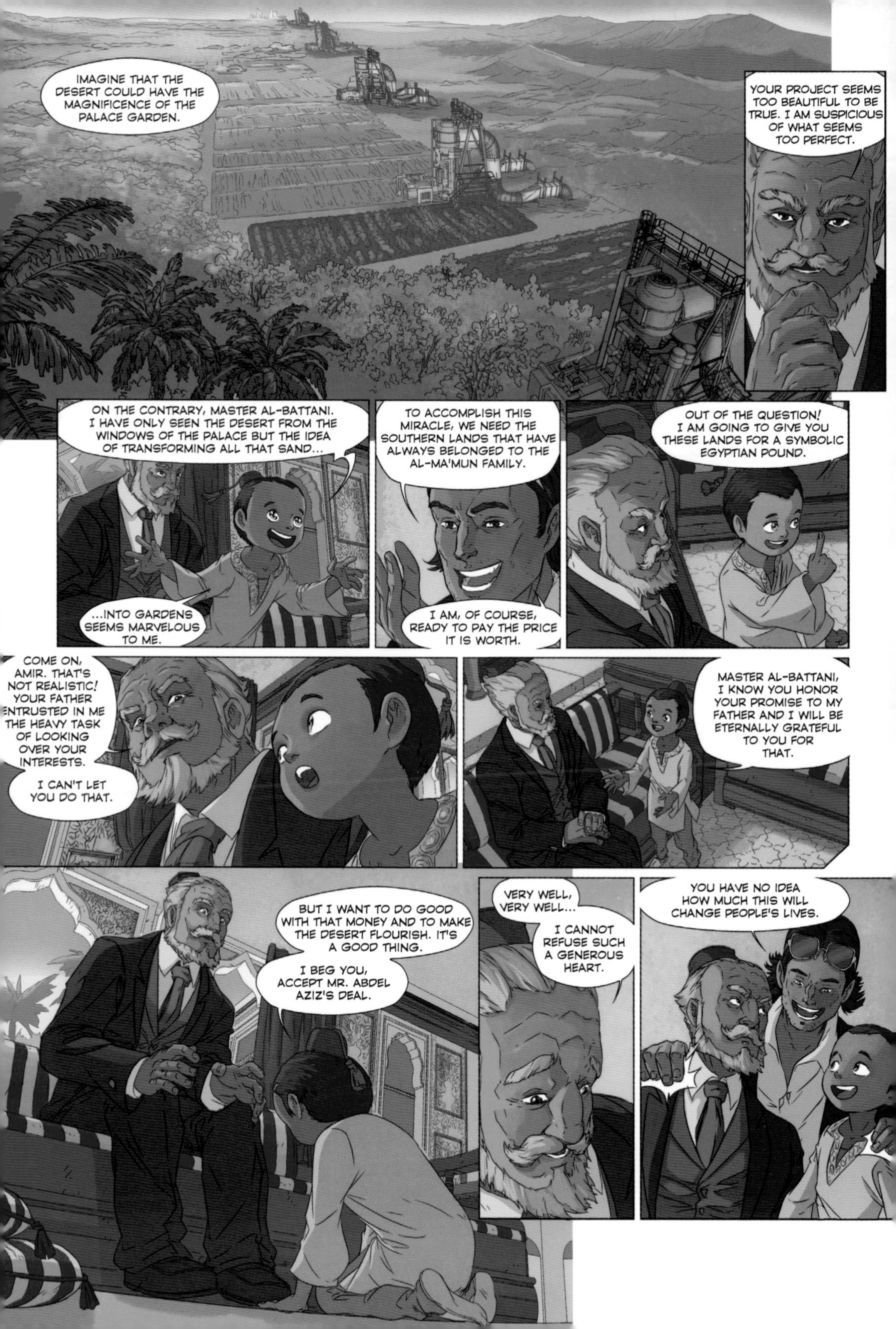
IMAGINE THAT THE DESERT COULD HAVE THE MAGNIFICENCE OF THE PALACE GARDEN.
YOUR PROJECT SEEMS TOO BEAUTIFUL TO BE TRUE. I AM SUSPICIOUS OF WHAT SEEMS TOO PERFECT.
ON THE CONTRARY, MASTER AL-BATTANI. I HAVE ONLY SEEN THE DESERT FROM THE WINDOWS OF THE PALACE BUT THE IDEA OF TRANSFORMING ALL THAT SAND...
...INTO GARDENS SEEMS MARVELOUS TO ME.
TO ACCOMPLISH THIS MIRACLE, WE NEED THE SOUTHERN LANDS THAT HAVE ALWAYS BELONGED TO THE AL-MA'MUN FAMILY.
I AM, OF COURSE, READY TO PAY THE PRICE IT IS WORTH.
OUT OF THE QUESTION! I AM GOING TO GIVE YOU THESE LANDS FOR A SYMBOLIC EGYPTIAN POUND.
COME ON, AMIR. THAT'S NOT REALISTIC! YOUR FATHER ENTRUSTED IN ME THE HEAVY TASK OF LOOKING OVER YOUR INTERESTS.
I CAN'T LET YOU DO THAT.
MASTER AL-BATTANI, I KNOW YOU HONOR YOUR PROMISE TO MY FATHER AND I WILL BE ETERNALLY GRATEFUL TO YOU FOR THAT.
BUT I WANT TO DO GOOD WITH THAT MONEY AND TO MAKE THE DESERT FLOURISH. IT'S A GOOD THING.
I BEG YOU, ACCEPT MR. ABDEL AZIZ'S DEAL.
VERY WELL, VERY WELL...
I CANNOT REFUSE SUCH A GENEROUS HEART.
YOU HAVE NO IDEA HOW MUCH THIS WILL CHANGE PEOPLE'S LIVES.

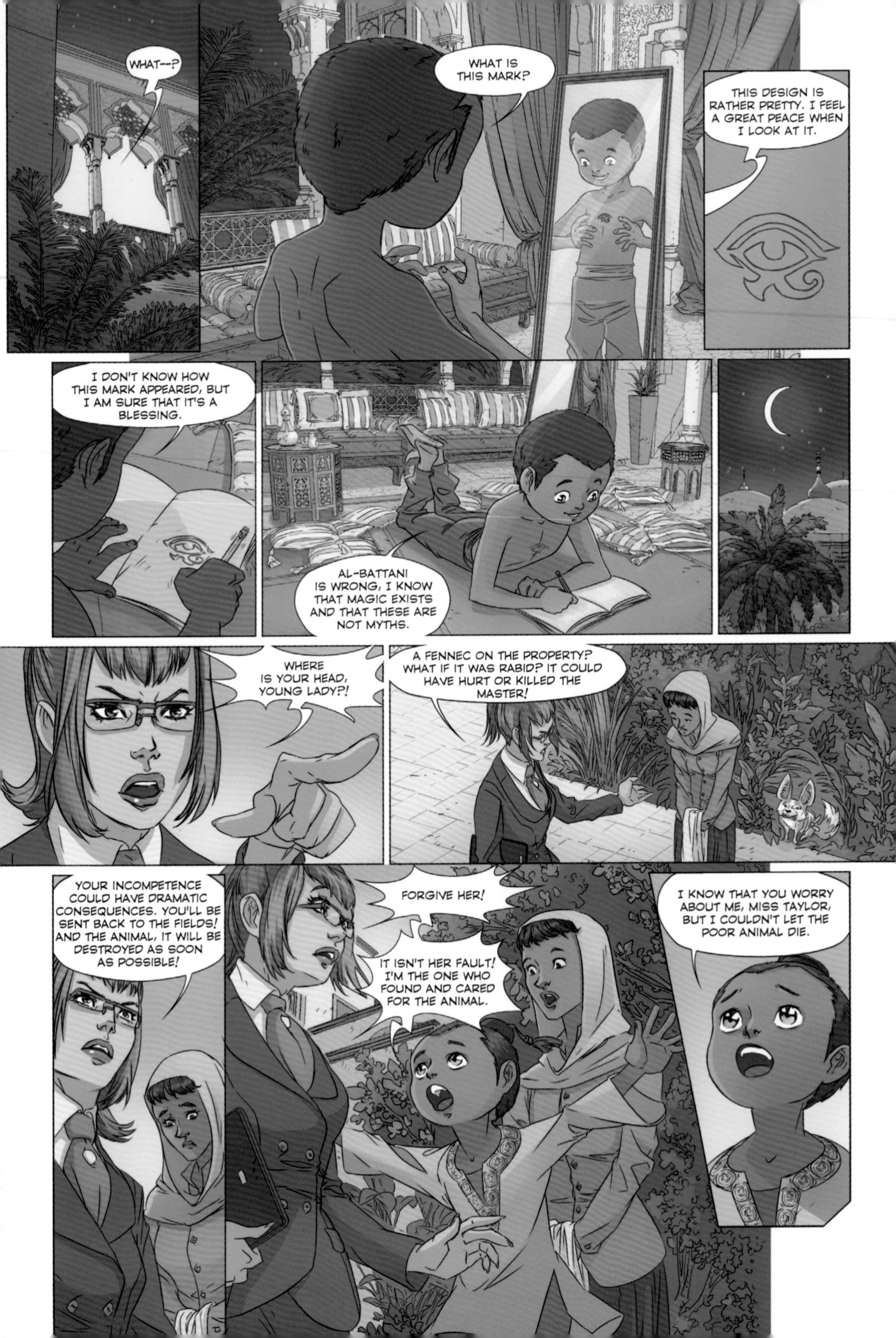
WHAT--?
WHAT IS THIS MARK?
THIS DESIGN IS RATHER PRETTY. I FEEL A GREAT PEACE WHEN I LOOK AT IT.
I DON'T KNOW HOW THIS MARK APPEARED, BUT I AM SURE THAT IT'S A BLESSING.
AL-BATTANI IS WRONG, I KNOW THAT MAGIC EXISTS AND THAT THESE ARE NOT MYTHS.
WHERE IS YOUR HEAD, YOUNG LADY?!
A FENNEC ON THE PROPERTY? WHAT IF IT WAS RABID? IT COULD HAVE HURT OR KILLED THE MASTER!
YOUR INCOMPETENCE COULD HAVE DRAMATIC CONSEQUENCES. YOU'LL BE SENT BACK TO THE FIELDS! AND THE ANIMAL, IT WILL BE DESTROYED AS SOON AS POSSIBLE!
FORGIVE HER!
IT ISN'T HER FAULT! I'M THE ONE WHO FOUND AND CARED FOR THE ANIMAL.
I KNOW THAT YOU WORRY ABOUT ME, MISS TAYLOR, BUT I COULDN'T LET THE POOR ANIMAL DIE.

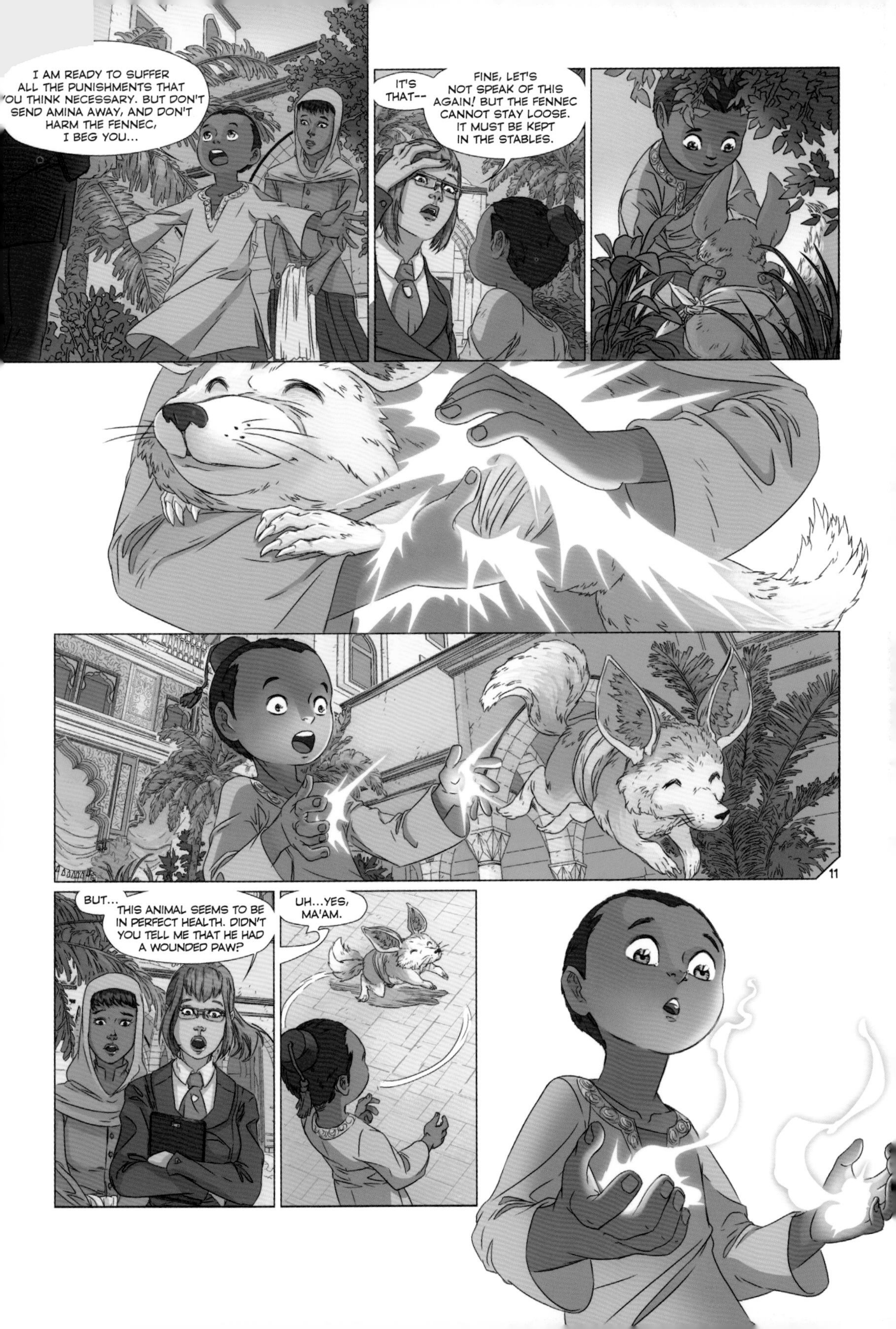
I AM READY TO SUFFER ALL THE PUNISHMENTS THAT 'OU THINK NECESSARY. BUT DON'T SEND AMINA AWAY, AND DON'T HARM THE FENNEC, I BEG YOU...
IT'S THAT--
FINE, LET'S NOT SPEAK OF THIS AGAIN! BUT THE FENNEC CANNOT STAY LOOSE. IT MUST BE KEPT IN THE STABLES.
BUT...
THIS ANIMAL SEEMS TO BE IN PERFECT HEALTH. DIDN'T YOU TELL ME THAT HE HAD A WOUNDED PAW?
UH...YES, MA'AM.

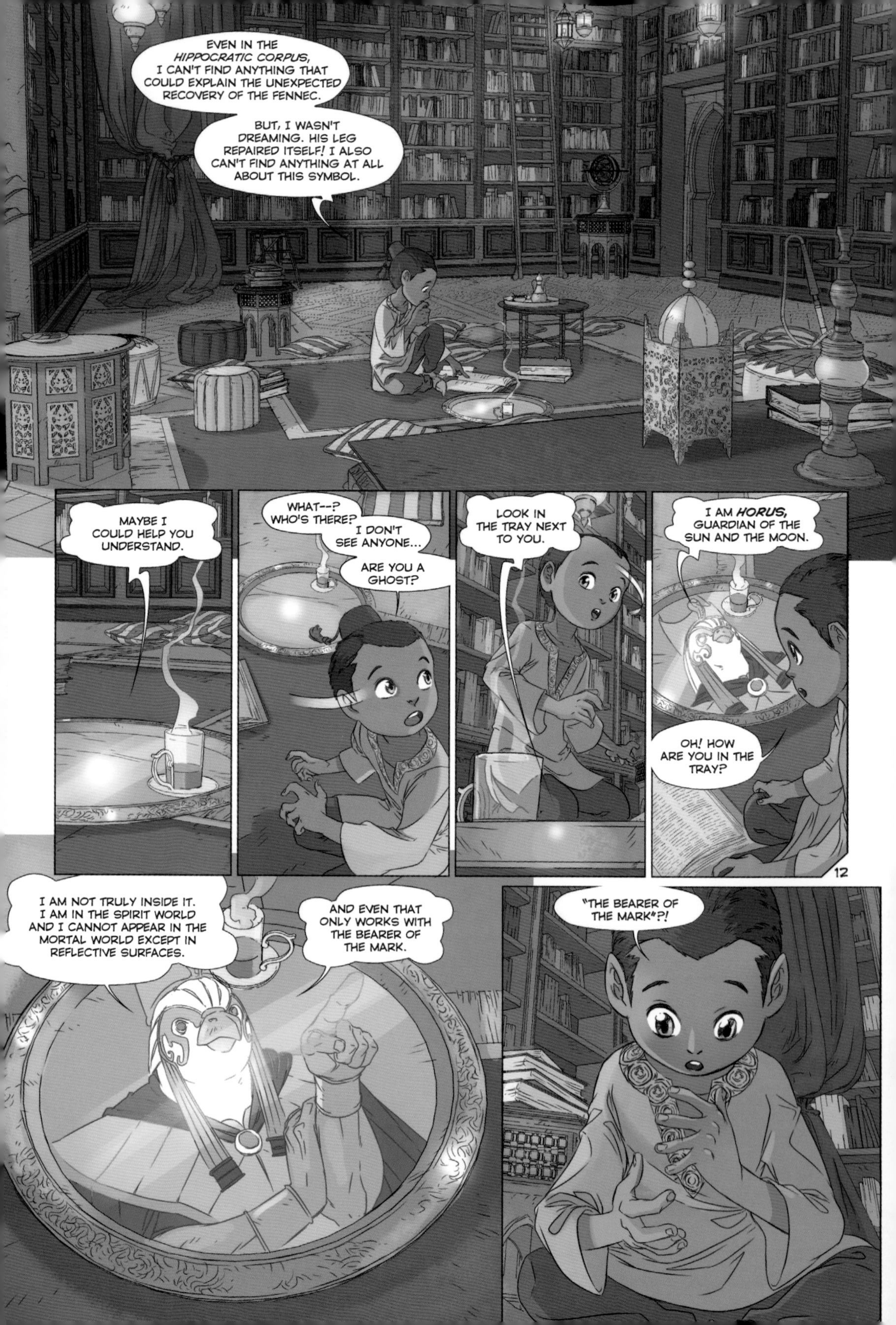
EVEN IN THE *HIPPOCRATIC CORPUS*, I CAN'T FIND ANYTHING THAT COULD EXPLAIN THE UNEXPECTED RECOVERY OF THE FENNEC.
BUT, I WASN'T DREAMING. HIS LEG REPAIRED ITSELF! I ALSO CAN'T FIND ANYTHING AT ALL ABOUT THIS SYMBOL.
MAYBE I COULD HELP YOU UNDERSTAND.
WHAT--? WHO'S THERE?
I DON'T SEE ANYONE...
ARE YOU A GHOST?
LOOK IN THE TRAY NEXT TO YOU.
I AM **HORUS,** GUARDIAN OF THE SUN AND THE MOON.
OH! HOW ARE YOU IN THE TRAY?
I AM NOT TRULY INSIDE IT. I AM IN THE SPIRIT WORLD AND I CANNOT APPEAR IN THE MORTAL WORLD EXCEPT IN REFLECTIVE SURFACES.
AND EVEN THAT ONLY WORKS WITH THE BEARER OF THE MARK.
"THE BEARER OF THE MARK"?!

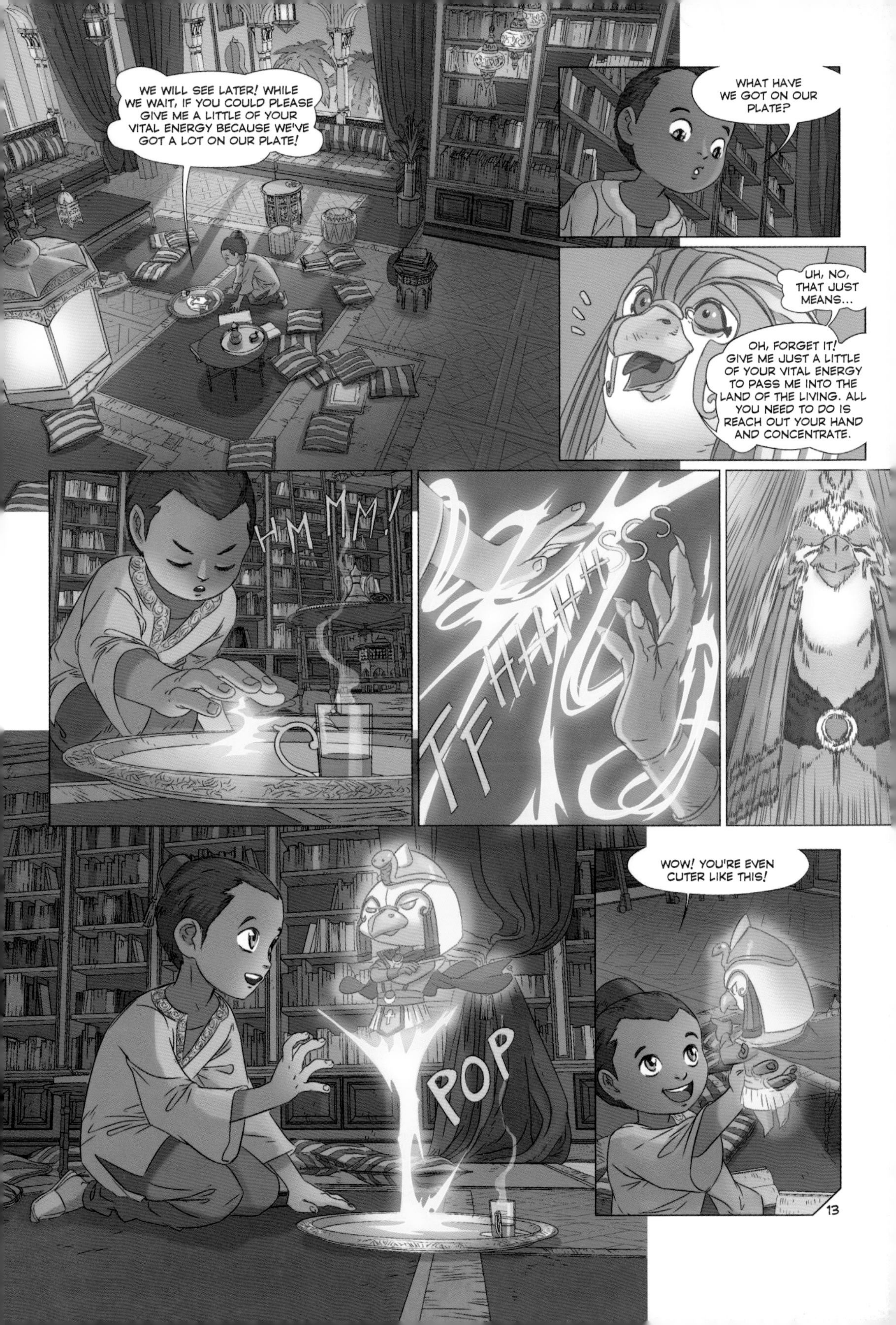
WE WILL SEE LATER! WHILE WE WAIT, IF YOU COULD PLEASE GIVE ME A LITTLE OF YOUR VITAL ENERGY BECAUSE WE'VE GOT A LOT ON OUR PLATE!
WHAT HAVE WE GOT ON OUR PLATE?
UH, NO, THAT JUST MEANS...
OH, FORGET IT! GIVE ME JUST A LITTLE OF YOUR VITAL ENERGY TO PASS ME INTO THE LAND OF THE LIVING. ALL YOU NEED TO DO IS REACH OUT YOUR HAND AND CONCENTRATE.
HMMM!
FFHHHHSSS
POP
WOW! YOU'RE EVEN CUTER LIKE THIS!

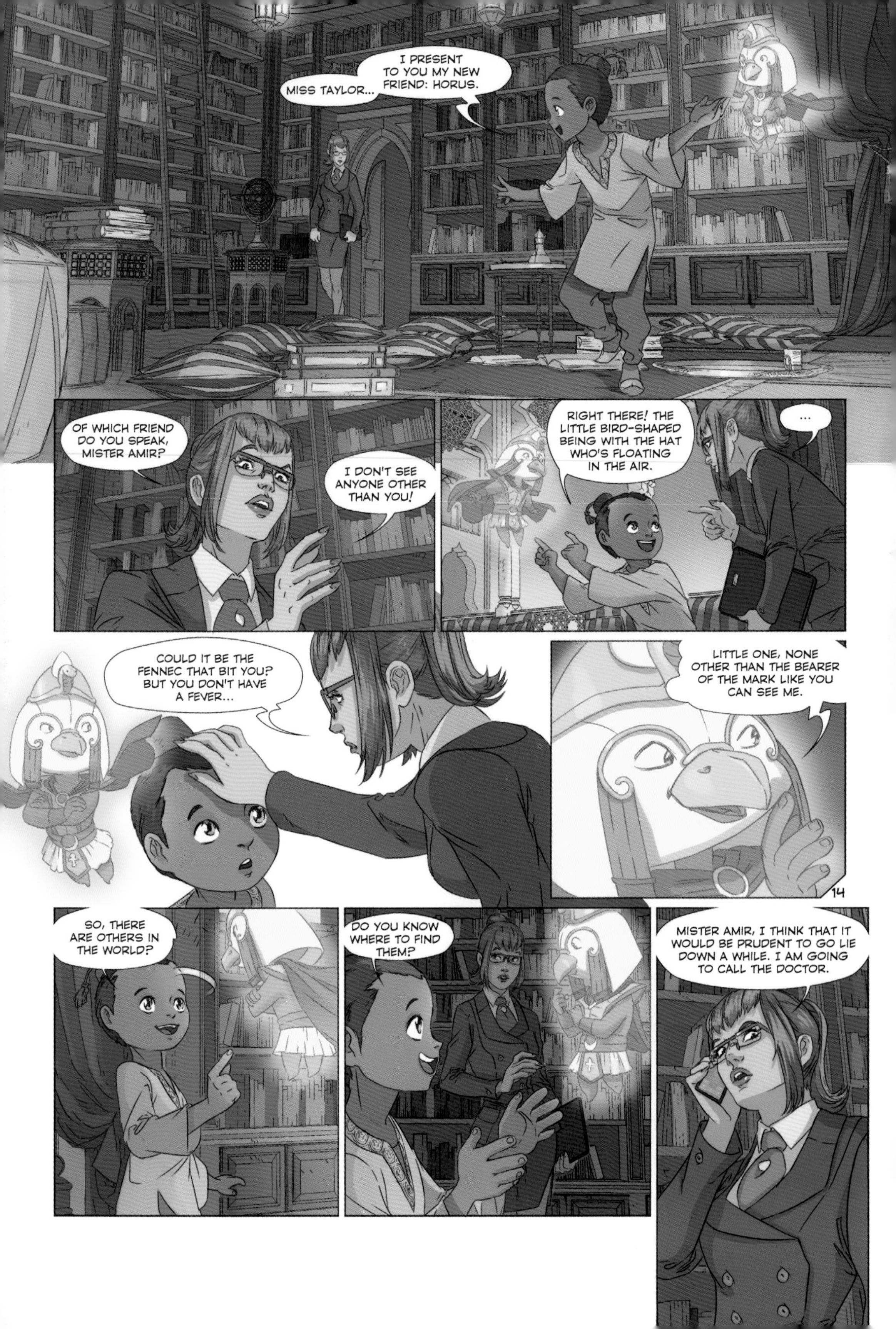
MISS TAYLOR...
I PRESENT TO YOU MY NEW FRIEND: HORUS.
OF WHICH FRIEND DO YOU SPEAK, MISTER AMIR?
I DON'T SEE ANYONE OTHER THAN YOU!
RIGHT THERE! THE LITTLE BIRD-SHAPED BEING WITH THE HAT WHO'S FLOATING IN THE AIR.
...
COULD IT BE THE FENNEC THAT BIT YOU? BUT YOU DON'T HAVE A FEVER...
LITTLE ONE, NONE OTHER THAN THE BEARER OF THE MARK LIKE YOU CAN SEE ME.
14
SO, THERE ARE OTHERS IN THE WORLD?
DO YOU KNOW WHERE TO FIND THEM?
MISTER AMIR, I THINK THAT IT WOULD BE PRUDENT TO GO LIE DOWN A WHILE. I AM GOING TO CALL THE DOCTOR.

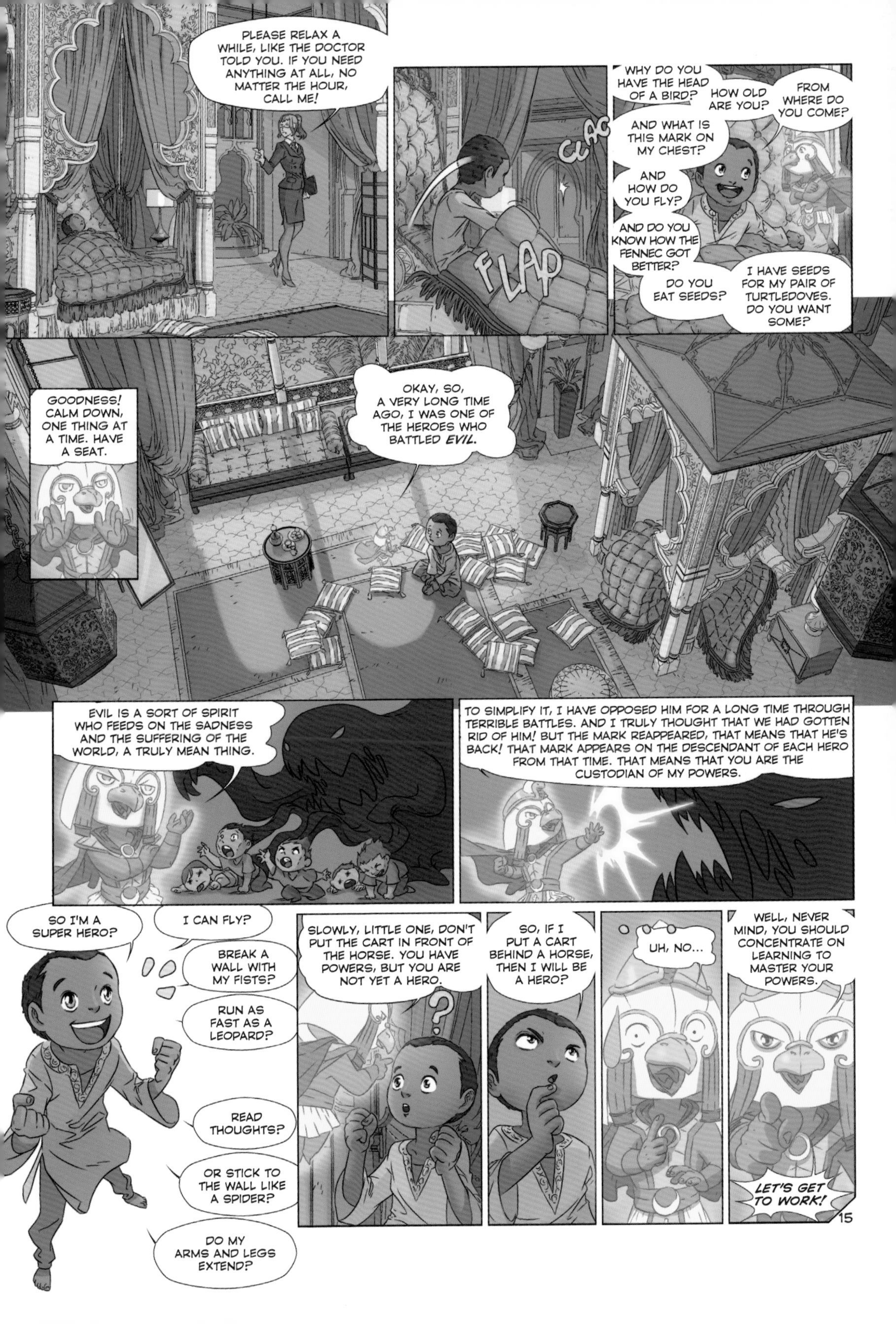
PLEASE RELAX A WHILE, LIKE THE DOCTOR TOLD YOU. IF YOU NEED ANYTHING AT ALL, NO MATTER THE HOUR, CALL ME!
CLAC
FLAP
WHY DO YOU HAVE THE HEAD OF A BIRD?
HOW OLD ARE YOU?
FROM WHERE DO YOU COME?
AND WHAT IS THIS MARK ON MY CHEST?
AND HOW DO YOU FLY?
AND DO YOU KNOW HOW THE FENNEC GOT BETTER?
DO YOU EAT SEEDS?
I HAVE SEEDS FOR MY PAIR OF TURTLEDOVES. DO YOU WANT SOME?
GOODNESS! CALM DOWN, ONE THING AT A TIME. HAVE A SEAT.
OKAY, SO, A VERY LONG TIME AGO, I WAS ONE OF THE HEROES WHO BATTLED EVIL.
EVIL IS A SORT OF SPIRIT WHO FEEDS ON THE SADNESS AND THE SUFFERING OF THE WORLD, A TRULY MEAN THING.
TO SIMPLIFY IT, I HAVE OPPOSED HIM FOR A LONG TIME THROUGH TERRIBLE BATTLES. AND I TRULY THOUGHT THAT WE HAD GOTTEN RID OF HIM! BUT THE MARK REAPPEARED, THAT MEANS THAT HE'S BACK! THAT MARK APPEARS ON THE DESCENDANT OF EACH HERO FROM THAT TIME. THAT MEANS THAT YOU ARE THE CUSTODIAN OF MY POWERS.
SO I'M A SUPER HERO?
I CAN FLY?
BREAK A WALL WITH MY FISTS?
RUN AS FAST AS A LEOPARD?
READ THOUGHTS?
OR STICK TO THE WALL LIKE A SPIDER?
DO MY ARMS AND LEGS EXTEND?
SLOWLY, LITTLE ONE, DON'T PUT THE CART IN FRONT OF THE HORSE. YOU HAVE POWERS, BUT YOU ARE NOT YET A HERO.
SO, IF I PUT A CART BEHIND A HORSE, THEN I WILL BE A HERO?
UH, NO...
WELL, NEVER MIND, YOU SHOULD CONCENTRATE ON LEARNING TO MASTER YOUR POWERS.
LET'S GET TO WORK!

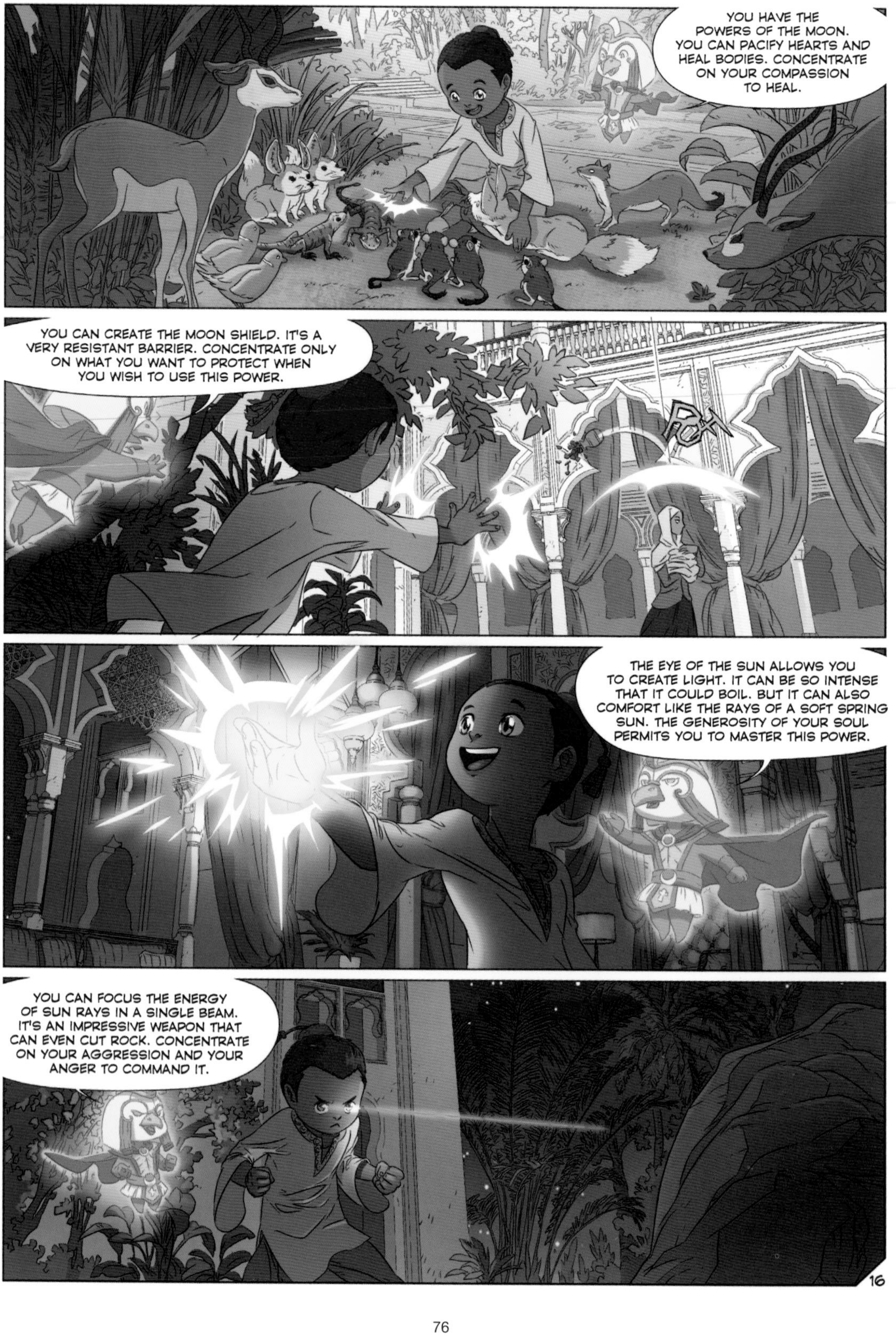
YOU HAVE THE POWERS OF THE MOON. YOU CAN PACIFY HEARTS AND HEAL BODIES. CONCENTRATE ON YOUR COMPASSION TO HEAL.
YOU CAN CREATE THE MOON SHIELD. IT'S A VERY RESISTANT BARRIER. CONCENTRATE ONLY ON WHAT YOU WANT TO PROTECT WHEN YOU WISH TO USE THIS POWER.
THE EYE OF THE SUN ALLOWS YOU TO CREATE LIGHT. IT CAN BE SO INTENSE THAT IT COULD BOIL. BUT IT CAN ALSO COMFORT LIKE THE RAYS OF A SOFT SPRING SUN. THE GENEROSITY OF YOUR SOUL PERMITS YOU TO MASTER THIS POWER.
YOU CAN FOCUS THE ENERGY OF SUN RAYS IN A SINGLE BEAM. IT'S AN IMPRESSIVE WEAPON THAT CAN EVEN CUT ROCK. CONCENTRATE ON YOUR AGGRESSION AND YOUR ANGER TO COMMAND IT.
16

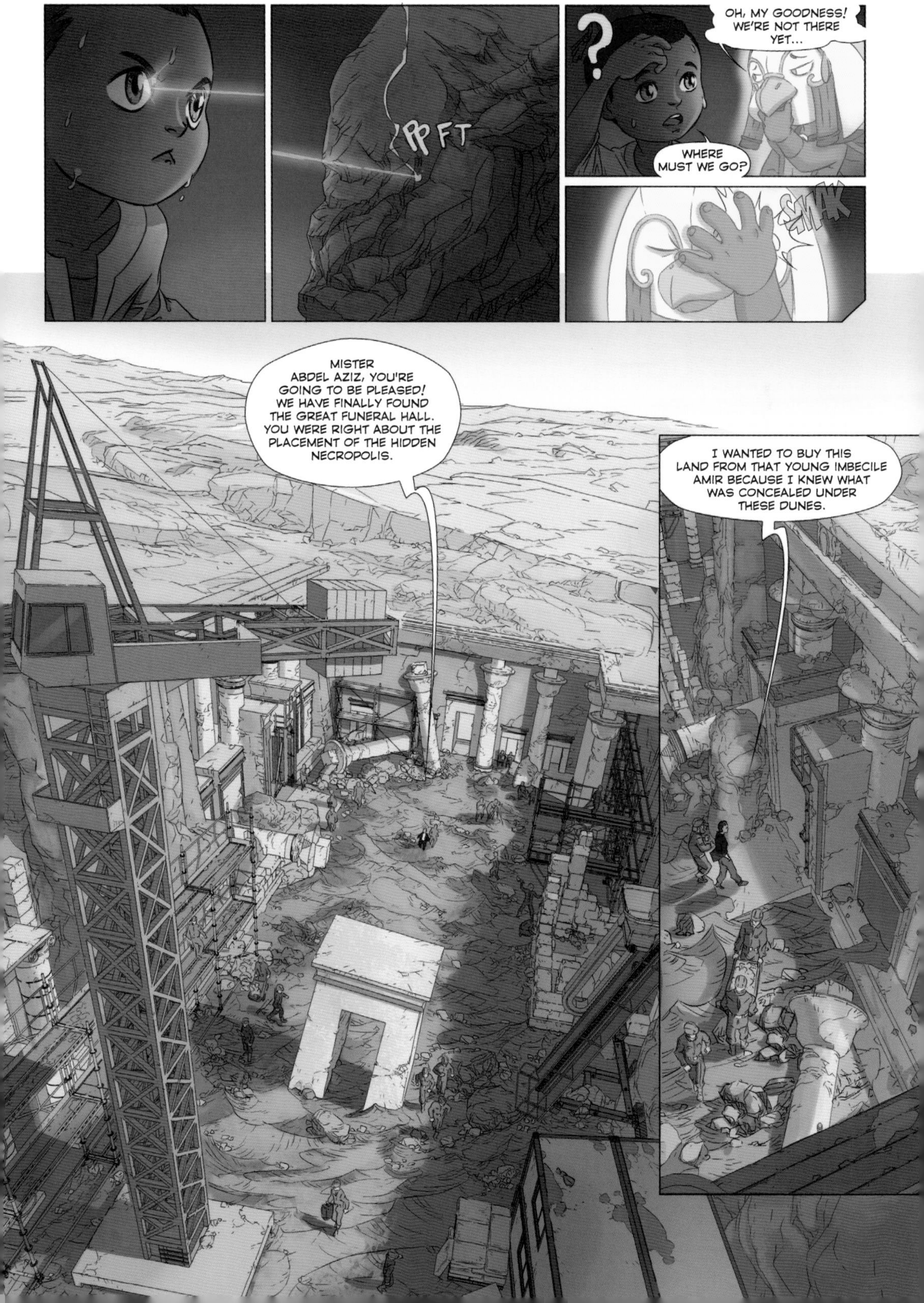
PPFT
OH, MY GOODNESS! WE'RE NOT THERE YET...
?
WHERE MUST WE GO?
SMAK
MISTER ABDEL AZIZ, YOU'RE GOING TO BE PLEASED! WE HAVE FINALLY FOUND THE GREAT FUNERAL HALL. YOU WERE RIGHT ABOUT THE PLACEMENT OF THE HIDDEN NECROPOLIS.
I WANTED TO BUY THIS LAND FROM THAT YOUNG IMBECILE AMIR BECAUSE I KNEW WHAT WAS CONCEALED UNDER THESE DUNES.

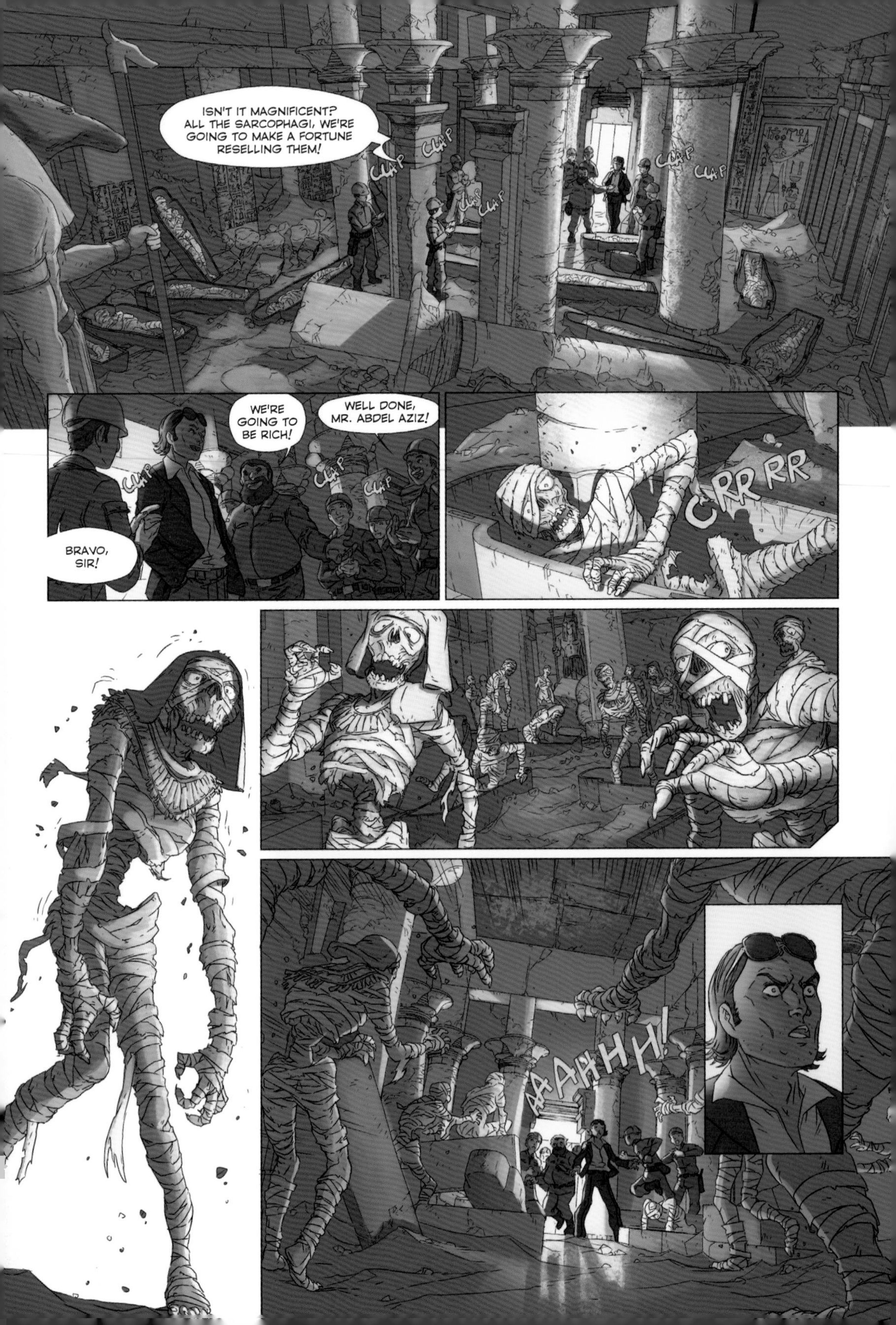
ISN'T IT MAGNIFICENT? ALL THE SARCOPHAGI, WE'RE GOING TO MAKE A FORTUNE RESELLING THEM!
CLAP CLAP
CLAP
CLAP CLAP
CLAP CLAP
CLAP
WE'RE GOING TO BE RICH!
WELL DONE, MR. ABDEL AZIZ!
CLAP
CLAP
BRAVO, SIR!
CRRRR
AAAHHH!

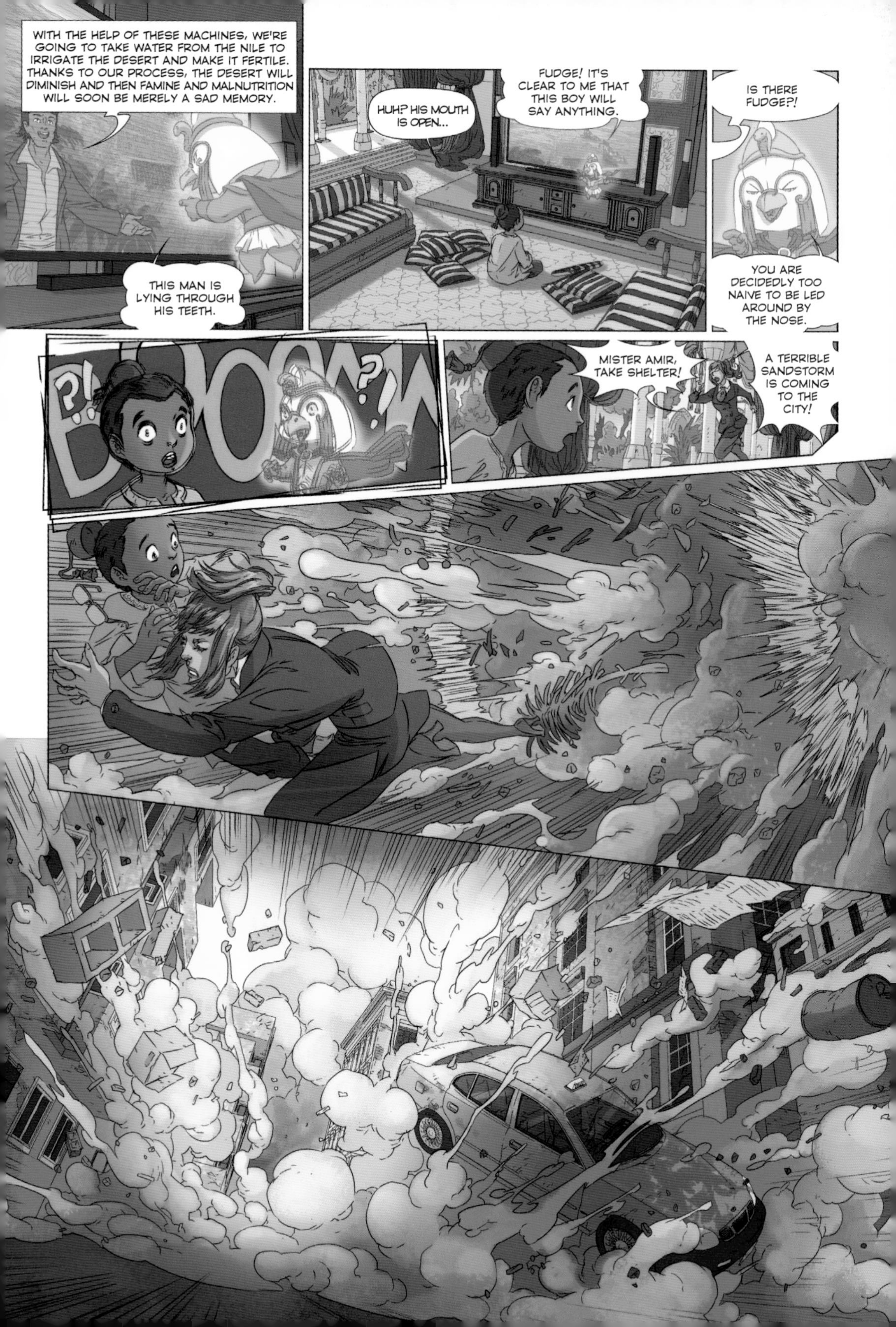
WITH THE HELP OF THESE MACHINES, WE'RE GOING TO TAKE WATER FROM THE NILE TO IRRIGATE THE DESERT AND MAKE IT FERTILE. THANKS TO OUR PROCESS, THE DESERT WILL DIMINISH AND THEN FAMINE AND MALNUTRITION WILL SOON BE MERELY A SAD MEMORY.
THIS MAN IS LYING THROUGH HIS TEETH.
HUH? HIS MOUTH IS OPEN...
FUDGE! IT'S CLEAR TO ME THAT THIS BOY WILL SAY ANYTHING.
IS THERE FUDGE?!
YOU ARE DECIDEDLY TOO NAIVE TO BE LED AROUND BY THE NOSE.
BOOOM
?!
?!
MISTER AMIR, TAKE SHELTER!
A TERRIBLE SANDSTORM IS COMING TO THE CITY!

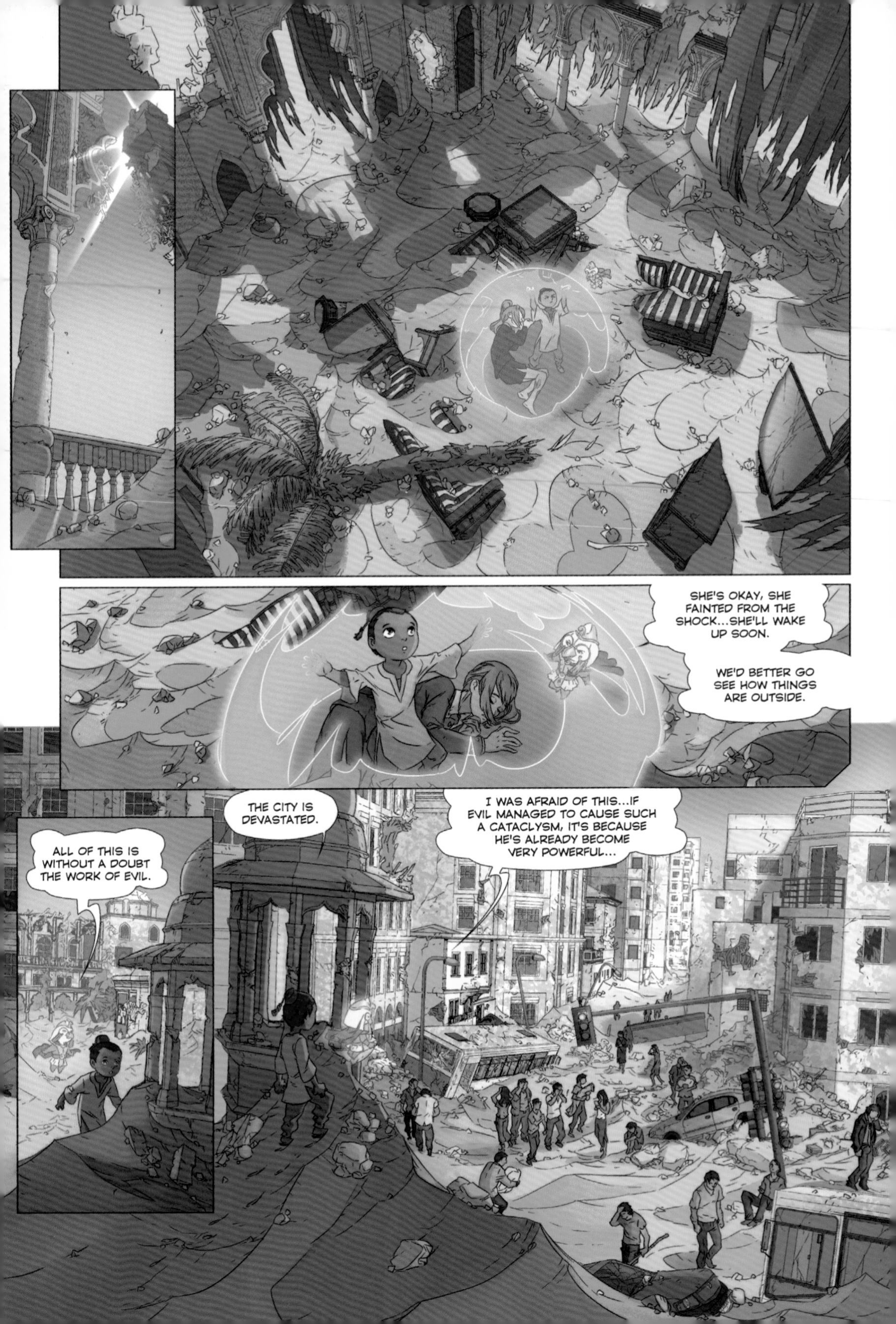
SHE'S OKAY, SHE FAINTED FROM THE SHOCK...SHE'LL WAKE UP SOON.
WE'D BETTER GO SEE HOW THINGS ARE OUTSIDE.
THE CITY IS DEVASTATED.
I WAS AFRAID OF THIS...IF EVIL MANAGED TO CAUSE SUCH A CATACLYSM, IT'S BECAUSE HE'S ALREADY BECOME VERY POWERFUL...
ALL OF THIS IS WITHOUT A DOUBT THE WORK OF EVIL.

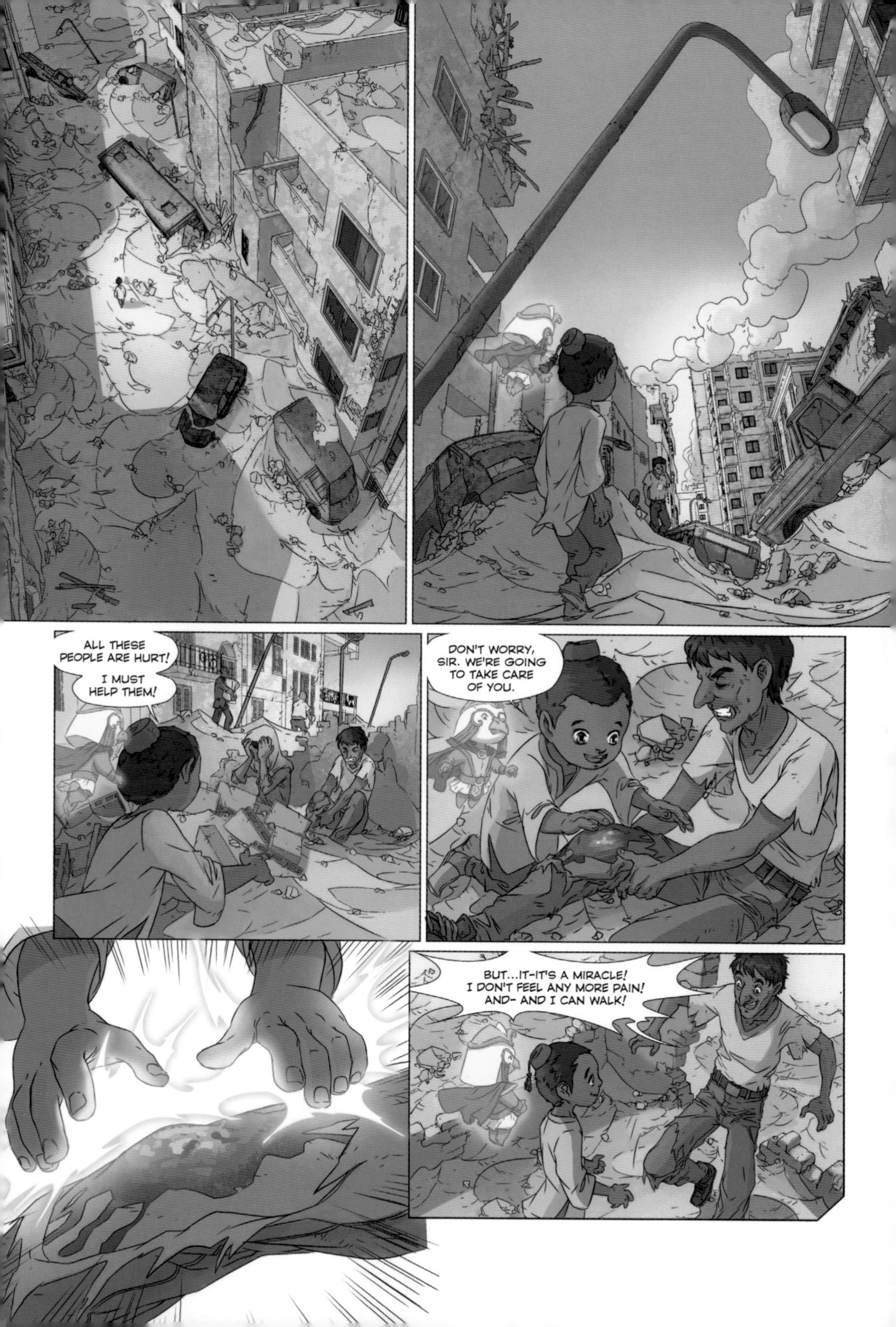
ALL THESE PEOPLE ARE HURT!
I MUST HELP THEM!
DON'T WORRY, SIR. WE'RE GOING TO TAKE CARE OF YOU.
BUT...IT-IT'S A MIRACLE! I DON'T FEEL ANY MORE PAIN! AND- AND I CAN WALK!

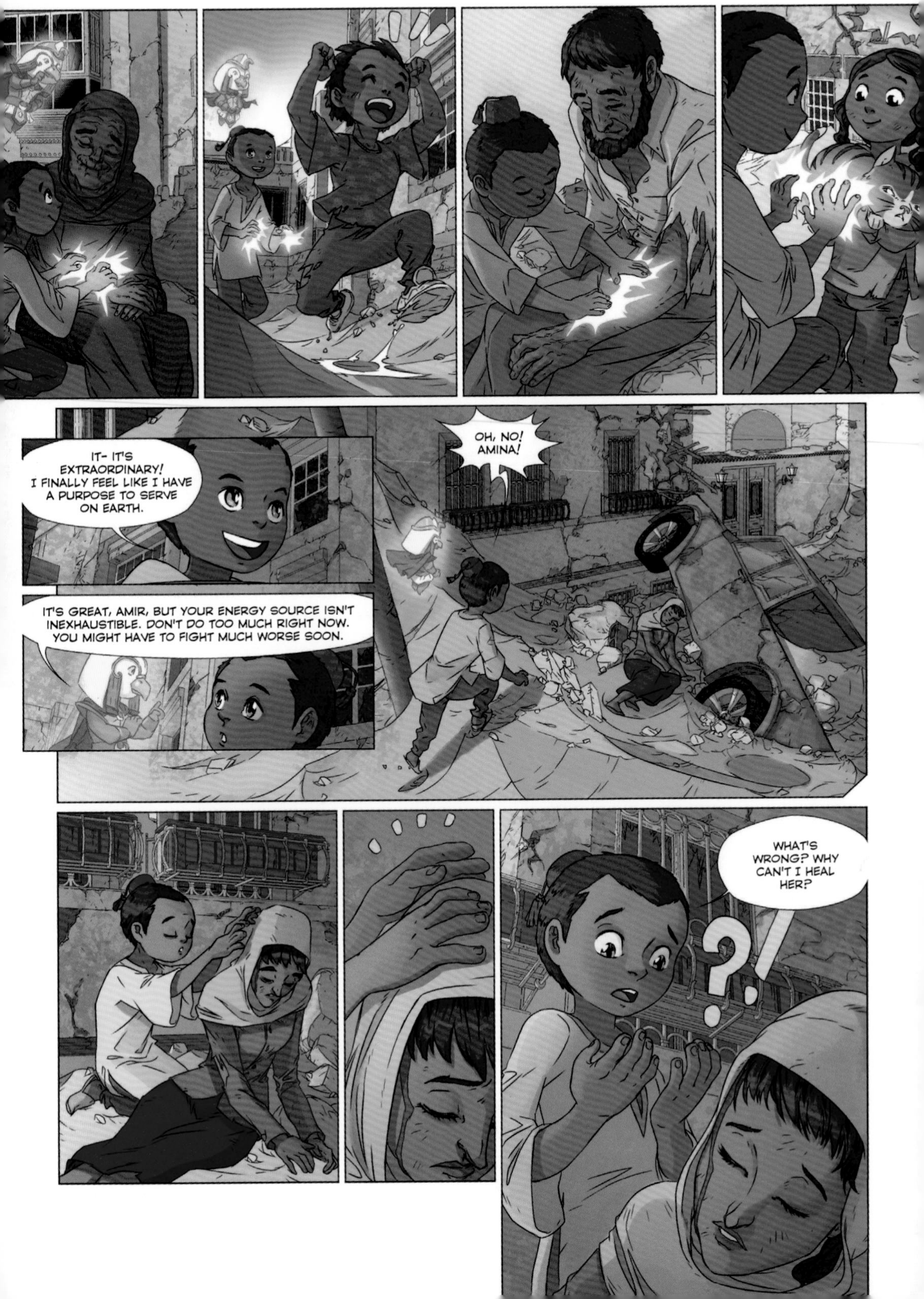

IT- IT'S EXTRAORDINARY! I FINALLY FEEL LIKE I HAVE A PURPOSE TO SERVE ON EARTH.
IT'S GREAT, AMIR, BUT YOUR ENERGY SOURCE ISN'T INEXHAUSTIBLE. DON'T DO TOO MUCH RIGHT NOW. YOU MIGHT HAVE TO FIGHT MUCH WORSE SOON.
OH, NO! AMINA!
WHAT'S WRONG? WHY CAN'T I HEAL HER?
?!

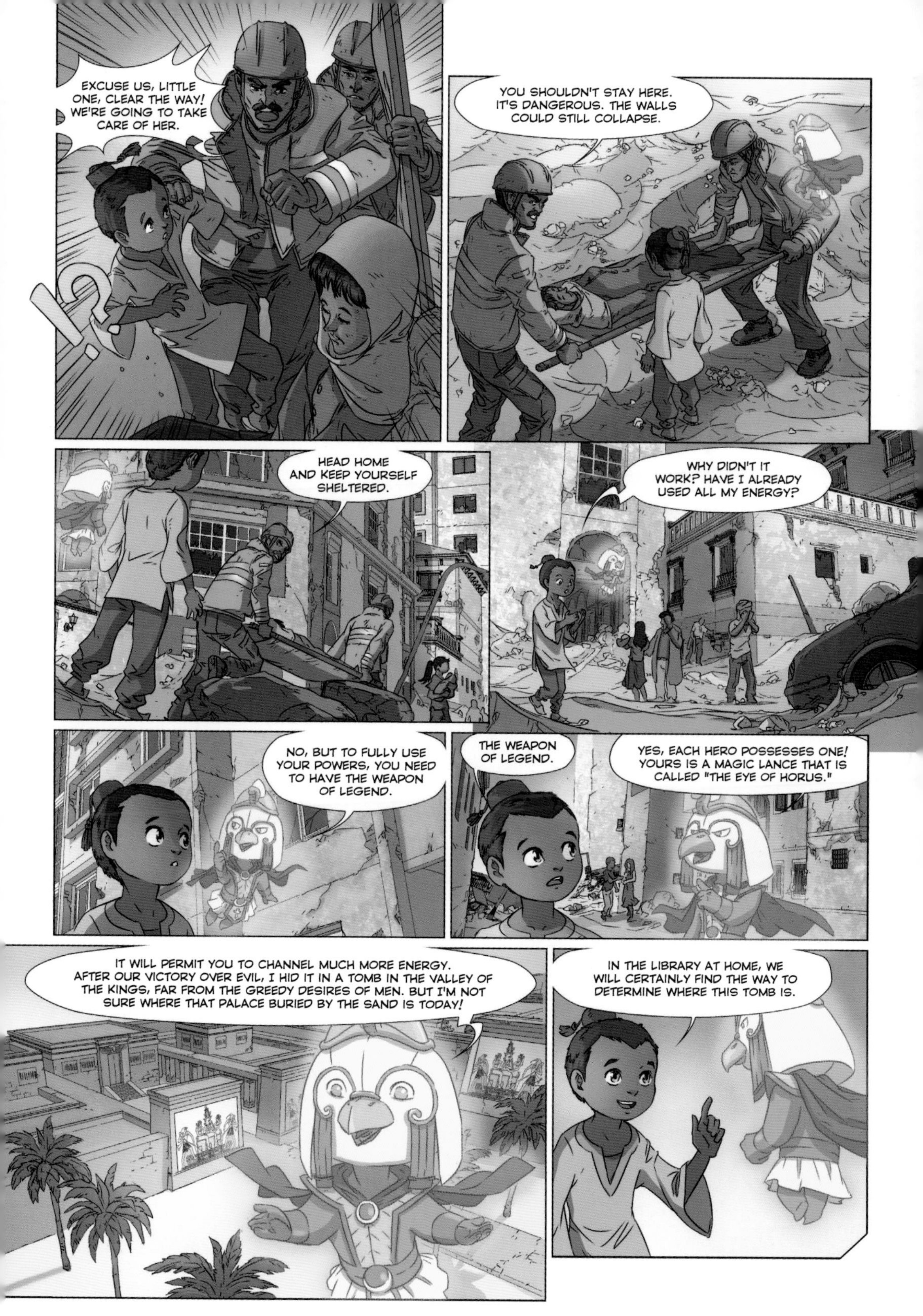

EXCUSE US, LITTLE ONE, CLEAR THE WAY! WE'RE GOING TO TAKE CARE OF HER.
!?
YOU SHOULDN'T STAY HERE. IT'S DANGEROUS. THE WALLS COULD STILL COLLAPSE.
HEAD HOME AND KEEP YOURSELF SHELTERED.
WHY DIDN'T IT WORK? HAVE I ALREADY USED ALL MY ENERGY?
NO, BUT TO FULLY USE YOUR POWERS, YOU NEED TO HAVE THE WEAPON OF LEGEND.
THE WEAPON OF LEGEND.
YES, EACH HERO POSSESSES ONE! YOURS IS A MAGIC LANCE THAT IS CALLED "THE EYE OF HORUS."
IT WILL PERMIT YOU TO CHANNEL MUCH MORE ENERGY. AFTER OUR VICTORY OVER EVIL, I HID IT IN A TOMB IN THE VALLEY OF THE KINGS, FAR FROM THE GREEDY DESIRES OF MEN. BUT I'M NOT SURE WHERE THAT PALACE BURIED BY THE SAND IS TODAY!
IN THE LIBRARY AT HOME, WE WILL CERTAINLY FIND THE WAY TO DETERMINE WHERE THIS TOMB IS.

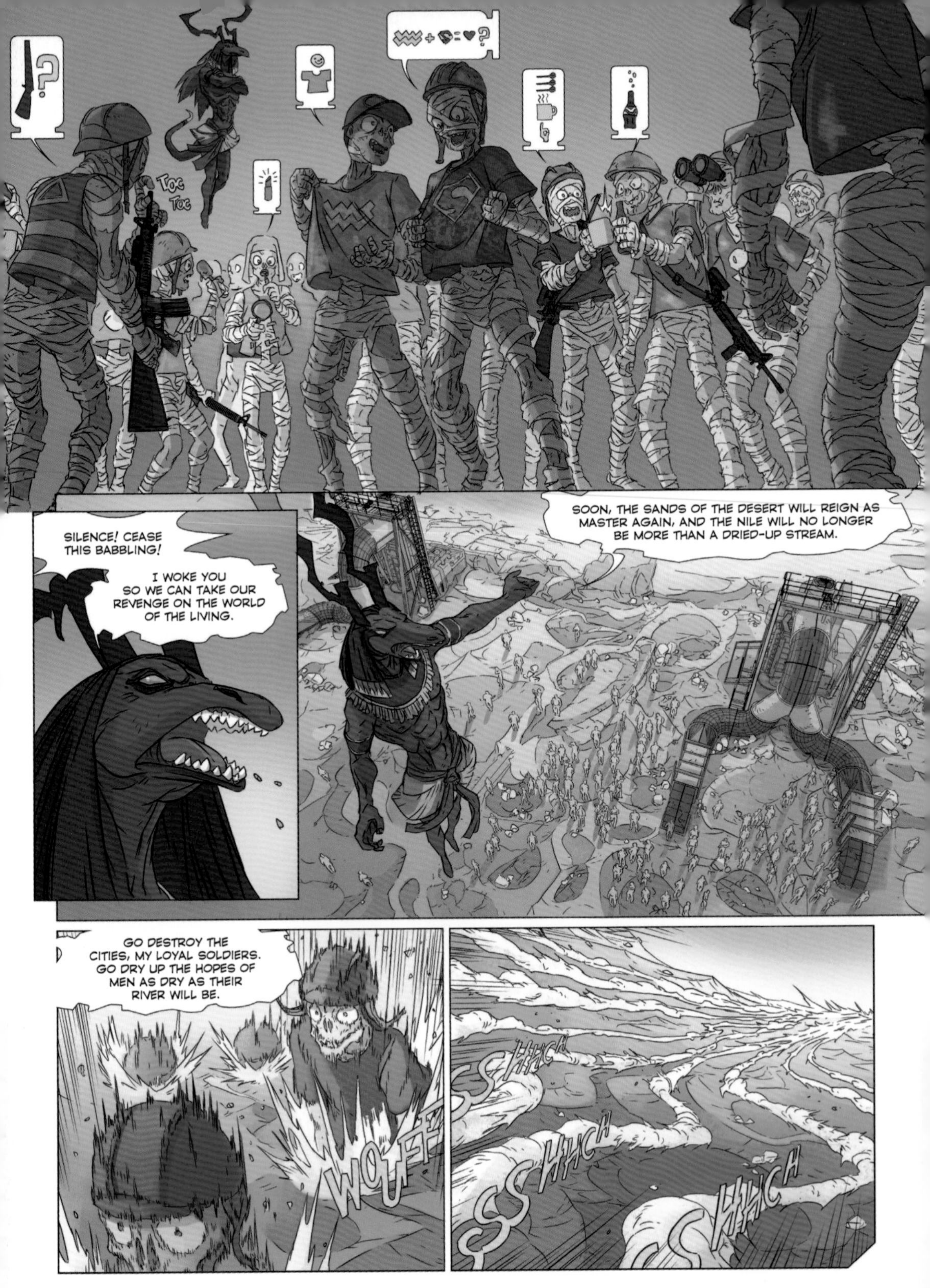
TOC TOC
SILENCE! CEASE THIS BABBLING!
I WOKE YOU SO WE CAN TAKE OUR REVENGE ON THE WORLD OF THE LIVING.
SOON, THE SANDS OF THE DESERT WILL REIGN AS MASTER AGAIN, AND THE NILE WILL NO LONGER BE MORE THAN A DRIED-UP STREAM.
GO DESTROY THE CITIES, MY LOYAL SOLDIERS. GO DRY UP THE HOPES OF MEN AS DRY AS THEIR RIVER WILL BE.
WOUFFF
SSHHCH
SSHHCH
SSHHCH

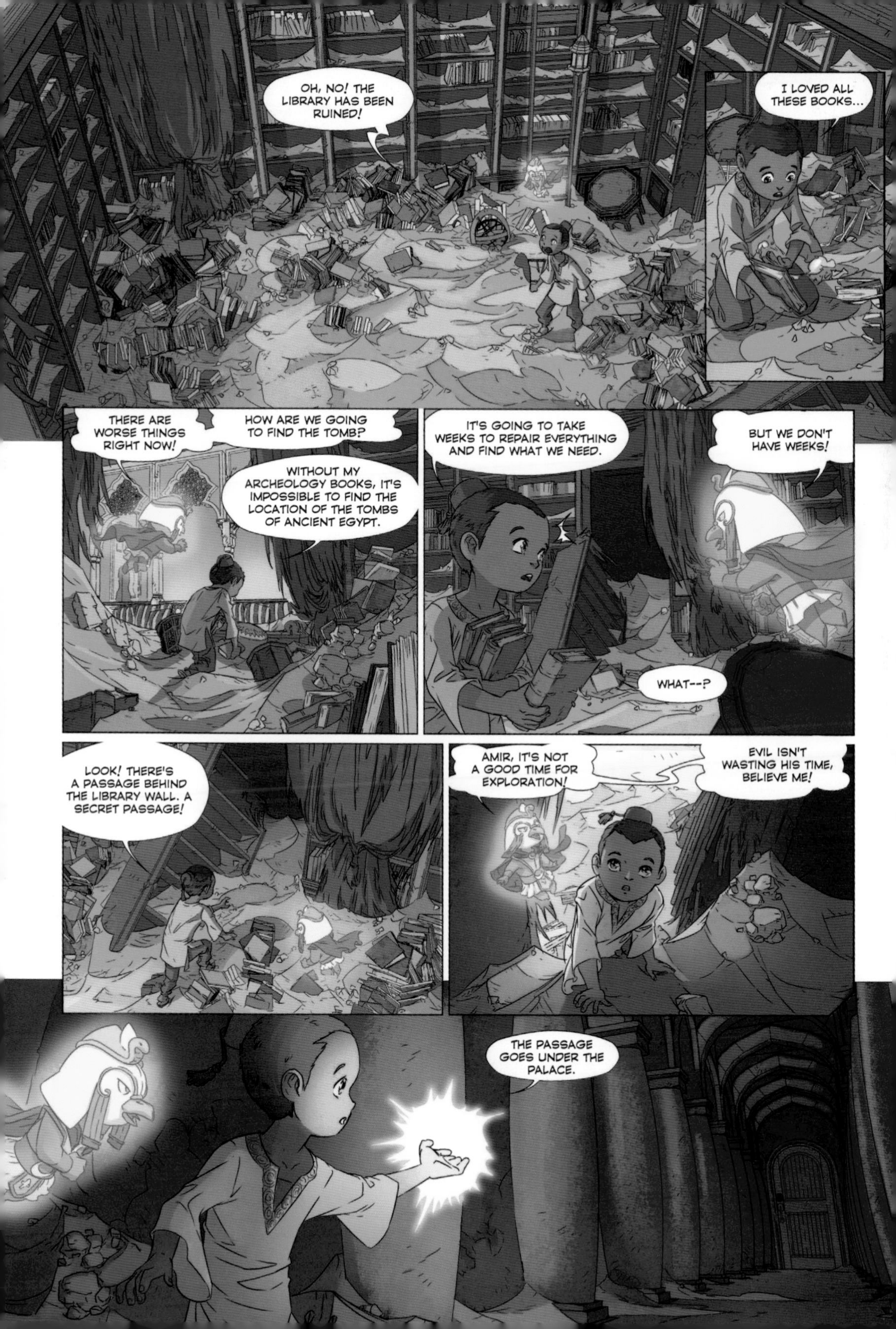

OH, NO! THE LIBRARY HAS BEEN RUINED!
I LOVED ALL THESE BOOKS...
THERE ARE WORSE THINGS RIGHT NOW!
HOW ARE WE GOING TO FIND THE TOMB?
WITHOUT MY ARCHEOLOGY BOOKS, IT'S IMPOSSIBLE TO FIND THE LOCATION OF THE TOMBS OF ANCIENT EGYPT.
IT'S GOING TO TAKE WEEKS TO REPAIR EVERYTHING AND FIND WHAT WE NEED.
BUT WE DON'T HAVE WEEKS!
WHAT--?
LOOK! THERE'S A PASSAGE BEHIND THE LIBRARY WALL. A SECRET PASSAGE!
AMIR, IT'S NOT A GOOD TIME FOR EXPLORATION!
EVIL ISN'T WASTING HIS TIME, BELIEVE ME!
THE PASSAGE GOES UNDER THE PALACE.

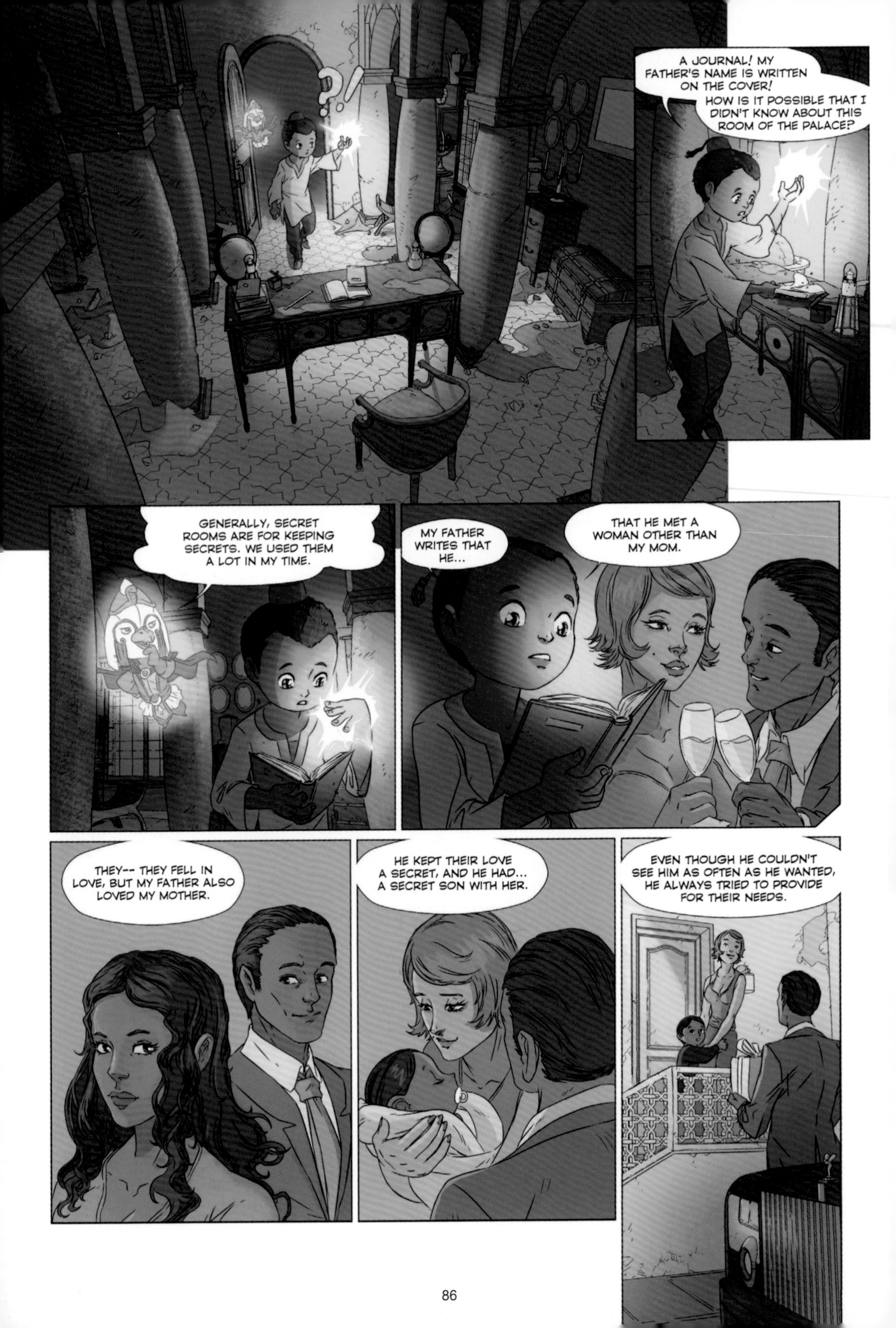
A JOURNAL! MY FATHER'S NAME IS WRITTEN ON THE COVER!
HOW IS IT POSSIBLE THAT I DIDN'T KNOW ABOUT THIS ROOM OF THE PALACE?
GENERALLY, SECRET ROOMS ARE FOR KEEPING SECRETS. WE USED THEM A LOT IN MY TIME.
MY FATHER WRITES THAT HE...
THAT HE MET A WOMAN OTHER THAN MY MOM.
THEY-- THEY FELL IN LOVE, BUT MY FATHER ALSO LOVED MY MOTHER.
HE KEPT THEIR LOVE A SECRET, AND HE HAD... A SECRET SON WITH HER.
EVEN THOUGH HE COULDN'T SEE HIM AS OFTEN AS HE WANTED, HE ALWAYS TRIED TO PROVIDE FOR THEIR NEEDS.

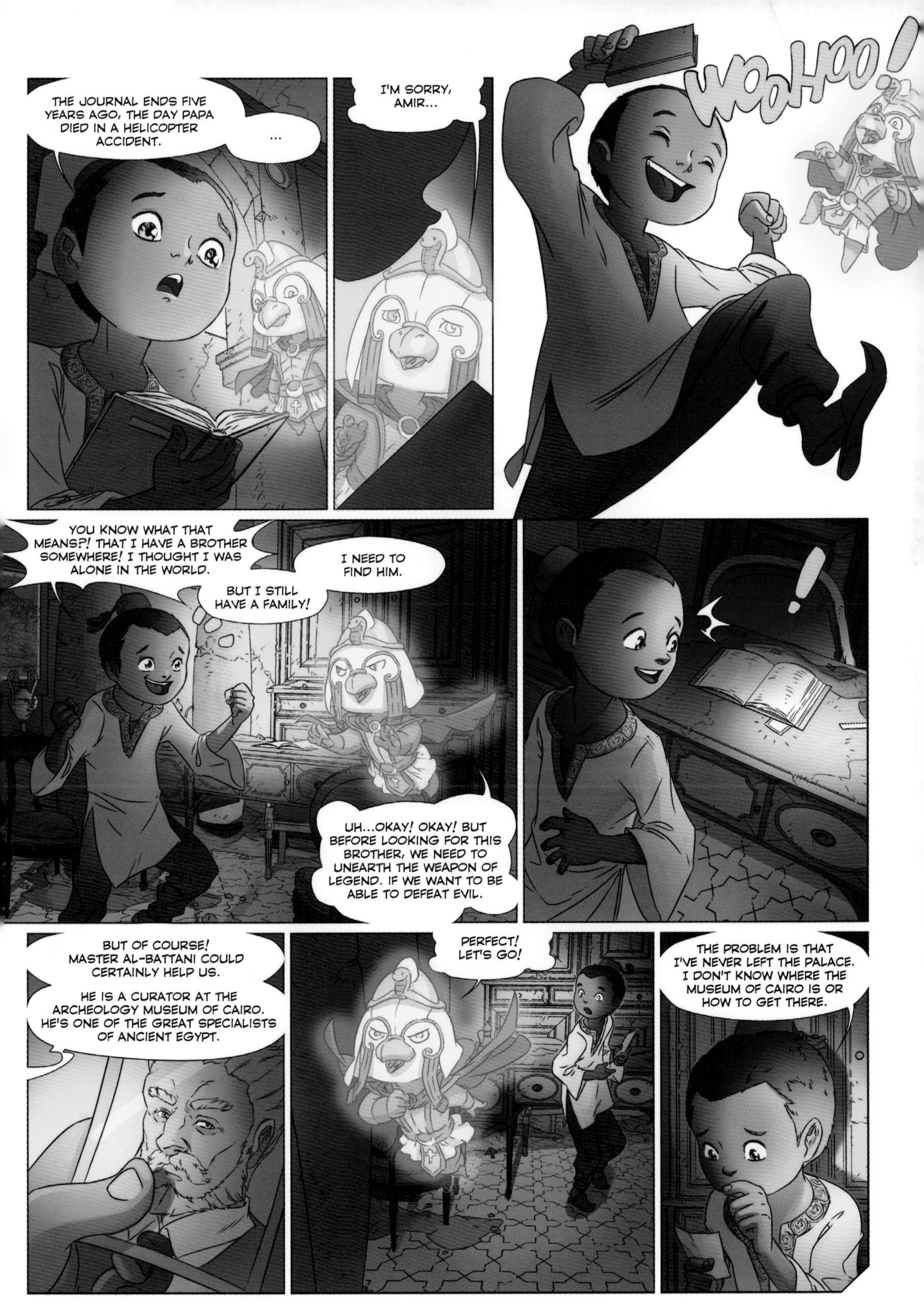
THE JOURNAL ENDS FIVE YEARS AGO, THE DAY PAPA DIED IN A HELICOPTER ACCIDENT.
...
I'M SORRY, AMIR...
WOOHOO!
YOU KNOW WHAT THAT MEANS?! THAT I HAVE A BROTHER SOMEWHERE! I THOUGHT I WAS ALONE IN THE WORLD.
BUT I STILL HAVE A FAMILY!
I NEED TO FIND HIM.
UH...OKAY! OKAY! BUT BEFORE LOOKING FOR THIS BROTHER, WE NEED TO UNEARTH THE WEAPON OF LEGEND. IF WE WANT TO BE ABLE TO DEFEAT EVIL.
!
BUT OF COURSE! MASTER AL-BATTANI COULD CERTAINLY HELP US.
HE IS A CURATOR AT THE ARCHEOLOGY MUSEUM OF CAIRO. HE'S ONE OF THE GREAT SPECIALISTS OF ANCIENT EGYPT.
PERFECT! LET'S GO!
THE PROBLEM IS THAT I'VE NEVER LEFT THE PALACE. I DON'T KNOW WHERE THE MUSEUM OF CAIRO IS OR HOW TO GET THERE.

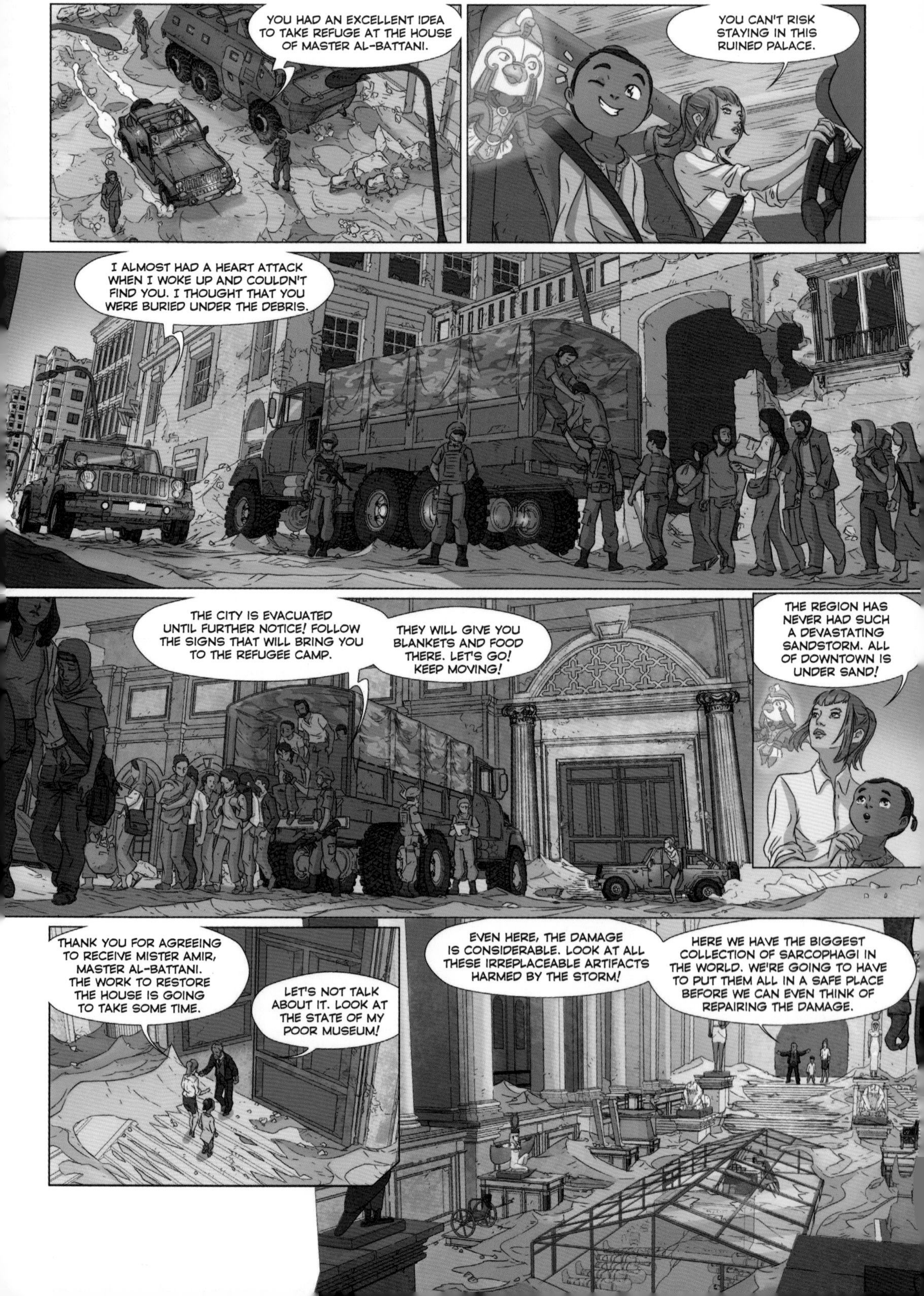
YOU HAD AN EXCELLENT IDEA TO TAKE REFUGE AT THE HOUSE OF MASTER AL-BATTANI.
YOU CAN'T RISK STAYING IN THIS RUINED PALACE.
I ALMOST HAD A HEART ATTACK WHEN I WOKE UP AND COULDN'T FIND YOU. I THOUGHT THAT YOU WERE BURIED UNDER THE DEBRIS.
THE CITY IS EVACUATED UNTIL FURTHER NOTICE! FOLLOW THE SIGNS THAT WILL BRING YOU TO THE REFUGEE CAMP.
THEY WILL GIVE YOU BLANKETS AND FOOD THERE. LET'S GO! KEEP MOVING!
THE REGION HAS NEVER HAD SUCH A DEVASTATING SANDSTORM. ALL OF DOWNTOWN IS UNDER SAND!
THANK YOU FOR AGREEING TO RECEIVE MISTER AMIR, MASTER AL-BATTANI. THE WORK TO RESTORE THE HOUSE IS GOING TO TAKE SOME TIME.
LET'S NOT TALK ABOUT IT. LOOK AT THE STATE OF MY POOR MUSEUM!
EVEN HERE, THE DAMAGE IS CONSIDERABLE. LOOK AT ALL THESE IRREPLACEABLE ARTIFACTS HARMED BY THE STORM!
HERE WE HAVE THE BIGGEST COLLECTION OF SARCOPHAGI IN THE WORLD. WE'RE GOING TO HAVE TO PUT THEM ALL IN A SAFE PLACE BEFORE WE CAN EVEN THINK OF REPAIRING THE DAMAGE.

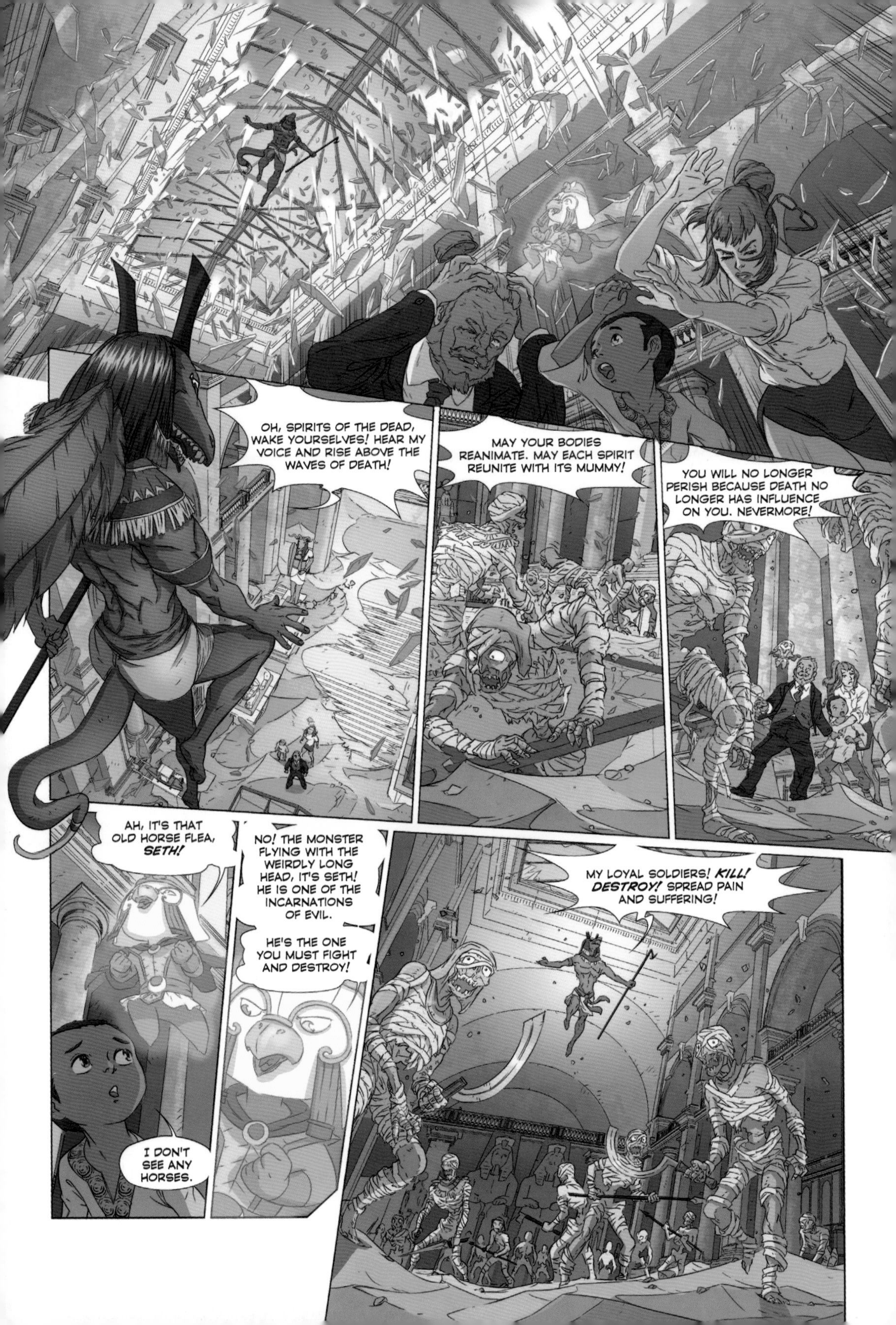

OH, SPIRITS OF THE DEAD, WAKE YOURSELVES! HEAR MY VOICE AND RISE ABOVE THE WAVES OF DEATH!
MAY YOUR BODIES REANIMATE. MAY EACH SPIRIT REUNITE WITH ITS MUMMY!
YOU WILL NO LONGER PERISH BECAUSE DEATH NO LONGER HAS INFLUENCE ON YOU. NEVERMORE!
AH, IT'S THAT OLD HORSE FLEA, SETH!
NO! THE MONSTER FLYING WITH THE WEIRDLY LONG HEAD, IT'S SETH! HE IS ONE OF THE INCARNATIONS OF EVIL.
HE'S THE ONE YOU MUST FIGHT AND DESTROY!
I DON'T SEE ANY HORSES.
MY LOYAL SOLDIERS! KILL! DESTROY! SPREAD PAIN AND SUFFERING!

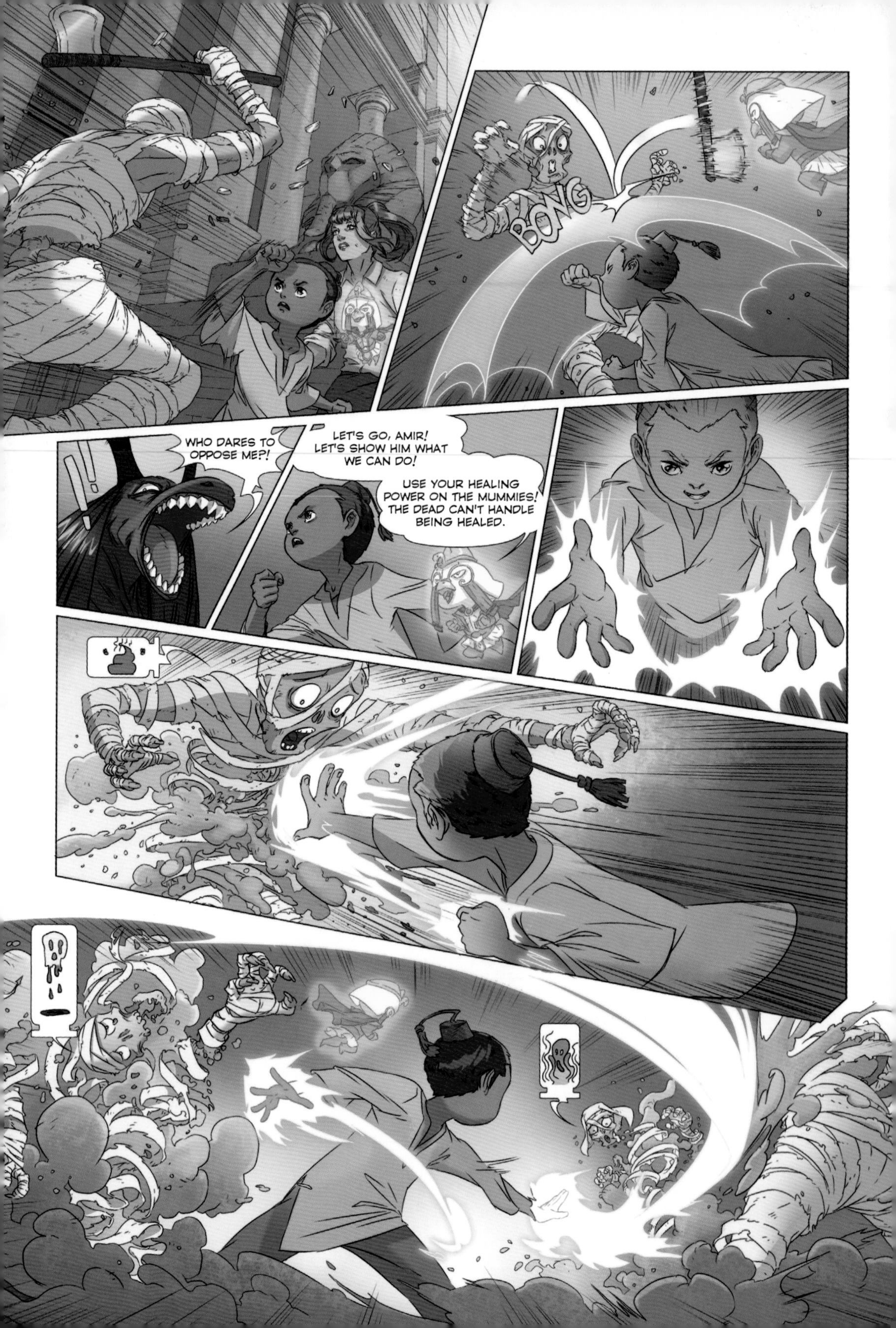
BONG
WHO DARES TO OPPOSE ME?!
!
LET'S GO, AMIR! LET'S SHOW HIM WHAT WE CAN DO!
USE YOUR HEALING POWER ON THE MUMMIES! THE DEAD CAN'T HANDLE BEING HEALED.

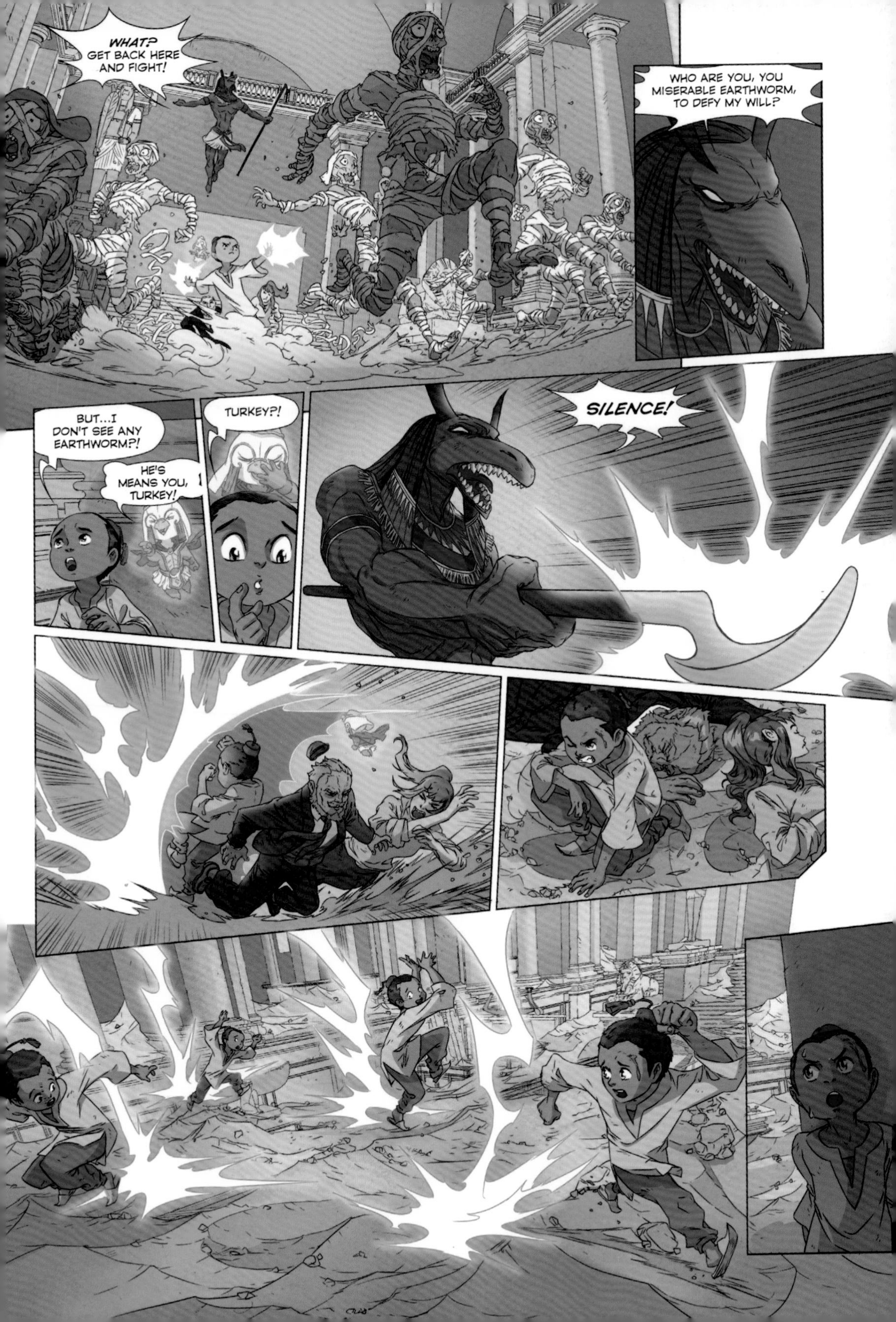
WHAT? GET BACK HERE AND FIGHT!
WHO ARE YOU, YOU MISERABLE EARTHWORM, TO DEFY MY WILL?
BUT...I DON'T SEE ANY EARTHWORM?!
HE'S MEANS YOU, TURKEY!
TURKEY?!
SILENCE!

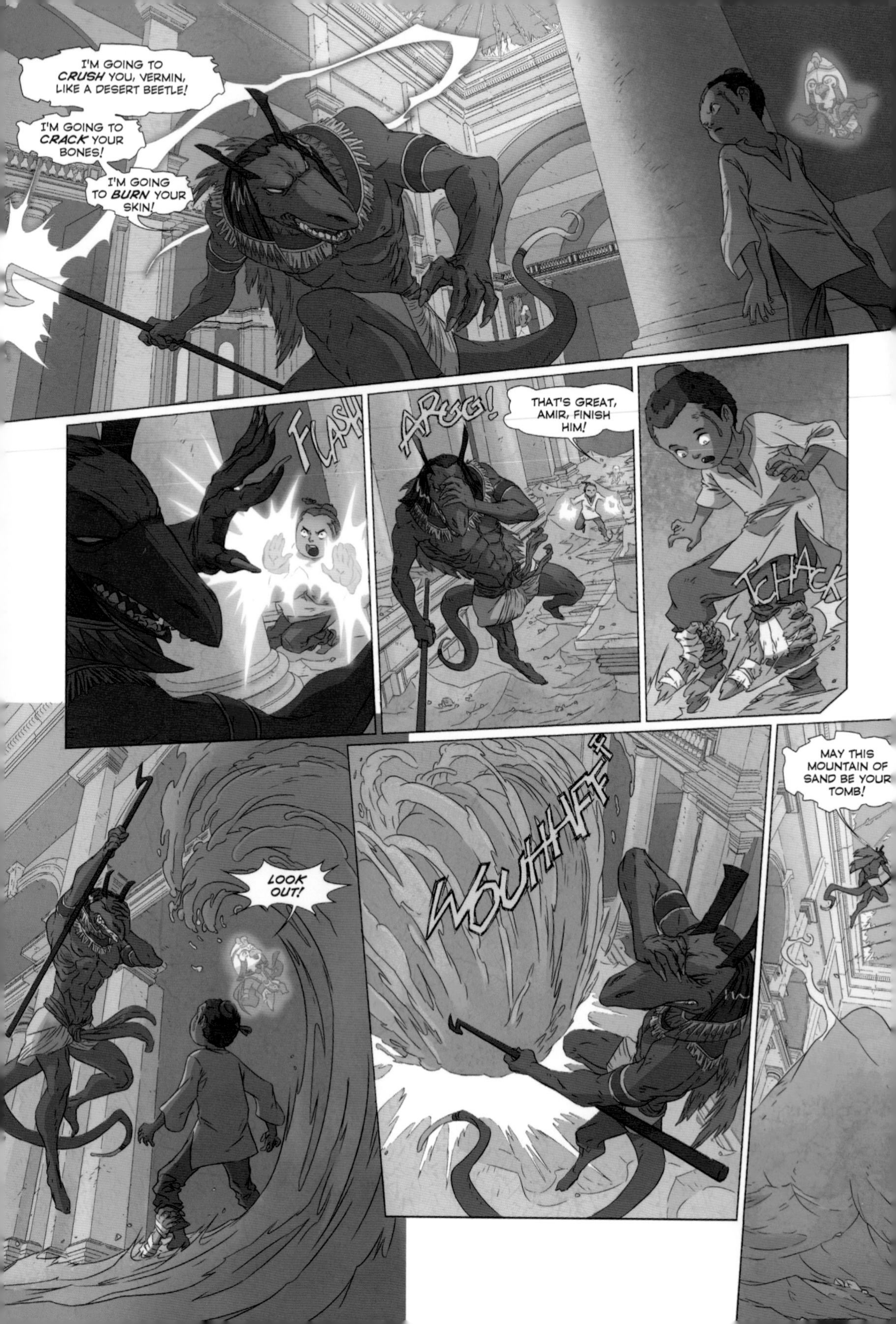
I'M GOING TO CRUSH YOU, VERMIN, LIKE A DESERT BEETLE!
I'M GOING TO CRACK YOUR BONES!
I'M GOING TO BURN YOUR SKIN!
FLASH
ARGG!
THAT'S GREAT, AMIR, FINISH HIM!
TCHACK
LOOK OUT!
WOUHHFF
MAY THIS MOUNTAIN OF SAND BE YOUR TOMB!

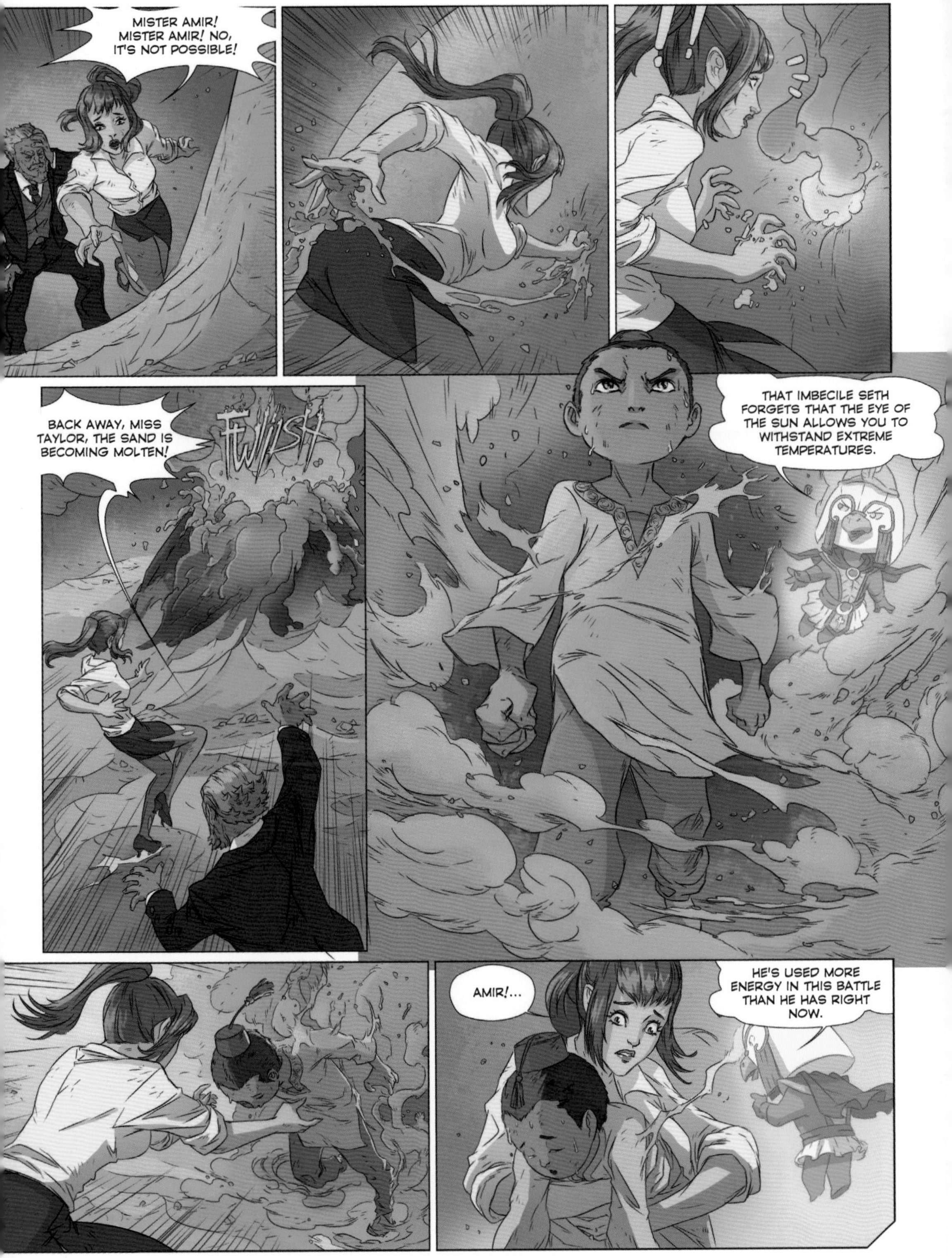
MISTER AMIR! MISTER AMIR! NO, IT'S NOT POSSIBLE!
BACK AWAY, MISS TAYLOR, THE SAND IS BECOMING MOLTEN!
FWISH
THAT IMBECILE SETH FORGETS THAT THE EYE OF THE SUN ALLOWS YOU TO WITHSTAND EXTREME TEMPERATURES.
AMIR!...
HE'S USED MORE ENERGY IN THIS BATTLE THAN HE HAS RIGHT NOW.

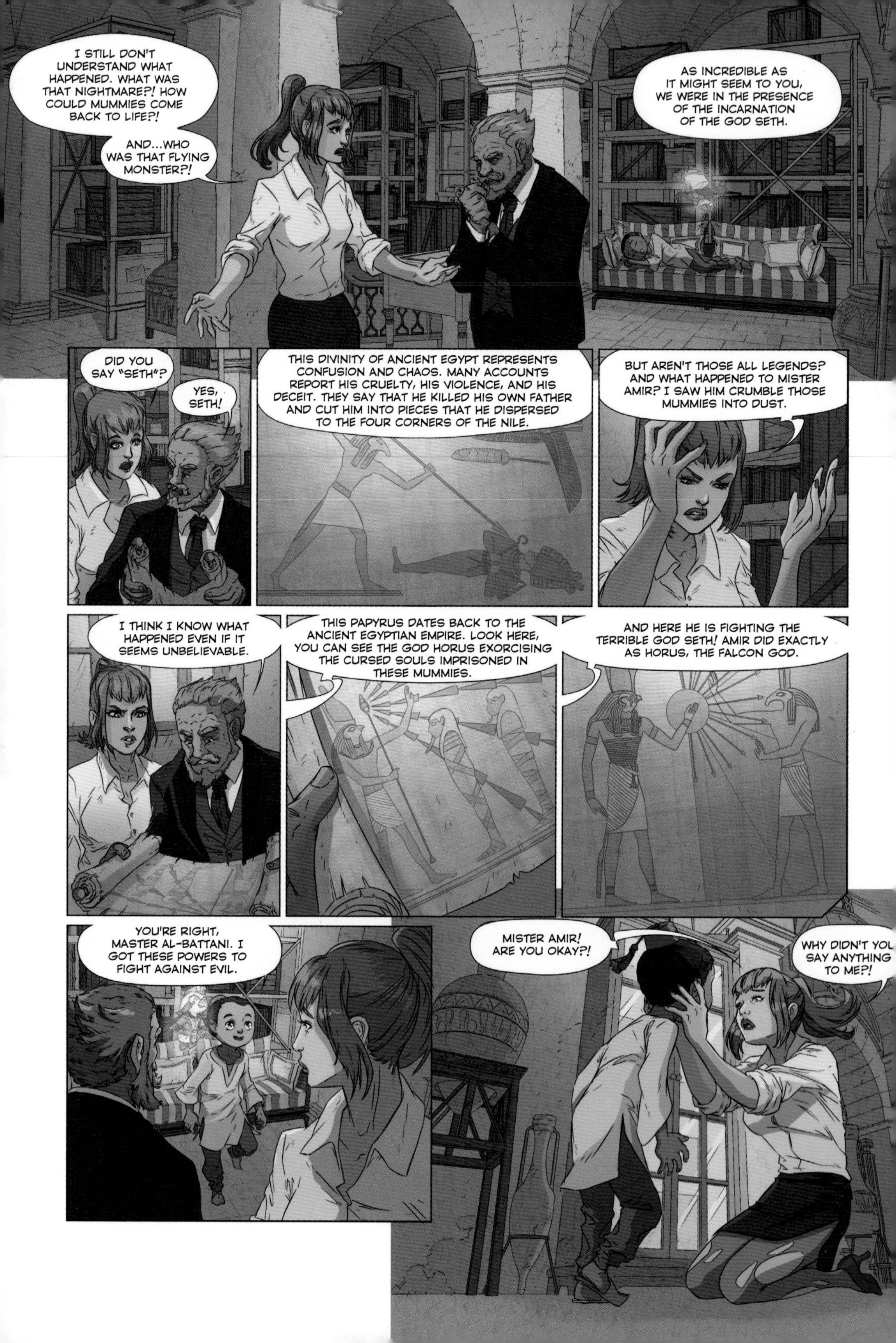
I STILL DON'T UNDERSTAND WHAT HAPPENED. WHAT WAS THAT NIGHTMARE?! HOW COULD MUMMIES COME BACK TO LIFE?!
AND...WHO WAS THAT FLYING MONSTER?!
AS INCREDIBLE AS IT MIGHT SEEM TO YOU, WE WERE IN THE PRESENCE OF THE INCARNATION OF THE GOD SETH.
DID YOU SAY "SETH"?
YES, SETH!
THIS DIVINITY OF ANCIENT EGYPT REPRESENTS CONFUSION AND CHAOS. MANY ACCOUNTS REPORT HIS CRUELTY, HIS VIOLENCE, AND HIS DECEIT. THEY SAY THAT HE KILLED HIS OWN FATHER AND CUT HIM INTO PIECES THAT HE DISPERSED TO THE FOUR CORNERS OF THE NILE.
BUT AREN'T THOSE ALL LEGENDS? AND WHAT HAPPENED TO MISTER AMIR? I SAW HIM CRUMBLE THOSE MUMMIES INTO DUST.
I THINK I KNOW WHAT HAPPENED EVEN IF IT SEEMS UNBELIEVABLE.
THIS PAPYRUS DATES BACK TO THE ANCIENT EGYPTIAN EMPIRE. LOOK HERE, YOU CAN SEE THE GOD HORUS EXORCISING THE CURSED SOULS IMPRISONED IN THESE MUMMIES.
AND HERE HE IS FIGHTING THE TERRIBLE GOD SETH! AMIR DID EXACTLY AS HORUS, THE FALCON GOD.
YOU'RE RIGHT, MASTER AL-BATTANI. I GOT THESE POWERS TO FIGHT AGAINST EVIL.
MISTER AMIR! ARE YOU OKAY?!
WHY DIDN'T YOU SAY ANYTHING TO ME?!

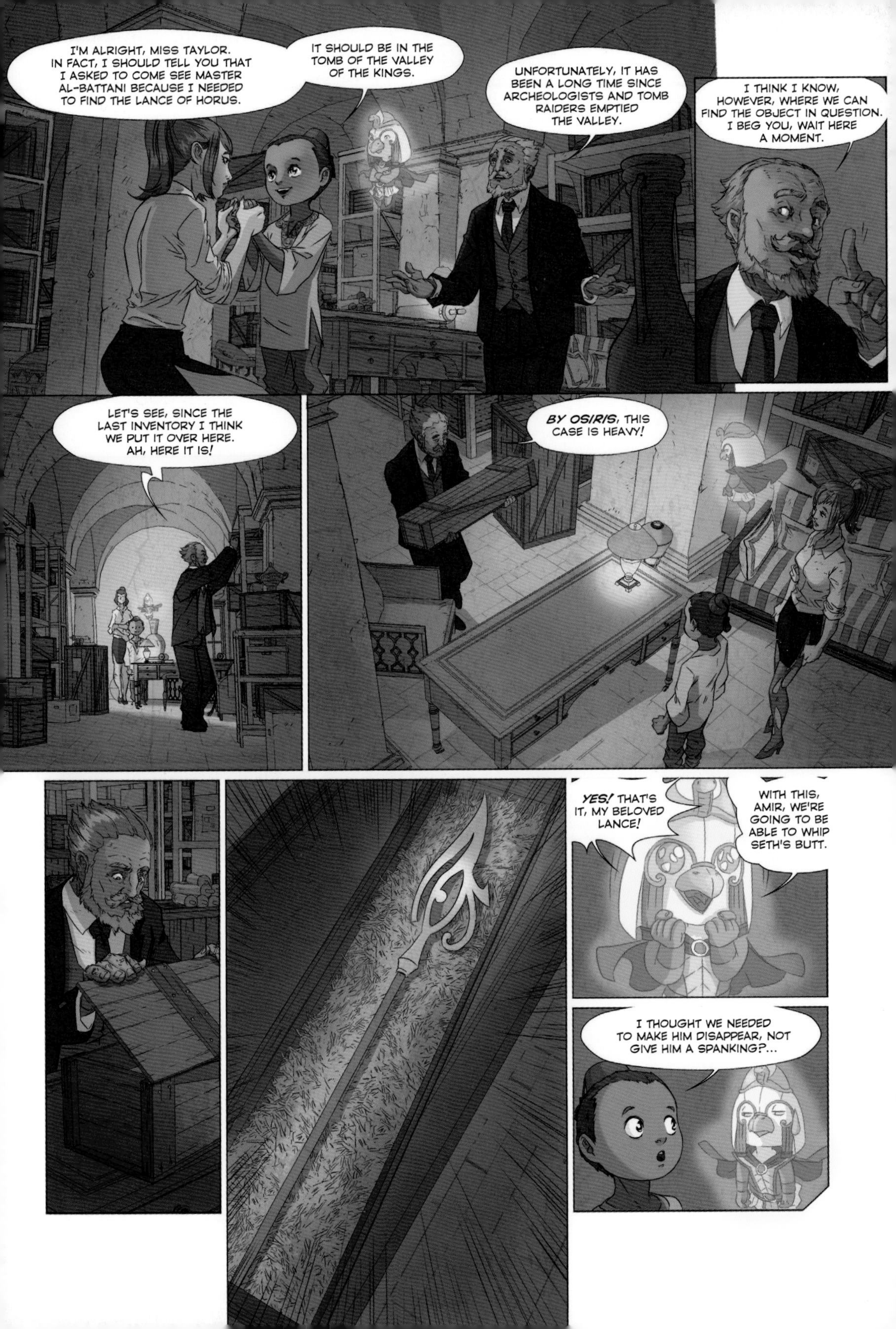
I'M ALRIGHT, MISS TAYLOR. IN FACT, I SHOULD TELL YOU THAT I ASKED TO COME SEE MASTER AL-BATTANI BECAUSE I NEEDED TO FIND THE LANCE OF HORUS.
IT SHOULD BE IN THE TOMB OF THE VALLEY OF THE KINGS.
UNFORTUNATELY, IT HAS BEEN A LONG TIME SINCE ARCHEOLOGISTS AND TOMB RAIDERS EMPTIED THE VALLEY.
I THINK I KNOW, HOWEVER, WHERE WE CAN FIND THE OBJECT IN QUESTION. I BEG YOU, WAIT HERE A MOMENT.
LET'S SEE, SINCE THE LAST INVENTORY I THINK WE PUT IT OVER HERE. AH, HERE IT IS!
BY OSIRIS, THIS CASE IS HEAVY!
YES! THAT'S IT, MY BELOVED LANCE!
WITH THIS, AMIR, WE'RE GOING TO BE ABLE TO WHIP SETH'S BUTT.
I THOUGHT WE NEEDED TO MAKE HIM DISAPPEAR, NOT GIVE HIM A SPANKING?...

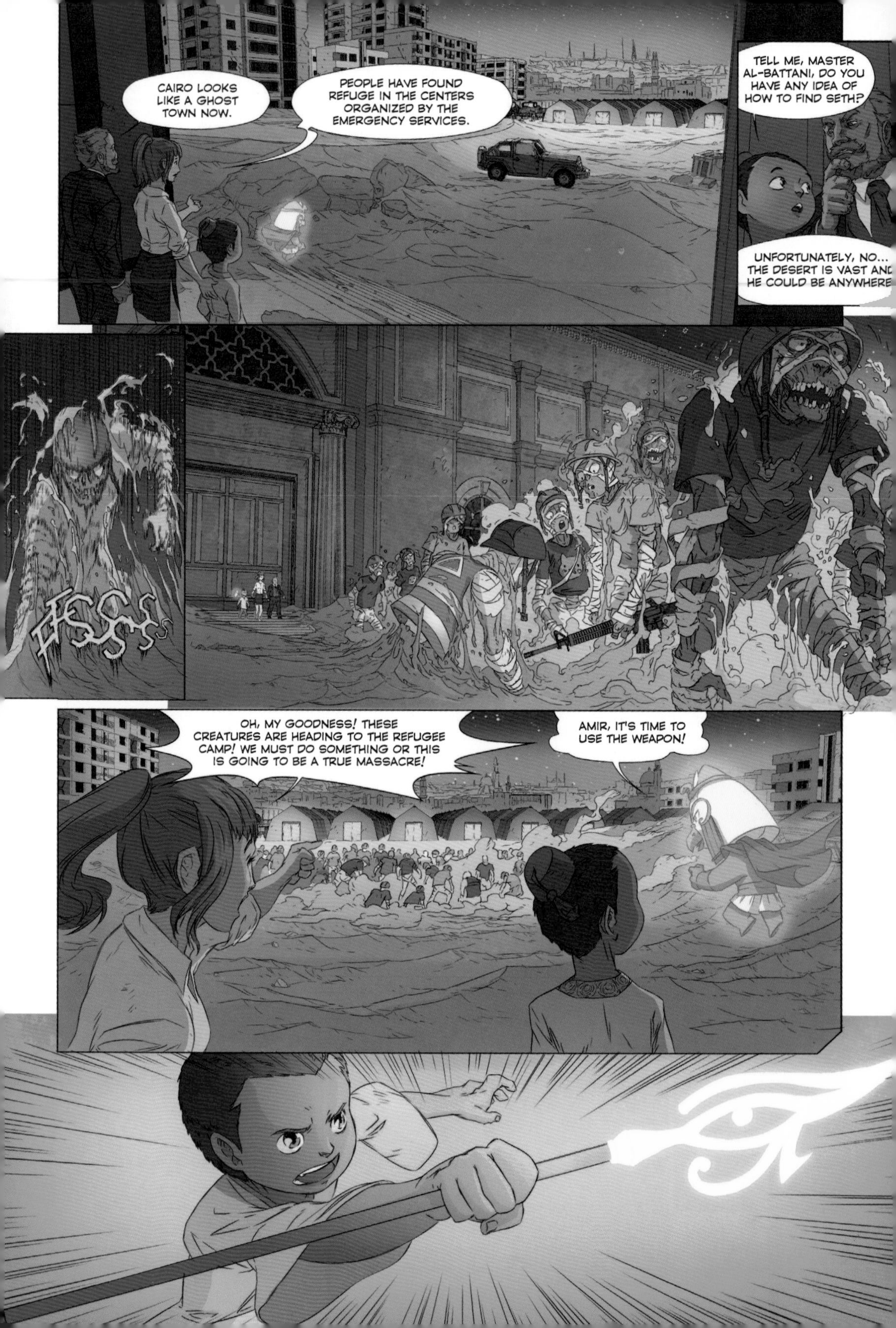

CAIRO LOOKS LIKE A GHOST TOWN NOW.
PEOPLE HAVE FOUND REFUGE IN THE CENTERS ORGANIZED BY THE EMERGENCY SERVICES.
TELL ME, MASTER AL-BATTANI, DO YOU HAVE ANY IDEA OF HOW TO FIND SETH?
UNFORTUNATELY, NO... THE DESERT IS VAST AND HE COULD BE ANYWHERE.
HSSSSS
OH, MY GOODNESS! THESE CREATURES ARE HEADING TO THE REFUGEE CAMP! WE MUST DO SOMETHING OR THIS IS GOING TO BE A TRUE MASSACRE!
AMIR, IT'S TIME TO USE THE WEAPON!

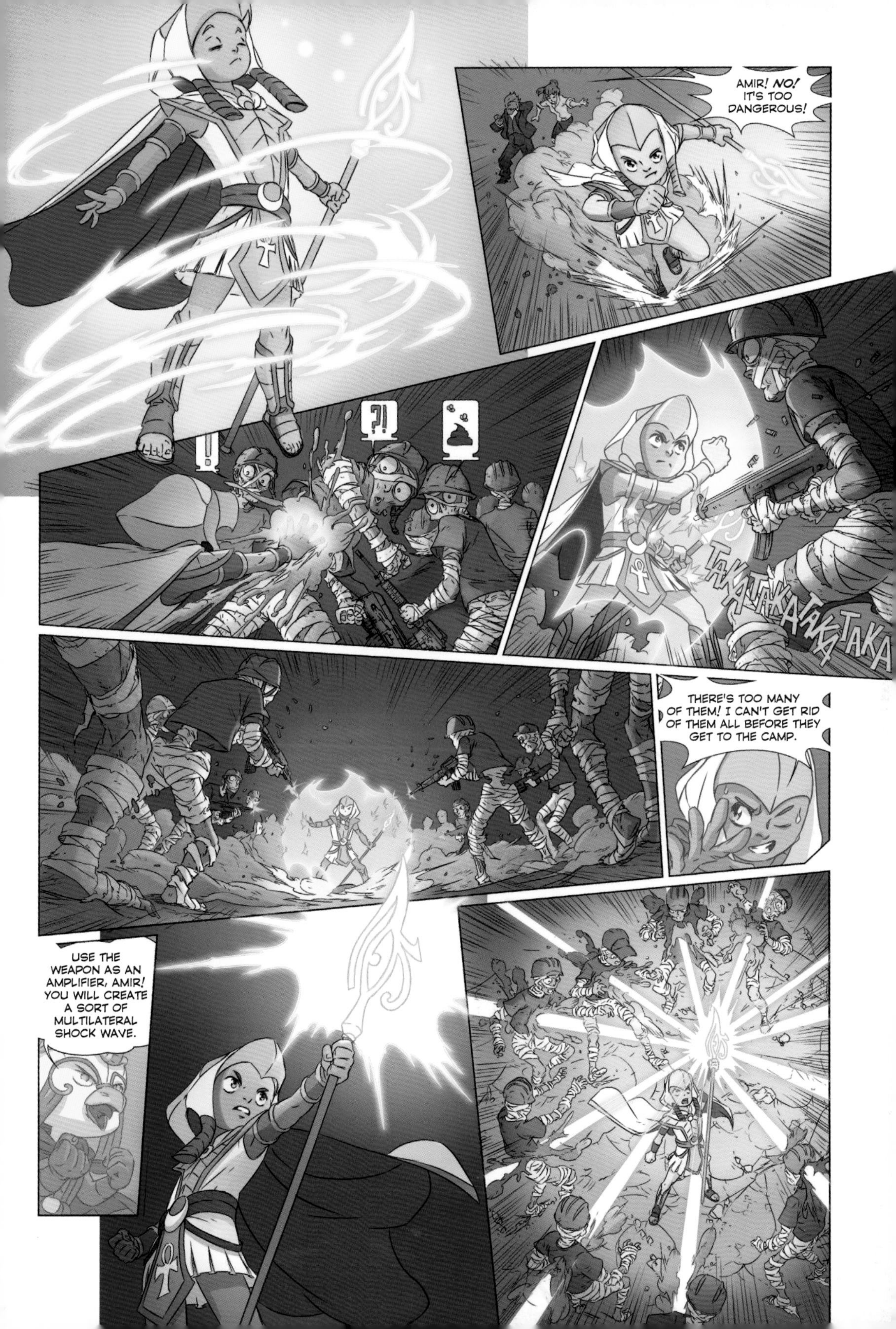
AMIR! NO! IT'S TOO DANGEROUS!
!
?!
TAKATAKATAKATAKATAKA
THERE'S TOO MANY OF THEM! I CAN'T GET RID OF THEM ALL BEFORE THEY GET TO THE CAMP.
USE THE WEAPON AS AN AMPLIFIER, AMIR! YOU WILL CREATE A SORT OF MULTILATERAL SHOCK WAVE.

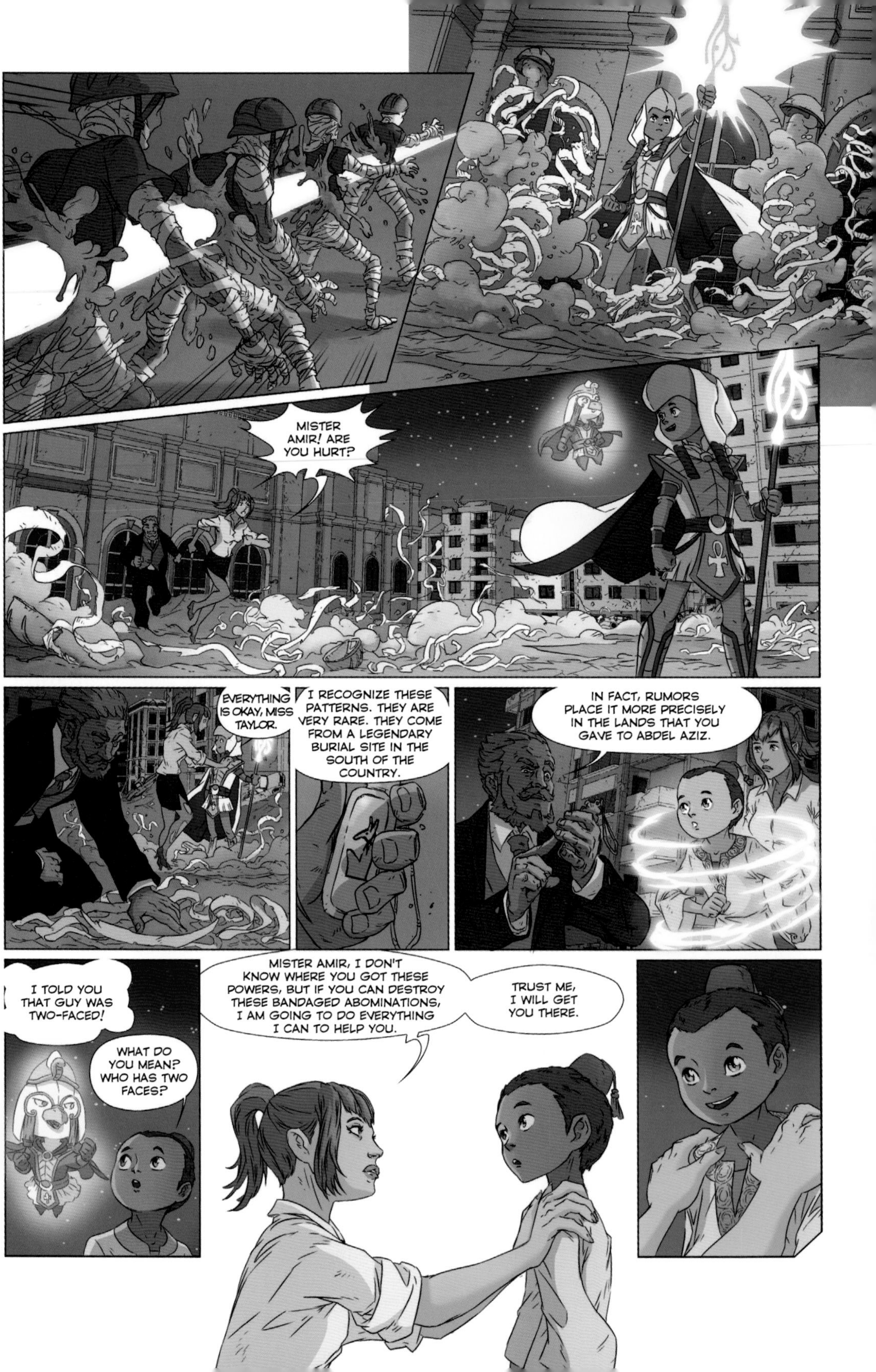
MISTER AMIR! ARE YOU HURT?
EVERYTHING IS OKAY, MISS TAYLOR.
I RECOGNIZE THESE PATTERNS. THEY ARE VERY RARE. THEY COME FROM A LEGENDARY BURIAL SITE IN THE SOUTH OF THE COUNTRY.
IN FACT, RUMORS PLACE IT MORE PRECISELY IN THE LANDS THAT YOU GAVE TO ABDEL AZIZ.
I TOLD YOU THAT GUY WAS TWO-FACED!
WHAT DO YOU MEAN? WHO HAS TWO FACES?
MISTER AMIR, I DON'T KNOW WHERE YOU GOT THESE POWERS, BUT IF YOU CAN DESTROY THESE BANDAGED ABOMINATIONS, I AM GOING TO DO EVERYTHING I CAN TO HELP YOU.
TRUST ME, I WILL GET YOU THERE.

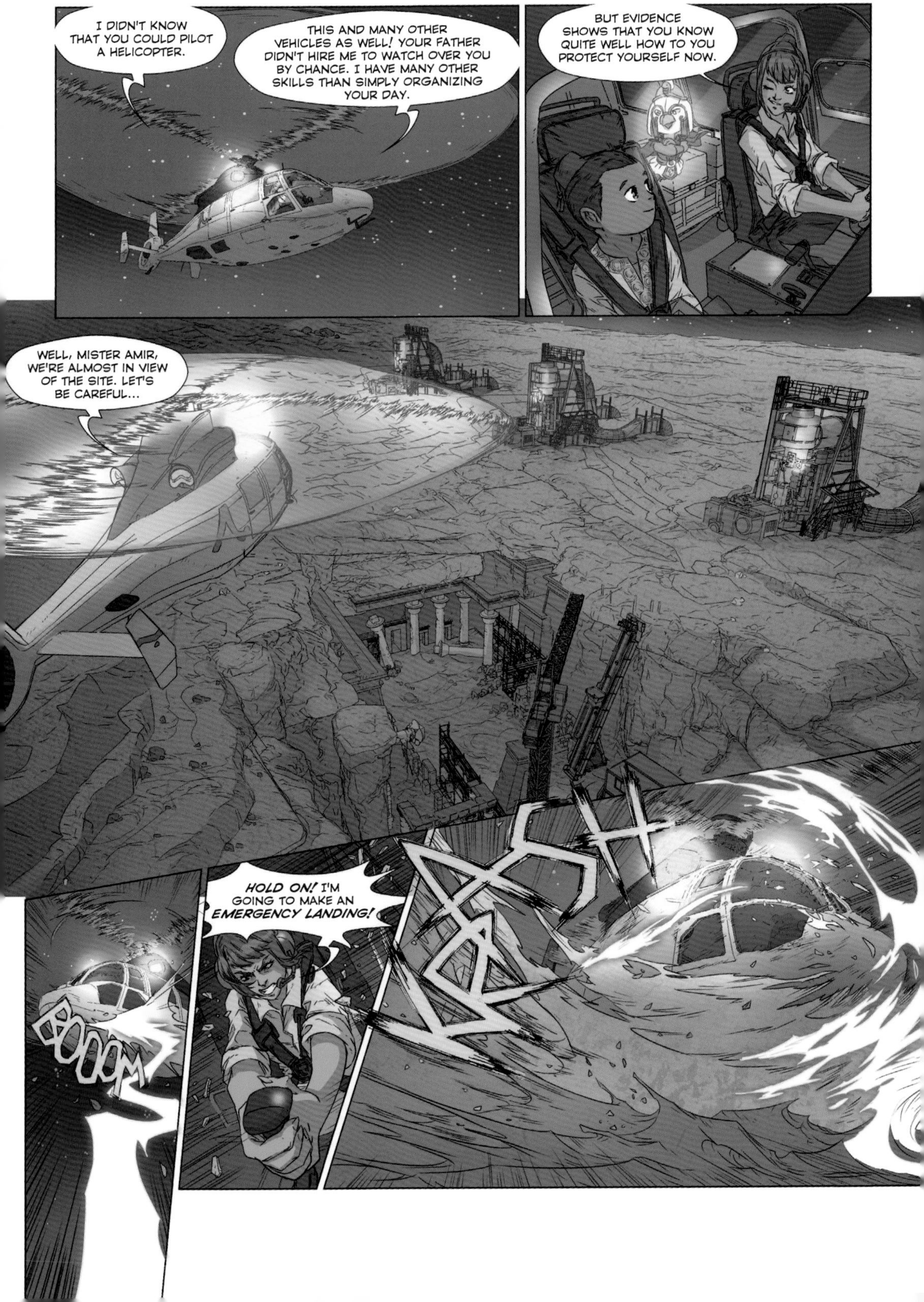
I DIDN'T KNOW THAT YOU COULD PILOT A HELICOPTER.
THIS AND MANY OTHER VEHICLES AS WELL! YOUR FATHER DIDN'T HIRE ME TO WATCH OVER YOU BY CHANCE. I HAVE MANY OTHER SKILLS THAN SIMPLY ORGANIZING YOUR DAY.
BUT EVIDENCE SHOWS THAT YOU KNOW QUITE WELL HOW TO YOU PROTECT YOURSELF NOW.
WELL, MISTER AMIR, WE'RE ALMOST IN VIEW OF THE SITE. LET'S BE CAREFUL...
BOOOM
HOLD ON! I'M GOING TO MAKE AN EMERGENCY LANDING!

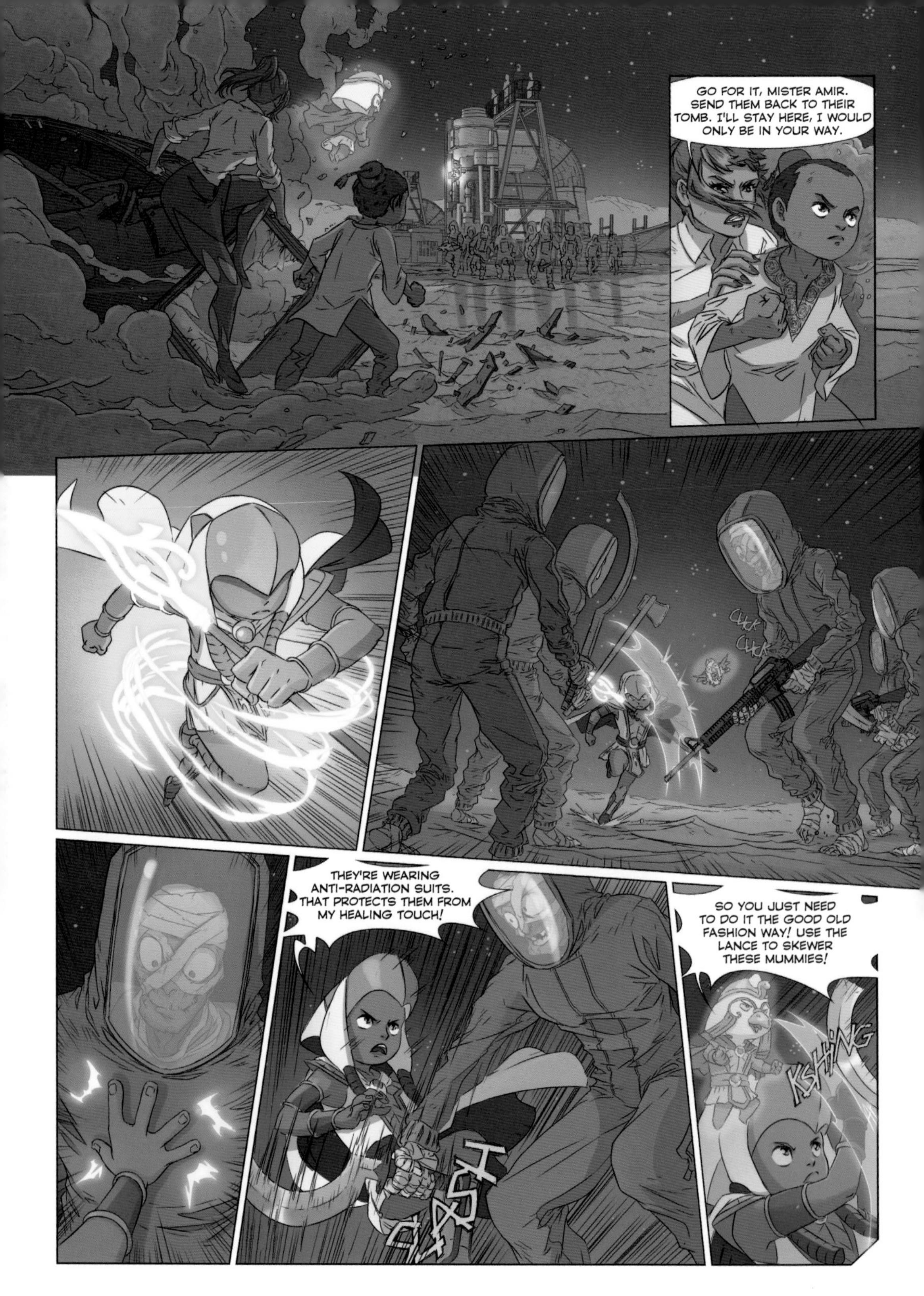
GO FOR IT, MISTER AMIR. SEND THEM BACK TO THEIR TOMB. I'LL STAY HERE, I WOULD ONLY BE IN YOUR WAY.
CLICK
CLICK
THEY'RE WEARING ANTI-RADIATION SUITS. THAT PROTECTS THEM FROM MY HEALING TOUCH!
CRASH
SO YOU JUST NEED TO DO IT THE GOOD OLD FASHION WAY! USE THE LANCE TO SKEWER THESE MUMMIES!
KSHING

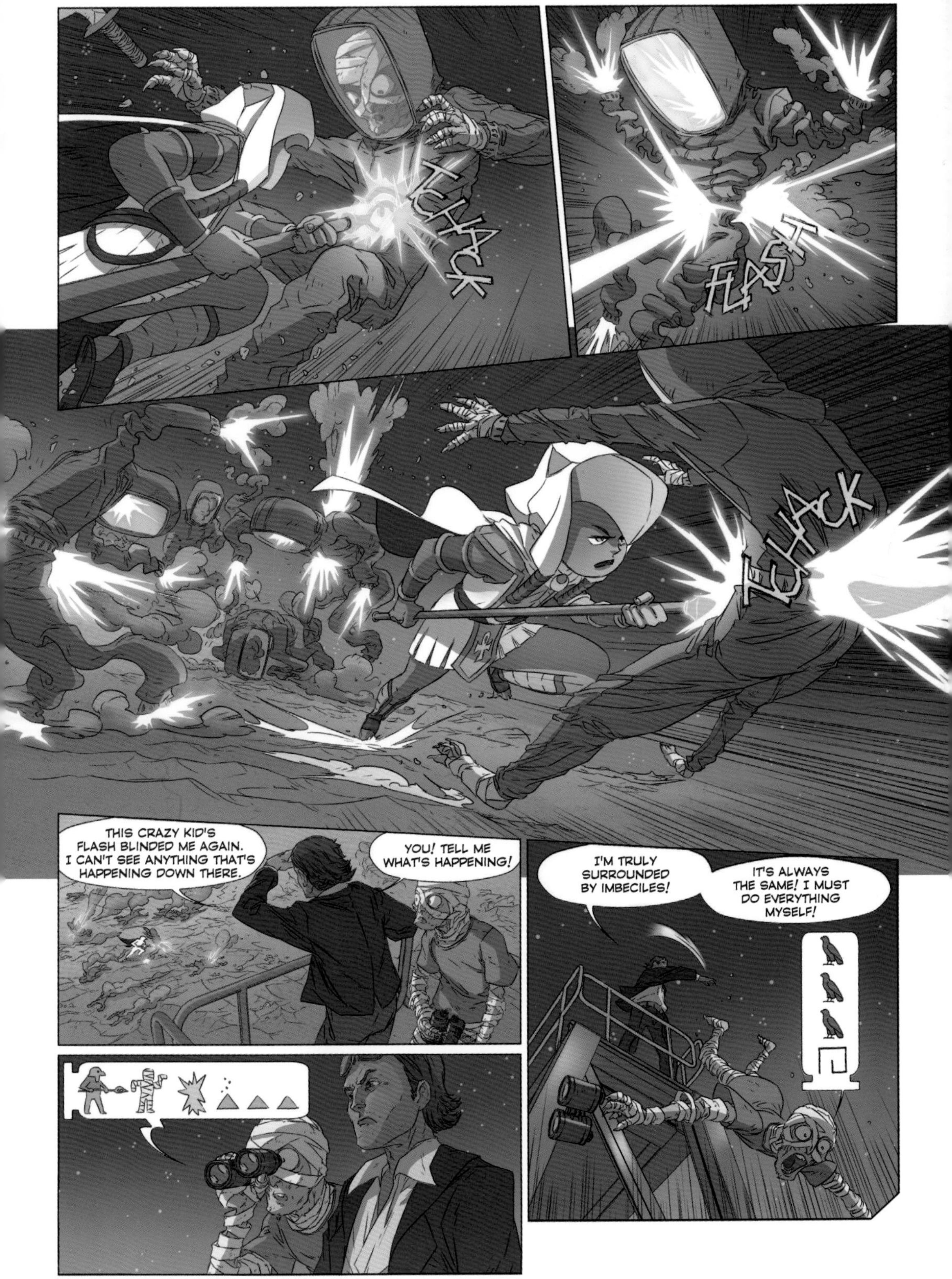

TCHACK
FLASH
TCHACK
THIS CRAZY KID'S FLASH BLINDED ME AGAIN. I CAN'T SEE ANYTHING THAT'S HAPPENING DOWN THERE.
YOU! TELL ME WHAT'S HAPPENING!
I'M TRULY SURROUNDED BY IMBECILES!
IT'S ALWAYS THE SAME! I MUST DO EVERYTHING MYSELF!

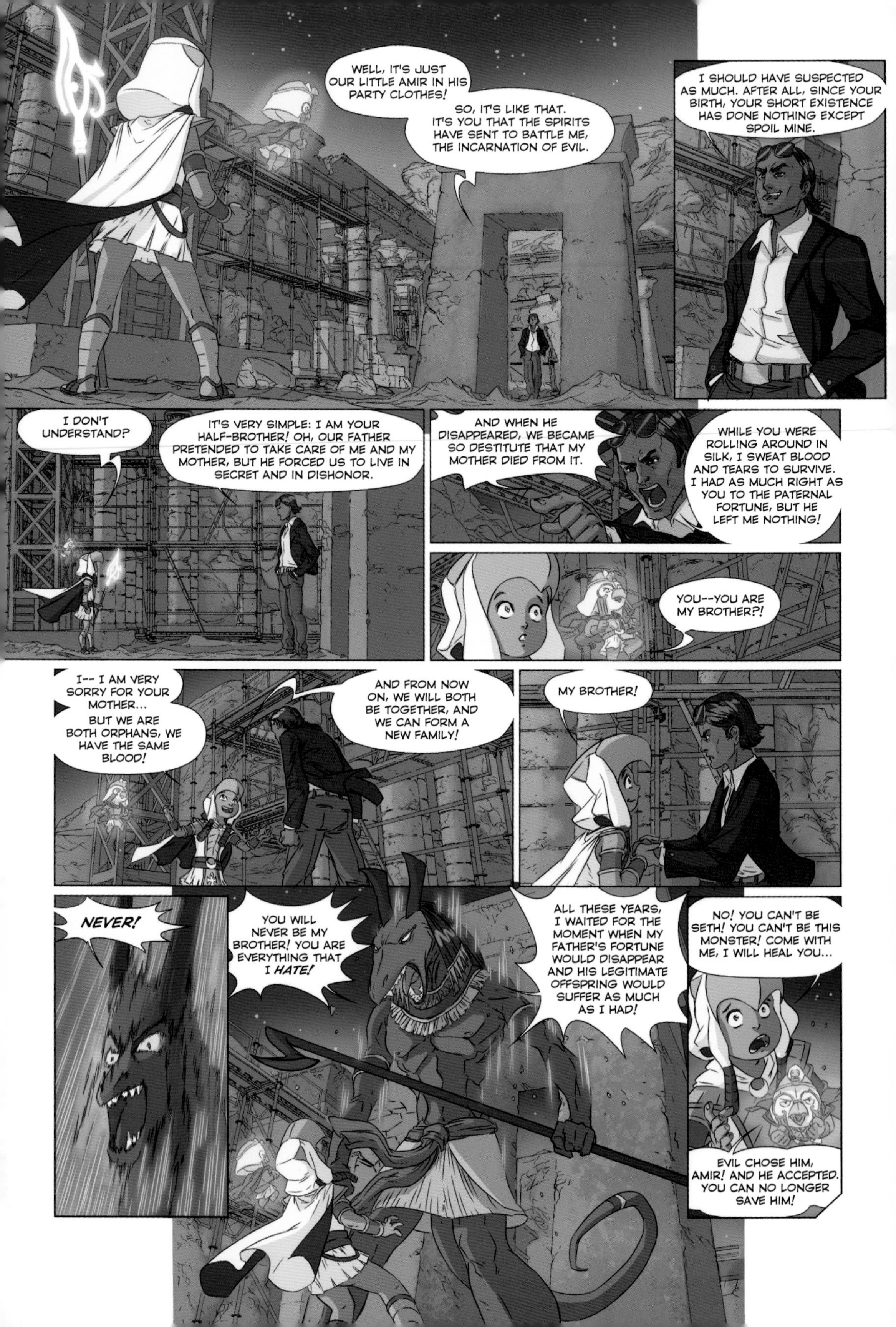
WELL, IT'S JUST OUR LITTLE AMIR IN HIS PARTY CLOTHES!
SO, IT'S LIKE THAT. IT'S YOU THAT THE SPIRITS HAVE SENT TO BATTLE ME, THE INCARNATION OF EVIL.
I SHOULD HAVE SUSPECTED AS MUCH. AFTER ALL, SINCE YOUR BIRTH, YOUR SHORT EXISTENCE HAS DONE NOTHING EXCEPT SPOIL MINE.
I DON'T UNDERSTAND?
IT'S VERY SIMPLE: I AM YOUR HALF-BROTHER! OH, OUR FATHER PRETENDED TO TAKE CARE OF ME AND MY MOTHER, BUT HE FORCED US TO LIVE IN SECRET AND IN DISHONOR.
AND WHEN HE DISAPPEARED, WE BECAME SO DESTITUTE THAT MY MOTHER DIED FROM IT.
WHILE YOU WERE ROLLING AROUND IN SILK, I SWEAT BLOOD AND TEARS TO SURVIVE. I HAD AS MUCH RIGHT AS YOU TO THE PATERNAL FORTUNE, BUT HE LEFT ME NOTHING!
YOU--YOU ARE MY BROTHER?!
I-- I AM VERY SORRY FOR YOUR MOTHER...
BUT WE ARE BOTH ORPHANS, WE HAVE THE SAME BLOOD!
AND FROM NOW ON, WE WILL BOTH BE TOGETHER, AND WE CAN FORM A NEW FAMILY!
MY BROTHER!
NEVER!
YOU WILL NEVER BE MY BROTHER! YOU ARE EVERYTHING THAT I HATE!
ALL THESE YEARS, I WAITED FOR THE MOMENT WHEN MY FATHER'S FORTUNE WOULD DISAPPEAR AND HIS LEGITIMATE OFFSPRING WOULD SUFFER AS MUCH AS I HAD!
NO! YOU CAN'T BE SETH! YOU CAN'T BE THIS MONSTER! COME WITH ME, I WILL HEAL YOU...
EVIL CHOSE HIM, AMIR! AND HE ACCEPTED. YOU CAN NO LONGER SAVE HIM!

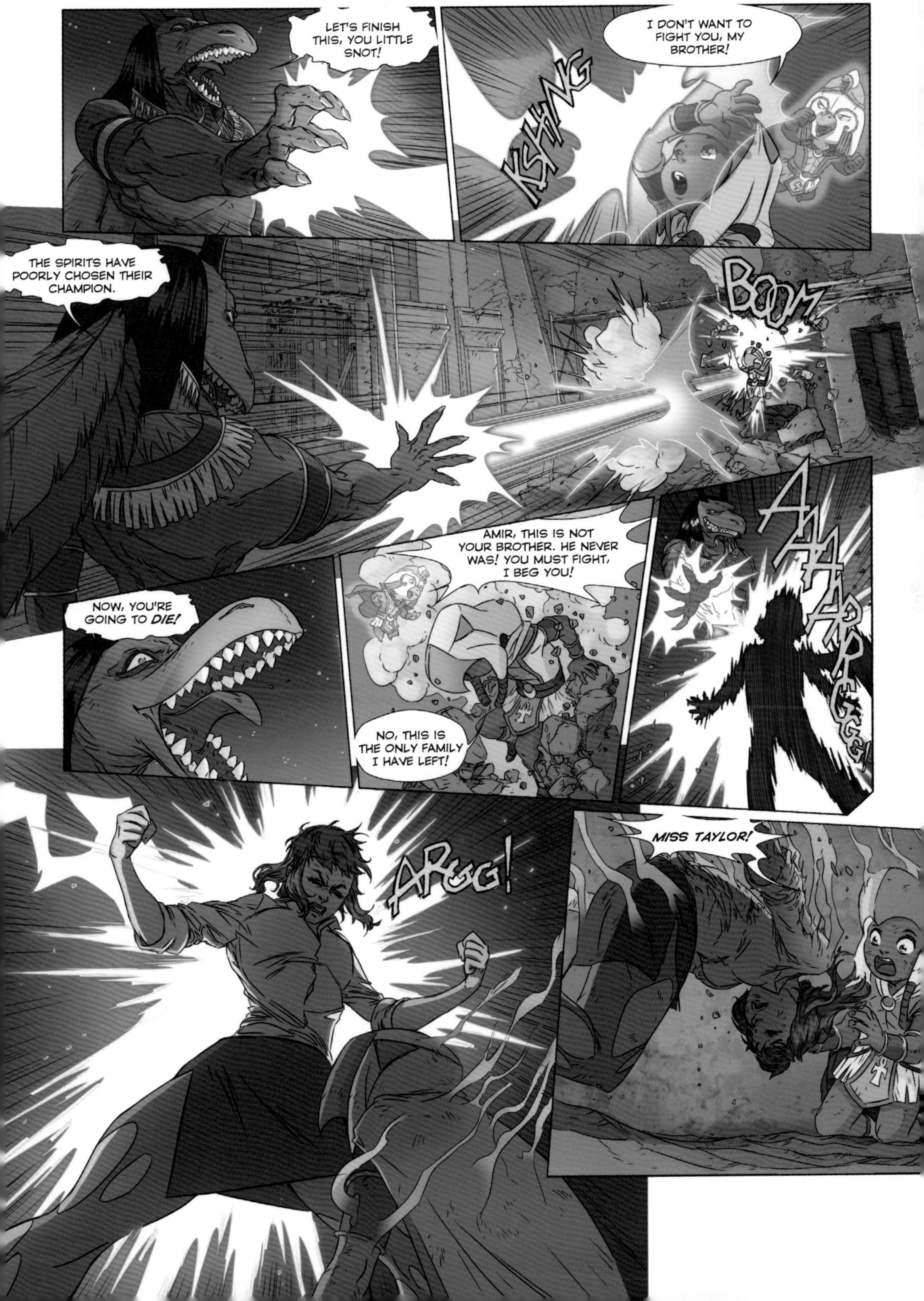

LET'S FINISH THIS, YOU LITTLE SNOT!
I DON'T WANT TO FIGHT YOU, MY BROTHER!
KSHING
THE SPIRITS HAVE POORLY CHOSEN THEIR CHAMPION.
BOOM!
NOW, YOU'RE GOING TO DIE!
AMIR, THIS IS NOT YOUR BROTHER. HE NEVER WAS! YOU MUST FIGHT, I BEG YOU!
NO, THIS IS THE ONLY FAMILY I HAVE LEFT!
AAAARGGGH!
ARGG!
MISS TAYLOR!

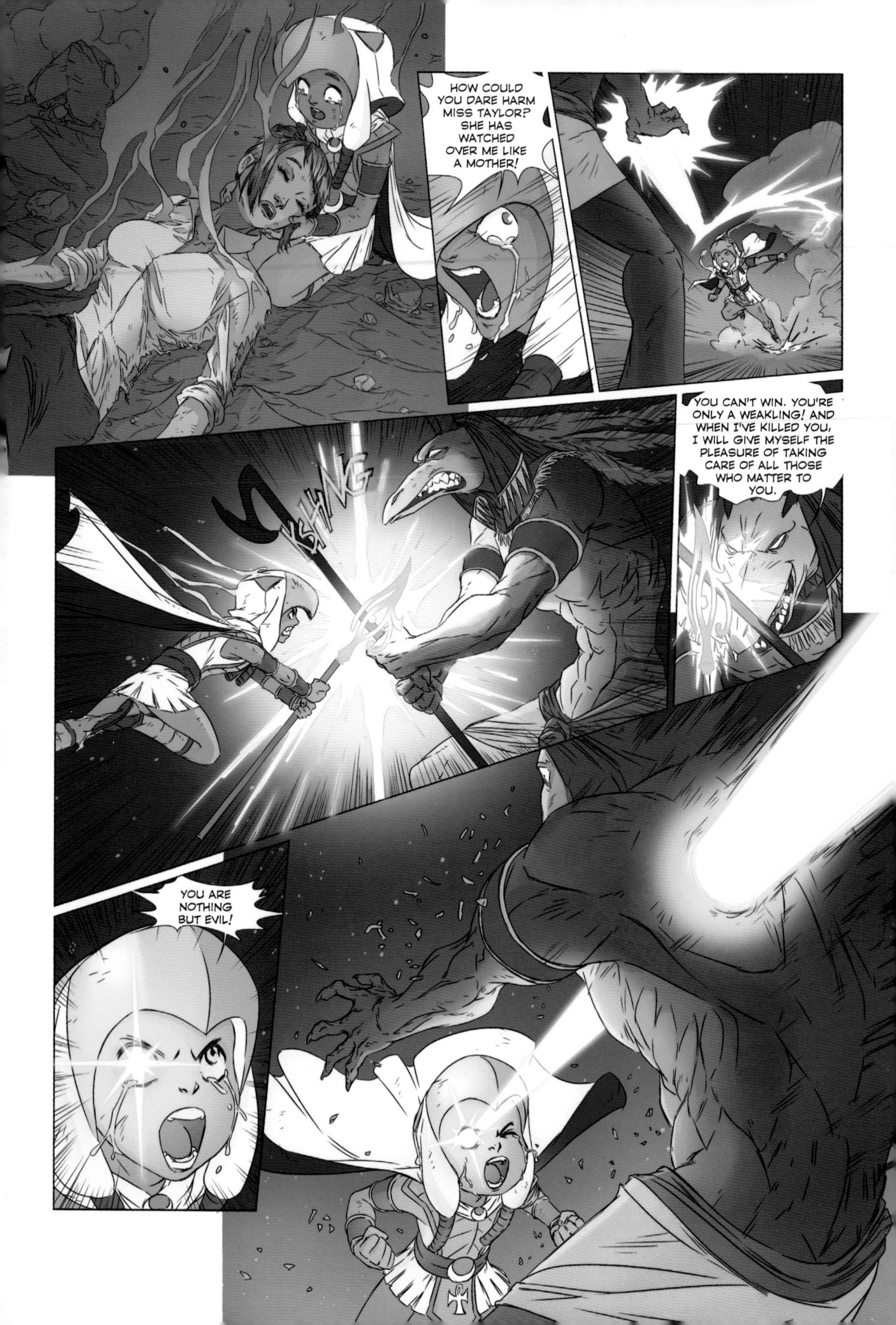
HOW COULD YOU DARE HARM MISS TAYLOR? SHE HAS WATCHED OVER ME LIKE A MOTHER!
SHHNG
YOU CAN'T WIN. YOU'RE ONLY A WEAKLING! AND WHEN I'VE KILLED YOU, I WILL GIVE MYSELF THE PLEASURE OF TAKING CARE OF ALL THOSE WHO MATTER TO YOU.
YOU ARE NOTHING BUT EVIL!

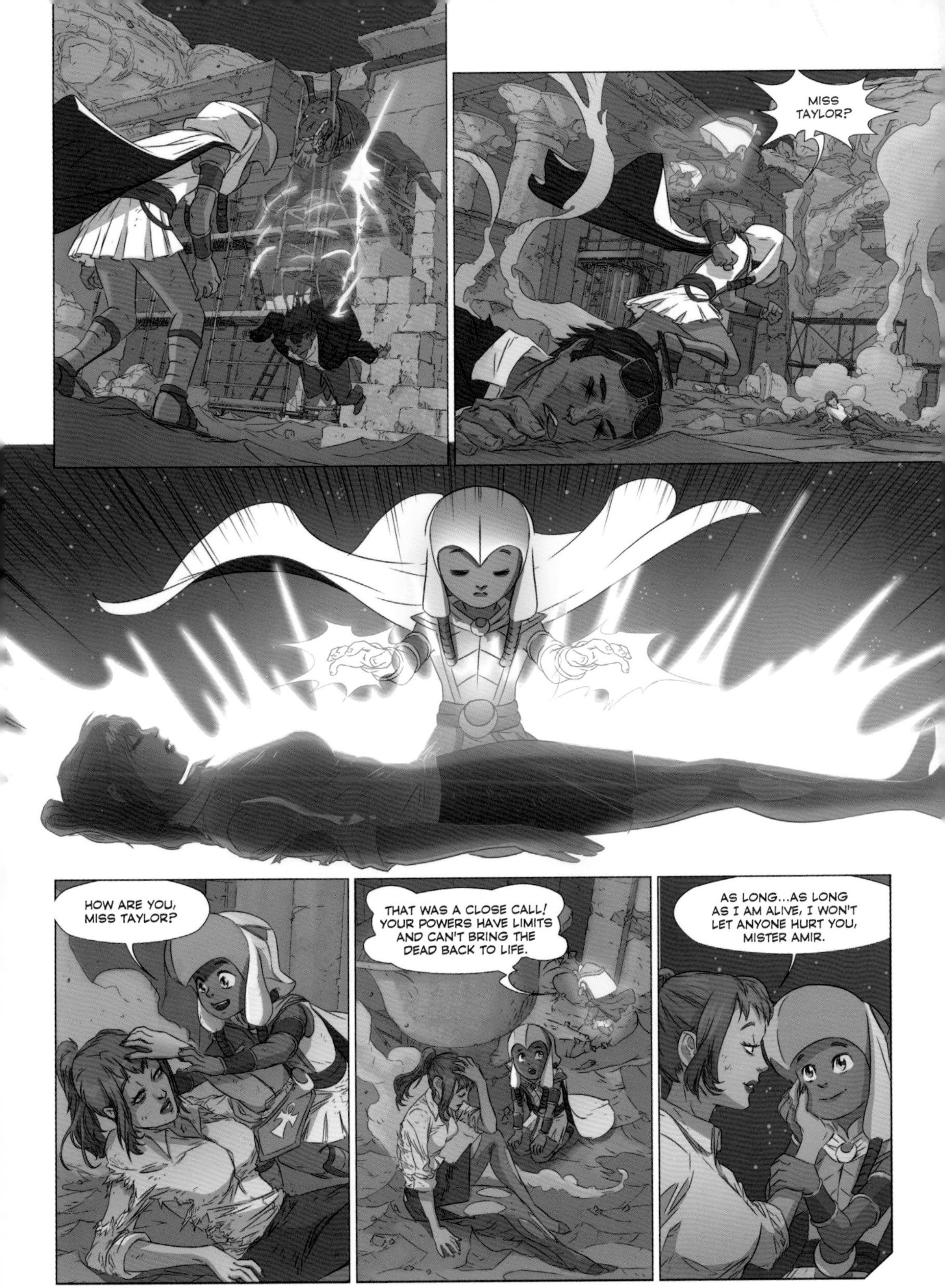
MISS TAYLOR?
HOW ARE YOU, MISS TAYLOR?
THAT WAS A CLOSE CALL! YOUR POWERS HAVE LIMITS AND CAN'T BRING THE DEAD BACK TO LIFE.
AS LONG...AS LONG AS I AM ALIVE, I WON'T LET ANYONE HURT YOU, MISTER AMIR.

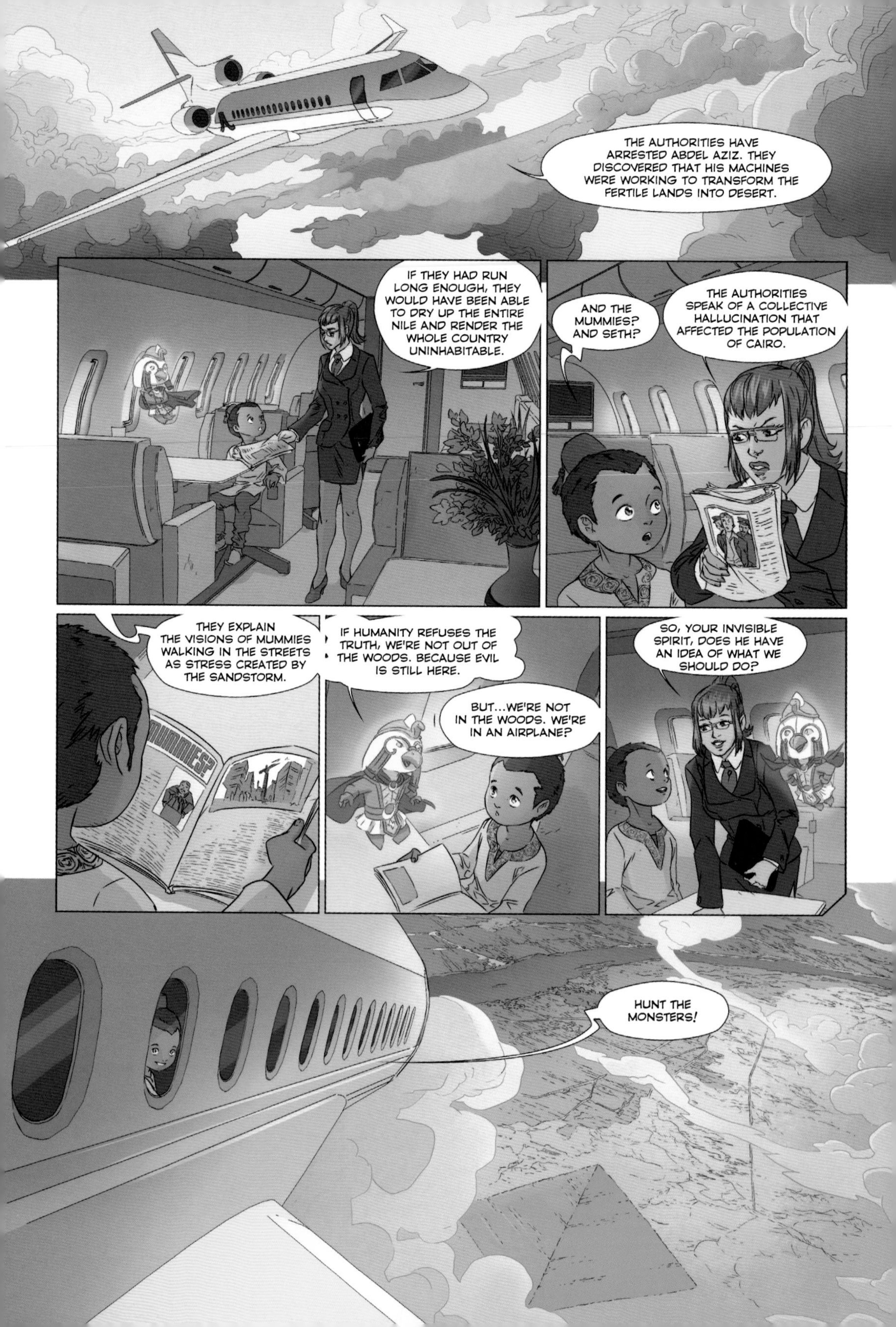
THE AUTHORITIES HAVE ARRESTED ABDEL AZIZ. THEY DISCOVERED THAT HIS MACHINES WERE WORKING TO TRANSFORM THE FERTILE LANDS INTO DESERT.
IF THEY HAD RUN LONG ENOUGH, THEY WOULD HAVE BEEN ABLE TO DRY UP THE ENTIRE NILE AND RENDER THE WHOLE COUNTRY UNINHABITABLE.
AND THE MUMMIES? AND SETH?
THE AUTHORITIES SPEAK OF A COLLECTIVE HALLUCINATION THAT AFFECTED THE POPULATION OF CAIRO.
THEY EXPLAIN THE VISIONS OF MUMMIES WALKING IN THE STREETS AS STRESS CREATED BY THE SANDSTORM.
MUMMIES?
IF HUMANITY REFUSES THE TRUTH, WE'RE NOT OUT OF THE WOODS. BECAUSE EVIL IS STILL HERE.
BUT...WE'RE NOT IN THE WOODS. WE'RE IN AN AIRPLANE?
SO, YOUR INVISIBLE SPIRIT, DOES HE HAVE AN IDEA OF WHAT WE SHOULD DO?
HUNT THE MONSTERS!

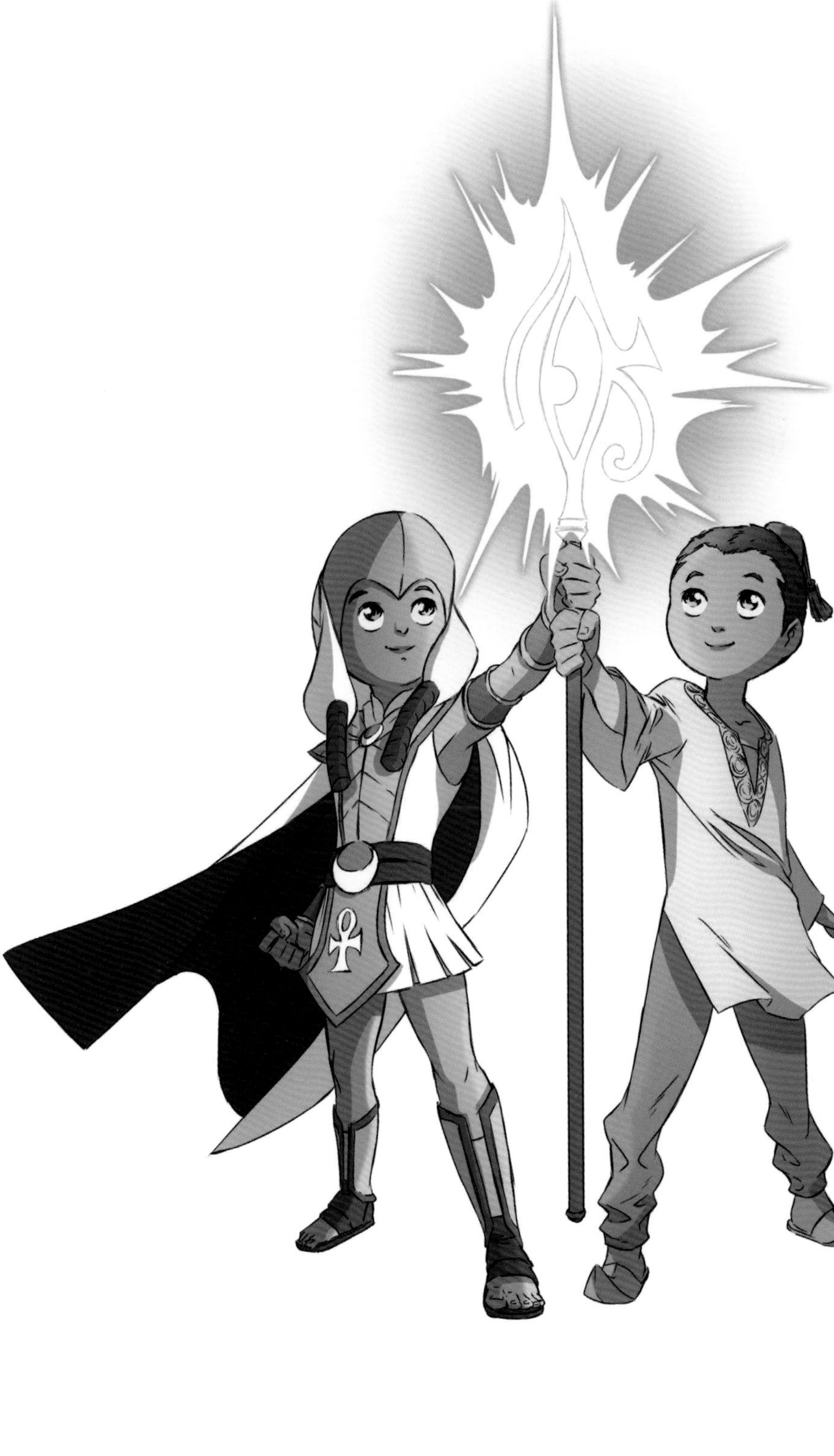

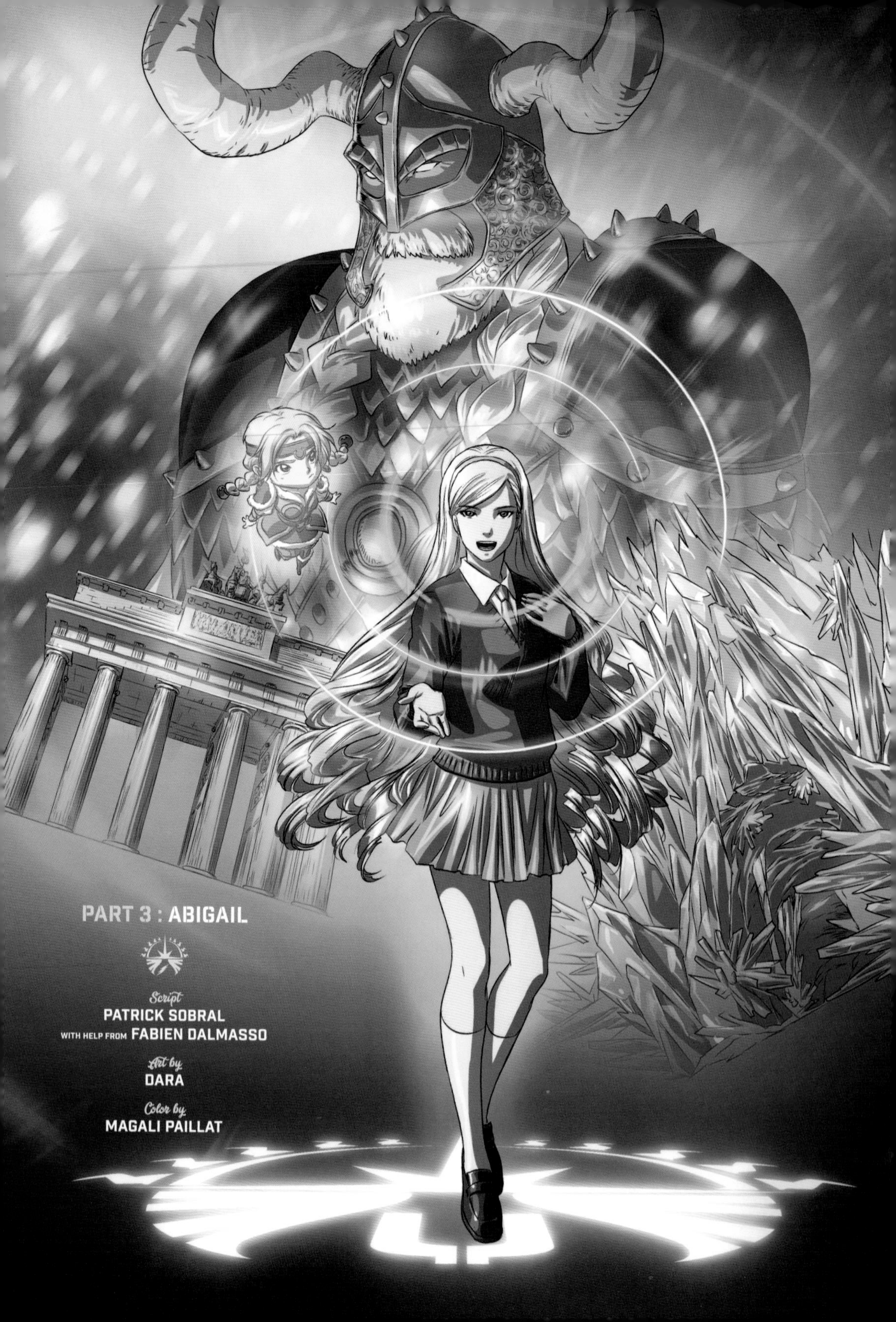

PART 3 : ABIGAIL

Script
PATRICK SOBRAL
WITH HELP FROM **FABIEN DALMASSO**

Art by
DARA

Color by
MAGALI PAILLAT

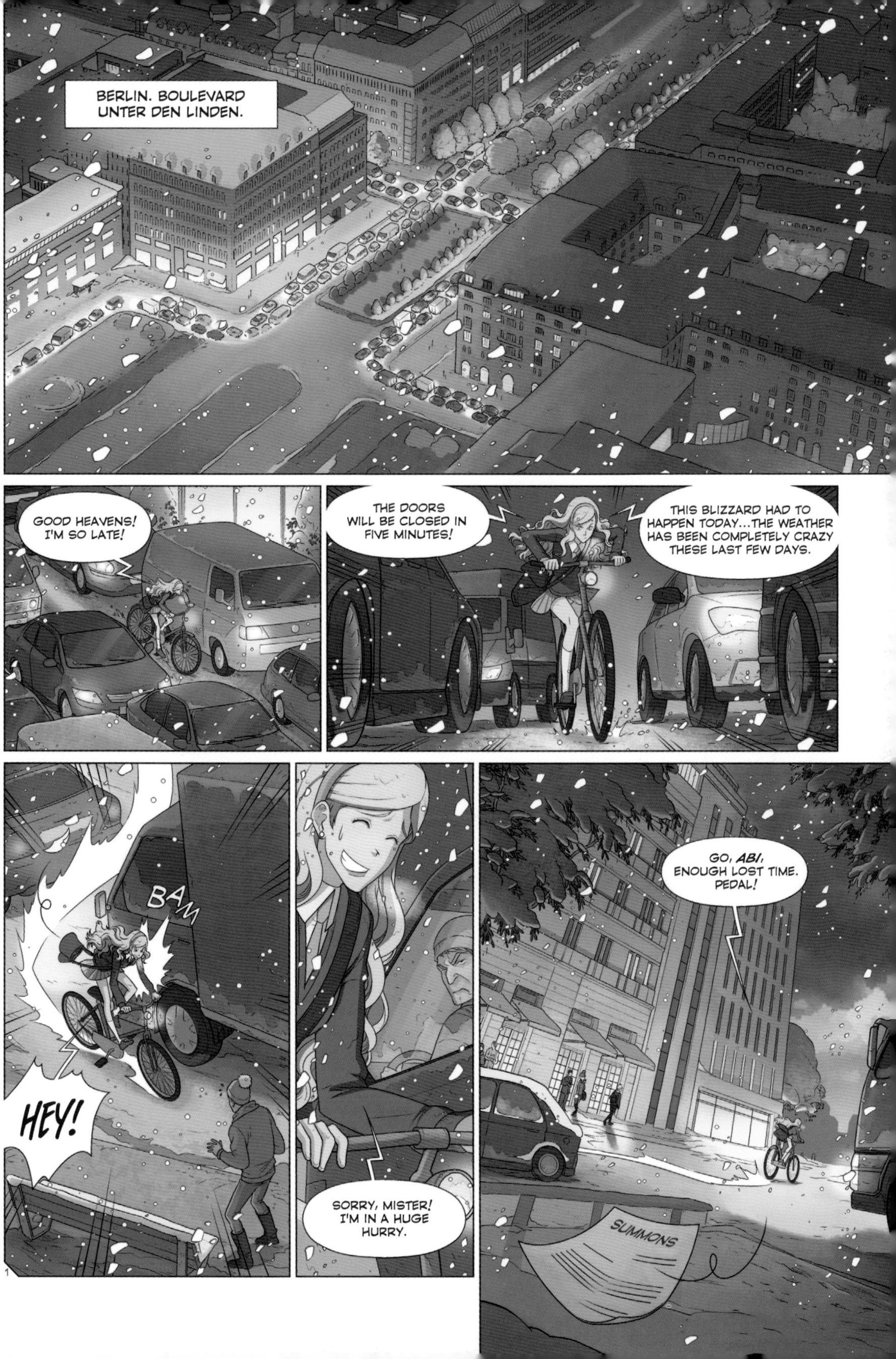
BERLIN. BOULEVARD UNTER DEN LINDEN.
GOOD HEAVENS! I'M SO LATE!
THE DOORS WILL BE CLOSED IN FIVE MINUTES!
THIS BLIZZARD HAD TO HAPPEN TODAY...THE WEATHER HAS BEEN COMPLETELY CRAZY THESE LAST FEW DAYS.
BAM
HEY!
SORRY, MISTER! I'M IN A HUGE HURRY.
GO, ABI, ENOUGH LOST TIME. PEDAL!
SUMMONS

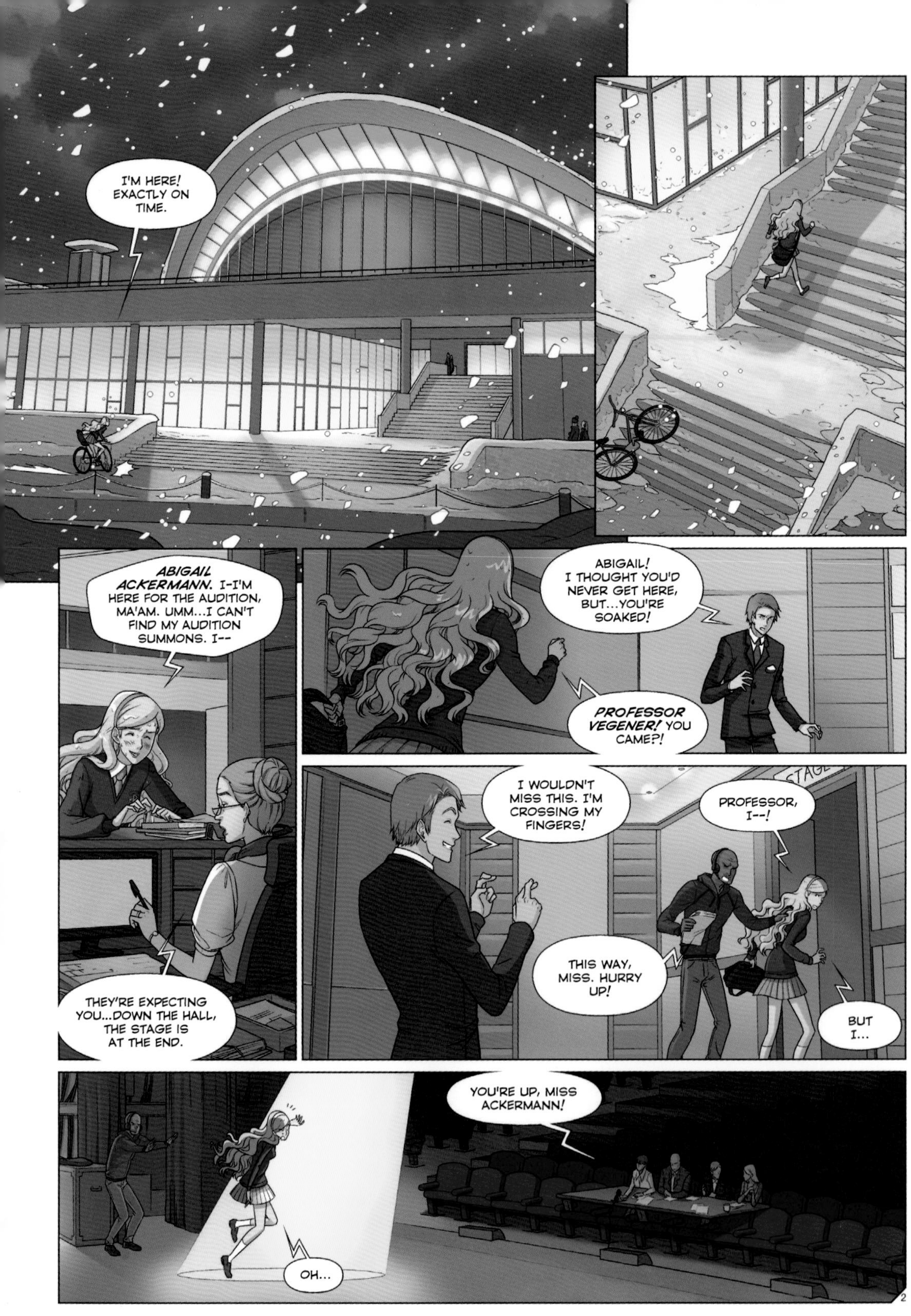

I'M HERE! EXACTLY ON TIME.
ABIGAIL ACKERMANN. I-I'M HERE FOR THE AUDITION, MA'AM. UMM...I CAN'T FIND MY AUDITION SUMMONS. I--
THEY'RE EXPECTING YOU...DOWN THE HALL, THE STAGE IS AT THE END.
ABIGAIL! I THOUGHT YOU'D NEVER GET HERE, BUT...YOU'RE SOAKED!
PROFESSOR VEGENER! YOU CAME?!
I WOULDN'T MISS THIS. I'M CROSSING MY FINGERS!
PROFESSOR, I--!
THIS WAY, MISS. HURRY UP!
BUT I...
YOU'RE UP, MISS ACKERMANN!
OH...
2

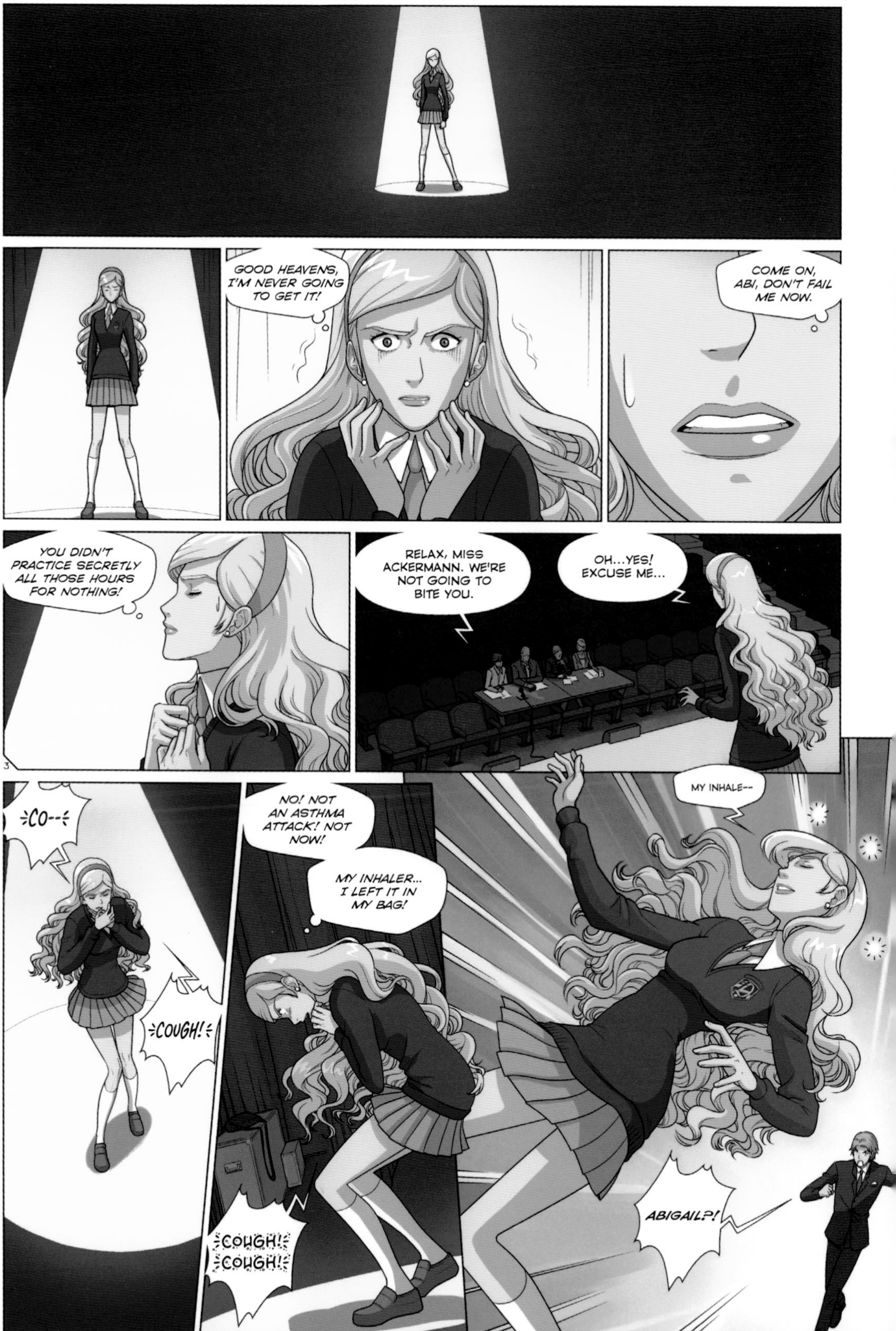
GOOD HEAVENS, I'M NEVER GOING TO GET IT!
COME ON, ABI, DON'T FAIL ME NOW.
YOU DIDN'T PRACTICE SECRETLY ALL THOSE HOURS FOR NOTHING!
RELAX, MISS ACKERMANN. WE'RE NOT GOING TO BITE YOU.
OH...YES! EXCUSE ME...
CO--
COUGH!
NO! NOT AN ASTHMA ATTACK! NOT NOW!
MY INHALER... I LEFT IT IN MY BAG!
COUGH! COUGH!
MY INHALE--
ABIGAIL?!

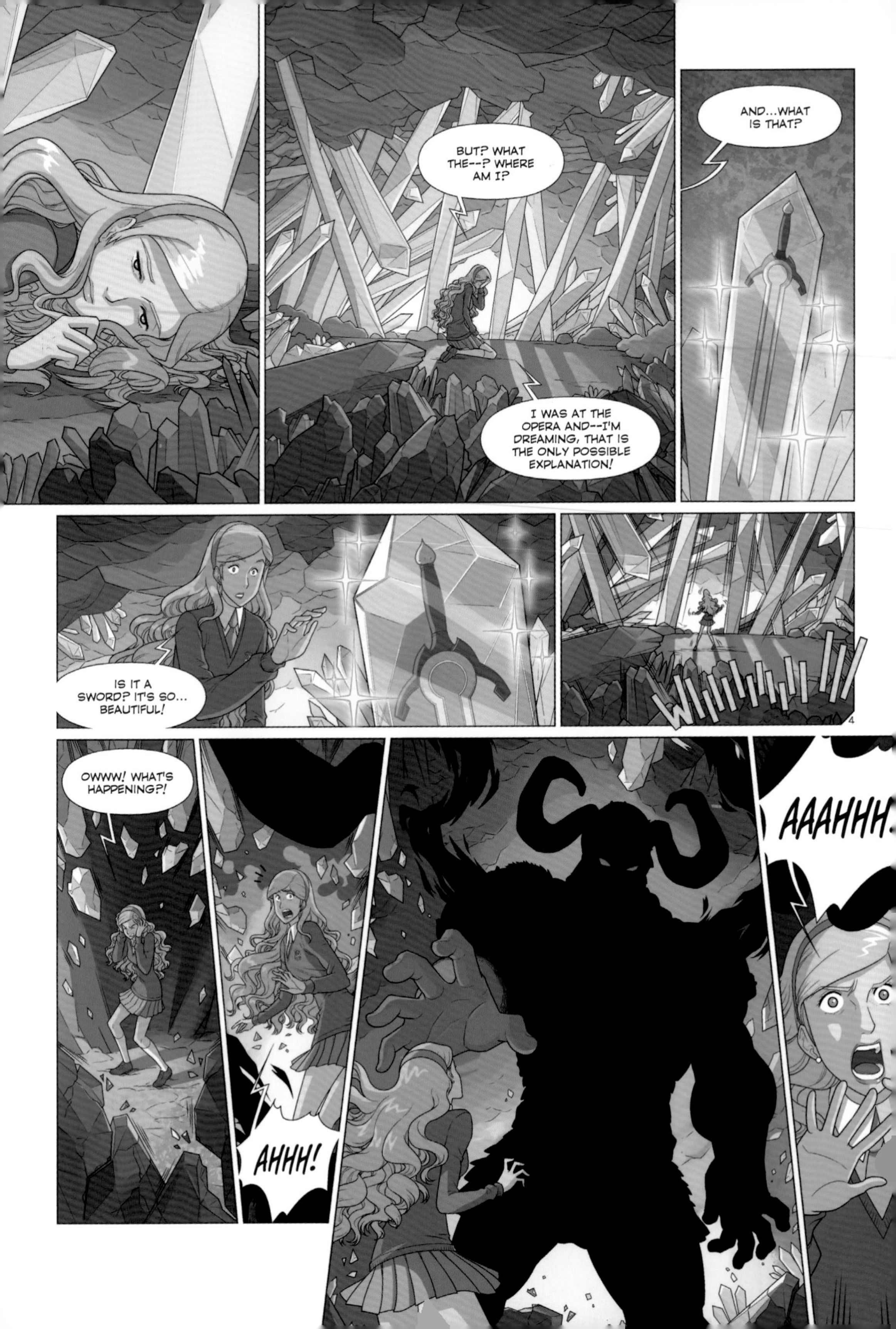
BUT? WHAT THE--? WHERE AM I?
I WAS AT THE OPERA AND--I'M DREAMING, THAT IS THE ONLY POSSIBLE EXPLANATION!
AND...WHAT IS THAT?
IS IT A SWORD? IT'S SO... BEAUTIFUL!
WHIIIIIIIIII
OWWW! WHAT'S HAPPENING?!
AHHH!
AAAHHH

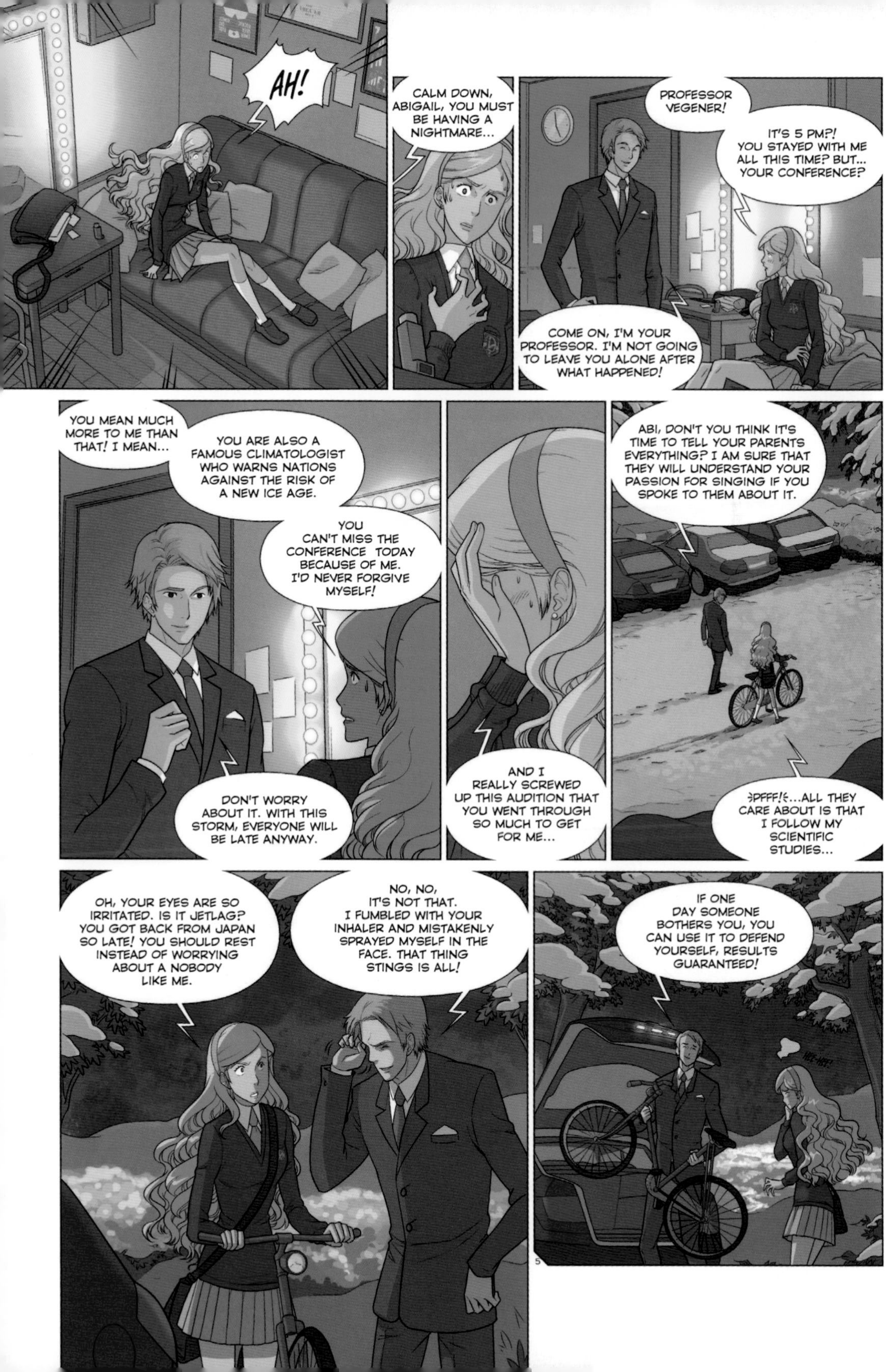
AH!
CALM DOWN, ABIGAIL, YOU MUST BE HAVING A NIGHTMARE...
PROFESSOR VEGENER!
IT'S 5 PM?! YOU STAYED WITH ME ALL THIS TIME? BUT... YOUR CONFERENCE?
COME ON, I'M YOUR PROFESSOR. I'M NOT GOING TO LEAVE YOU ALONE AFTER WHAT HAPPENED!
YOU MEAN MUCH MORE TO ME THAN THAT! I MEAN...
YOU ARE ALSO A FAMOUS CLIMATOLOGIST WHO WARNS NATIONS AGAINST THE RISK OF A NEW ICE AGE.
YOU CAN'T MISS THE CONFERENCE TODAY BECAUSE OF ME. I'D NEVER FORGIVE MYSELF!
DON'T WORRY ABOUT IT. WITH THIS STORM, EVERYONE WILL BE LATE ANYWAY.
AND I REALLY SCREWED UP THIS AUDITION THAT YOU WENT THROUGH SO MUCH TO GET FOR ME...
ABI, DON'T YOU THINK IT'S TIME TO TELL YOUR PARENTS EVERYTHING? I AM SURE THAT THEY WILL UNDERSTAND YOUR PASSION FOR SINGING IF YOU SPOKE TO THEM ABOUT IT.
PFFF!...ALL THEY CARE ABOUT IS THAT I FOLLOW MY SCIENTIFIC STUDIES...
OH, YOUR EYES ARE SO IRRITATED. IS IT JETLAG? YOU GOT BACK FROM JAPAN SO LATE! YOU SHOULD REST INSTEAD OF WORRYING ABOUT A NOBODY LIKE ME.
NO, NO, IT'S NOT THAT. I FUMBLED WITH YOUR INHALER AND MISTAKENLY SPRAYED MYSELF IN THE FACE. THAT THING STINGS IS ALL!
IF ONE DAY SOMEONE BOTHERS YOU, YOU CAN USE IT TO DEFEND YOURSELF, RESULTS GUARANTEED!

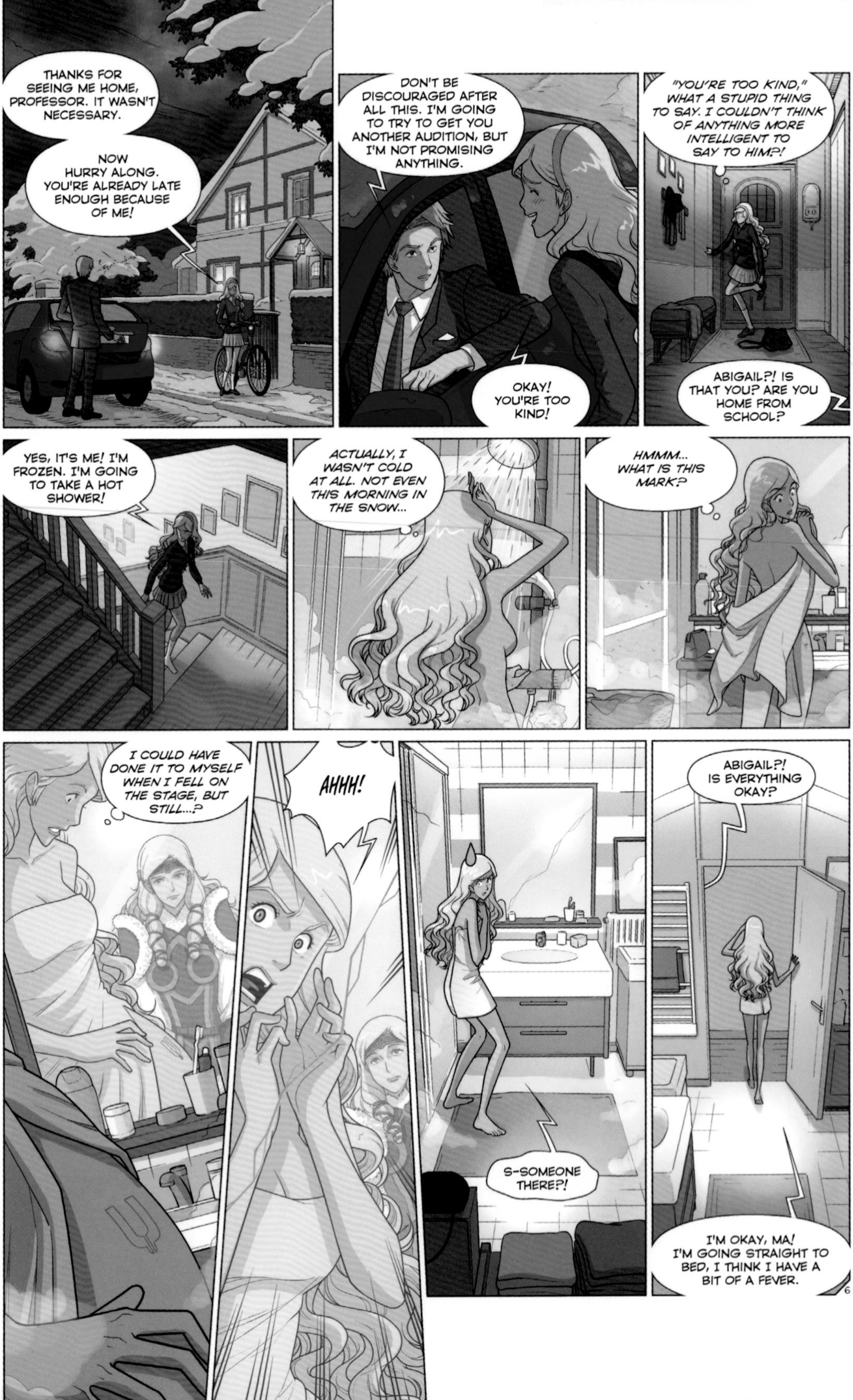
THANKS FOR SEEING ME HOME, PROFESSOR. IT WASN'T NECESSARY.
NOW HURRY ALONG. YOU'RE ALREADY LATE ENOUGH BECAUSE OF ME!
DON'T BE DISCOURAGED AFTER ALL THIS. I'M GOING TO TRY TO GET YOU ANOTHER AUDITION, BUT I'M NOT PROMISING ANYTHING.
OKAY! YOU'RE TOO KIND!
"YOU'RE TOO KIND," WHAT A STUPID THING TO SAY. I COULDN'T THINK OF ANYTHING MORE INTELLIGENT TO SAY TO HIM?!
ABIGAIL?! IS THAT YOU? ARE YOU HOME FROM SCHOOL?
YES, IT'S ME! I'M FROZEN. I'M GOING TO TAKE A HOT SHOWER!
ACTUALLY, I WASN'T COLD AT ALL. NOT EVEN THIS MORNING IN THE SNOW...
HMMM... WHAT IS THIS MARK?
I COULD HAVE DONE IT TO MYSELF WHEN I FELL ON THE STAGE, BUT STILL...?
AHHH!
S-SOMEONE THERE?!
ABIGAIL?! IS EVERYTHING OKAY?
I'M OKAY, MA! I'M GOING STRAIGHT TO BED, I THINK I HAVE A BIT OF A FEVER.

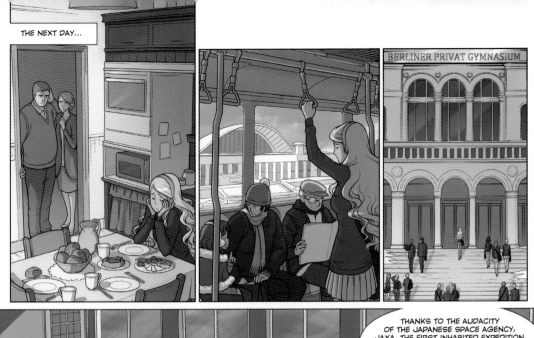

BERLINER PRIVAT GYMNASIUM

THANKS TO THE AUDACITY OF THE JAPANESE SPACE AGENCY, JAXA, THE FIRST INHABITED EXPEDITION HAS JUST RETURNED FROM A VOYAGE OF TWENTY MONTHS TO MARS, OF WHICH FOUR WERE SPENT ON THE SURFACE. THIS FEAT OF MODERN SCIENCE WILL--

AH...

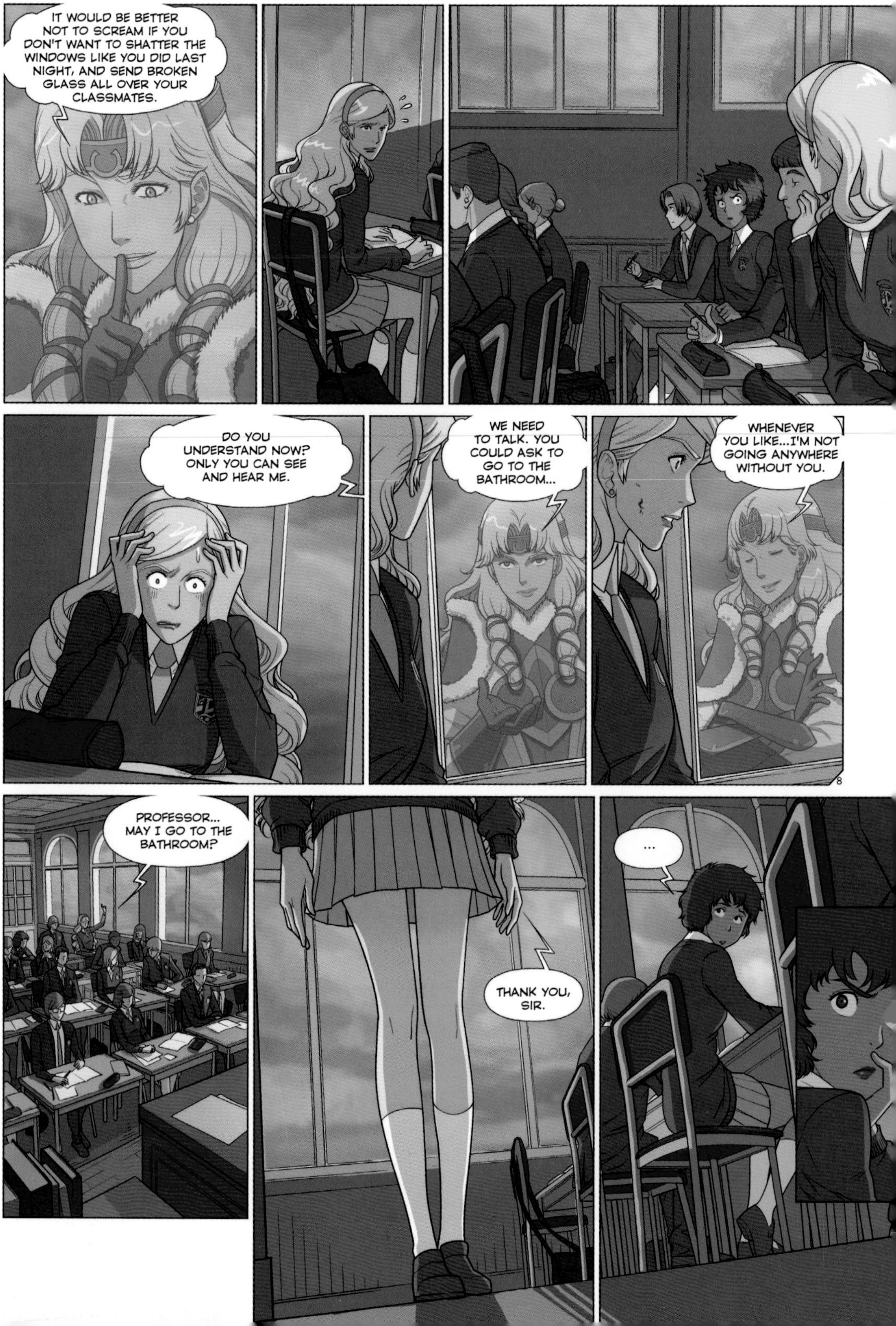
IT WOULD BE BETTER NOT TO SCREAM IF YOU DON'T WANT TO SHATTER THE WINDOWS LIKE YOU DID LAST NIGHT, AND SEND BROKEN GLASS ALL OVER YOUR CLASSMATES.
DO YOU UNDERSTAND NOW? ONLY YOU CAN SEE AND HEAR ME.
WE NEED TO TALK. YOU COULD ASK TO GO TO THE BATHROOM...
WHENEVER YOU LIKE...I'M NOT GOING ANYWHERE WITHOUT YOU.
8
PROFESSOR... MAY I GO TO THE BATHROOM?
THANK YOU, SIR.
...

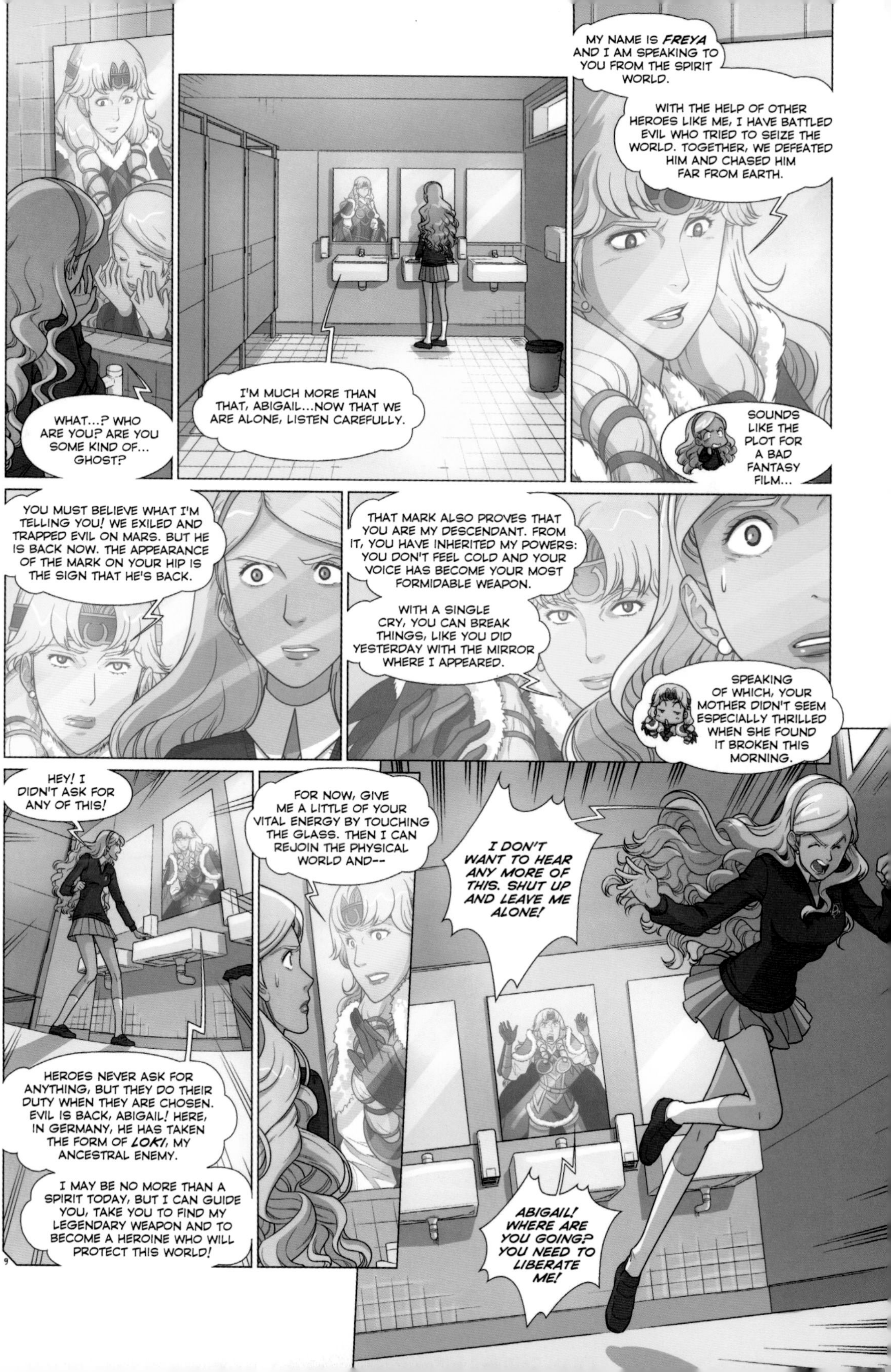
WHAT...? WHO ARE YOU? ARE YOU SOME KIND OF... GHOST?
I'M MUCH MORE THAN THAT, ABIGAIL...NOW THAT WE ARE ALONE, LISTEN CAREFULLY.
MY NAME IS FREYA AND I AM SPEAKING TO YOU FROM THE SPIRIT WORLD.
WITH THE HELP OF OTHER HEROES LIKE ME, I HAVE BATTLED EVIL WHO TRIED TO SEIZE THE WORLD. TOGETHER, WE DEFEATED HIM AND CHASED HIM FAR FROM EARTH.
SOUNDS LIKE THE PLOT FOR A BAD FANTASY FILM...
YOU MUST BELIEVE WHAT I'M TELLING YOU! WE EXILED AND TRAPPED EVIL ON MARS. BUT HE IS BACK NOW. THE APPEARANCE OF THE MARK ON YOUR HIP IS THE SIGN THAT HE'S BACK.
THAT MARK ALSO PROVES THAT YOU ARE MY DESCENDANT. FROM IT, YOU HAVE INHERITED MY POWERS: YOU DON'T FEEL COLD AND YOUR VOICE HAS BECOME YOUR MOST FORMIDABLE WEAPON.
WITH A SINGLE CRY, YOU CAN BREAK THINGS, LIKE YOU DID YESTERDAY WITH THE MIRROR WHERE I APPEARED.
SPEAKING OF WHICH, YOUR MOTHER DIDN'T SEEM ESPECIALLY THRILLED WHEN SHE FOUND IT BROKEN THIS MORNING.
HEY! I DIDN'T ASK FOR ANY OF THIS!
HEROES NEVER ASK FOR ANYTHING, BUT THEY DO THEIR DUTY WHEN THEY ARE CHOSEN. EVIL IS BACK, ABIGAIL! HERE, IN GERMANY, HE HAS TAKEN THE FORM OF LOKI, MY ANCESTRAL ENEMY.
I MAY BE NO MORE THAN A SPIRIT TODAY, BUT I CAN GUIDE YOU, TAKE YOU TO FIND MY LEGENDARY WEAPON AND TO BECOME A HEROINE WHO WILL PROTECT THIS WORLD!
FOR NOW, GIVE ME A LITTLE OF YOUR VITAL ENERGY BY TOUCHING THE GLASS. THEN I CAN REJOIN THE PHYSICAL WORLD AND--
I DON'T WANT TO HEAR ANY MORE OF THIS. SHUT UP AND LEAVE ME ALONE!
ABIGAIL! WHERE ARE YOU GOING? YOU NEED TO LIBERATE ME!

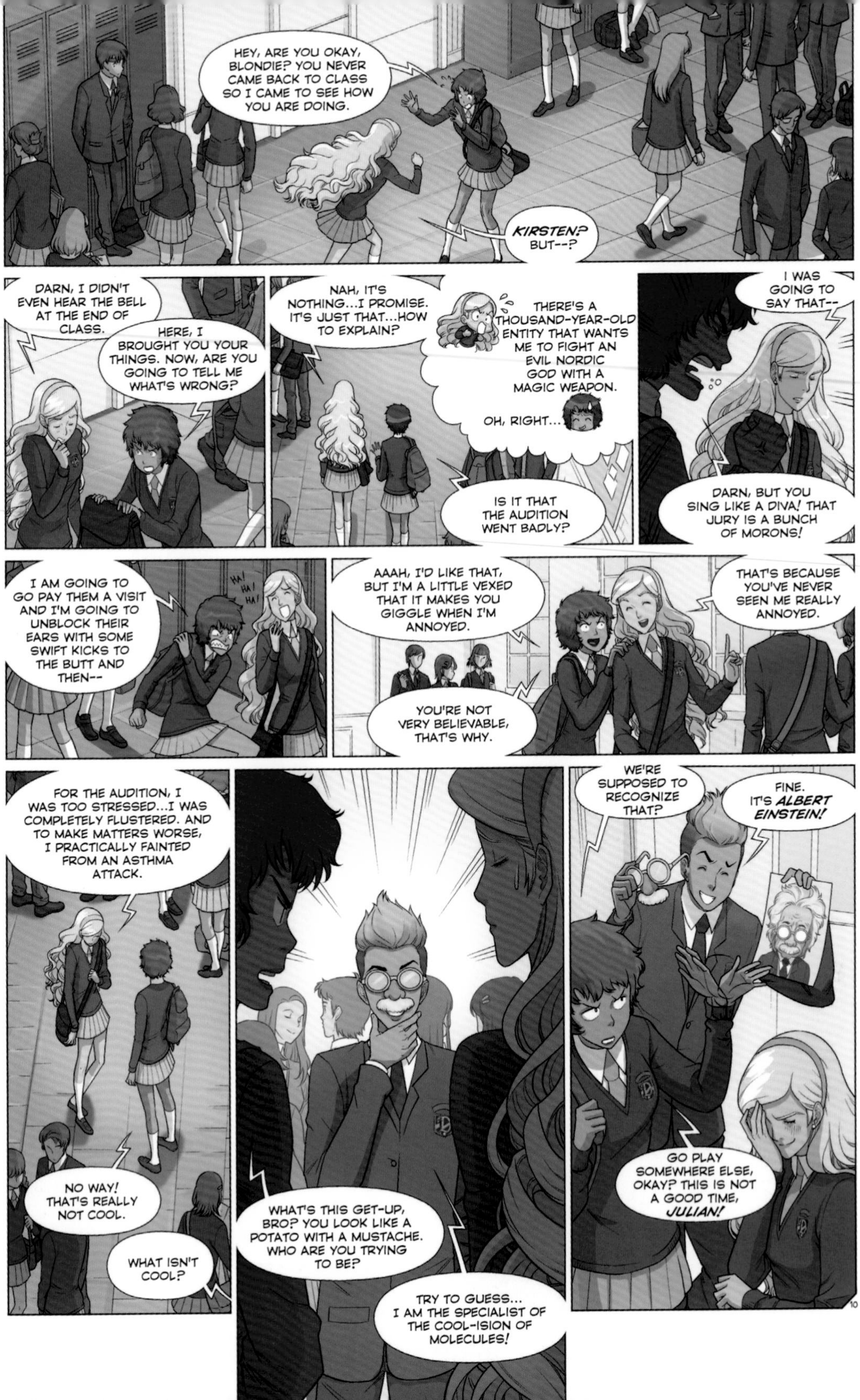
HEY, ARE YOU OKAY, BLONDIE? YOU NEVER CAME BACK TO CLASS SO I CAME TO SEE HOW YOU ARE DOING.
KIRSTEN? BUT--?
DARN, I DIDN'T EVEN HEAR THE BELL AT THE END OF CLASS.
HERE, I BROUGHT YOU YOUR THINGS. NOW, ARE YOU GOING TO TELL ME WHAT'S WRONG?
NAH, IT'S NOTHING...I PROMISE. IT'S JUST THAT...HOW TO EXPLAIN?
THERE'S A THOUSAND-YEAR-OLD ENTITY THAT WANTS ME TO FIGHT AN EVIL NORDIC GOD WITH A MAGIC WEAPON.
OH, RIGHT...
IS IT THAT THE AUDITION WENT BADLY?
I WAS GOING TO SAY THAT--
DARN, BUT YOU SING LIKE A DIVA! THAT JURY IS A BUNCH OF MORONS!
I AM GOING TO GO PAY THEM A VISIT AND I'M GOING TO UNBLOCK THEIR EARS WITH SOME SWIFT KICKS TO THE BUTT AND THEN--
HA! HA! HA!
AAAH, I'D LIKE THAT, BUT I'M A LITTLE VEXED THAT IT MAKES YOU GIGGLE WHEN I'M ANNOYED.
THAT'S BECAUSE YOU'VE NEVER SEEN ME REALLY ANNOYED.
YOU'RE NOT VERY BELIEVABLE, THAT'S WHY.
FOR THE AUDITION, I WAS TOO STRESSED...I WAS COMPLETELY FLUSTERED. AND TO MAKE MATTERS WORSE, I PRACTICALLY FAINTED FROM AN ASTHMA ATTACK.
NO WAY! THAT'S REALLY NOT COOL.
WHAT ISN'T COOL?
WHAT'S THIS GET-UP, BRO? YOU LOOK LIKE A POTATO WITH A MUSTACHE. WHO ARE YOU TRYING TO BE?
TRY TO GUESS... I AM THE SPECIALIST OF THE COOL-ISION OF MOLECULES!
WE'RE SUPPOSED TO RECOGNIZE THAT?
FINE. IT'S ALBERT EINSTEIN!
GO PLAY SOMEWHERE ELSE, OKAY? THIS IS NOT A GOOD TIME, JULIAN!

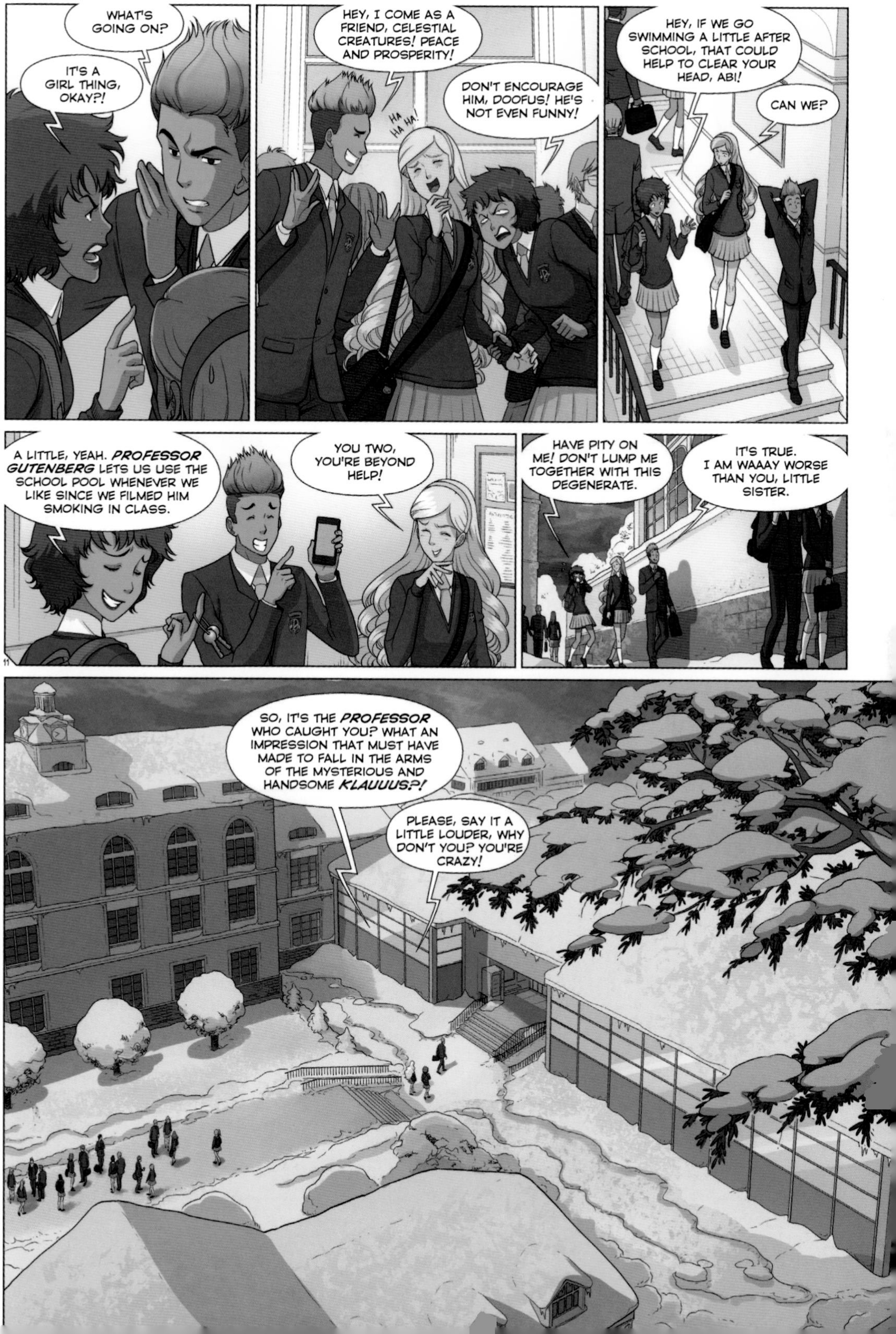
WHAT'S GOING ON?
IT'S A GIRL THING, OKAY?!
HEY, I COME AS A FRIEND, CELESTIAL CREATURES! PEACE AND PROSPERITY!
HA HA HA!
DON'T ENCOURAGE HIM, DOOFUS! HE'S NOT EVEN FUNNY!
HEY, IF WE GO SWIMMING A LITTLE AFTER SCHOOL, THAT COULD HELP TO CLEAR YOUR HEAD, ABI!
CAN WE?
A LITTLE, YEAH. PROFESSOR GUTENBERG LETS US USE THE SCHOOL POOL WHENEVER WE LIKE SINCE WE FILMED HIM SMOKING IN CLASS.
YOU TWO, YOU'RE BEYOND HELP!
HAVE PITY ON ME! DON'T LUMP ME TOGETHER WITH THIS DEGENERATE.
IT'S TRUE. I AM WAAAY WORSE THAN YOU, LITTLE SISTER.
SO, IT'S THE PROFESSOR WHO CAUGHT YOU? WHAT AN IMPRESSION THAT MUST HAVE MADE TO FALL IN THE ARMS OF THE MYSTERIOUS AND HANDSOME KLAUUUS?!
PLEASE, SAY IT A LITTLE LOUDER, WHY DON'T YOU? YOU'RE CRAZY!

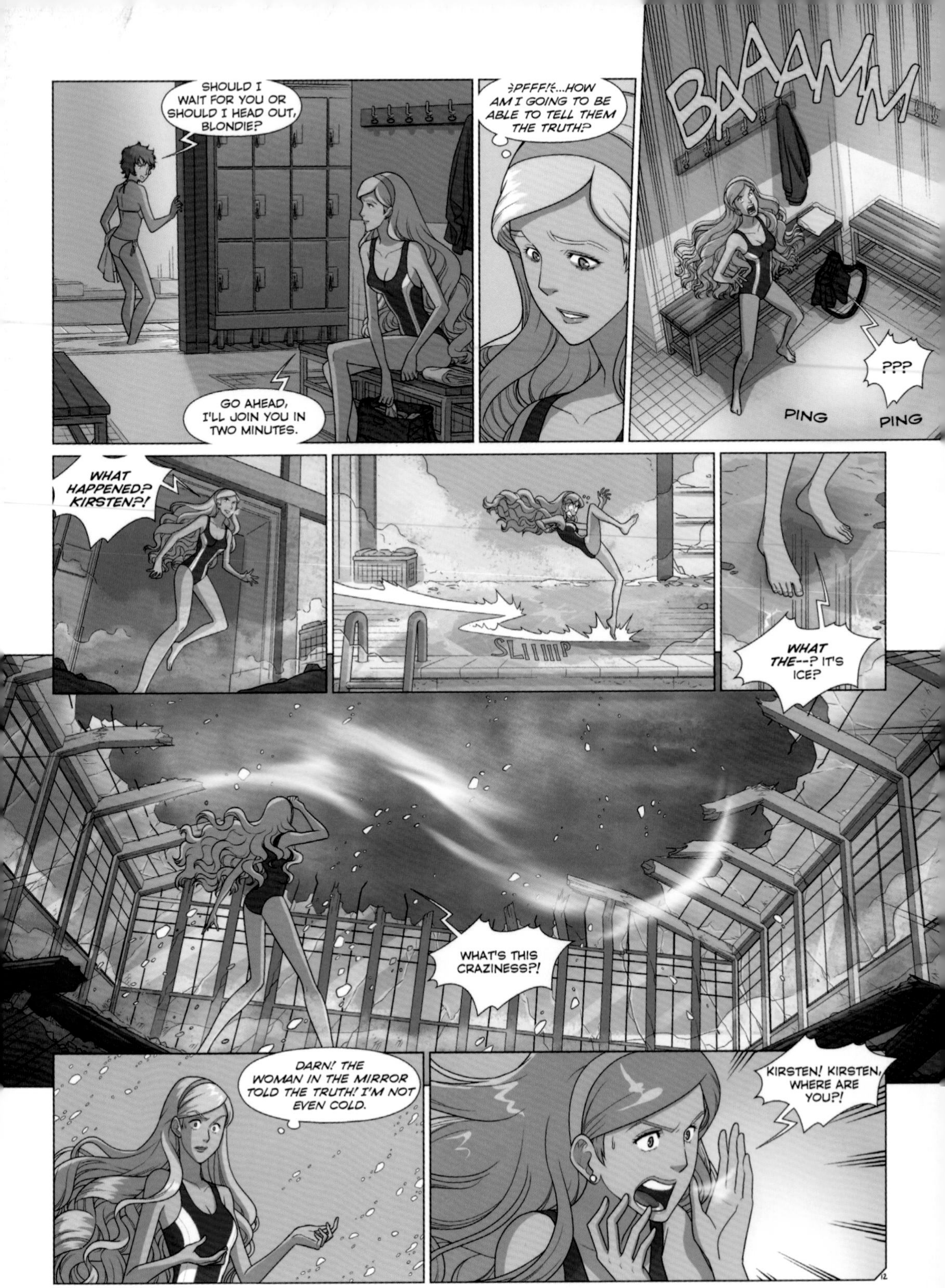
SHOULD I WAIT FOR YOU OR SHOULD I HEAD OUT, BLONDIE?
GO AHEAD, I'LL JOIN YOU IN TWO MINUTES.
PFFFF!...HOW AM I GOING TO BE ABLE TO TELL THEM THE TRUTH?
BAAAMM!!
???
PING
PING
WHAT HAPPENED? KIRSTEN?!
SLIIIIP
WHAT THE--? IT'S ICE?
WHAT'S THIS CRAZINESS?!
DARN! THE WOMAN IN THE MIRROR TOLD THE TRUTH! I'M NOT EVEN COLD.
KIRSTEN! KIRSTEN, WHERE ARE YOU?!

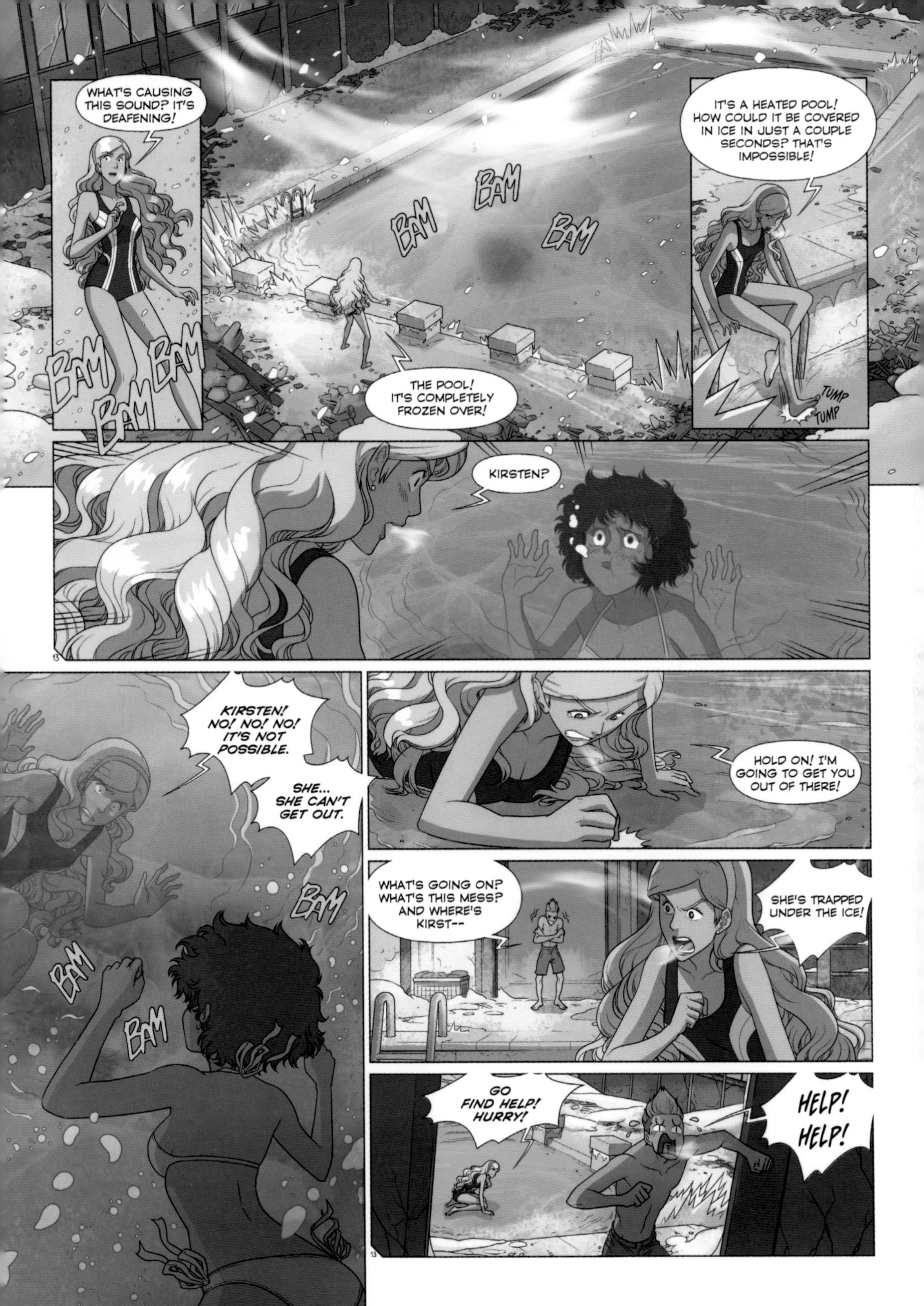
WHAT'S CAUSING THIS SOUND? IT'S DEAFENING!
BAM BAM BAM BAM
BAM BAM BAM
THE POOL! IT'S COMPLETELY FROZEN OVER!
IT'S A HEATED POOL! HOW COULD IT BE COVERED IN ICE IN JUST A COUPLE SECONDS? THAT'S IMPOSSIBLE!
TUMP TUMP
KIRSTEN?
KIRSTEN! NO! NO! NO! IT'S NOT POSSIBLE.
SHE... SHE CAN'T GET OUT.
BAM
BAM
BAM
HOLD ON! I'M GOING TO GET YOU OUT OF THERE!
WHAT'S GOING ON? WHAT'S THIS MESS? AND WHERE'S KIRST--
SHE'S TRAPPED UNDER THE ICE!
GO FIND HELP! HURRY!
HELP! HELP!

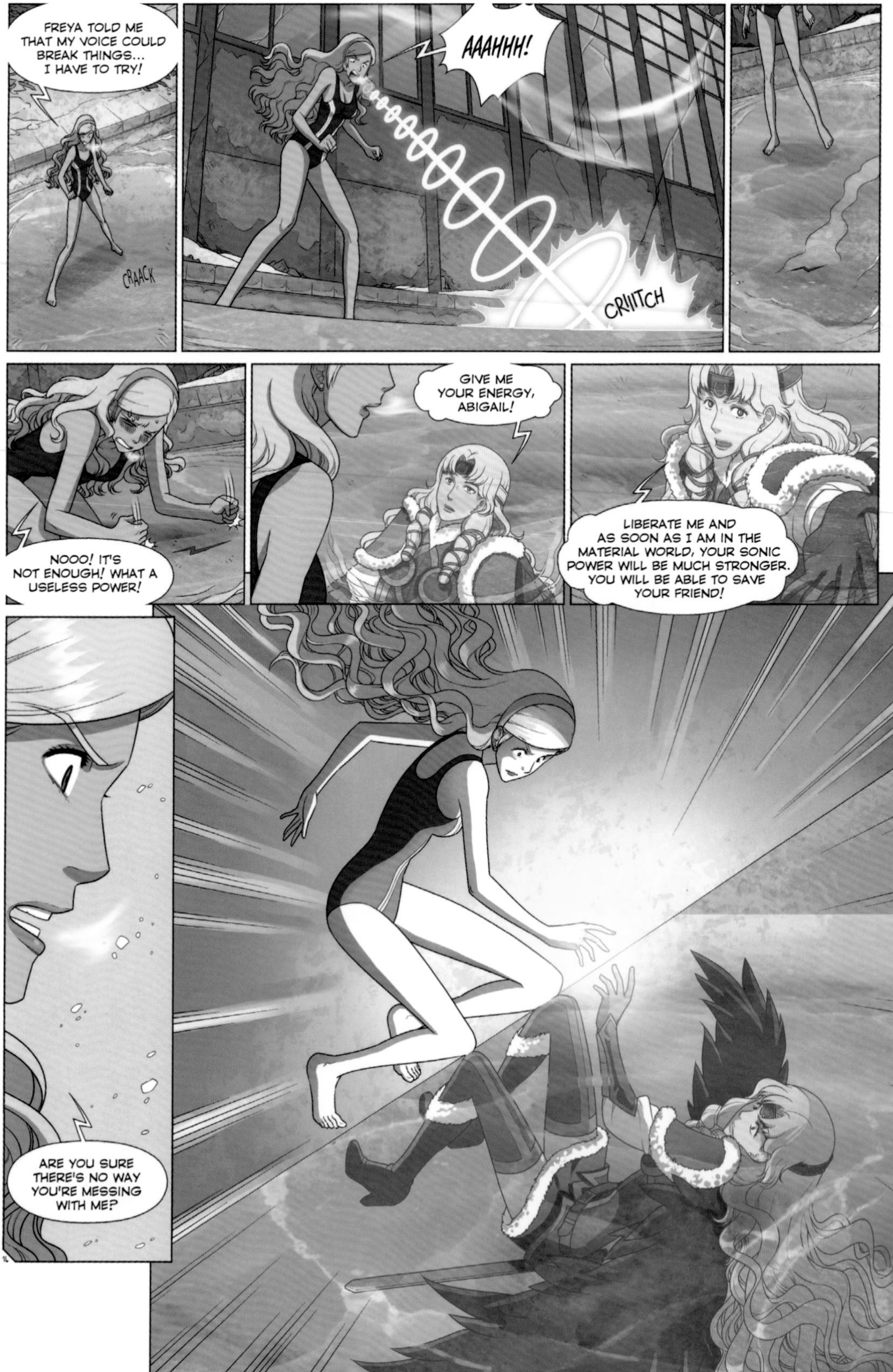

FREYA TOLD ME THAT MY VOICE COULD BREAK THINGS... I HAVE TO TRY!
CRAACK
AAAHHH!
CRIIITCH
NOOO! IT'S NOT ENOUGH! WHAT A USELESS POWER!
GIVE ME YOUR ENERGY, ABIGAIL!
LIBERATE ME AND AS SOON AS I AM IN THE MATERIAL WORLD, YOUR SONIC POWER WILL BE MUCH STRONGER. YOU WILL BE ABLE TO SAVE YOUR FRIEND!
ARE YOU SURE THERE'S NO WAY YOU'RE MESSING WITH ME?

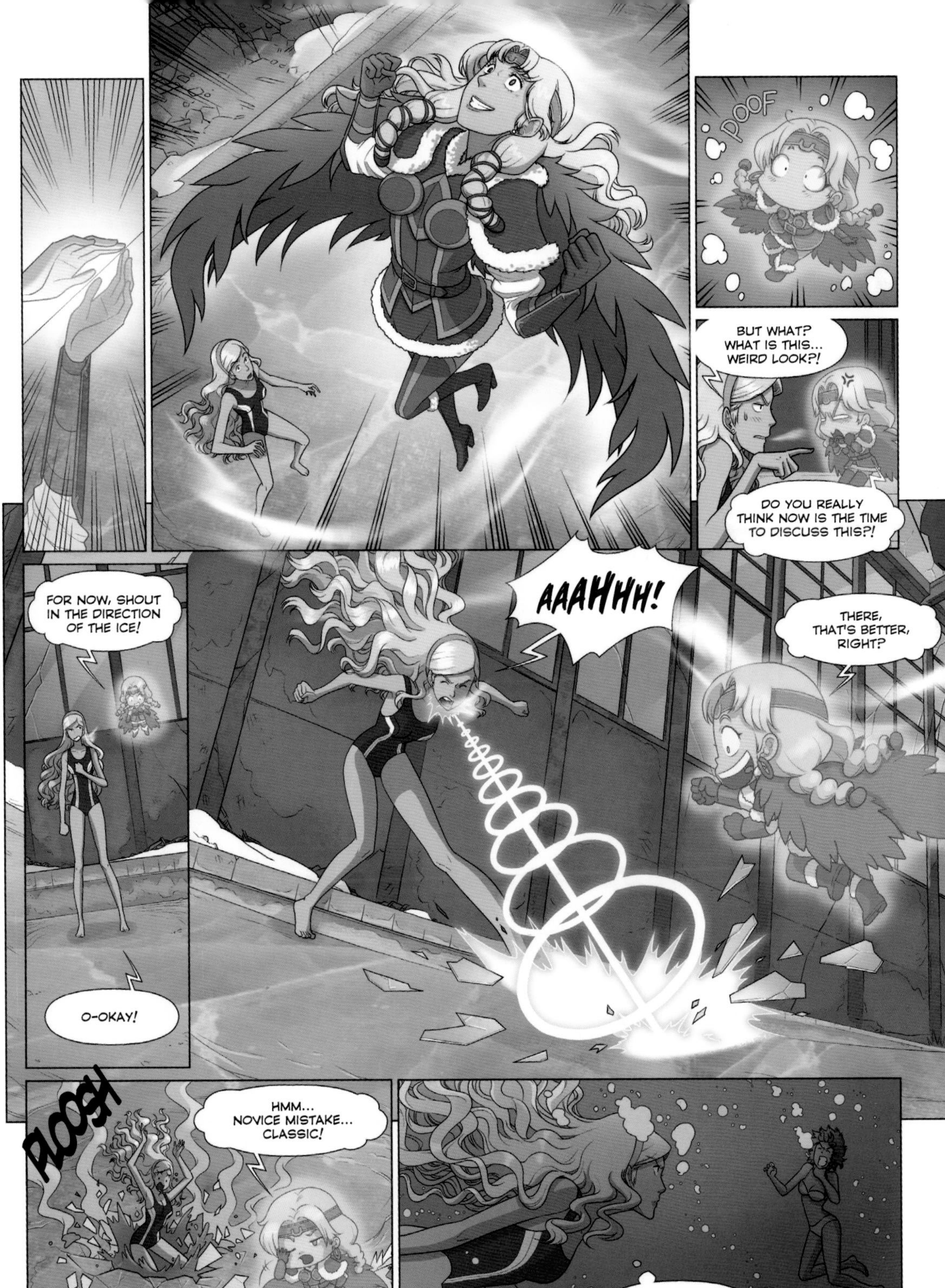
POOF
BUT WHAT? WHAT IS THIS... WEIRD LOOK?!
DO YOU REALLY THINK NOW IS THE TIME TO DISCUSS THIS?!
FOR NOW, SHOUT IN THE DIRECTION OF THE ICE!
O-OKAY!
AAAHHH!
THERE, THAT'S BETTER, RIGHT?
PLOOSH
HMM... NOVICE MISTAKE... CLASSIC!
HOLD ON, KIRSTEN! I'M COMING!

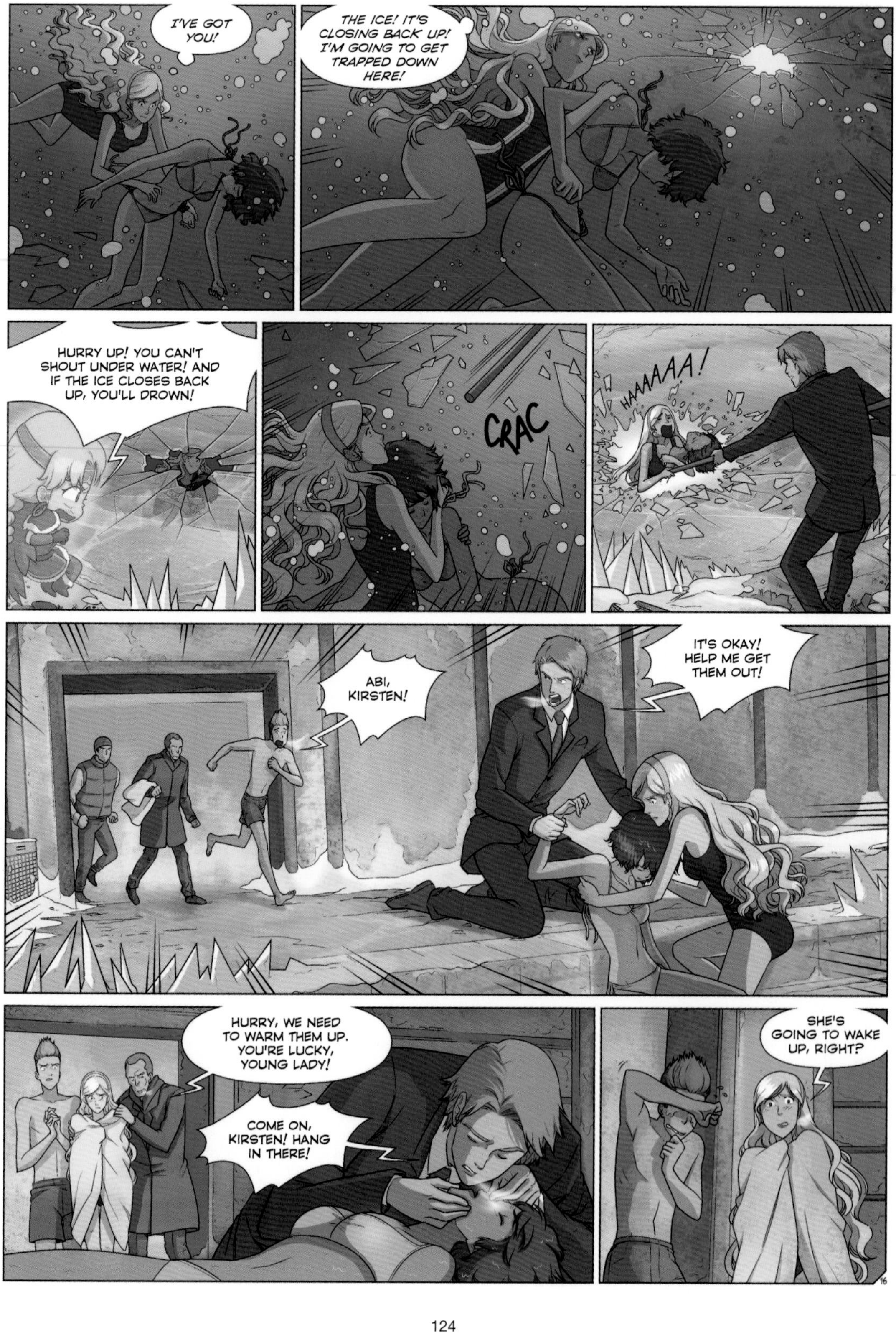

I'VE GOT YOU!
THE ICE! IT'S CLOSING BACK UP! I'M GOING TO GET TRAPPED DOWN HERE!
HURRY UP! YOU CAN'T SHOUT UNDER WATER! AND IF THE ICE CLOSES BACK UP, YOU'LL DROWN!
CRAC
HAAAAAA!
ABI, KIRSTEN!
IT'S OKAY! HELP ME GET THEM OUT!
HURRY, WE NEED TO WARM THEM UP. YOU'RE LUCKY, YOUNG LADY!
COME ON, KIRSTEN! HANG IN THERE!
SHE'S GOING TO WAKE UP, RIGHT?
16

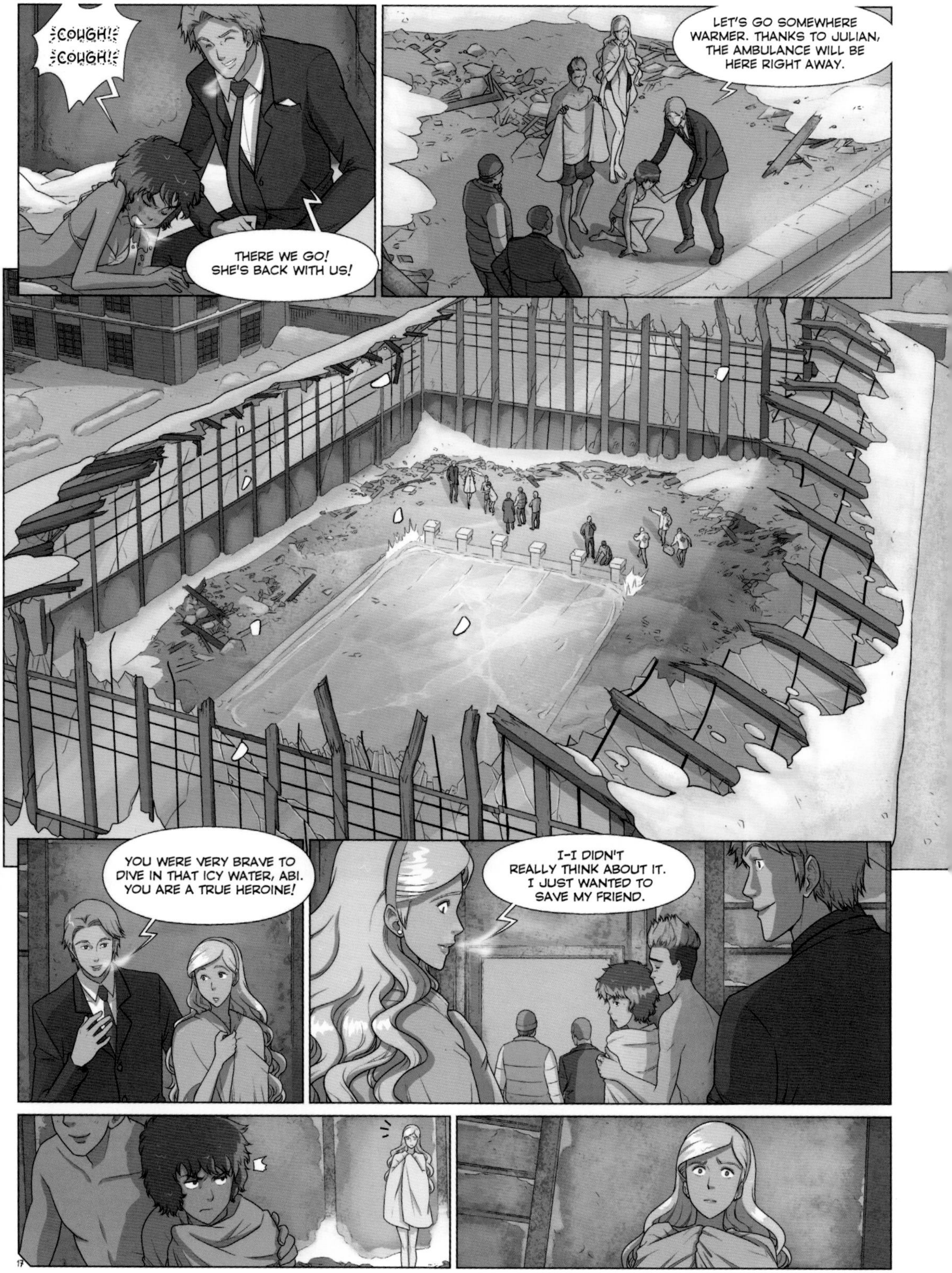
COUGH!! COUGH!!
THERE WE GO! SHE'S BACK WITH US!
LET'S GO SOMEWHERE WARMER. THANKS TO JULIAN, THE AMBULANCE WILL BE HERE RIGHT AWAY.
YOU WERE VERY BRAVE TO DIVE IN THAT ICY WATER, ABI. YOU ARE A TRUE HEROINE!
I-I DIDN'T REALLY THINK ABOUT IT. I JUST WANTED TO SAVE MY FRIEND.

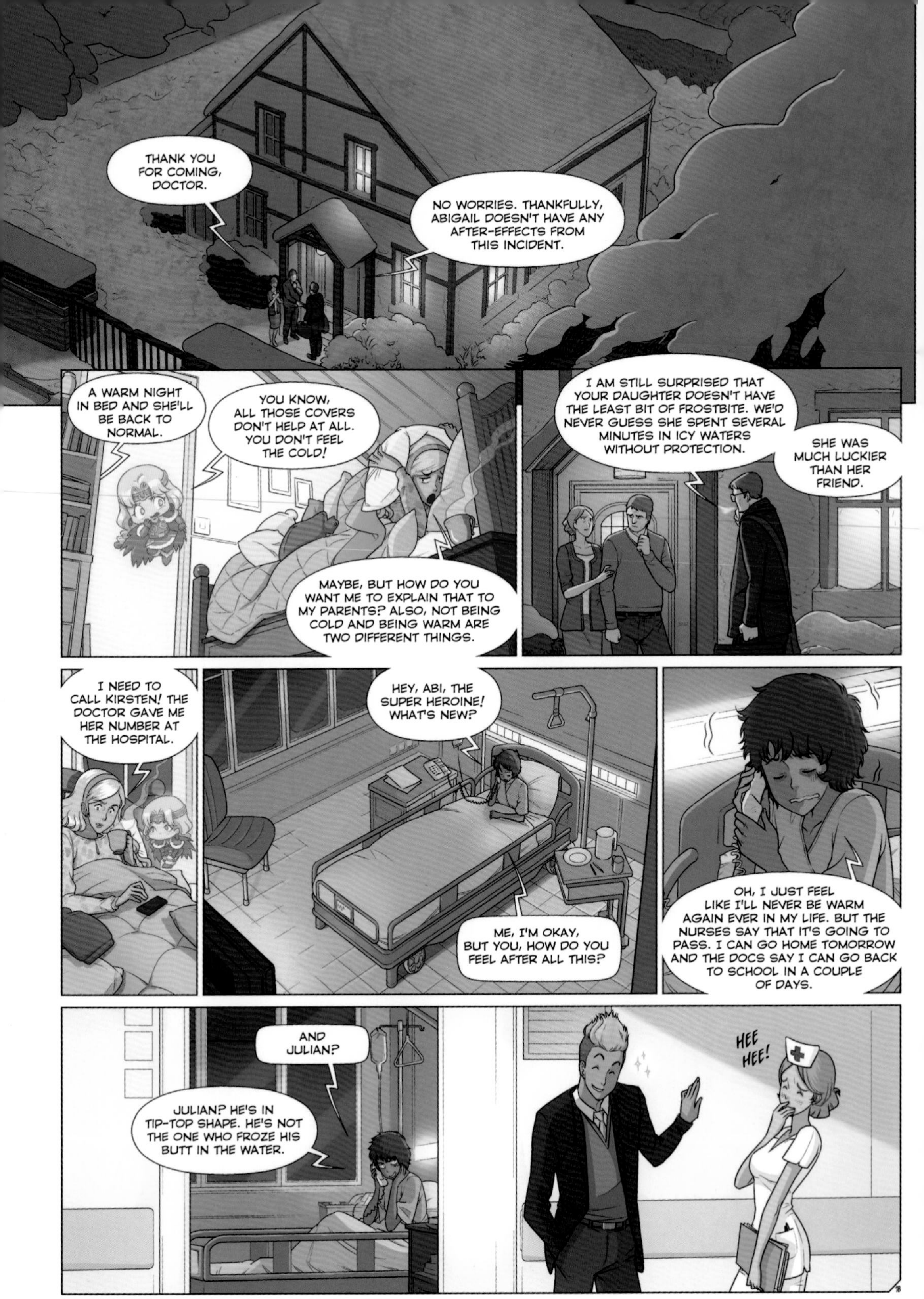
THANK YOU FOR COMING, DOCTOR.
NO WORRIES. THANKFULLY, ABIGAIL DOESN'T HAVE ANY AFTER-EFFECTS FROM THIS INCIDENT.
A WARM NIGHT IN BED AND SHE'LL BE BACK TO NORMAL.
YOU KNOW, ALL THOSE COVERS DON'T HELP AT ALL. YOU DON'T FEEL THE COLD!
MAYBE, BUT HOW DO YOU WANT ME TO EXPLAIN THAT TO MY PARENTS? ALSO, NOT BEING COLD AND BEING WARM ARE TWO DIFFERENT THINGS.
I AM STILL SURPRISED THAT YOUR DAUGHTER DOESN'T HAVE THE LEAST BIT OF FROSTBITE. WE'D NEVER GUESS SHE SPENT SEVERAL MINUTES IN ICY WATERS WITHOUT PROTECTION.
SHE WAS MUCH LUCKIER THAN HER FRIEND.
I NEED TO CALL KIRSTEN! THE DOCTOR GAVE ME HER NUMBER AT THE HOSPITAL.
HEY, ABI, THE SUPER HEROINE! WHAT'S NEW?
ME, I'M OKAY, BUT YOU, HOW DO YOU FEEL AFTER ALL THIS?
OH, I JUST FEEL LIKE I'LL NEVER BE WARM AGAIN EVER IN MY LIFE. BUT THE NURSES SAY THAT IT'S GOING TO PASS. I CAN GO HOME TOMORROW AND THE DOCS SAY I CAN GO BACK TO SCHOOL IN A COUPLE OF DAYS.
AND JULIAN?
JULIAN? HE'S IN TIP-TOP SHAPE. HE'S NOT THE ONE WHO FROZE HIS BUTT IN THE WATER.
HEE HEE!

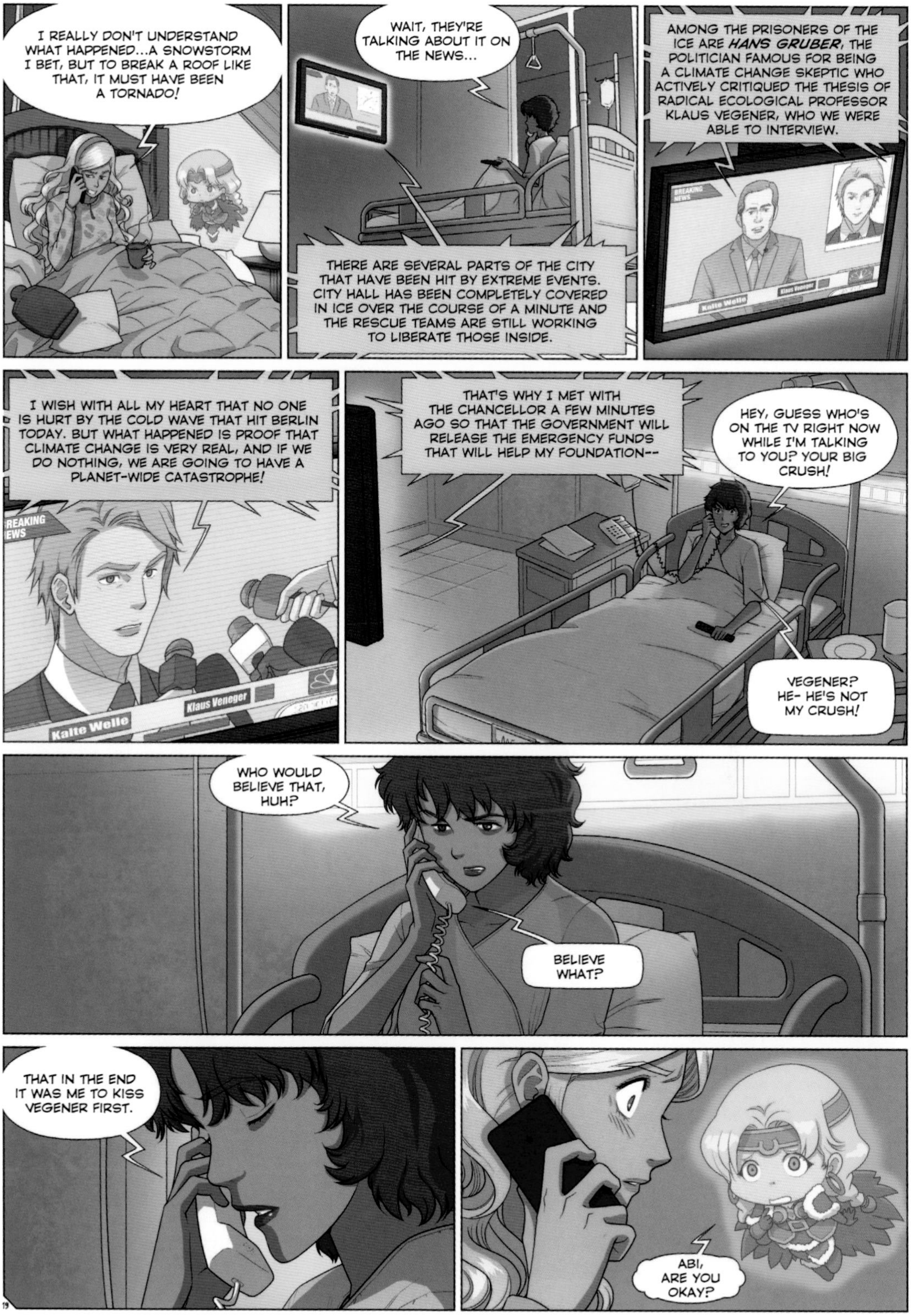
I REALLY DON'T UNDERSTAND WHAT HAPPENED...A SNOWSTORM I BET, BUT TO BREAK A ROOF LIKE THAT, IT MUST HAVE BEEN A TORNADO!
WAIT, THEY'RE TALKING ABOUT IT ON THE NEWS...
THERE ARE SEVERAL PARTS OF THE CITY THAT HAVE BEEN HIT BY EXTREME EVENTS. CITY HALL HAS BEEN COMPLETELY COVERED IN ICE OVER THE COURSE OF A MINUTE AND THE RESCUE TEAMS ARE STILL WORKING TO LIBERATE THOSE INSIDE.
AMONG THE PRISONERS OF THE ICE ARE HANS GRUBER, THE POLITICIAN FAMOUS FOR BEING A CLIMATE CHANGE SKEPTIC WHO ACTIVELY CRITIQUED THE THESIS OF RADICAL ECOLOGICAL PROFESSOR KLAUS VEGENER, WHO WE WERE ABLE TO INTERVIEW.
I WISH WITH ALL MY HEART THAT NO ONE IS HURT BY THE COLD WAVE THAT HIT BERLIN TODAY. BUT WHAT HAPPENED IS PROOF THAT CLIMATE CHANGE IS VERY REAL, AND IF WE DO NOTHING, WE ARE GOING TO HAVE A PLANET-WIDE CATASTROPHE!
Klaus Veneger
Kalte Welle
THAT'S WHY I MET WITH THE CHANCELLOR A FEW MINUTES AGO SO THAT THE GOVERNMENT WILL RELEASE THE EMERGENCY FUNDS THAT WILL HELP MY FOUNDATION--
HEY, GUESS WHO'S ON THE TV RIGHT NOW WHILE I'M TALKING TO YOU? YOUR BIG CRUSH!
VEGENER? HE- HE'S NOT MY CRUSH!
WHO WOULD BELIEVE THAT, HUH?
BELIEVE WHAT?
THAT IN THE END IT WAS ME TO KISS VEGENER FIRST.
ABI, ARE YOU OKAY?

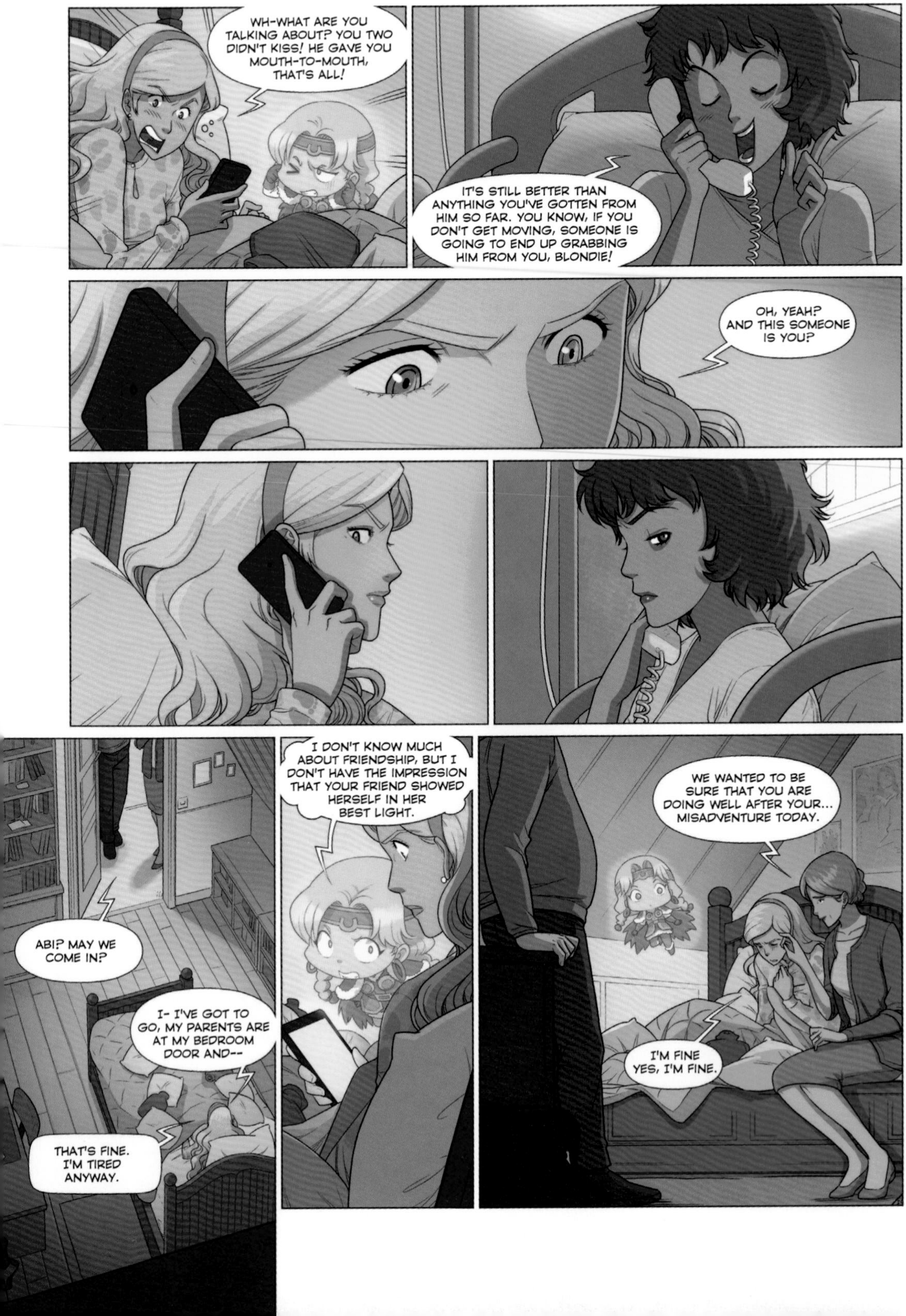
WH-WHAT ARE YOU TALKING ABOUT? YOU TWO DIDN'T KISS! HE GAVE YOU MOUTH-TO-MOUTH, THAT'S ALL!
IT'S STILL BETTER THAN ANYTHING YOU'VE GOTTEN FROM HIM SO FAR. YOU KNOW, IF YOU DON'T GET MOVING, SOMEONE IS GOING TO END UP GRABBING HIM FROM YOU, BLONDIE!
OH, YEAH? AND THIS SOMEONE IS YOU?
ABI? MAY WE COME IN?
I- I'VE GOT TO GO, MY PARENTS ARE AT MY BEDROOM DOOR AND--
THAT'S FINE. I'M TIRED ANYWAY.
I DON'T KNOW MUCH ABOUT FRIENDSHIP, BUT I DON'T HAVE THE IMPRESSION THAT YOUR FRIEND SHOWED HERSELF IN HER BEST LIGHT.
WE WANTED TO BE SURE THAT YOU ARE DOING WELL AFTER YOUR... MISADVENTURE TODAY.
I'M FINE YES, I'M FINE.

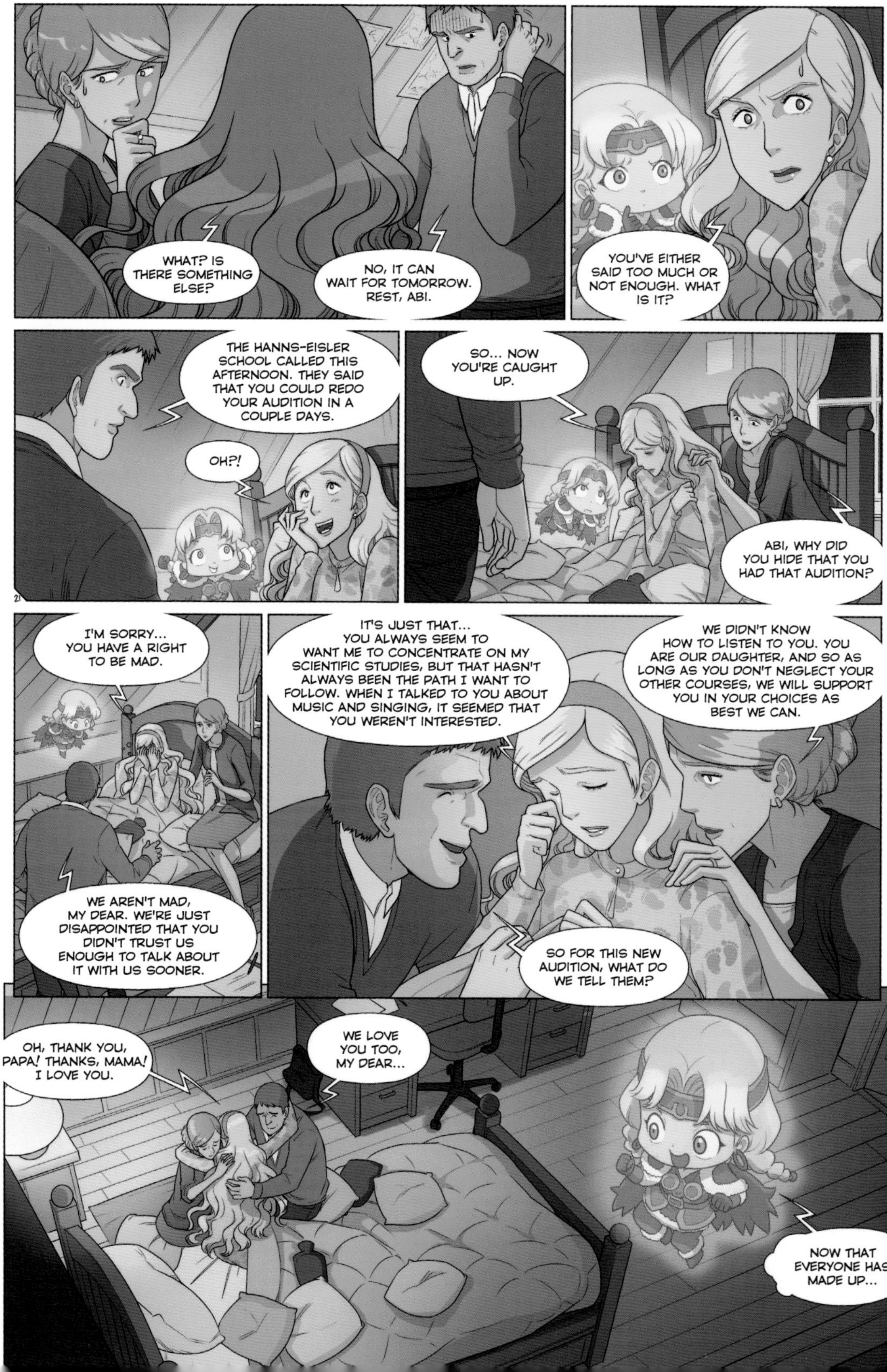
WHAT? IS THERE SOMETHING ELSE?
NO, IT CAN WAIT FOR TOMORROW. REST, ABI.
YOU'VE EITHER SAID TOO MUCH OR NOT ENOUGH. WHAT IS IT?
THE HANNS-EISLER SCHOOL CALLED THIS AFTERNOON. THEY SAID THAT YOU COULD REDO YOUR AUDITION IN A COUPLE DAYS.
OH?!
SO... NOW YOU'RE CAUGHT UP.
ABI, WHY DID YOU HIDE THAT YOU HAD THAT AUDITION?
I'M SORRY... YOU HAVE A RIGHT TO BE MAD.
WE AREN'T MAD, MY DEAR. WE'RE JUST DISAPPOINTED THAT YOU DIDN'T TRUST US ENOUGH TO TALK ABOUT IT WITH US SOONER.
IT'S JUST THAT... YOU ALWAYS SEEM TO WANT ME TO CONCENTRATE ON MY SCIENTIFIC STUDIES, BUT THAT HASN'T ALWAYS BEEN THE PATH I WANT TO FOLLOW. WHEN I TALKED TO YOU ABOUT MUSIC AND SINGING, IT SEEMED THAT YOU WEREN'T INTERESTED.
WE DIDN'T KNOW HOW TO LISTEN TO YOU. YOU ARE OUR DAUGHTER, AND SO AS LONG AS YOU DON'T NEGLECT YOUR OTHER COURSES, WE WILL SUPPORT YOU IN YOUR CHOICES AS BEST WE CAN.
SO FOR THIS NEW AUDITION, WHAT DO WE TELL THEM?
OH, THANK YOU, PAPA! THANKS, MAMA! I LOVE YOU.
WE LOVE YOU TOO, MY DEAR...
NOW THAT EVERYONE HAS MADE UP...

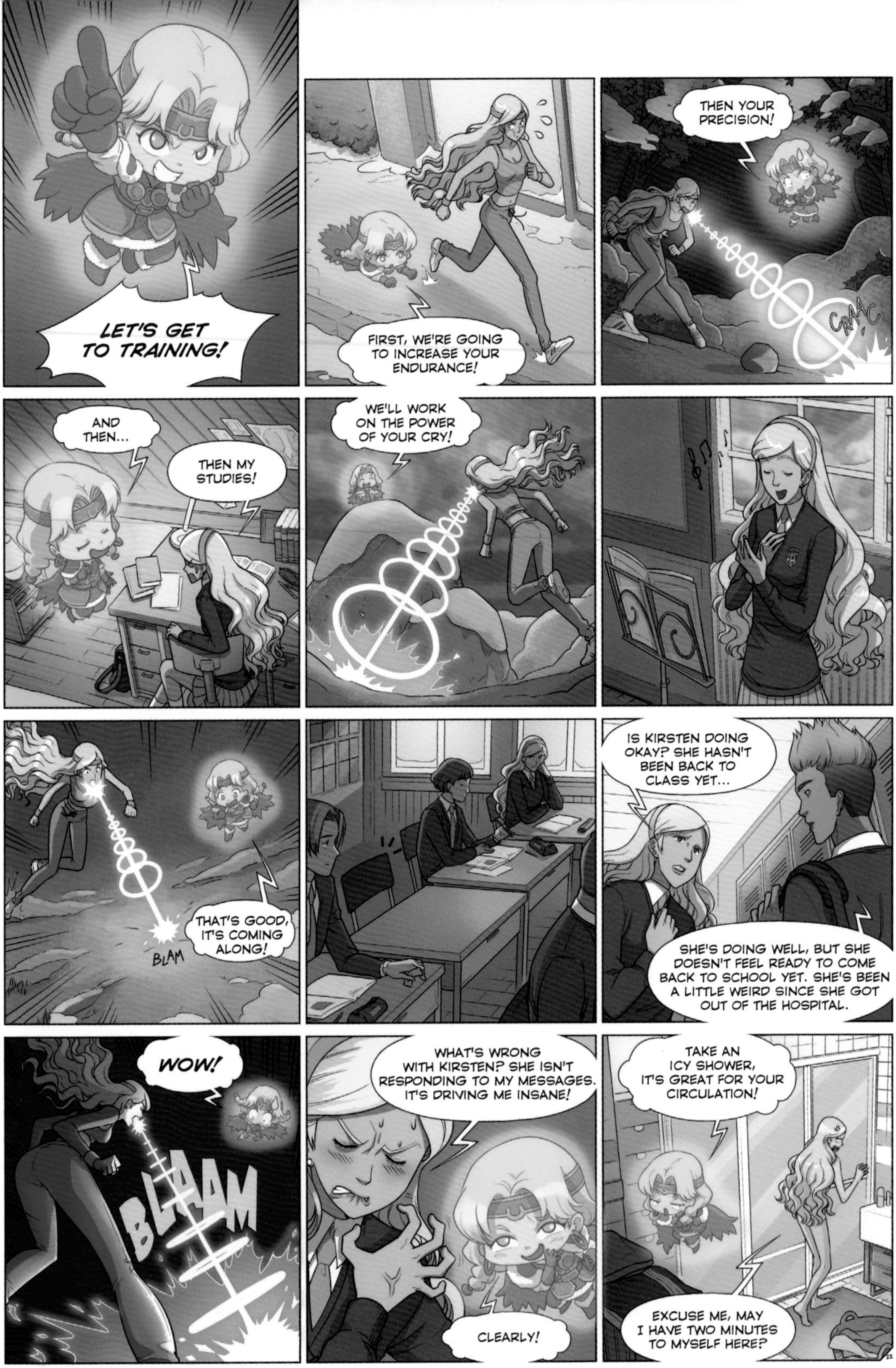

LET'S GET TO TRAINING!
FIRST, WE'RE GOING TO INCREASE YOUR ENDURANCE!
THEN YOUR PRECISION!
CRAAC
AND THEN...
THEN MY STUDIES!
WE'LL WORK ON THE POWER OF YOUR CRY!
THAT'S GOOD, IT'S COMING ALONG!
BLAM
IS KIRSTEN DOING OKAY? SHE HASN'T BEEN BACK TO CLASS YET...
SHE'S DOING WELL, BUT SHE DOESN'T FEEL READY TO COME BACK TO SCHOOL YET. SHE'S BEEN A LITTLE WEIRD SINCE SHE GOT OUT OF THE HOSPITAL.
WOW!
BLAAM
WHAT'S WRONG WITH KIRSTEN? SHE ISN'T RESPONDING TO MY MESSAGES. IT'S DRIVING ME INSANE!
CLEARLY!
TAKE AN ICY SHOWER, IT'S GREAT FOR YOUR CIRCULATION!
EXCUSE ME, MAY I HAVE TWO MINUTES TO MYSELF HERE?

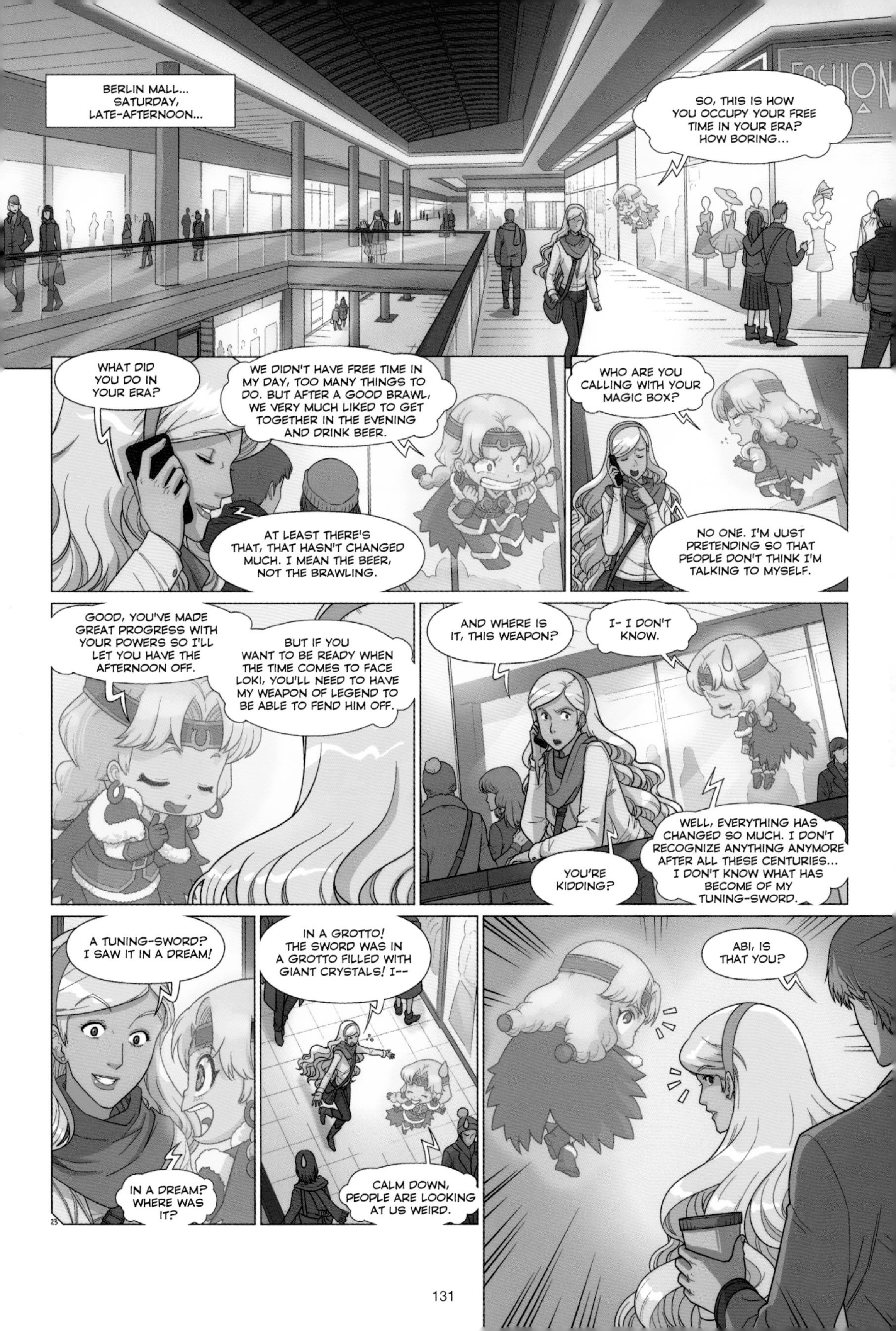
BERLIN MALL... SATURDAY, LATE-AFTERNOON...
SO, THIS IS HOW YOU OCCUPY YOUR FREE TIME IN YOUR ERA? HOW BORING...
WHAT DID YOU DO IN YOUR ERA?
WE DIDN'T HAVE FREE TIME IN MY DAY, TOO MANY THINGS TO DO. BUT AFTER A GOOD BRAWL, WE VERY MUCH LIKED TO GET TOGETHER IN THE EVENING AND DRINK BEER.
AT LEAST THERE'S THAT, THAT HASN'T CHANGED MUCH. I MEAN THE BEER, NOT THE BRAWLING.
WHO ARE YOU CALLING WITH YOUR MAGIC BOX?
NO ONE. I'M JUST PRETENDING SO THAT PEOPLE DON'T THINK I'M TALKING TO MYSELF.
GOOD, YOU'VE MADE GREAT PROGRESS WITH YOUR POWERS SO I'LL LET YOU HAVE THE AFTERNOON OFF.
BUT IF YOU WANT TO BE READY WHEN THE TIME COMES TO FACE LOKI, YOU'LL NEED TO HAVE MY WEAPON OF LEGEND TO BE ABLE TO FEND HIM OFF.
AND WHERE IS IT, THIS WEAPON?
I- I DON'T KNOW.
WELL, EVERYTHING HAS CHANGED SO MUCH. I DON'T RECOGNIZE ANYTHING ANYMORE AFTER ALL THESE CENTURIES... I DON'T KNOW WHAT HAS BECOME OF MY TUNING-SWORD.
YOU'RE KIDDING?
A TUNING-SWORD? I SAW IT IN A DREAM!
IN A DREAM? WHERE WAS IT?
IN A GROTTO! THE SWORD WAS IN A GROTTO FILLED WITH GIANT CRYSTALS! I--
CALM DOWN, PEOPLE ARE LOOKING AT US WEIRD.
ABI, IS THAT YOU?
23

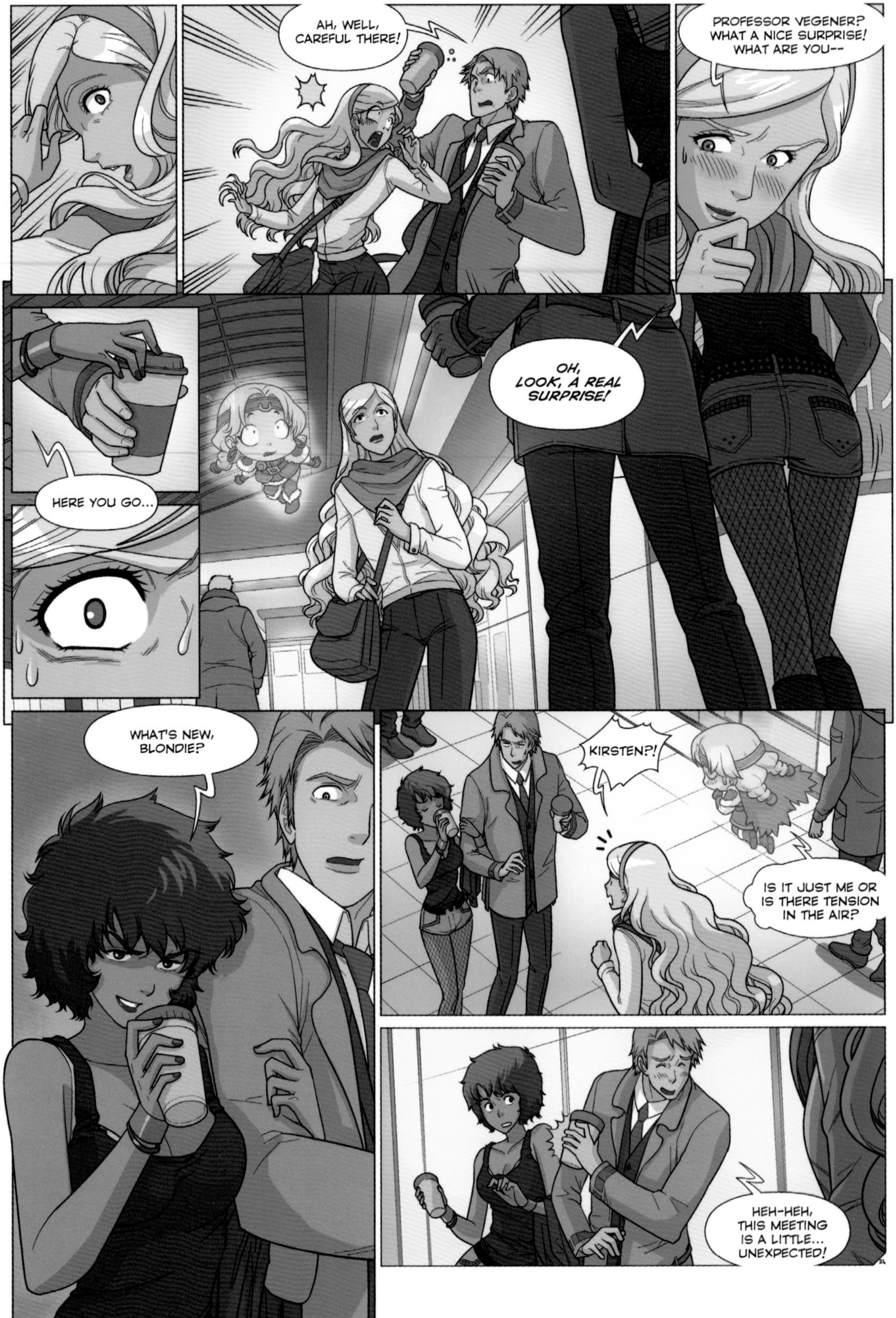
AH, WELL, CAREFUL THERE!
PROFESSOR VEGENER? WHAT A NICE SURPRISE! WHAT ARE YOU--
HERE YOU GO...
OH, LOOK, A REAL SURPRISE!
WHAT'S NEW, BLONDIE?
KIRSTEN?!
IS IT JUST ME OR IS THERE TENSION IN THE AIR?
HEH-HEH, THIS MEETING IS A LITTLE... UNEXPECTED!

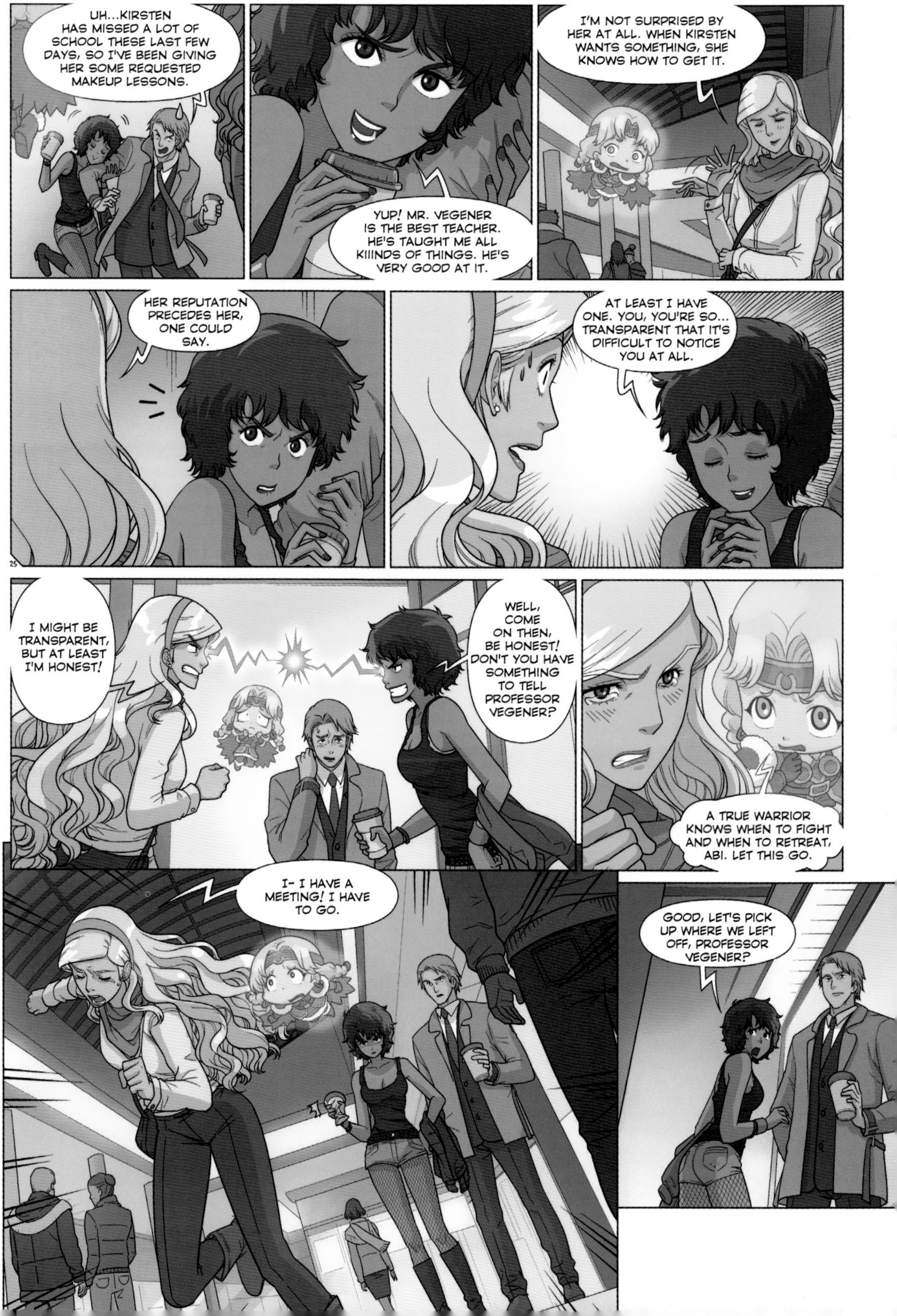
UH...KIRSTEN HAS MISSED A LOT OF SCHOOL THESE LAST FEW DAYS, SO I'VE BEEN GIVING HER SOME REQUESTED MAKEUP LESSONS.
YUP! MR. VEGENER IS THE BEST TEACHER. HE'S TAUGHT ME ALL KIIINDS OF THINGS. HE'S VERY GOOD AT IT.
I'M NOT SURPRISED BY HER AT ALL. WHEN KIRSTEN WANTS SOMETHING, SHE KNOWS HOW TO GET IT.
HER REPUTATION PRECEDES HER, ONE COULD SAY.
AT LEAST I HAVE ONE. YOU, YOU'RE SO... TRANSPARENT THAT IT'S DIFFICULT TO NOTICE YOU AT ALL.
I MIGHT BE TRANSPARENT, BUT AT LEAST I'M HONEST!
WELL, COME ON THEN, BE HONEST! DON'T YOU HAVE SOMETHING TO TELL PROFESSOR VEGENER?
A TRUE WARRIOR KNOWS WHEN TO FIGHT AND WHEN TO RETREAT, ABI. LET THIS GO.
I- I HAVE A MEETING! I HAVE TO GO.
GOOD, LET'S PICK UP WHERE WE LEFT OFF, PROFESSOR VEGENER?

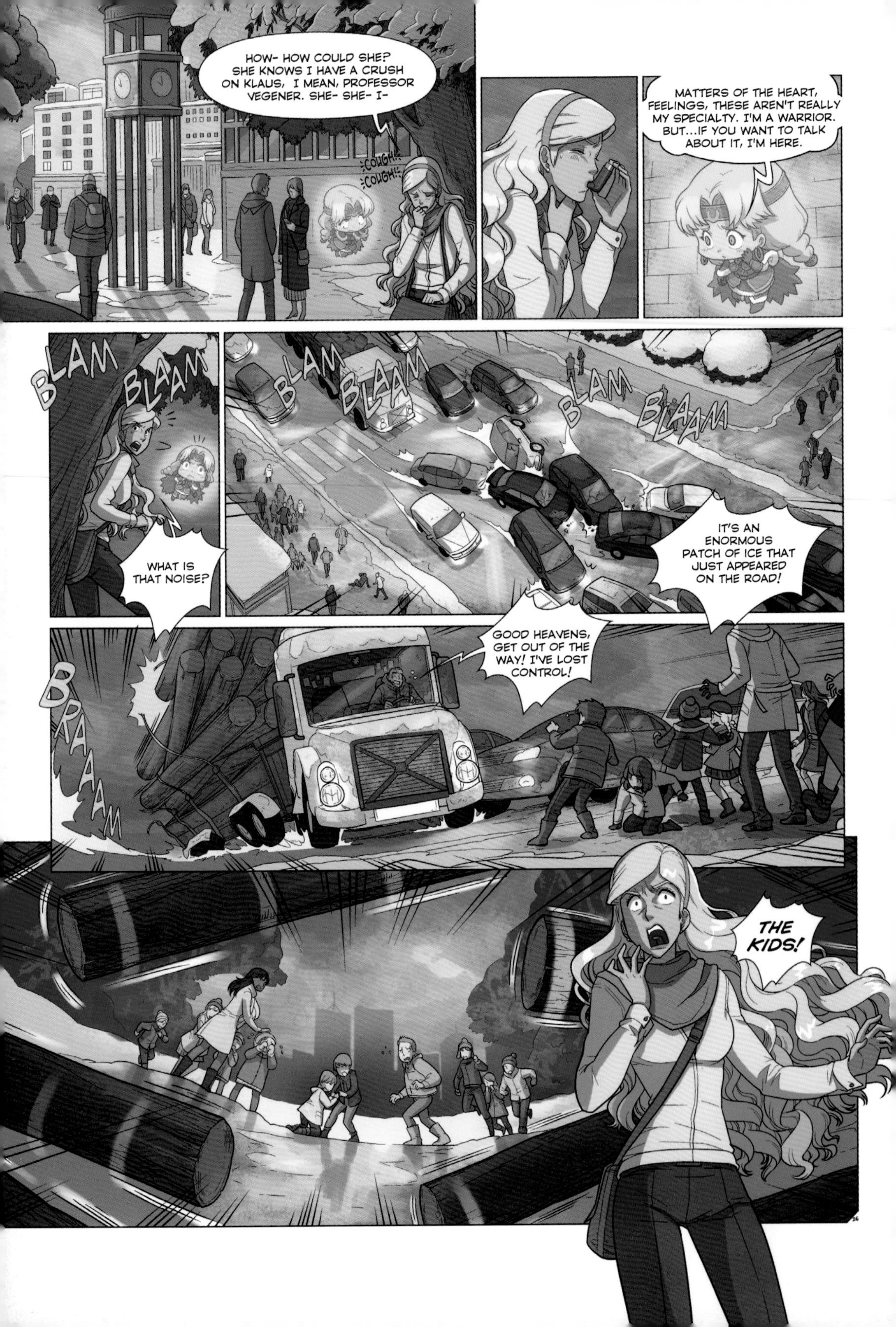
HOW- HOW COULD SHE? SHE KNOWS I HAVE A CRUSH ON KLAUS, I MEAN, PROFESSOR VEGENER. SHE- SHE- I-
COUGH! COUGH!
MATTERS OF THE HEART, FEELINGS, THESE AREN'T REALLY MY SPECIALTY. I'M A WARRIOR. BUT...IF YOU WANT TO TALK ABOUT IT, I'M HERE.
BLAM
BLAAM
WHAT IS THAT NOISE?
BLAM
BLAAM
BLAM
BLAAM
IT'S AN ENORMOUS PATCH OF ICE THAT JUST APPEARED ON THE ROAD!
GOOD HEAVENS, GET OUT OF THE WAY! I'VE LOST CONTROL!
BRAAAAM
THE KIDS!

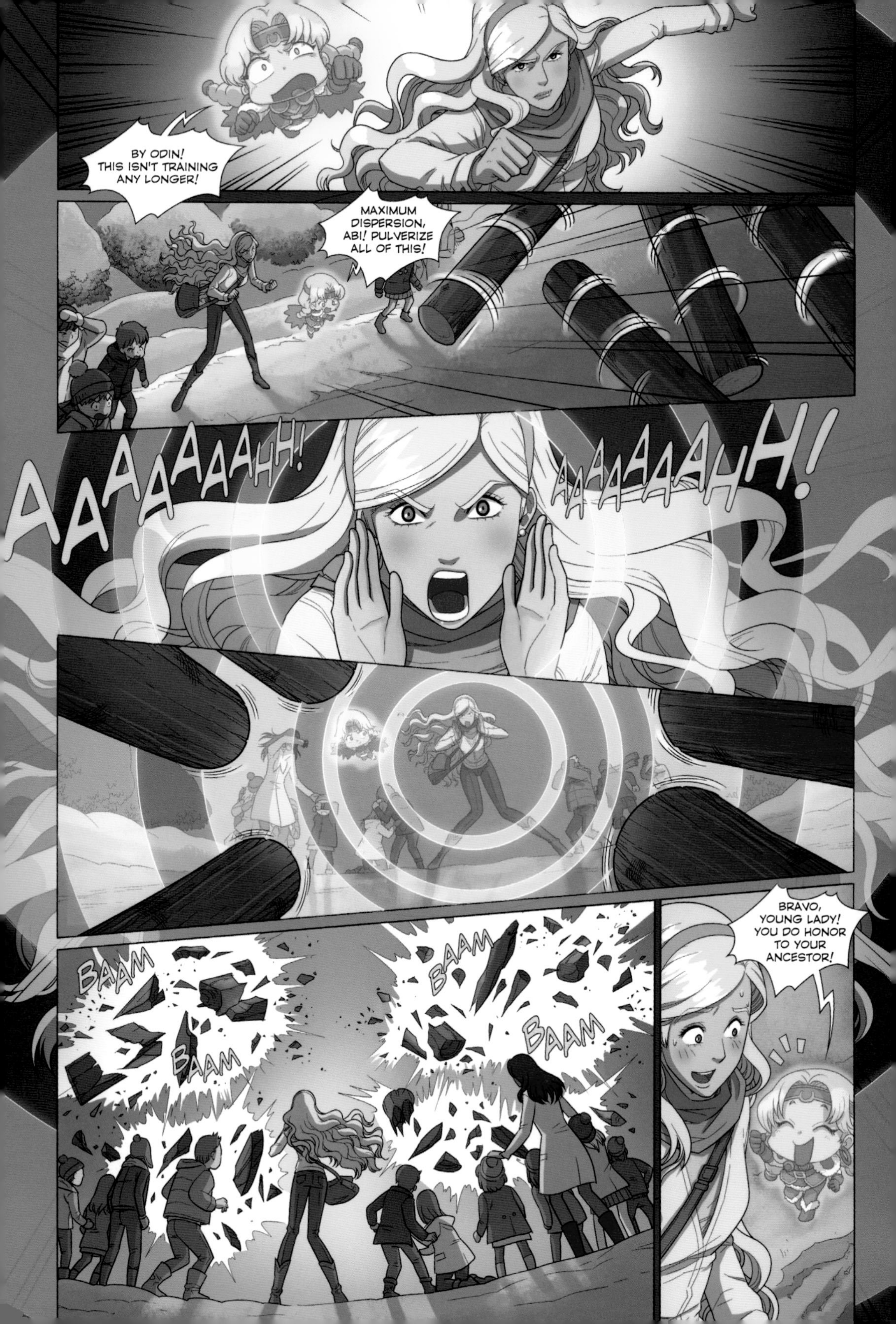
BY ODIN! THIS ISN'T TRAINING ANY LONGER!
MAXIMUM DISPERSION, ABI! PULVERIZE ALL OF THIS!
AAAAAAAHH!
AAAAAAAAHH!
BAAM
BAAM
BAAM
BAAM
BRAVO, YOUNG LADY! YOU DO HONOR TO YOUR ANCESTOR!

WHAT WAS THAT PATCH OF ICE THAT CAME OUT OF NOWHERE?

THERE'S MAGIC BEHIND IT, I CAN SENSE IT.

IT HAS NOTHING TO DO WITH CLIMATE CHANGE. EVERYTHING BEARS THE SIGNATURE OF LOKI.

HIS WITCHCRAFT IS THE SOURCE OF THESE GLACIAL EVENTS, I'M SURE OF IT.

BUT WHY IS HE DOING THIS? AND WHERE IS HE?

WELL, HE COULD BE REINCARNATED AS ANYONE. IT WON'T BE OBVIOUS RIGHT AWAY, BUT WE SHOULD HURRY TO FIND HIM TO BRING AN END TO HIS SCHEMES. FOR NOW, THERE HAVEN'T BEEN ANY VICTIMS, BUT THAT MIGHT NOT CONTINUE TO BE THE CASE.

DO YOU FEEL READY?

THERE'S ONLY ME TO BATTLE LOKI, SO I HAVE TO LEAVE MY PERSONAL PROBLEMS ASIDE. MY HEARTBREAK CAN WAIT. AND LIKE YOU TOLD ME WHEN WE MET "HEROES DO THEIR DUTY WHEN THEY ARE CHOSEN."

OH, RIGHT, I SAID THAT? SOUNDS LIKE A SPELL TO ME, ACTUALLY.

SO, LET'S GET YOUR SWORD AND DEFEAT THIS LOKI!

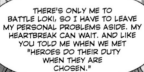

THE NEXT DAY...

IT'S HERE! THE SCHOOL'S LIBRARY HAS A GOOD NUMBER OF BOOKS ON GEOLOGY.

WHAT AN IMPRESSIVE COLLECTION OF BOOKS! NOTHING COMPARED TO MY ERA. I MUST SAY, WE DIDN'T READ MUCH BACK THEN...

I'M GOING TO FIND WHAT WE WANT.

THAT'S IT! IT'S THE GROTTO THAT I SAW IN MY DREAM.

WHERE IS IT?

QUIET, PLEASE, I'M READING. AND YOU SHOULD BE DOING THE SAME.

SORRY, I ONLY READ THE NORDIC RUNES.

SO, THIS SAYS THAT GROTTO HAS BECOME A TOURIST SPOT FOR GEOLOGY ENTHUSIASTS SINCE ITS DISCOVERY ABOUT TWENTY YEARS AGO.

IS IT FAR?

NO, WE'RE LUCKY! IT'S ONLY TWENTY-FIVE MILES FROM BERLIN.

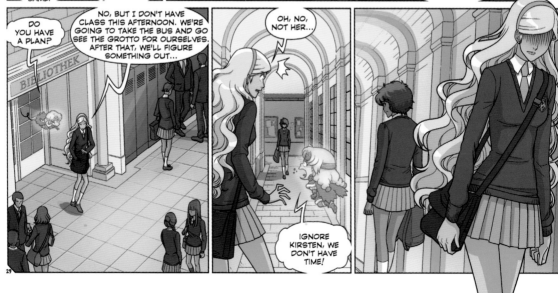

DO YOU HAVE A PLAN?

NO, BUT I DON'T HAVE CLASS THIS AFTERNOON. WE'RE GOING TO TAKE THE BUS AND GO SEE THE GROTTO FOR OURSELVES. AFTER THAT, WE'LL FIGURE SOMETHING OUT...

BIBLIOTHEK

OH, NO, NOT HER...

IGNORE KIRSTEN, WE DON'T HAVE TIME!

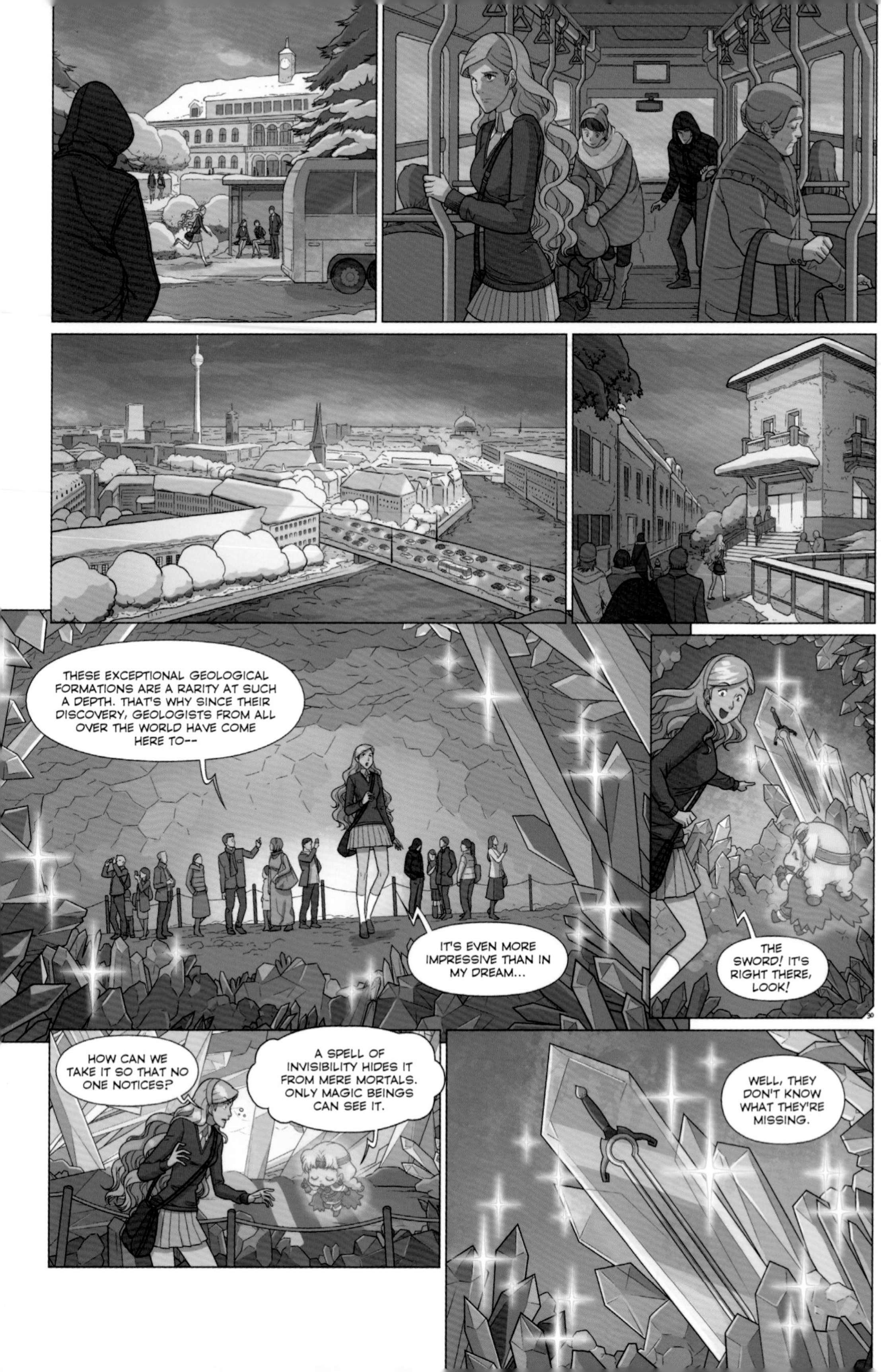
THESE EXCEPTIONAL GEOLOGICAL FORMATIONS ARE A RARITY AT SUCH A DEPTH. THAT'S WHY SINCE THEIR DISCOVERY, GEOLOGISTS FROM ALL OVER THE WORLD HAVE COME HERE TO--
IT'S EVEN MORE IMPRESSIVE THAN IN MY DREAM...
THE SWORD! IT'S RIGHT THERE, LOOK!
HOW CAN WE TAKE IT SO THAT NO ONE NOTICES?
A SPELL OF INVISIBILITY HIDES IT FROM MERE MORTALS. ONLY MAGIC BEINGS CAN SEE IT.
WELL, THEY DON'T KNOW WHAT THEY'RE MISSING.

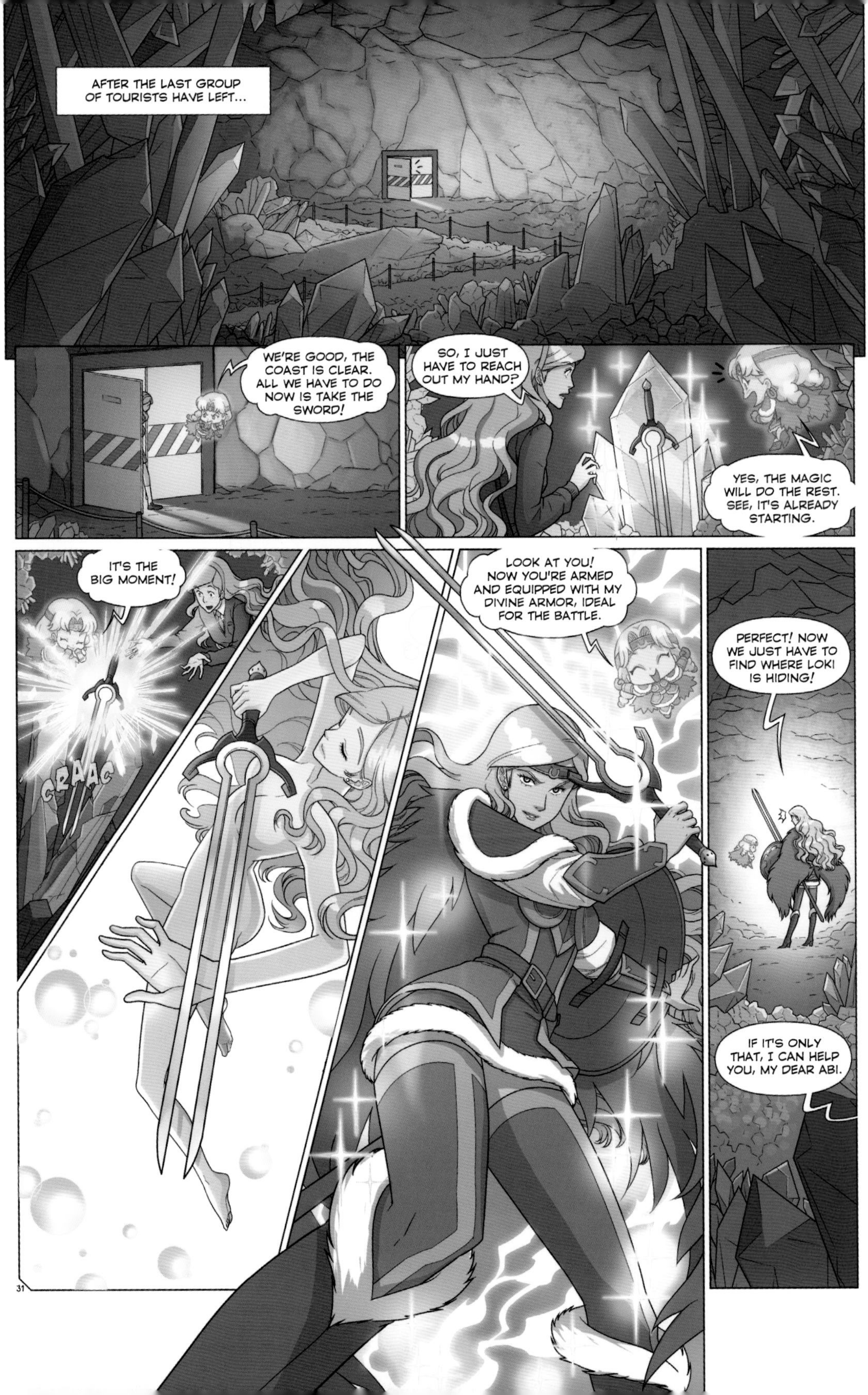
AFTER THE LAST GROUP OF TOURISTS HAVE LEFT...
WE'RE GOOD, THE COAST IS CLEAR. ALL WE HAVE TO DO NOW IS TAKE THE SWORD!
SO, I JUST HAVE TO REACH OUT MY HAND?
YES, THE MAGIC WILL DO THE REST. SEE, IT'S ALREADY STARTING.
IT'S THE BIG MOMENT!
CRAAC
LOOK AT YOU! NOW YOU'RE ARMED AND EQUIPPED WITH MY DIVINE ARMOR, IDEAL FOR THE BATTLE.
PERFECT! NOW WE JUST HAVE TO FIND WHERE LOKI IS HIDING!
IF IT'S ONLY THAT, I CAN HELP YOU, MY DEAR ABI.

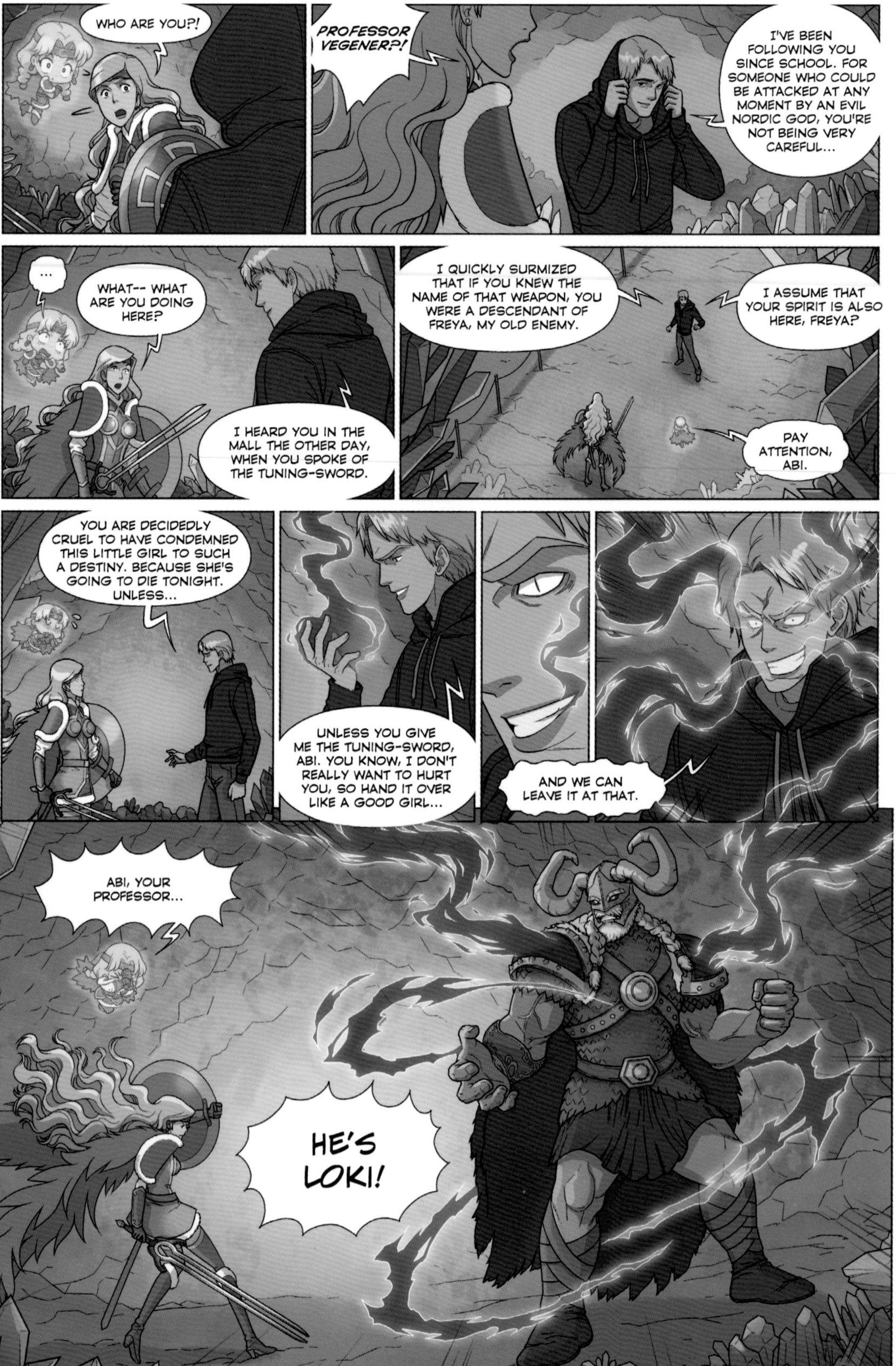
WHO ARE YOU?!
PROFESSOR VEGENER?!
I'VE BEEN FOLLOWING YOU SINCE SCHOOL. FOR SOMEONE WHO COULD BE ATTACKED AT ANY MOMENT BY AN EVIL NORDIC GOD, YOU'RE NOT BEING VERY CAREFUL...
...
WHAT-- WHAT ARE YOU DOING HERE?
I HEARD YOU IN THE MALL THE OTHER DAY, WHEN YOU SPOKE OF THE TUNING-SWORD.
I QUICKLY SURMIZED THAT IF YOU KNEW THE NAME OF THAT WEAPON, YOU WERE A DESCENDANT OF FREYA, MY OLD ENEMY.
I ASSUME THAT YOUR SPIRIT IS ALSO HERE, FREYA?
PAY ATTENTION, ABI.
YOU ARE DECIDEDLY CRUEL TO HAVE CONDEMNED THIS LITTLE GIRL TO SUCH A DESTINY. BECAUSE SHE'S GOING TO DIE TONIGHT. UNLESS...
UNLESS YOU GIVE ME THE TUNING-SWORD, ABI. YOU KNOW, I DON'T REALLY WANT TO HURT YOU, SO HAND IT OVER LIKE A GOOD GIRL...
AND WE CAN LEAVE IT AT THAT.
ABI, YOUR PROFESSOR...
HE'S LOKI!

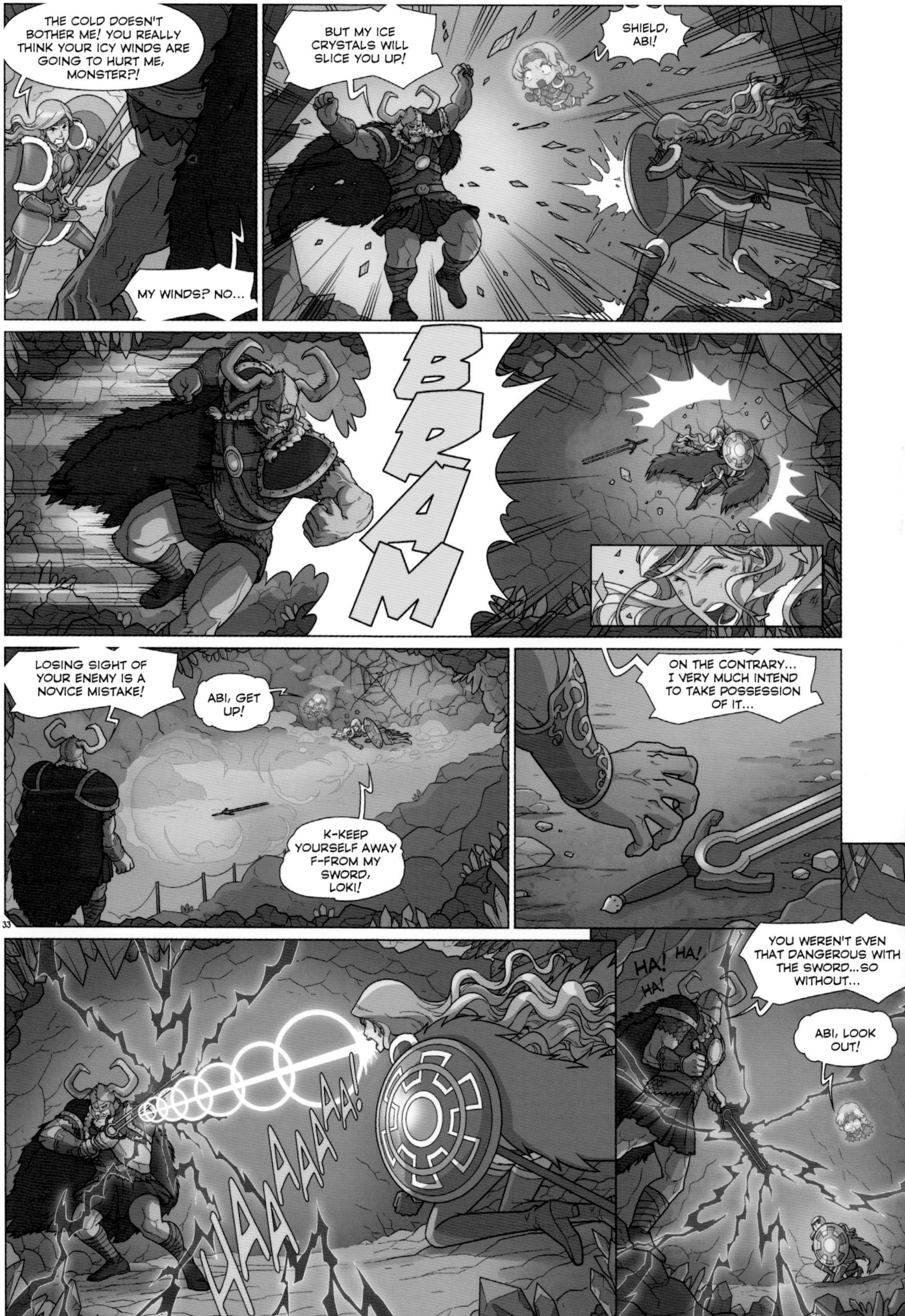

THE COLD DOESN'T BOTHER ME! YOU REALLY THINK YOUR ICY WINDS ARE GOING TO HURT ME, MONSTER?!
MY WINDS? NO...
BUT MY ICE CRYSTALS WILL SLICE YOU UP!
SHIELD, ABI!
BRAM
LOSING SIGHT OF YOUR ENEMY IS A NOVICE MISTAKE!
ABI, GET UP!
K-KEEP YOURSELF AWAY F-FROM MY SWORD, LOKI!
ON THE CONTRARY... I VERY MUCH INTEND TO TAKE POSSESSION OF IT...
HAAAAAAAA!
HA! HA! HA!
YOU WEREN'T EVEN THAT DANGEROUS WITH THE SWORD...SO WITHOUT...
ABI, LOOK OUT!

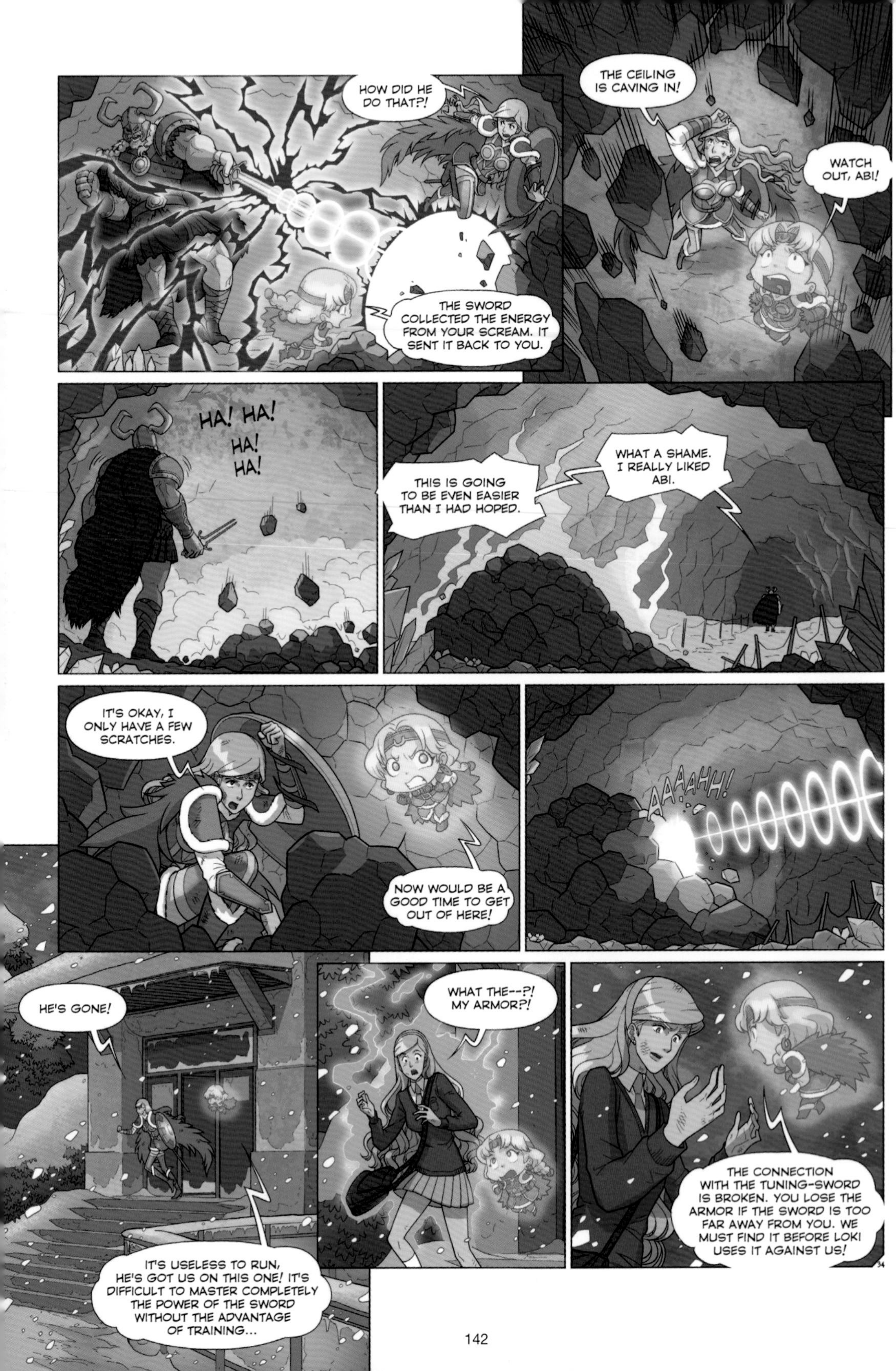
HOW DID HE DO THAT?!
THE SWORD COLLECTED THE ENERGY FROM YOUR SCREAM. IT SENT IT BACK TO YOU.
THE CEILING IS CAVING IN!
WATCH OUT, ABI!
HA! HA! HA! HA!
THIS IS GOING TO BE EVEN EASIER THAN I HAD HOPED.
WHAT A SHAME. I REALLY LIKED ABI.
IT'S OKAY, I ONLY HAVE A FEW SCRATCHES.
NOW WOULD BE A GOOD TIME TO GET OUT OF HERE!
AAAAHH!
HE'S GONE!
IT'S USELESS TO RUN, HE'S GOT US ON THIS ONE! IT'S DIFFICULT TO MASTER COMPLETELY THE POWER OF THE SWORD WITHOUT THE ADVANTAGE OF TRAINING...
WHAT THE--?! MY ARMOR?!
THE CONNECTION WITH THE TUNING-SWORD IS BROKEN. YOU LOSE THE ARMOR IF THE SWORD IS TOO FAR AWAY FROM YOU. WE MUST FIND IT BEFORE LOKI USES IT AGAINST US!

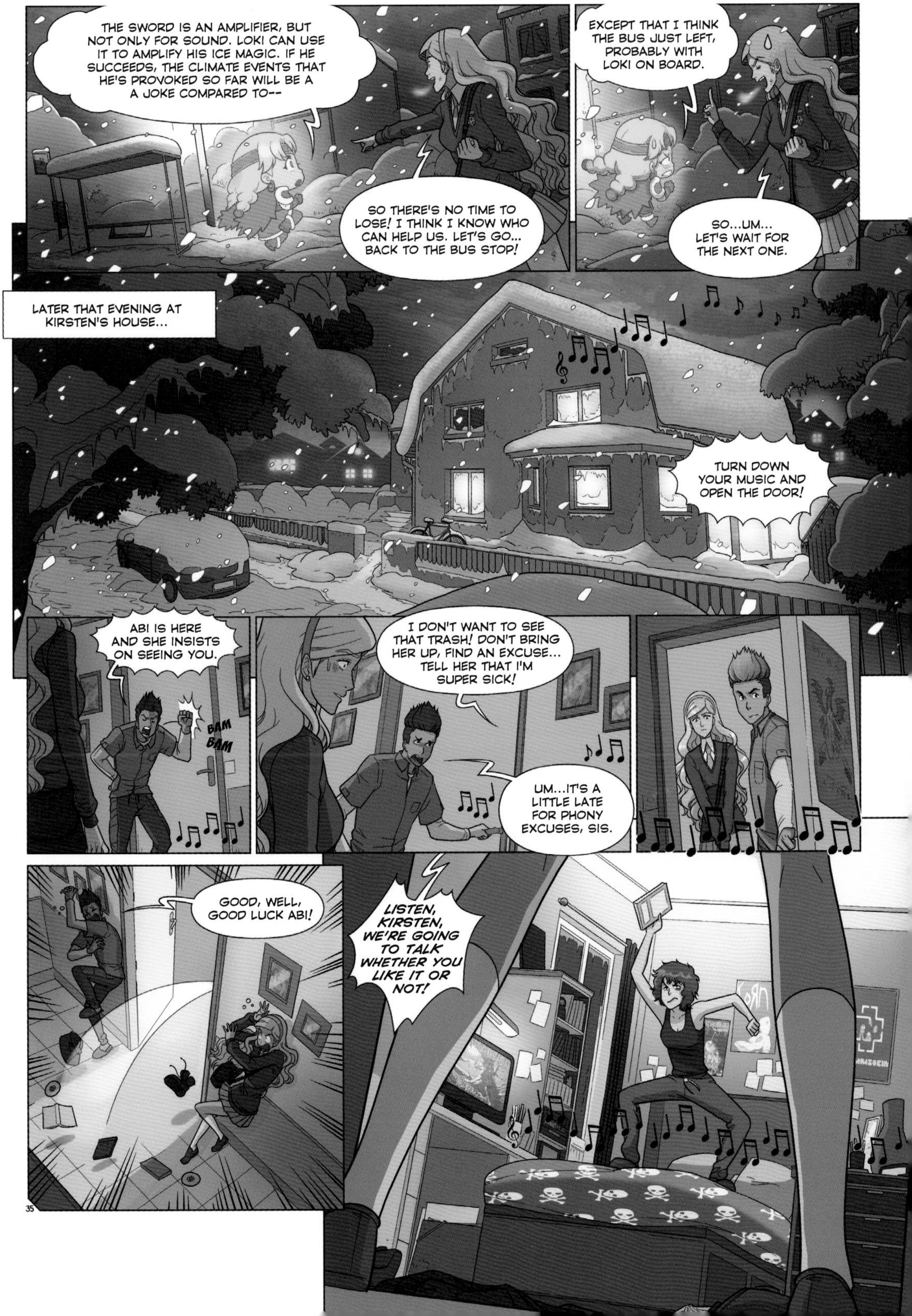
THE SWORD IS AN AMPLIFIER, BUT NOT ONLY FOR SOUND. LOKI CAN USE IT TO AMPLIFY HIS ICE MAGIC. IF HE SUCCEEDS, THE CLIMATE EVENTS THAT HE'S PROVOKED SO FAR WILL BE A A JOKE COMPARED TO--
SO THERE'S NO TIME TO LOSE! I THINK I KNOW WHO CAN HELP US. LET'S GO... BACK TO THE BUS STOP!
EXCEPT THAT I THINK THE BUS JUST LEFT, PROBABLY WITH LOKI ON BOARD.
SO...UM... LET'S WAIT FOR THE NEXT ONE.
LATER THAT EVENING AT KIRSTEN'S HOUSE...
TURN DOWN YOUR MUSIC AND OPEN THE DOOR!
ABI IS HERE AND SHE INSISTS ON SEEING YOU.
BAM
BAM
I DON'T WANT TO SEE THAT TRASH! DON'T BRING HER UP, FIND AN EXCUSE... TELL HER THAT I'M SUPER SICK!
UM...IT'S A LITTLE LATE FOR PHONY EXCUSES, SIS.
GOOD, WELL, GOOD LUCK ABI!
LISTEN, KIRSTEN, WE'RE GOING TO TALK WHETHER YOU LIKE IT OR NOT!

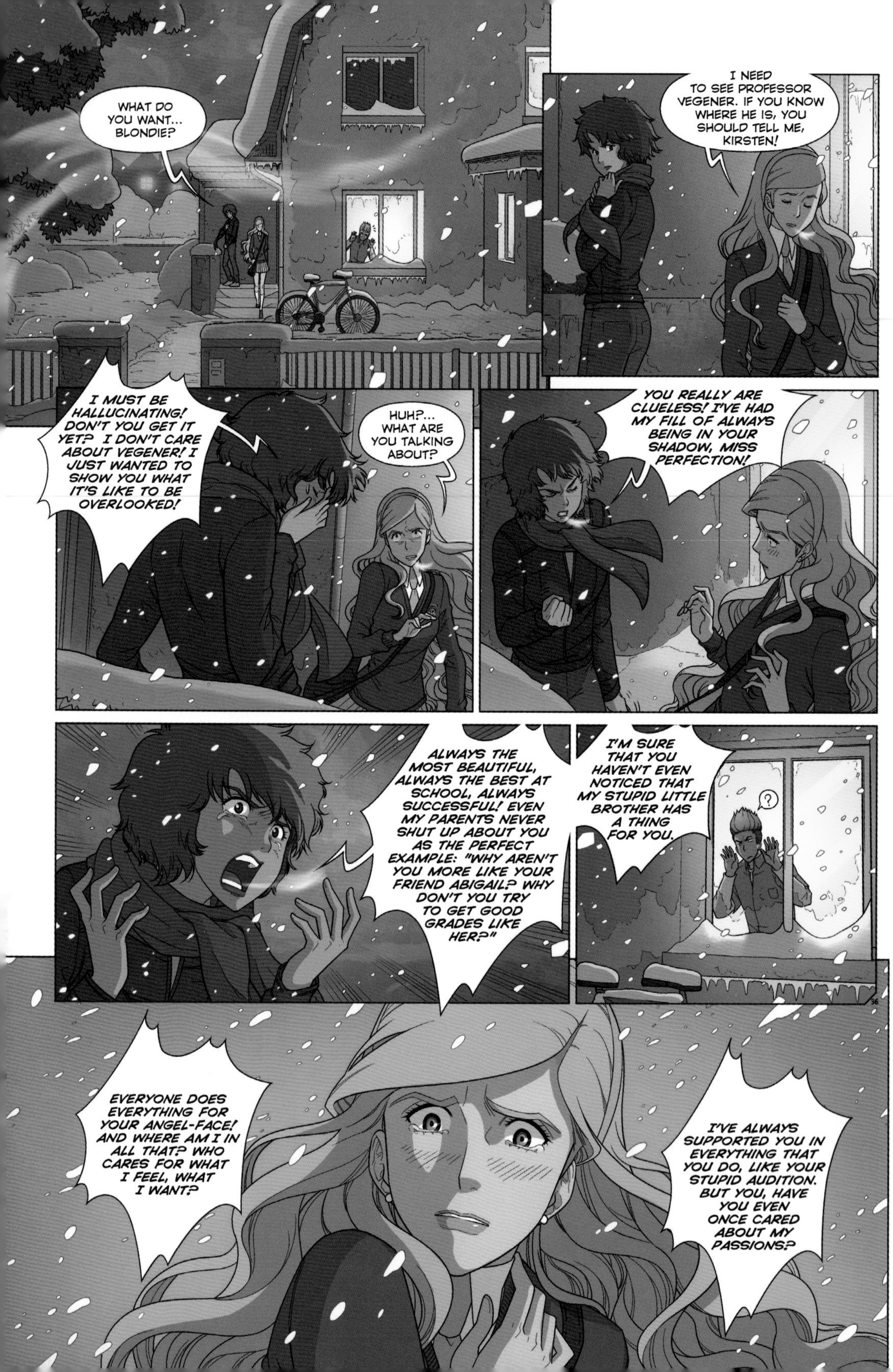
WHAT DO YOU WANT... BLONDIE?
I NEED TO SEE PROFESSOR VEGENER. IF YOU KNOW WHERE HE IS, YOU SHOULD TELL ME, KIRSTEN!
I MUST BE HALLUCINATING! DON'T YOU GET IT YET? I DON'T CARE ABOUT VEGENER! I JUST WANTED TO SHOW YOU WHAT IT'S LIKE TO BE OVERLOOKED!
HUH?... WHAT ARE YOU TALKING ABOUT?
YOU REALLY ARE CLUELESS! I'VE HAD MY FILL OF ALWAYS BEING IN YOUR SHADOW, MISS PERFECTION!
ALWAYS THE MOST BEAUTIFUL, ALWAYS THE BEST AT SCHOOL, ALWAYS SUCCESSFUL! EVEN MY PARENTS NEVER SHUT UP ABOUT YOU AS THE PERFECT EXAMPLE: "WHY AREN'T YOU MORE LIKE YOUR FRIEND ABIGAIL? WHY DON'T YOU TRY TO GET GOOD GRADES LIKE HER?"
I'M SURE THAT YOU HAVEN'T EVEN NOTICED THAT MY STUPID LITTLE BROTHER HAS A THING FOR YOU.
?
EVERYONE DOES EVERYTHING FOR YOUR ANGEL-FACE! AND WHERE AM I IN ALL THAT? WHO CARES FOR WHAT I FEEL, WHAT I WANT?
I'VE ALWAYS SUPPORTED YOU IN EVERYTHING THAT YOU DO, LIKE YOUR STUPID AUDITION. BUT YOU, HAVE YOU EVEN ONCE CARED ABOUT MY PASSIONS?

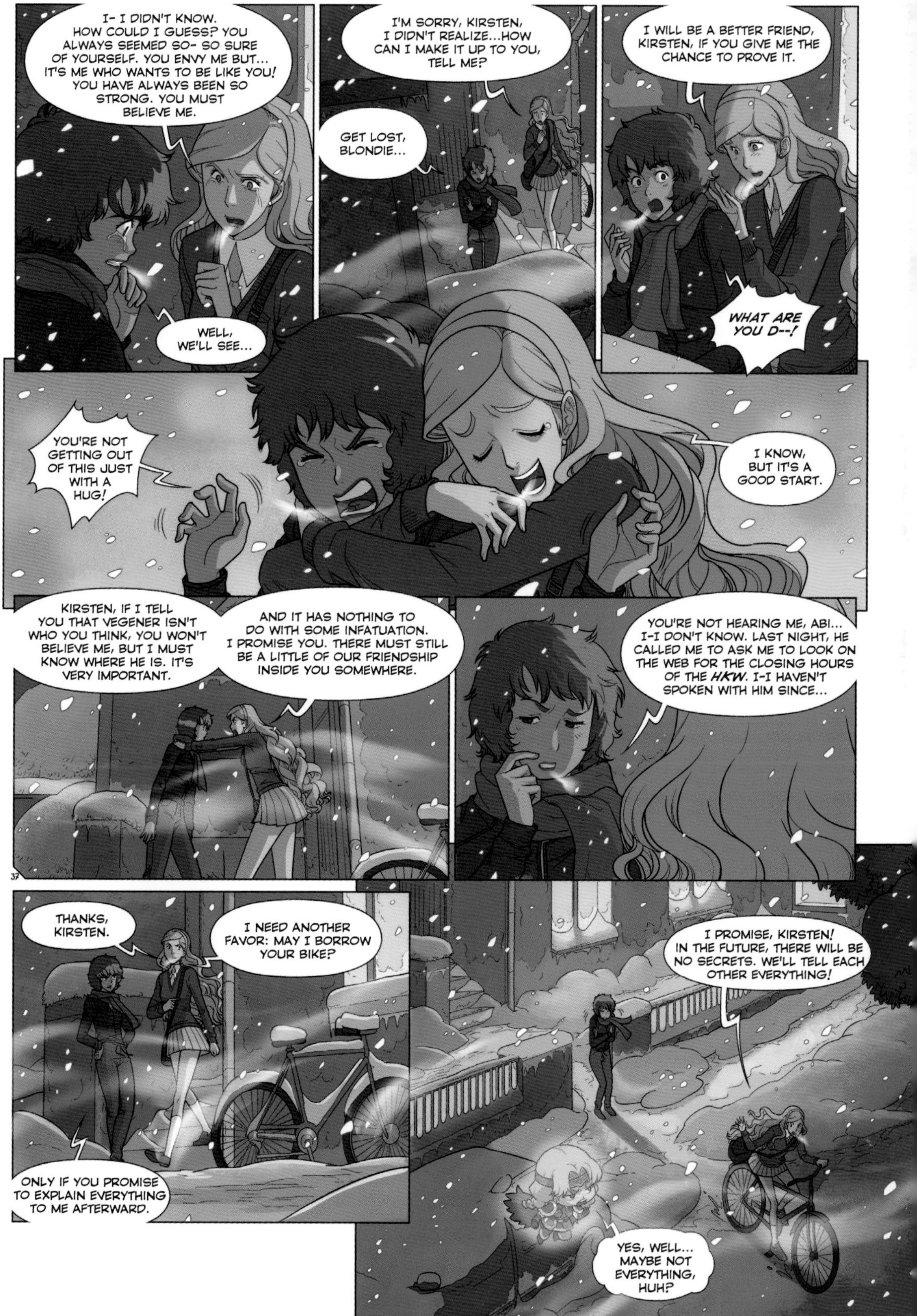
I- I DIDN'T KNOW. HOW COULD I GUESS? YOU ALWAYS SEEMED SO- SO SURE OF YOURSELF. YOU ENVY ME BUT... IT'S ME WHO WANTS TO BE LIKE YOU! YOU HAVE ALWAYS BEEN SO STRONG. YOU MUST BELIEVE ME.
WELL, WE'LL SEE...
I'M SORRY, KIRSTEN, I DIDN'T REALIZE...HOW CAN I MAKE IT UP TO YOU, TELL ME?
GET LOST, BLONDIE...
I WILL BE A BETTER FRIEND, KIRSTEN, IF YOU GIVE ME THE CHANCE TO PROVE IT.
WHAT ARE YOU D--!
YOU'RE NOT GETTING OUT OF THIS JUST WITH A HUG!
I KNOW, BUT IT'S A GOOD START.
KIRSTEN, IF I TELL YOU THAT VEGENER ISN'T WHO YOU THINK, YOU WON'T BELIEVE ME, BUT I MUST KNOW WHERE HE IS. IT'S VERY IMPORTANT.
AND IT HAS NOTHING TO DO WITH SOME INFATUATION. I PROMISE YOU. THERE MUST STILL BE A LITTLE OF OUR FRIENDSHIP INSIDE YOU SOMEWHERE.
YOU'RE NOT HEARING ME, ABI... I-I DON'T KNOW. LAST NIGHT, HE CALLED ME TO ASK ME TO LOOK ON THE WEB FOR THE CLOSING HOURS OF THE HKW. I-I HAVEN'T SPOKEN WITH HIM SINCE...
THANKS, KIRSTEN.
I NEED ANOTHER FAVOR: MAY I BORROW YOUR BIKE?
ONLY IF YOU PROMISE TO EXPLAIN EVERYTHING TO ME AFTERWARD.
I PROMISE, KIRSTEN! IN THE FUTURE, THERE WILL BE NO SECRETS. WE'LL TELL EACH OTHER EVERYTHING!
YES, WELL... MAYBE NOT EVERYTHING, HUH?

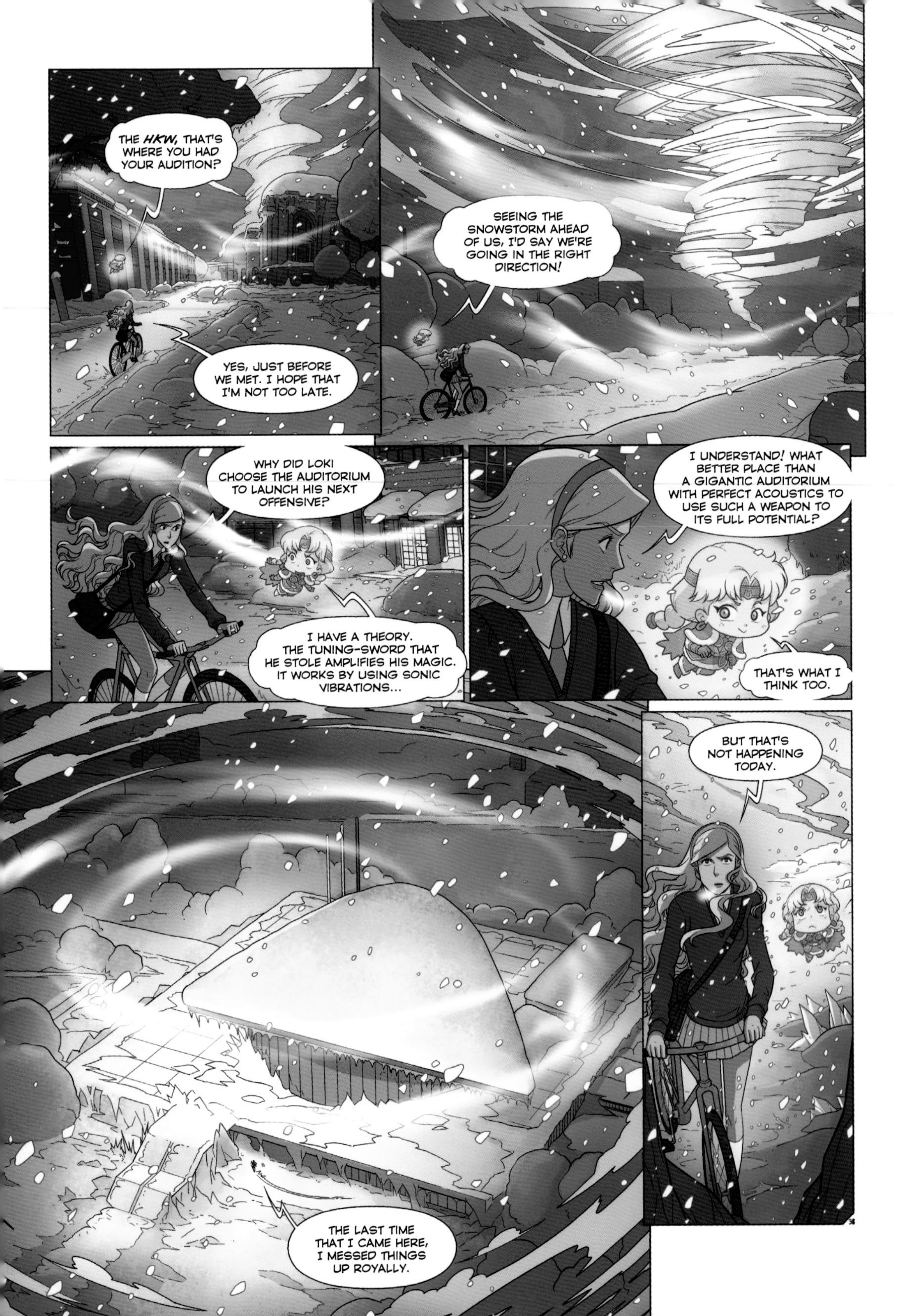

THE HKW, THAT'S WHERE YOU HAD YOUR AUDITION?
YES, JUST BEFORE WE MET. I HOPE THAT I'M NOT TOO LATE.
SEEING THE SNOWSTORM AHEAD OF US, I'D SAY WE'RE GOING IN THE RIGHT DIRECTION!
WHY DID LOKI CHOOSE THE AUDITORIUM TO LAUNCH HIS NEXT OFFENSIVE?
I HAVE A THEORY. THE TUNING-SWORD THAT HE STOLE AMPLIFIES HIS MAGIC. IT WORKS BY USING SONIC VIBRATIONS...
I UNDERSTAND! WHAT BETTER PLACE THAN A GIGANTIC AUDITORIUM WITH PERFECT ACOUSTICS TO USE SUCH A WEAPON TO ITS FULL POTENTIAL?
THAT'S WHAT I THINK TOO.
THE LAST TIME THAT I CAME HERE, I MESSED THINGS UP ROYALLY.
BUT THAT'S NOT HAPPENING TODAY.

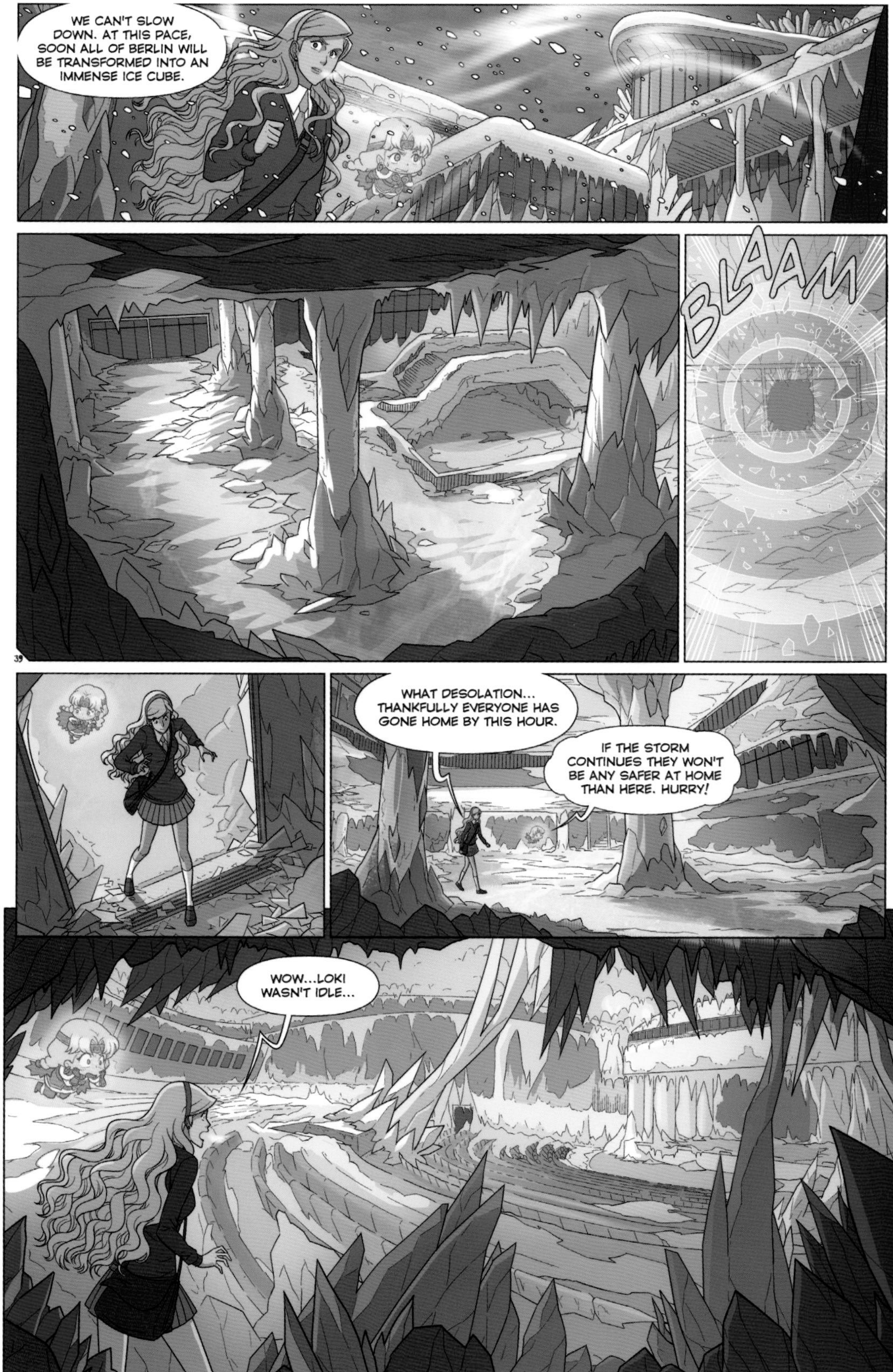
WE CAN'T SLOW DOWN. AT THIS PACE, SOON ALL OF BERLIN WILL BE TRANSFORMED INTO AN IMMENSE ICE CUBE.
BLAAM
WHAT DESOLATION... THANKFULLY EVERYONE HAS GONE HOME BY THIS HOUR.
IF THE STORM CONTINUES THEY WON'T BE ANY SAFER AT HOME THAN HERE. HURRY!
WOW...LOKI WASN'T IDLE...

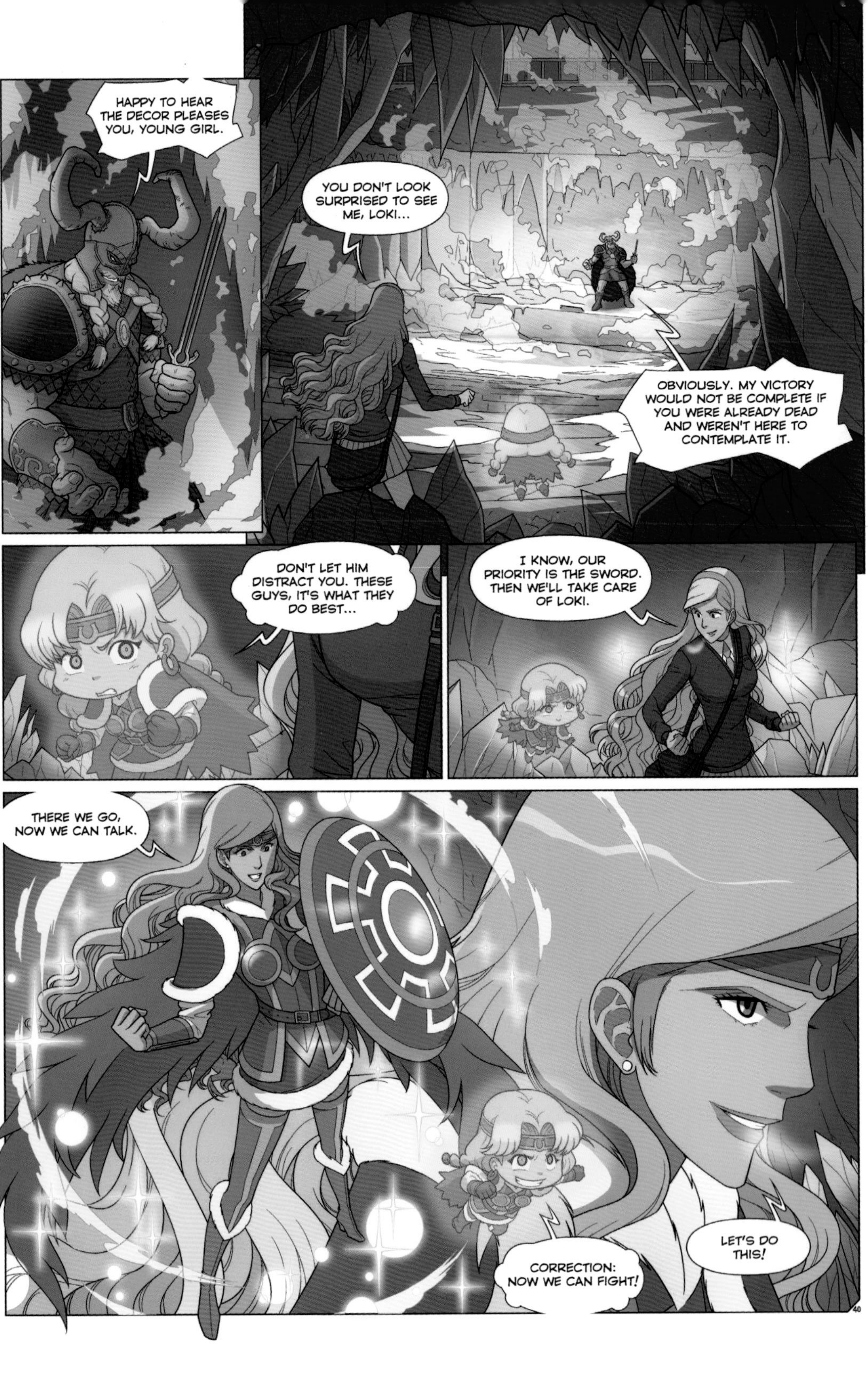

HAPPY TO HEAR THE DECOR PLEASES YOU, YOUNG GIRL.
YOU DON'T LOOK SURPRISED TO SEE ME, LOKI...
OBVIOUSLY. MY VICTORY WOULD NOT BE COMPLETE IF YOU WERE ALREADY DEAD AND WEREN'T HERE TO CONTEMPLATE IT.
DON'T LET HIM DISTRACT YOU. THESE GUYS, IT'S WHAT THEY DO BEST...
I KNOW, OUR PRIORITY IS THE SWORD. THEN WE'LL TAKE CARE OF LOKI.
THERE WE GO, NOW WE CAN TALK.
CORRECTION: NOW WE CAN FIGHT!
LET'S DO THIS!
40

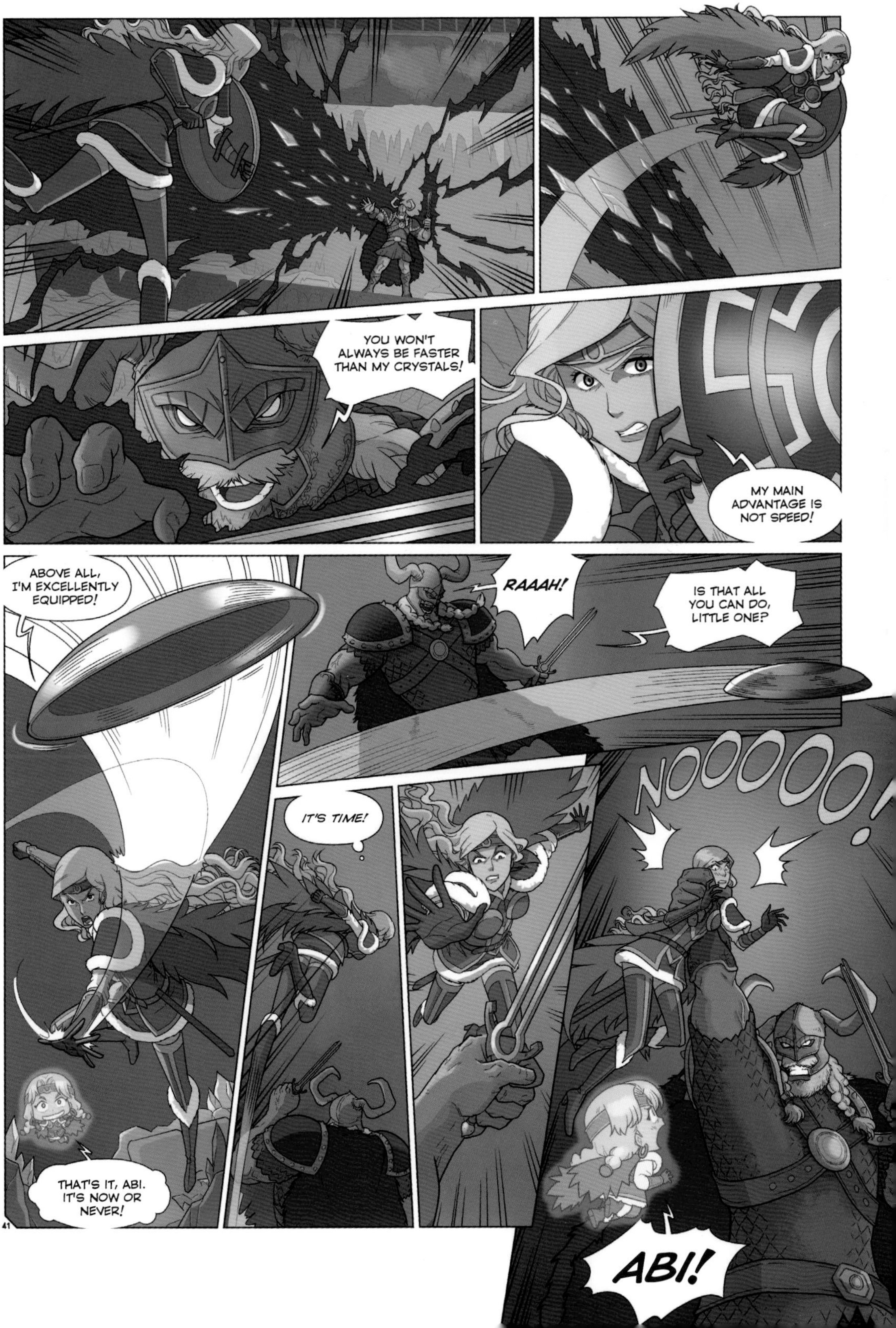
YOU WON'T ALWAYS BE FASTER THAN MY CRYSTALS!
MY MAIN ADVANTAGE IS NOT SPEED!
ABOVE ALL, I'M EXCELLENTLY EQUIPPED!
RAAAH!
IS THAT ALL YOU CAN DO, LITTLE ONE?
THAT'S IT, ABI. IT'S NOW OR NEVER!
IT'S TIME!
NOOOOOO!
ABI!

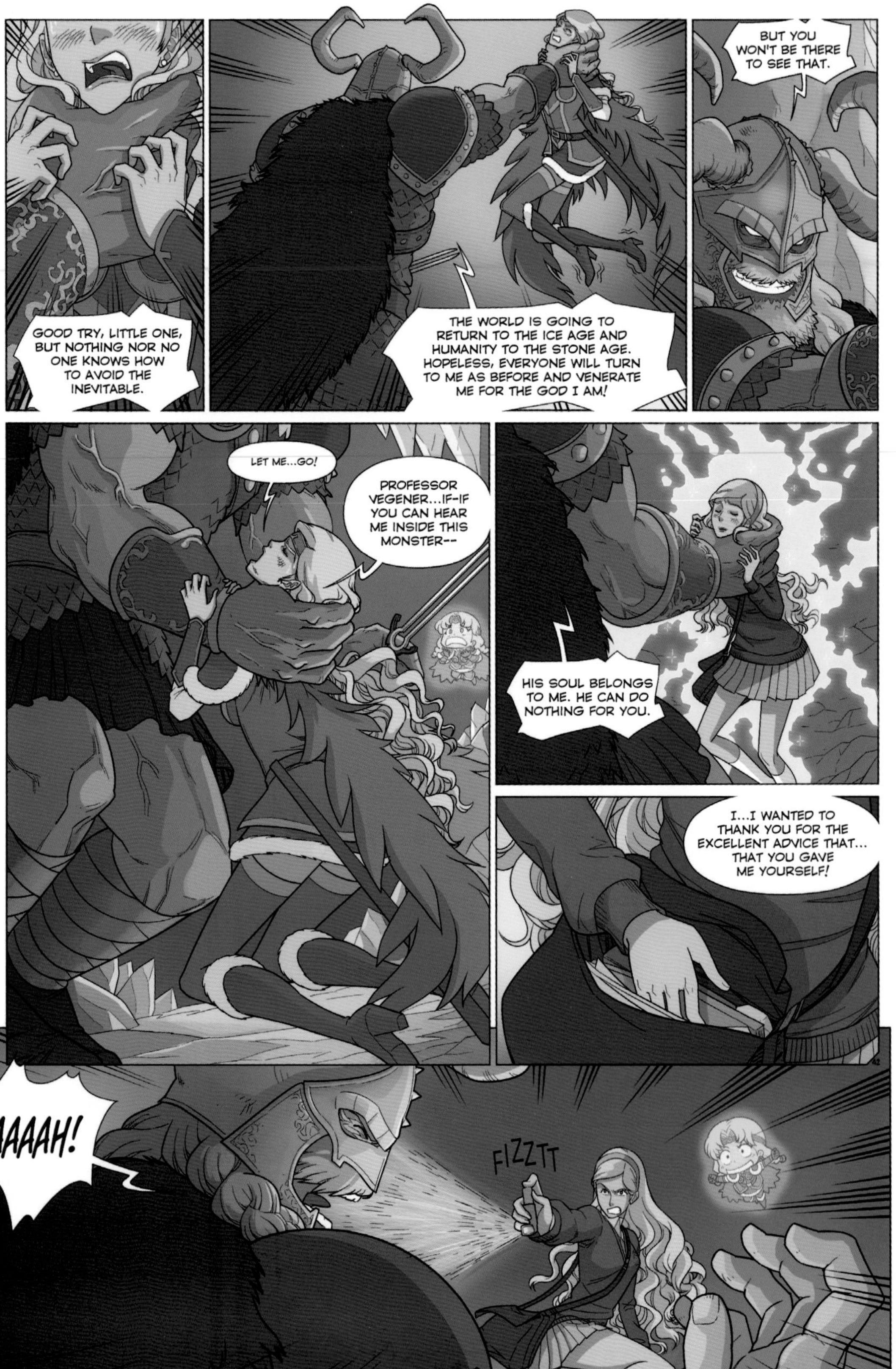
GOOD TRY, LITTLE ONE, BUT NOTHING NOR NO ONE KNOWS HOW TO AVOID THE INEVITABLE.
THE WORLD IS GOING TO RETURN TO THE ICE AGE AND HUMANITY TO THE STONE AGE. HOPELESS, EVERYONE WILL TURN TO ME AS BEFORE AND VENERATE ME FOR THE GOD I AM!
BUT YOU WON'T BE THERE TO SEE THAT.
LET ME...GO!
PROFESSOR VEGENER...IF-IF YOU CAN HEAR ME INSIDE THIS MONSTER--
HIS SOUL BELONGS TO ME. HE CAN DO NOTHING FOR YOU.
I...I WANTED TO THANK YOU FOR THE EXCELLENT ADVICE THAT... THAT YOU GAVE ME YOURSELF!
AAAAH!
FIZZTT

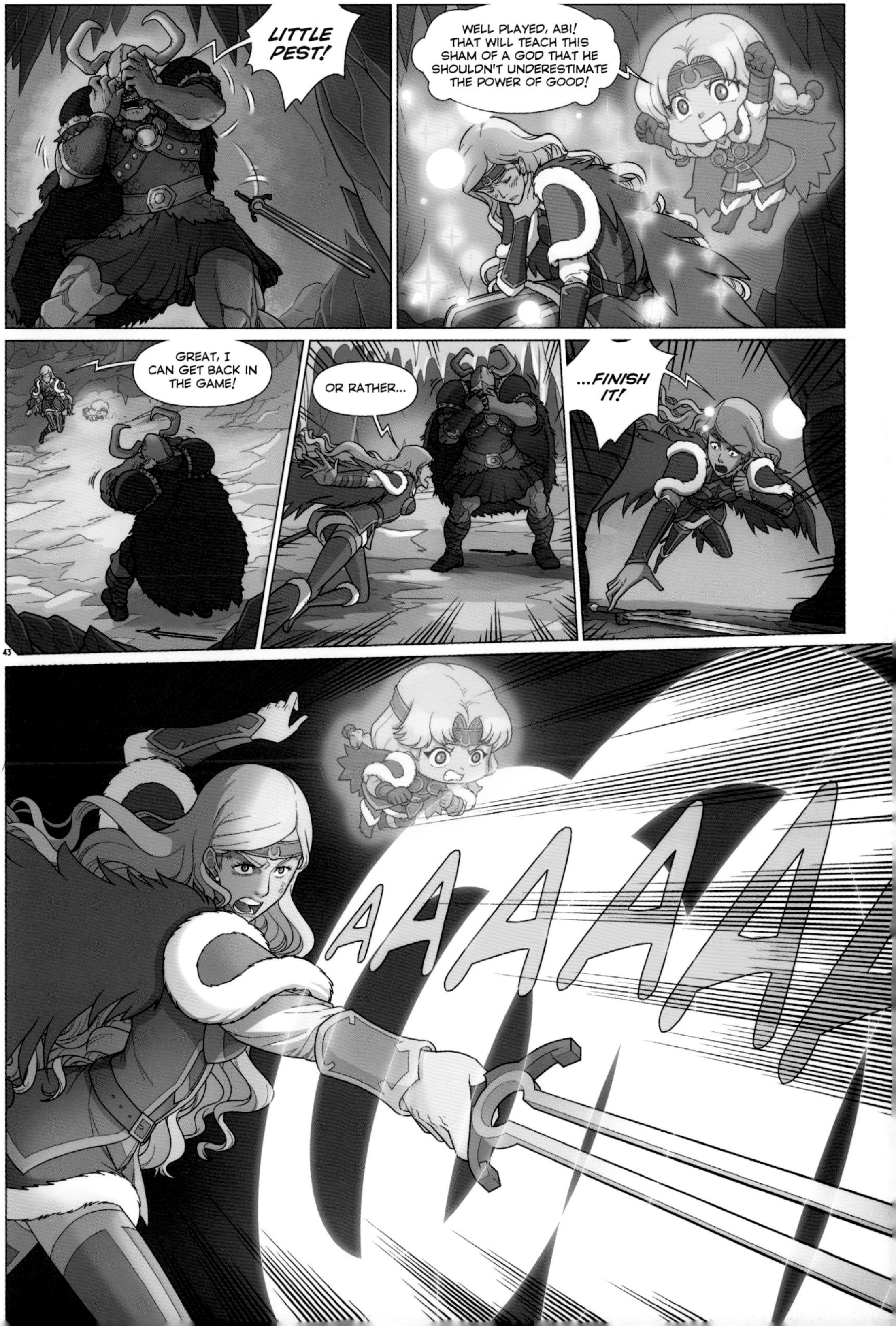
LITTLE PEST!
WELL PLAYED, ABI! THAT WILL TEACH THIS SHAM OF A GOD THAT HE SHOULDN'T UNDERESTIMATE THE POWER OF GOOD!
GREAT, I CAN GET BACK IN THE GAME!
OR RATHER...
...FINISH IT!
AAAAAA

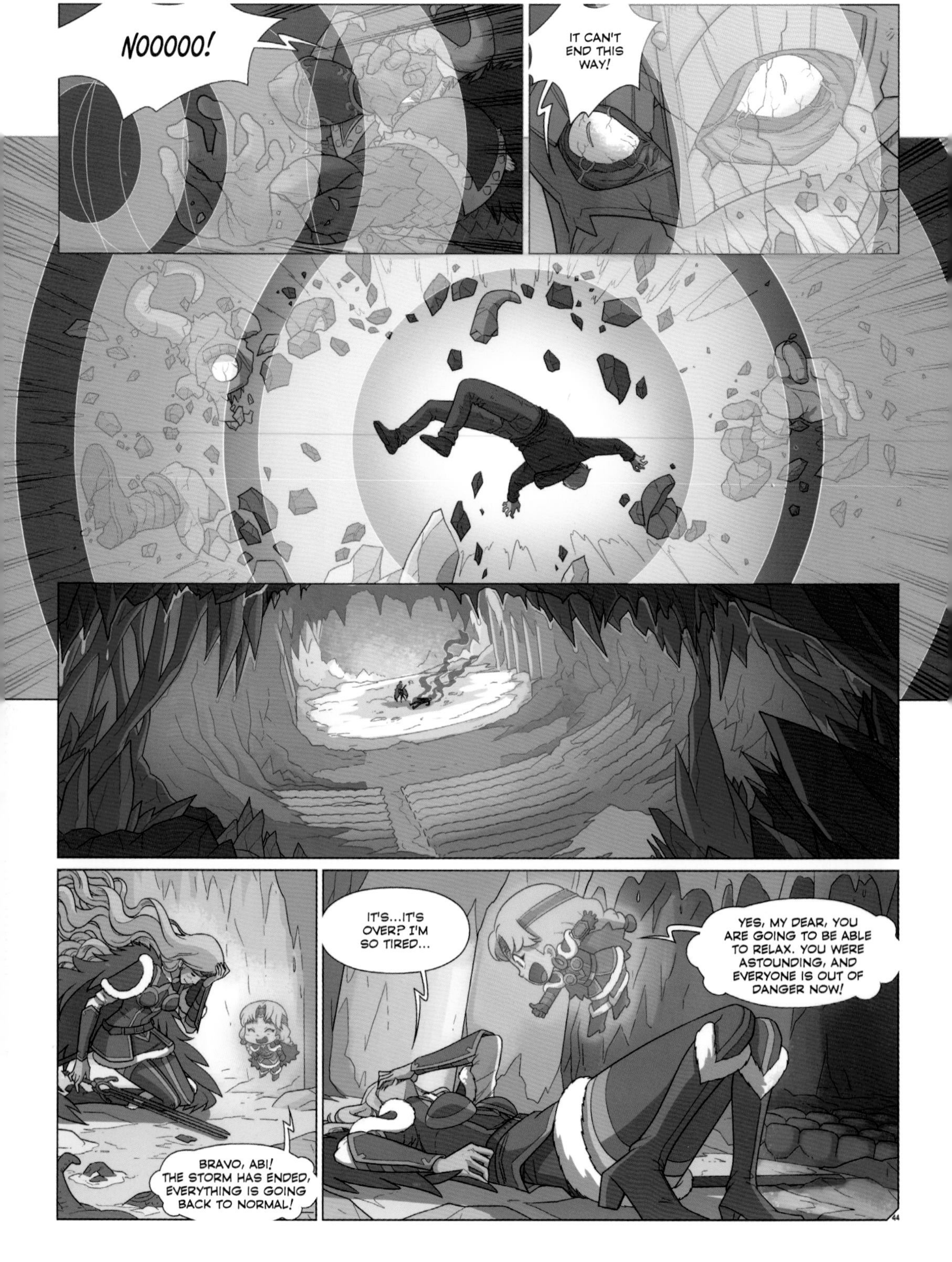
NOOOOO!
IT CAN'T END THIS WAY!
IT'S...IT'S OVER? I'M SO TIRED...
YES, MY DEAR, YOU ARE GOING TO BE ABLE TO RELAX. YOU WERE ASTOUNDING, AND EVERYONE IS OUT OF DANGER NOW!
BRAVO, ABI! THE STORM HAS ENDED, EVERYTHING IS GOING BACK TO NORMAL!
44

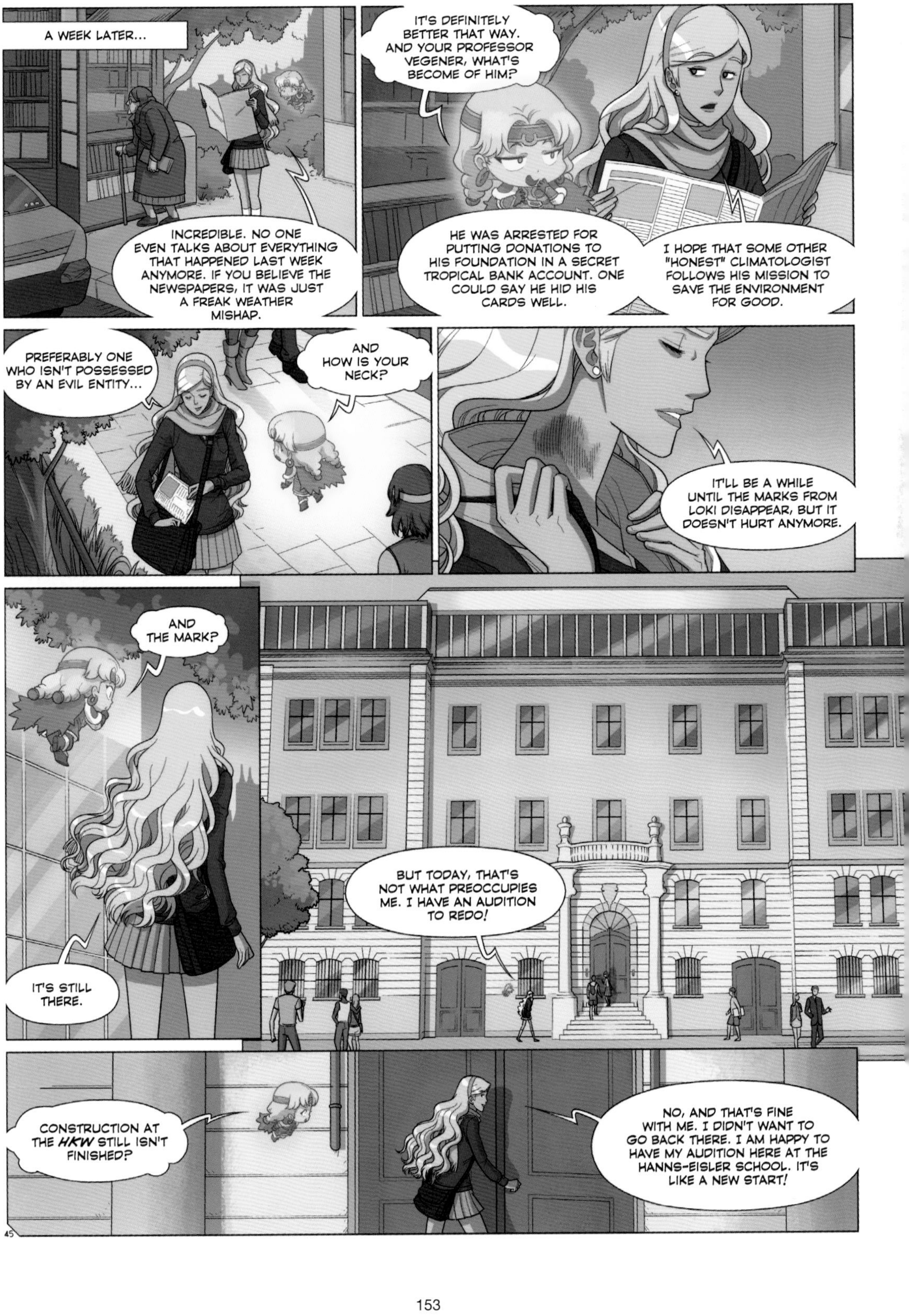
A WEEK LATER...
INCREDIBLE. NO ONE EVEN TALKS ABOUT EVERYTHING THAT HAPPENED LAST WEEK ANYMORE. IF YOU BELIEVE THE NEWSPAPERS, IT WAS JUST A FREAK WEATHER MISHAP.
IT'S DEFINITELY BETTER THAT WAY. AND YOUR PROFESSOR VEGENER, WHAT'S BECOME OF HIM?
HE WAS ARRESTED FOR PUTTING DONATIONS TO HIS FOUNDATION IN A SECRET TROPICAL BANK ACCOUNT. ONE COULD SAY HE HID HIS CARDS WELL.
I HOPE THAT SOME OTHER "HONEST" CLIMATOLOGIST FOLLOWS HIS MISSION TO SAVE THE ENVIRONMENT FOR GOOD.
PREFERABLY ONE WHO ISN'T POSSESSED BY AN EVIL ENTITY...
AND HOW IS YOUR NECK?
IT'LL BE A WHILE UNTIL THE MARKS FROM LOKI DISAPPEAR, BUT IT DOESN'T HURT ANYMORE.
AND THE MARK?
IT'S STILL THERE.
BUT TODAY, THAT'S NOT WHAT PREOCCUPIES ME. I HAVE AN AUDITION TO REDO!
CONSTRUCTION AT THE *HKW* STILL ISN'T FINISHED?
NO, AND THAT'S FINE WITH ME. I DIDN'T WANT TO GO BACK THERE. I AM HAPPY TO HAVE MY AUDITION HERE AT THE HANNS-EISLER SCHOOL. IT'S LIKE A NEW START!
45

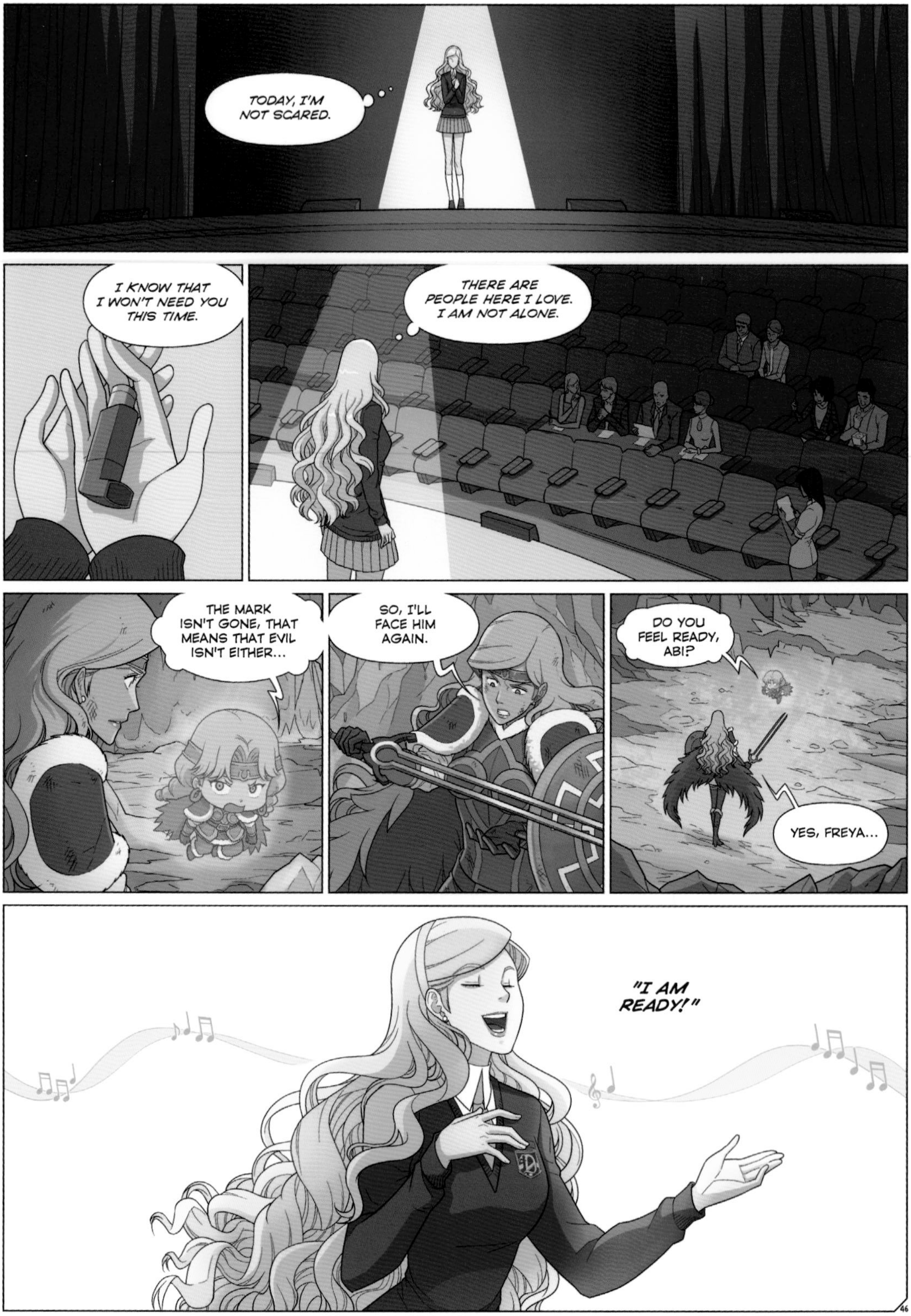
TODAY, I'M NOT SCARED.
I KNOW THAT I WON'T NEED YOU THIS TIME.
THERE ARE PEOPLE HERE I LOVE. I AM NOT ALONE.
THE MARK ISN'T GONE, THAT MEANS THAT EVIL ISN'T EITHER...
SO, I'LL FACE HIM AGAIN.
DO YOU FEEL READY, ABI?
YES, FREYA...
"I AM READY!"
46

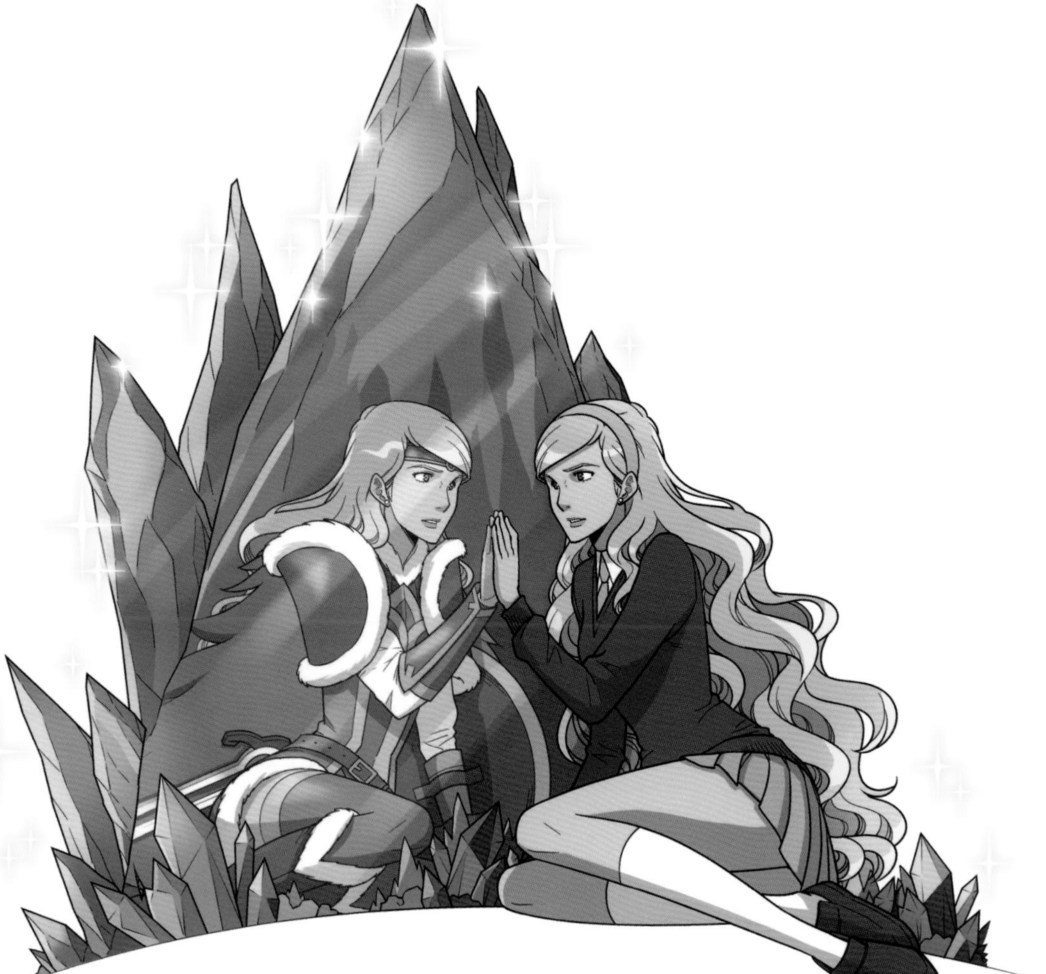

WATCH OUT FOR PAPERCUTZ

Welcome to the prestigious premiere of THE MYTHICS #1 "Heroes Reborn," created by Patrick Sobral, Patricia Lyfoung, and Philippe Ogaki, written by Philippe Ogaki, Patrick Sobral, and Fabien Dalmasso, and drawn by Jenny, Philippe Ogaki, and Dara—a veritable pantheon of comicbook gods—brought to you by Papercutz, those earth-bound heroes dedicated to publishing great graphic novels for all ages. I'm Jim Salicrup, Editor-in-Chief and a fount of Myth-information, here with some exciting news. First, we're excited about THE MYTHICS. In this volume, you've met Yuko, Amir, and Abigail, but they only comprise have of the new gods that are here to save us all. In THE MYTHICS #2 "Apocalypse Ahead" you'll get to meet the remaining three.

And if that wasn't exciting enough (I mean, gods returning to earth…!), we also want to share some Papercutz publishing news that's so exciting, it was even in The New York Times! So exciting, I'm going to tell you all about it right now…

Papercutz has managed to get the North American rights to publish perhaps the most successful comics series in the world—ASTERIX! Now some of you may not have heard of this Asterix fella, so let's take a quick journey in time…

We're back in the year 50 BC in the ancient country of Gaul, located where France, Belgium, and the Southern Netherlands are today. All of Gaul has been conquered by the Romans… well, not all of it. One tiny village, inhabited by indomitable Gauls, resists the invaders again and again. That doesn't make it easy for the garrisons of Roman soldiers surrounding the village in fortified camps.

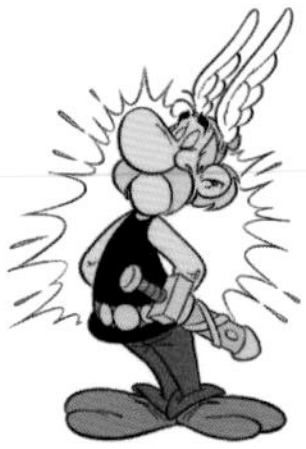
Asterix

So, how's it possible that a small village can hold its own against the mighty Roman Empire? The answer is this guy…

Asterix. A shrewd, little warrior of keen intellect… and superhuman strength. Asterix gets his superhuman strength from a magic potion. But he's not alone.

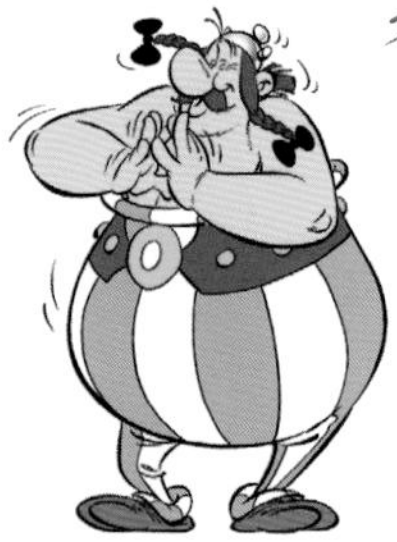
Obelix

Obelix is Asterix's inseparable friend. He too has superhuman strength. He's a menhir (tall, upright stone monuments) deliveryman, he loves eating wild boar, and getting into brawls. Obelix is always ready to drop everything to go off on a new adventure with Asterix.

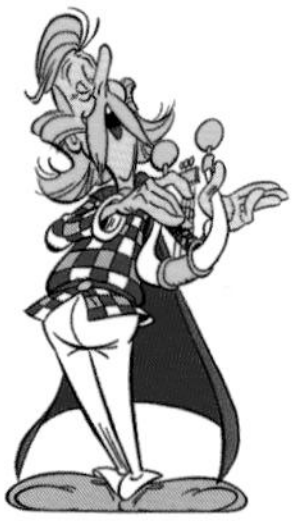
Cacofonix

Panoramix, the village's venerable Druid, gathers mistletoe and prepares magic potions. His greatest success is the power potion. When a villager drinks this magical elixir he or she is temporarily granted super-strength. This is just one of the Druid's potions! And now you know why this small village can survive, despite seemingly impossible odds. While we're here, we may as well meet a few other gauls…

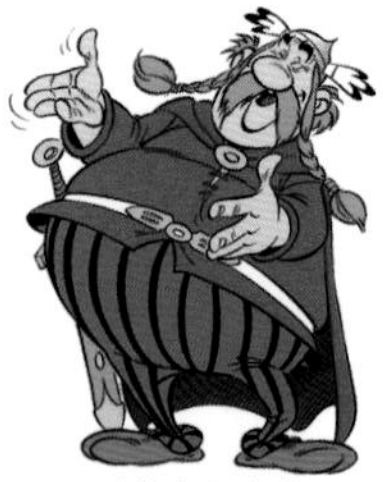
Vitalstatistix

Cacofonix is the bard—the village poet. Opinions about his talents are divided: he thinks he's awesome, everybody else think he's awful, but when he doesn't say anything, he's a cheerful companion and well-liked…

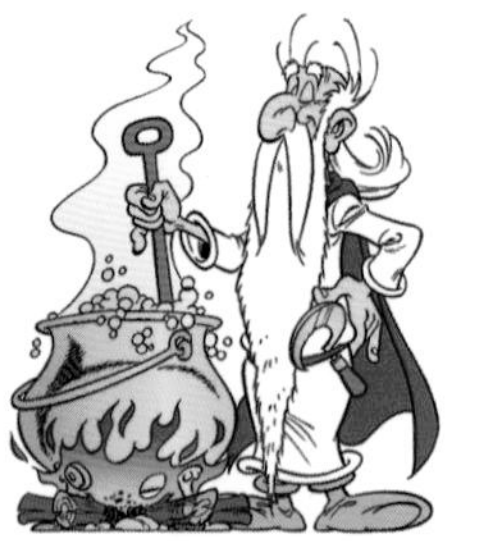
Panoramix

Vitalstatistix, finally, is the village's chief. Majestic, courageous, and irritable, the old warrior is respected by his men and feared by his enemies. Vitalstatistix has only one fear: that the sky will fall on his head but, as he says himself, "That'll be the day!"

There are plenty more characters around here, but you've met enough for now. It's time we get back to the palatial Papercutz offices, and wrap this up. Now, where did we park our time machine…? Lets take a quick trip to the future and meet THE ONLY LIVING GIRL!

Thanks, Jim

STAY IN TOUCH!

EMAIL:	salicrup@papercutz.com
WEB:	www.papercutz.com
TWITTER:	@papercutzgn
FACEBOOK:	PAPERCUTZGRAPHICNOVELS
REGULAR MAIL:	Papercutz, 160 Broadway, Suite 700, East Wing, New York, NY 10038

Special preview of THE ONLY LIVING GIRL #1
"The Island at the Edge of Infinity"

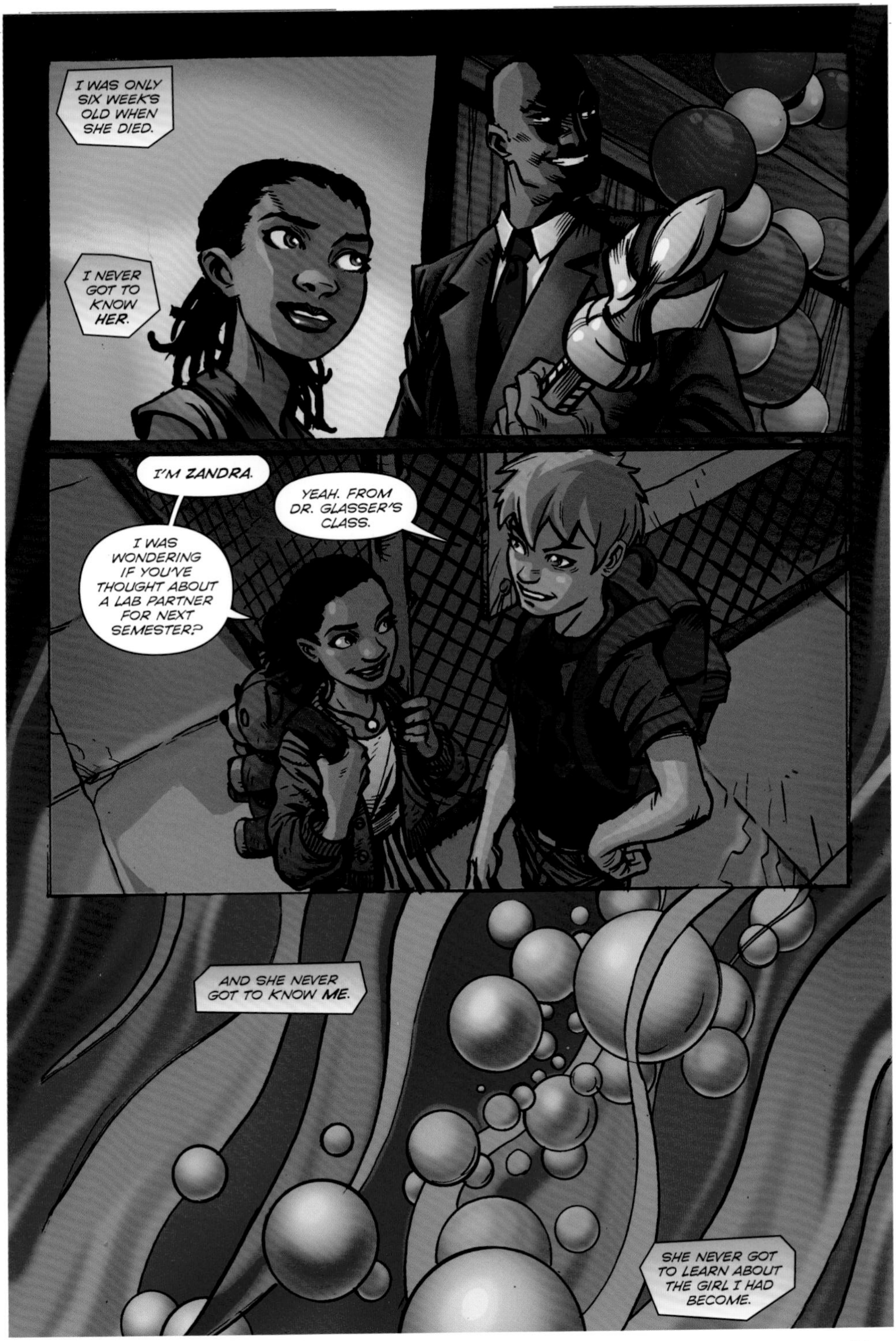
I WAS ONLY SIX WEEKS OLD WHEN SHE DIED.
I NEVER GOT TO KNOW HER.
I'M ZANDRA.
I WAS WONDERING IF YOU'VE THOUGHT ABOUT A LAB PARTNER FOR NEXT SEMESTER?
YEAH. FROM DR. GLASSER'S CLASS.
AND SHE NEVER GOT TO KNOW ME.
SHE NEVER GOT TO LEARN ABOUT THE GIRL I HAD BECOME.

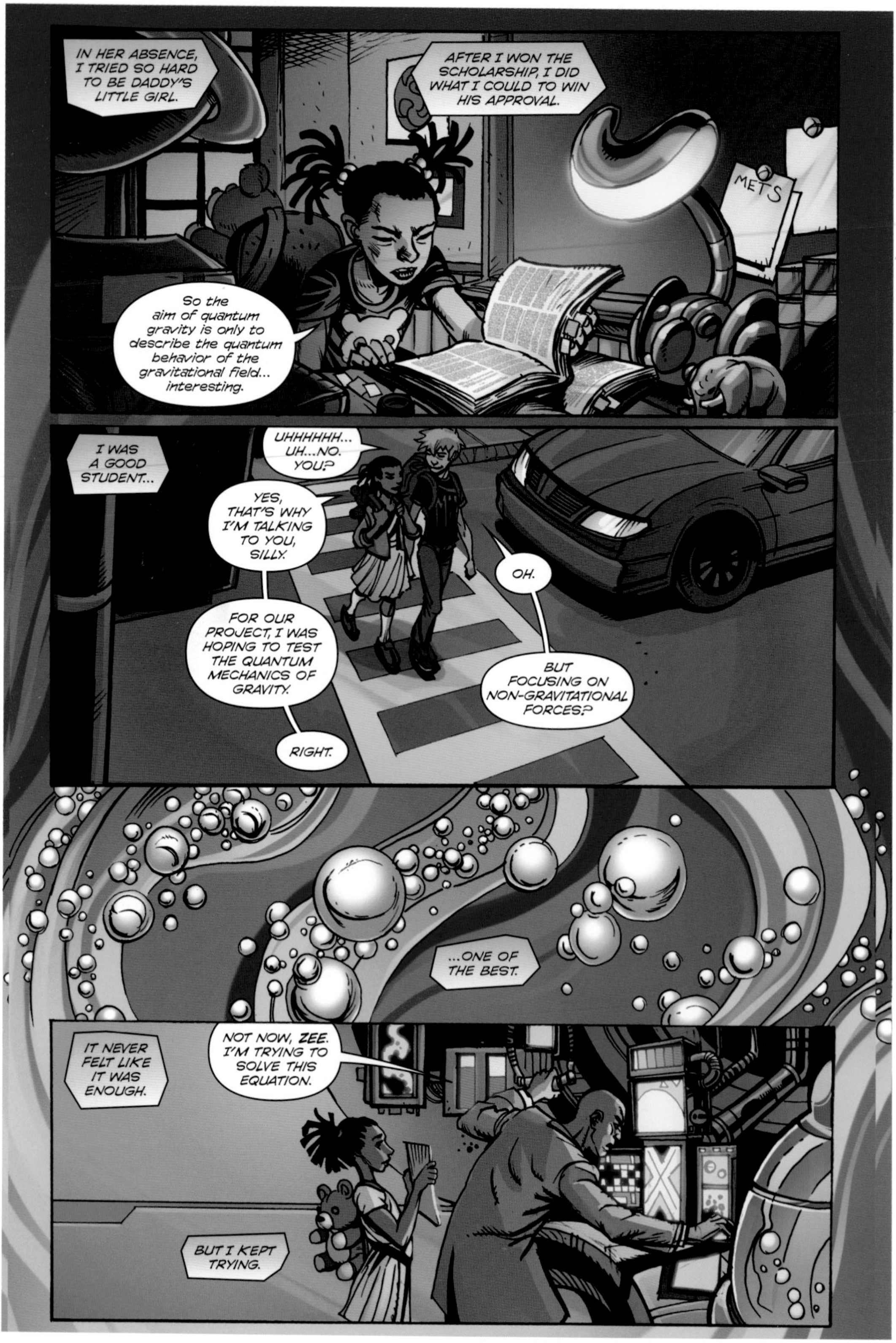

IN HER ABSENCE, I TRIED SO HARD TO BE DADDY'S LITTLE GIRL.
AFTER I WON THE SCHOLARSHIP, I DID WHAT I COULD TO WIN HIS APPROVAL.
METS
So the aim of quantum gravity is only to describe the quantum behavior of the gravitational field... interesting.
I WAS A GOOD STUDENT...
UHHHHHH... UH...NO. YOU?
YES, THAT'S WHY I'M TALKING TO YOU, SILLY.
OH.
FOR OUR PROJECT, I WAS HOPING TO TEST THE QUANTUM MECHANICS OF GRAVITY.
BUT FOCUSING ON NON-GRAVITATIONAL FORCES?
RIGHT.
...ONE OF THE BEST.
IT NEVER FELT LIKE IT WAS ENOUGH.
NOT NOW, ZEE. I'M TRYING TO SOLVE THIS EQUATION.
BUT I KEPT TRYING.

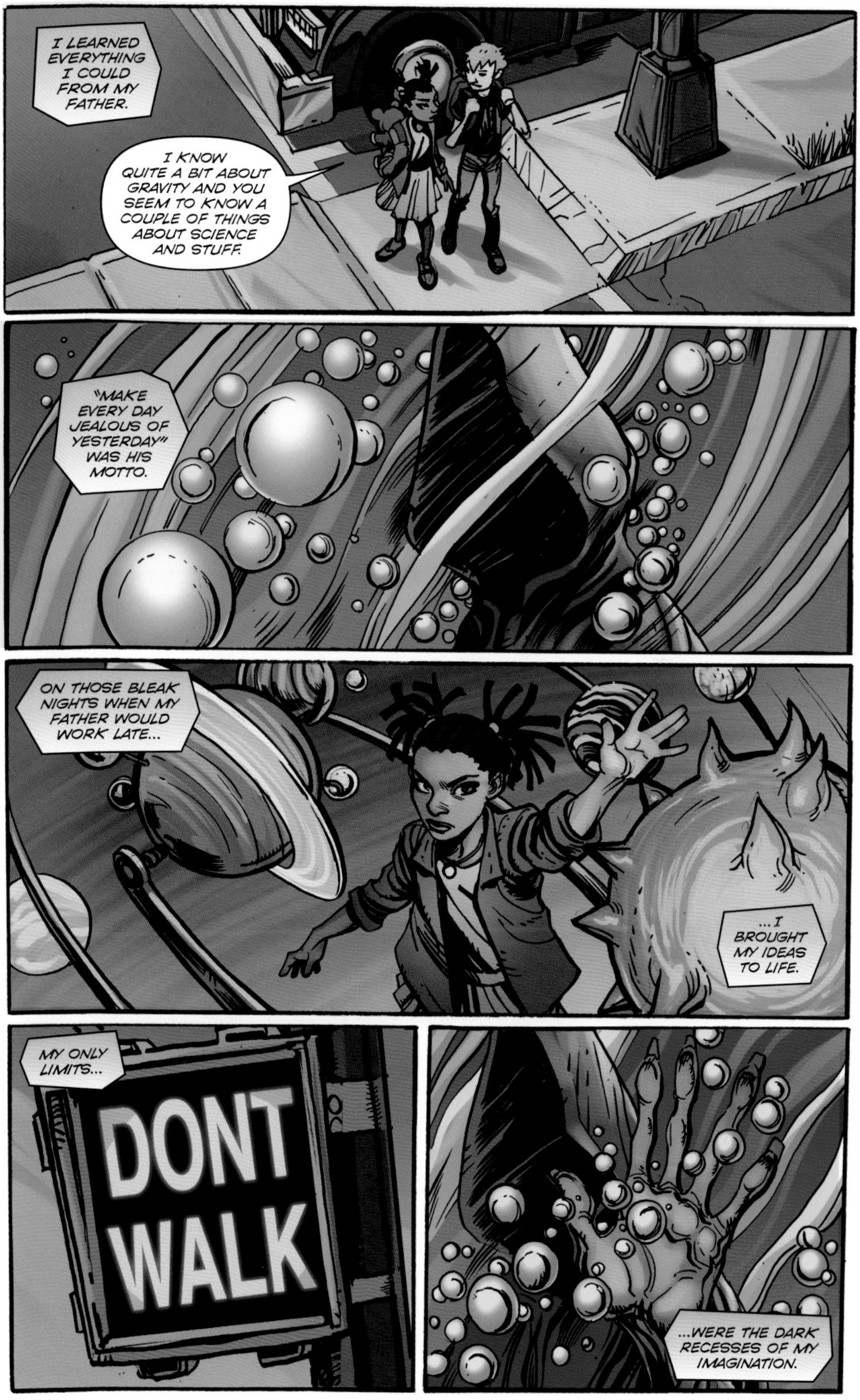
I LEARNED EVERYTHING I COULD FROM MY FATHER.
I KNOW QUITE A BIT ABOUT GRAVITY AND YOU SEEM TO KNOW A COUPLE OF THINGS ABOUT SCIENCE AND STUFF.
"MAKE EVERY DAY JEALOUS OF YESTERDAY" WAS HIS MOTTO.
ON THOSE BLEAK NIGHTS WHEN MY FATHER WOULD WORK LATE...
...I BROUGHT MY IDEAS TO LIFE.
MY ONLY LIMITS...
DONT WALK
...WERE THE DARK RECESSES OF MY IMAGINATION.

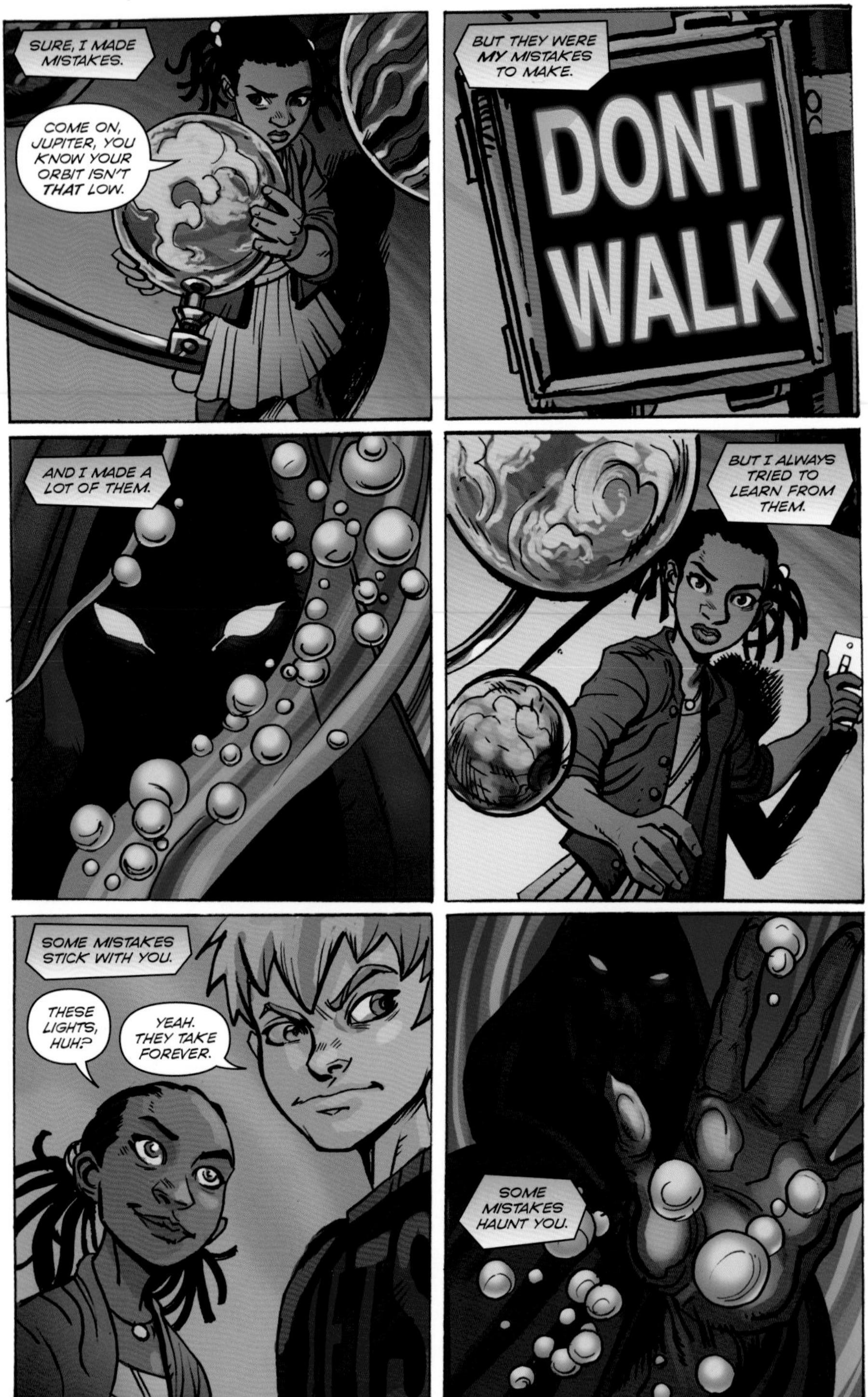
SURE, I MADE MISTAKES.
COME ON, JUPITER, YOU KNOW YOUR ORBIT ISN'T THAT LOW.
BUT THEY WERE MY MISTAKES TO MAKE.
DONT WALK
AND I MADE A LOT OF THEM.
BUT I ALWAYS TRIED TO LEARN FROM THEM.
SOME MISTAKES STICK WITH YOU.
THESE LIGHTS, HUH?
YEAH. THEY TAKE FOREVER.
SOME MISTAKES HAUNT YOU.